P9-CSW-674

ILLUSIONS

KATHERINE STONE

ILLUSIONS

KENSINGTON BOOKS

KENSINGTON BOOKS are published by

Kensington Publishing Corp.
475 Park Avenue South
New York, NY 10016

Copyright © 1994 by Katherine Stone

Library of Congress Card Catalog Number: 93-080088
ISBN   0-8217-4453-4

All rights reserved. No part of this book may be reproduced in any form or by any means without the prior written consent of the Publisher, excepting brief quotes used in reviews.

Kensington Books is a trademark of Kensington Publishing Corp.

First Printing: February, 1994

Printed in the United States of America

Prologue

Saint-Jean-Cap-Ferrat, France
November 11, 1959

"There's a second baby . . ."

Those were the last words Claudia Green heard before she lost consciousness—and the first ones she remembered when she awakened.

She was in her bedroom at the villa, the same room in which she had given birth. The room was softly illuminated now by the golden glow of a porcelain lamp, and as her light blue eyes surveyed its shadows, Claudia saw that during the deep sleep to which she had been forced—by a cloth of ether held gently but firmly over her mouth and nose—all traces of the magnificent drama of nature that had occurred here had been removed. The bedroom bore no memories of the recent birth, and as she had slept, she herself had been bathed and clothed in a fresh cotton nightgown.

How long had she been lost in that deep and dreamless sleep?

Just a few hours, she realized as she gazed outside. The first baby, a healthy little boy who had announced his safe arrival with a robust cry, had been born shortly after midnight. The moonless winter sky above was inky black still, but as her eyes drifted eastward toward the horizon she saw that dawn was near, its pale golden fingers already gently caressing the edges of the dark black cloak of night.

Claudia hoped that this new day would be a glorious one, a radiant and smiling welcome to her just-born babies.

Her attention was suddenly, unceremoniously, drawn from the splendor of the awakening sky back into the shadowed room as the bedroom door clicked open—without even a knock of warning.

Why *should* Victor Kincaid knock? No intrusion could be as intimate as what she had already done with this darkly handsome man who was in all ways—except the most private one—a virtual stranger. Together she and Victor Kincaid had created two new lives, and he had been in this room, watching intently as she had given birth to those babies.

"We are about to leave," Victor told her, his voice polite and formal as always. Almost as an afterthought he asked, "Are you all right?"

"Yes. Thank you. The babies are already strong enough to travel?"

"Babies?" Victor echoed with surprise. "There is only one baby, Claudia."

"No," she countered bravely to the stern dark eyes. "I'm very sure that there was a second one."

After a moment the dark sternness relented slightly and Victor admitted with a sigh, "Yes. There was a second baby, also a boy. The doctor could tell even before he was delivered that he would not survive. That's why you were given the ether, in hopes that you wouldn't remember."

"Oh. I see," Claudia answered softly. "Where is he?"

"With us," Victor lied swiftly, without even a heartbeat's delay. Embellishing further, he assured her, "Rachel and I will find a beautiful and peaceful place for him."

"Thank you," Claudia murmured quietly, suddenly swept by a grief for the baby son who had died that far surpassed the sadness she felt about the healthy son she would never see. The son who had survived would have a life filled with happiness.

How Claudia wished she had been able to give such happiness to both of her babies.

"You will not forget our agreement, Claudia," Victor said to the light blue eyes that had become blurred with wistful sadness. His voice was very cold, his words a command not a question. You *will not* forget.

"No," Claudia replied as the sharpness in his tone forced her to focus. "I won't forget. I will never tell anyone, and I will never try to see him."

"Good." The quietly uttered word seemed laced with threat, as if there were an unspoken, perhaps unspeakable, consequence that might befall her should she dare to break their agreement. When he was convinced that she understood, Victor withdrew a long white envelope from the inside pocket of his impeccably tailored jacket. "This contains your plane ticket, enough cash for the trip, and the passbook for the bank in Boston."

Claudia took the envelope but didn't open it. She knew that the ticket to Boston, undoubtedly first class, would be there, and that there would be more cash than she had ever before held in her hands, and that the amount of money deposited in her name in the bank would be the small fortune that Victor had promised. As she gazed at the pristine white envelope, Claudia felt a sudden impulse to hand it back to him.

She didn't want to revoke their agreement, of course. By giving him away, she had given her son the greatest gift she had to give. But from the very beginning, her offer had been about helping, not about money, a generous wish to do whatever she could to alleviate the anguish she had seen in Rachel Kincaid's eyes. Victor Kincaid had never understood that money was not a motive—or perhaps he had simply not wanted to be in any kind of emotional debt . . . or jeopardy. It was he who had placed a dollar amount on their agreement.

And if she gave that fortune back to him now, even if she explained that she was revoking the payment *not* the solemn promise, he wouldn't understand; and he and Rachel would be forever plagued with the fearful worry that someday she might come to reclaim her baby.

So the envelope remained in her hand, and eventually she lifted her gaze from the pristine white to his intense dark blue eyes.

"I've hired a woman to stay here with you while you convalesce," Victor continued. "Her name is Francesca. She believes that I am taking the baby to the United States for medical treatment and that you will join me as soon as you are able to travel."

Claudia nodded her solemn agreement to maintain that story. Then, sensing Victor's restlessness to leave, and feeling as always her own uneasiness in the powerful presence of this intimate stranger, she said quietly, "Well, then, good-bye."

"Good-bye, Claudia."

She watched in silence as he left, never giving voice to the urgent whispers of her heart. *Love him, Victor. Please love him and treasure him and make him feel safe and wanted—always.*

The whispers flowed from her heart on a river of emotion which, finding no escape through the silent lips, flooded her eyes with a torrent of tears. Taking her blurred gaze from the door beyond which Victor Kincaid had vanished forever, she turned once again toward the world outside. The sky was pure gold now, and the Mediterranean sparkled a brilliant sapphire, and the glittering blue and gold portrait was framed in the luxuriance of lavender bougainvilleas.

Before her shimmered the glorious day that she had hoped would greet her son. With the realization her tears began to subside, allowing the wondrous day to come into ever clearer focus. And as it did, Claudia felt a sense of peace.

Her son would be loved and cherished. Of that Claudia had no doubt. True, Victor Kincaid had always been wary and distant with her; and true, too, with her he had dealt only in money not emotion. But from the beginning Claudia had seen in his dark eyes how very much he wanted his baby.

The beginning . . . not quite eleven months before . . . in a hospital in Los Angeles . . . on Christmas Day . . .

* * *

Claudia had been a volunteer, the most dedicated and reliable the hospital had. When the director of volunteers balked at her request to work every day during the Christmas holidays, including Christmas Day, Claudia had swiftly assured him that she truly loved being there—and that her family, who proudly shared the dream of her becoming a doctor, understood and approved.

It was true that Claudia loved being at the hospital. Indeed, it was the only place where Claudia Green had ever felt at home, or safe, or wanted, or needed. As a high school volunteer, the official tasks assigned to her were quite trivial: wheeling patients to various destinations in the hospital, making certain that water pitchers on nightstands were full, delivering flowers from the nurses' stations to the patients' rooms. But it was what she did unofficially—and by deep instinct—that made her feel needed: the gentle smiles of comfort, the wise words that were so beyond her years, the soft hugs when there were no words to speak.

It was true that she loved being at the hospital. And it was also true that she dreamed of becoming a doctor. But it was not true that she shared her dream with a loving family. Claudia had no family—at least not one which had ever wanted her. She had been left on the doorstep of the orphanage as a newborn, her name chosen by someone with a slight interest in first names but none whatsoever in the last. A first name might endure, but a last name would change the moment the child was adopted. As a result, at the time of her arrival at the West Los Angeles orphanage all last names assigned to its residents were simply colors. Had she been placed on the doorstep a few hours earlier—or later—Claudia Green might have been Claudia Black or Gold or White or Brown.

No one expected the surname Green to endure, but it had . . . because no one ever came to give her another one. The nation was at war when Claudia was born. Couples were separated by the conflict and not searching to adopt; and when the war was over, the couples who had survived celebrated by joyfully creating their own babies; and when the few people who did come in search of a child looked at her, their eyes were critical—and they always made another choice, as if she was unworthy of being loved.

That was why her own parents had abandoned her, of course. And that was why, over and over, she was rejected by others as well. They were drawn to her, beckoned by the golden hair that glittered like a halo, but on closer inspection their hopeful smiles faded and swiftly, so swiftly, they moved on to inspect another child. Perhaps it was her shyness that drove the potential parents away; or perhaps it was the huge blue eyes which by age three were already haunted, having seen far too much to sparkle with joy; or perhaps it was the beautiful yet solemn face that knew no reason for laughter—indeed, knew truths that might inhibit laughter for an entire lifetime.

School was Claudia's first sanctuary. She was very bright; her remarkable brilliance allowed her to escape from the stark lone-liness and cruel truths of her own life into the wonders of learning. The hospital was her second sanctuary, discovered after she overheard classmates discussing the fact that volunteer work would "look good" on their college applications. Claudia had never even thought about college—she had always been solely focused on the immense task of simply surviving from day to day—and what appealed to her about volunteering at the hospital wasn't its possible future benefit to her, but instead the prospect of helping others now.

At the hospital Claudia's shyness was conquered by her compassion, and the heavy curtain of somberness that had al-ways veiled her lovely face was lifted, and the icy ghosts that had always before haunted her bright blue eyes were melted by a deep inner warmth. Claudia knew that she herself would never be loved, but she made a wondrous discovery: love lived within her. It was there, deep inside, a tiny fragile bud that had been waiting to blossom into a bountiful bouquet to be shared and given away. For now the only gifts she could give were emotional ones; but one day, she vowed bravely, the gift of compassion would be embellished by the talents of her bright mind and delicate hands.

Claudia met Rachel Kincaid on Christmas Day, two hours after Rachel had miscarried the fifth baby that she and her husband Victor had conceived. Claudia was delivering a water pitcher, but the moment she entered the stark private room, she wished she had been delivering flowers instead. Rachel was alone in the room, and the anguish in her eyes was too deep for tears, and Claudia felt a rush of compassion, as always. But this time the emotion Claudia felt was stronger than ever before, because the sad woman looked so very much like her. The eyes were the same remarkable blue, and her silky hair glittered like spun gold, and her lovely features held the same delicacy.

Rachel Kincaid could have been a long-lost and much-beloved older sister.

As Claudia sat beside the bed, Rachel shared with her the immense sadness of having lost so many unborn babies, and the painful truth that her delicacy was in fact a horrible frailty, and the greater and even more painful truth that her doctor had admonished her to stop trying to have children. It was becoming far too dangerous to her own health, the doctor had said—a grim truth which at that very moment the doctor was sharing with her husband.

But, Rachel pleaded softly, how could she stop trying when she and her husband both wanted a baby so desperately?

Claudia was about to quietly suggest that perhaps there was a shy and lonely little girl in an orphanage somewhere, desperate for the gentle love that Rachel could so obviously give, but before she could make that suggestion, Victor Kincaid entered the room. Claudia couldn't read his dark blue eyes, but she saw clearly the painful apology in Rachel's. Rachel wanted to give her husband *his* baby, an heir that would carry the strong and powerful Kincaid bloodlines.

Claudia left the room shortly after Victor entered, but the

memory of Rachel's almost fearful anguish lingered in her compassionate heart . . . and sometime during that sleepless Christmas night Claudia Green's bright mind, in concert with her generous heart, formulated a brave and extraordinary idea.

The day after Christmas was Friday. Victor Kincaid was at work. It was there, in his imposing office at Triple Crown Studios, that Claudia presented her remarkable idea to him.

She and Victor hadn't actually spoken the day before, so now she introduced herself formally, as Mrs. Thomas Green, a widow whose husband had been killed in an accident the year before. She would never fall in love again, she said with quiet and confident calm. There would never be another man with whom she would want to share her life or have a family. Since her husband's death, her plans to be a wife—and someday a mother—had been irrevocably replaced by plans to become a doctor, to spend the rest of her life helping others.

She had been very touched by Rachel's sadness, Claudia told Victor. And she had thought of a way that she could help: by giving him—them—the baby that Rachel couldn't.

As one of Triple Crown's two vice presidents, Victor Kincaid was accustomed to hearing "pitches." Indeed, he spent much of his time listening to the ideas of writers and directors who very much hoped to convince him to provide the financial support that would enable their creative visions to come to life on the silver screen. Victor had the uncanny—and immensely valuable—ability to almost immediately distinguish ideas which would succeed from ones that were destined to fail. He also had the ability to listen to all pitches with inscrutable calm, his handsome face as impassive listening to ideas he knew to be disastrous as it was when hearing ones that were destined to be blockbusters.

Now, as this young woman sat before him, quietly proposing this most extraordinary plan, Victor's face remained impassive as always. But his mind spun and his heart raced—because sometime within the next two years he and Rachel needed to present Rachel's father, Bradford Barrington Chase, with a grandbaby, a child that Bradford would believe without question was descended from his own blue, blue blood.

Bradford Barrington Chase was a man who by virtue of his privileged birth should simply have been handed everything he ever wanted on a silver platter. But it hadn't happened that way; and Bradford, who had far more initiative than petulance, had adjusted brilliantly. From boyhood he had had two passions: racehorses and motion pictures. Heir to Barrington Farm, his childhood home in the heart of Kentucky's most blue-blooded bluegrass country, he vowed aloud that he would have a Triple Crown winner by the time he was thirty. He came close, twice having horses that won two of the Crown's three glittering jewels, but his thirtieth birthday came and went without the coveted treasure itself.

Someday he would have a horse that would win the Triple Crown, Bradford amended then, adjusting to the setback but by no means accepting it as absolute. In the meantime he would pursue his other lifelong passion. He would make movies.

Bradford Barrington Chase moved from Kentucky to Hollywood and founded Triple Crown Studios. Within a few years of his arrival in Tinseltown he had won virtually all the races at the box office, jewel after dazzling jewel. His life seemed to be back on track, filled with golden trophies on silver platters, but it faltered again when his wife gave birth to the only children they would ever have—identical twin daughters . . . not the sons he had always wanted.

Bradford adjusted to this immense disappointment by raising Rachel and Rebecca as if they were sons. He expected each daughter to be a reflection of himself, to have a competitive energy and limitless drive that matched his own. The twin girls were remarkably identical in their physical features but remarkably dissimilar in all other ways. Rebecca was a ravishing portrait of boundless confidence, fearless and strong; whereas Rachel, uncertain and frail, was afraid even of her own shadow. In every

competition to which they were inevitably thrown by their relentlessly demanding father, Rebecca always won, finally win-
ning the most cherished prize of all: her father's true affection
. . . and his forgiveness that she was merely a daughter.

Bradford Chase chose the occasion of his twin daughters'
twenty-first birthday to announce publicly the ultimate competition in which the girls would compete—the race for control of
Triple Crown Studios. He was planning to retire from the movie
business in ten years, he told the rich and powerful who had
assembled at the lavish gala held in honor of the milestone
birthdays. He would dedicate the rest of his life to his still-
unfulfilled quest to own a horse that would win the Derby, the
Preakness, and the Belmont. On his retirement, each daughter
would be given half of his motion picture empire—providing
that by then she had married and given him a grandchild. If only
one twin met the requirement for inheritance, then she alone
would become the new owner of Hollywood's most powerful
studio.

On the face of it, Bradford Chase had for the first time
created a competition in which Rachel at least had a fighting
chance. Of the two sisters, it was Rachel who would make the
better mother. In fact, she would make a wonderful mother.

But what chance did frail and timid Rachel Chase have to
attract the kind of man of whom her father would approve?
Bradford's approval was an unspoken yet essential ingredient in
the competition. There would be fortune-hunters, of course,
men who would profess their undying love for the frail heiress—but they would be swiftly dismissed by Bradford. He
would accept as sons-in-law only the kind of men who were the
sons he himself would have had, dynamic and talented men
who were savvy in the ways of Hollywood and capable of
carrying on the tradition of Triple Crown. All others would be
rejected. And if either daughter dared to marry a man of whom
he did not approve? She would promptly be disowned, and the
competition would be over.

It seemed that Rachel would lose by default, because it was

beyond imagination that the kind of man of whom her father would approve would ever want her . . .

Victor Kincaid had been so entrenched in producing *Mardi Gras* for Paramount that it was months before he became aware of the astonishing announcement that Bradford Barrington Chase had made. By then Rebecca Chase was already engaged to Michael Lancaster, her father's right-hand man and Rebecca's lover for the past year. Which left only Rachel for Victor— Rachel, who should have been exactly as beautiful as her ravishing twin, but whose intrinsic beauty was remarkably undermined by her frailty and lack of confidence.

Rachel fell deeply and desperately in love with black-haired, blue-eyed, leading man handsome Victor Kincaid; and even though everyone—including Rachel—knew that Victor was interested in her fortune, his successes at Paramount had been so stunning that Bradford Chase welcomed him with open arms. Indeed, the man who had spent his life studying the bloodlines of Thoroughbreds anticipated with unconcealed eagerness the grandchild who would mingle his own financial and marketing wizardry with the astonishing creative genius of Victor Kincaid.

Victor and Rachel conceived for the first time on their wedding night. That baby, and all the subsequent ones, were lost before the end of the first trimester. If Bradford Chase was touched by the plight of his frail daughter, he didn't show it. *He wanted a Chase-Kincaid grandchild.*

Rebecca was equally insensitive to the anguish of the twin for whom she had always felt only contempt. As of two and a half years before Bradford's anticipated retirement, Rebecca and Michael hadn't yet even tried to conceive. But they were *practicing,* Rebecca announced, her brilliant blue eyes glowing with the golden confidence that had never shone in her twin's. She had no doubt that she and Michael would "get it right" the first time they tried, she said, and until then she most assuredly did not want to distort her sleek sexy body, nor disrupt her fast-paced life of parties and travel, with "Daddy's little retirement foal." Rebecca had already laid claim to her father's name. Her baby, boy or girl, would be Bradford Barrington Lancaster.

Victor Kincaid loved things—power, wealth, fame, creative freedom—not people. But he felt oddly protective of the frail wife who loved him so much. He knew that despite the doctor's warning that it might cost her her own life, Rachel would continue to try to have the baby who would give her husband what he so desperately wanted—and without which he would probably leave her. Victor's creative mind had searched frantically for other solutions but had found none that were satisfactory. Even the most secret of adoptions was fraught with problems. He could probably keep tight control of the secret with money, but all the money in the world wouldn't ensure that as the adopted infant grew he would resemble either a Chase or a Kincaid.

Victor Kincaid had been unable to solve the dilemma that confronted him; but now, sitting before him, was a woman who could have been a sister to Rachel and Rebecca—and she was proposing that she be a stand-in for his wife in the most intimate and important creation of his life.

Victor's mind was already far beyond the extraordinary proposal. He was already mentally scripting and directing the production itself. Once the pregnancy was a certainty, he would send Mrs. Green to the South of France, to a secluded villa in one of the tiny picturesque towns overlooking the Mediterranean. He and Rachel would follow later, on their yearly six-week trip to Europe, but at the end of the six weeks he would return alone with the joyous news that while away Rachel had realized that she was pregnant—five months already, more than two months beyond the point at which she had lost her other babies. It seemed safest for her to remain right where she was, he would explain to her father and sister. The tranquil beauty of the Côte d'Azur would be nurturing for her, and he would return to be with her as her due date neared. The staff at the villa would be told that Rachel and Mrs. Green were sisters, and that Mrs. Green was his wife, and . . . *it would work.*

It would work and no one would know.

Victor Kincaid spent much of his life listening to pitches. Most were delivered with an energy that was almost desperate, a plea that the vision that meant so much to its creator would ignite something in Victor as well. But as Mrs. Thomas Green presented the most imaginative *and most valuable* pitch that Victor Kincaid had ever heard, there was no desperate energy, just a quiet and unassuming calm.

"How much money did you have in mind, Mrs. Green?" he asked finally, his calm matching hers.

None, Claudia thought. This wasn't about money. And she was, she believed, as much a beneficiary of her plan as Rachel and Victor would be. By giving her baby to them, Claudia was giving her child the most wonderful gift she could imagine: a lifetime of happiness and love. The lessons of her own lonely and loveless life had taught her with unquestioned certainty that no man would ever fall in love with her. This was the only way that she could ever offer a baby of hers a happy home with a loving mother *and* father.

Claudia wanted nothing, but as she searched the face of Victor Kincaid, she realized that he was not the kind of man who would want to owe anyone a debt of emotional gratitude—nor did Claudia want either Rachel or Victor to feel indebted to her. Some tangible agreement was necessary. Claudia Green was freeing Rachel and Victor Kincaid from their anguish. Perhaps they could free her from hers. She didn't need much money, just enough to never have to return to the orphanage. She could find a tiny room in a boardinghouse, a place of her own where she could live while she earned money for college and medical school . . .

A small amount of money was all that Claudia needed to be free. But as she was thinking of the best way to tell him that, Victor Kincaid offered her a fortune.

As Claudia gazed at the magnificent winter dawn, she remembered that day in Victor's office, and the days—and nights—that had followed. It had been easy to convince Victor that she was old enough to have been married and widowed; the haunted sadness of her blue eyes did that. And what of her virginal fear when the man whose intense dark eyes had at last revealed how very much he wanted the baby had arrived to create that miracle with her? Somehow, for the baby to whom she was giving a lifetime of happiness and love, she had concealed her fear.

For a shivering moment Claudia made herself remember the coolly calculated precision of the act which had created the miracle of life. Then, with relief, she moved on to the happier memories: the sunny days spent at the villa with Rachel, their quiet friendship, Rachel's gentle assurances that she would love the baby with all her heart.

And now the baby was born. What would he look like? Claudia wondered. His hair would undoubtedly be the color of midnight, Victor's lustrous black conquering her own glittering gold. And her baby's eyes? Her own eyes were light blue, and Victor's dark blue ones were almost black—so slate blue perhaps, or maybe even gray. And what would he *be* like, this son she would never even see? Very bright, of course, as both she and Victor were. And if he could just have her compassion, and Victor's creative genius, and Rachel's gentleness . . .

Claudia was startled from her reverie by the sound of gravel crunching beneath the wheels of a car. They were leaving now, as Victor had said they would, and Rachel hadn't even come to say good-bye. Rachel was with her son, Claudia reminded herself, where she belonged. And, she realized, gentle and uncertain Rachel had probably been fearful of seeing doubt in the light blue eyes that were so very much like her own.

You wouldn't have seen doubt, Rachel, Claudia thought. You would have seen only great joy for the baby boy who lived . . . and deep sadness for the infant son who had not.

*   *   *

Victor Kincaid did not permit his eyes to drift at all as they traveled past the small church where a few hours earlier, in the middle of the cold moonless night, he had left his other son.

The decision to leave one baby behind had been absolutely necessary. Bradford Chase would gratefully accept the miracle of this grandchild—this grand*son*—but it would be pushing too far the bounds of credulity to pretend that frail Rachel had given birth to twins. Even if Bradford accepted it simply because he wanted to, Rebecca would expose the lie. She had a vested interest now. As if by a sixth sense, she had conceived at almost the same moment that Claudia had; and, Victor imagined, by the time he and Rachel and his son reached Los Angeles, Rebecca would have already presented her father with *her* new baby. Victor secretly hoped that Bradford Barrington Lancaster would be a little girl; but even if Rebecca had borne a baby boy, he knew that his own son—Victor Chase Kincaid—would please the patriarch very much.

It had been necessary to leave one of his twin sons behind, and Victor had accomplished the task with quick and unemotional efficiency. Thankfully, the decision had been made beforehand that Victor "the husband"—but not Rachel "the sister"—would witness the delivery. Rachel waited in her far-away bedroom, finally taking the sleeping pills that Victor had suggested so that she would be well rested to care for the baby who would, if the labor progressed as expected, be delivered sometime during the night.

By two A.M. the doctor and nurses were gone, paid handsomely in cash by Victor. There had been special bonuses for the nurses who had bathed Claudia so gently that she hadn't fully awakened. And there had been an extra special bonus for the doctor who had agreed to simply sign the birth certificates, leaving Victor to fill in the details before presenting them to the appropriate agency in the United States.

The twin baby boys had been bathed and wrapped in soft blankets; and at two A.M., when Victor had gone to them, they had been sleeping peacefully, curled together as one.

They were quite identical, Victor had realized as he gazed at them. Even if they hadn't been, he wouldn't have wasted any time deciding which one to keep and which one to give away. He needed to act quickly, decisively, while Rachel, Claudia, and the babies all slept.

It didn't matter to Victor Kincaid which twin he kept and which one he gave away. Either baby boy assured him of his half of Triple Crown.

It didn't matter to Victor.

But it mattered very much to the tiny infant who was left near the altar of the small church in Saint-Jean-Cap-Ferrat in the middle of that cold and moonless November night.

PART
ONE

Chapter One

San Francisco
May 14, 1994

Sea Witch rocked gently against her moorings in San Francisco's exclusive Marina Yacht Club. Inside the sleek sailboat Chase Carlton was fastening the pearl studs of the dress shirt that he had rented along with the black silk tuxedo.

Someday, Chase knew, it would be cost effective to buy a tuxedo of his own. It was remarkable how often the women who were drawn to him came from the innermost circle of San Francisco's rich and privileged elite. They loved the casual—and so sexy—indifference of the jeans he almost always wore, his obvious contempt for tradition and his even more obvious unwillingness to be tamed. But they wanted to see him in tuxedos as well, because Chase Carlton was stunning in the austerely tailored evening clothes, an impeccably dressed panther, an elegant image of tautly controlled strength: graceful, powerful, wild still—and untamable always.

Tonight's tuxedo was for the opera, opening night of this season's production of *Otello.* Chase anticipated with both pleasure and need the evening that lay ahead. The pleasures were obvious—the magic of the music followed by the intimacies of passion he would share with Vanessa—and he needed to become lost in the intoxication of both; because what he needed most of all was a respite from the vivid images of horror that had blazed relentlessly in his mind for the past three months.

The images were images of death, and the feelings that accompanied them were pure evil. Both belonged to someone else, a man who murdered for his own pleasure, but it was Chase's extraordinary "gift" to be able to journey into the mind of such a man, to understand his evil, to *feel* the emotions that drove him to kill and kill again—and eventually, through that journey, to find a way to put an end to the murderer's lethal lust.

Long before the revelation of his gift, women had wanted Chase Carlton—the graceful power of his sensual body, the smoldering passion of his winter-gray eyes, the dark dangers which lurked in the shadows of his heart; but his inexplicable ability to know the innermost thoughts and feelings and desires of murderers enhanced even more Chase's already compelling allure. Chase never shared with his lovers the cases with which he was involved, not one detail, not ever, not even when the killer was dead or captured and the books and movies that fed society's insatiable fascination with such psychopaths were well under way. And even to the police and FBI he revealed only what was necessary to put an end to the killings.

Most of what Chase learned from his voyages into evil was truly unspeakable—and never forgettable—a private torment that screamed silently within him, further isolating the orphan who had been destined to a life of solitary anguish from the moment he had been left in the cold darkness near the altar of a small church in the South of France.

At the triumphant conclusion of each case Chase would vow to his already badly damaged heart that he would never again make the journey into evil. He would seal the solemn vow by escaping to the welcoming tranquility of the sea, balming his deep wounds first with the soothing sounds of wind and waves, and then, when he could sing again, with the sounds of his own music. He would always plan to simply sail forever, to become lost for eternity in the vastness of the sea; but inevitably the powerful pull of the invisible force that had guided him throughout his life would compel him to return—and when he did, there would be another case already waiting for him. The families of the victims would be so desperate, pleading for a tiny glimmer of hope in their immense grief, a whisper of justice amid the thunder of their loss . . . and even though for Chase it would be a private descent into hell and madness, he would agree to help.

Chase neither expected nor wanted anything in return for the help he gave. But because of his extraordinary gift, he had been given an extraordinary gift in return: *Sea Witch,* his sleek black fifty-foot sailboat. The case had been in Denver, away from the solace of the sea that was so necessary to him always—especially when he was involved in a journey of death. The brutal murders of the young women there had been crescendo-ing, and the police had no clues, and as Chase had gazed at the photographs of the savaged victims he had begun to feel whatever it was that connected him to evil . . . and he had agreed.

Chase Carlton had almost died in Denver, a true and final death, not simply the irrevocable death of spirit that came with each case. He had no memory of his brush with death—the concussion had given him a lasting amnesia—but the police had arrived in time to witness the drama that had been played out on the ledge of the building. As Chase wrestled to keep the killer's hunting knife from plunging into his own heart, he and the murderer fell. The killer died on the pavement five flights below, but Chase's fall had been broken after two stories by another ledge. His skull was fractured, and it was a week before he awakened, and months before the memories that had been violently thrust into darkness reappeared from their shadows.

When the real estate tycoon father of one of the victims presented Chase with a check for five million dollars, his first impulse was to flatly refuse. But the girl's parents persisted, and when it became obvious how very much it meant to them, a tangible way to express their gratitude that their beloved daughter's death had been solved and a chance to do *something* after so many anguished months of helplessness, Chase graciously accepted their remarkable gift.

He bought *Sea Witch* and placed the remainder of the fortune in safe, conservative investments. Then, because the Denver case had almost cost him his life as well as his heart and spirit and soul, he set sail on a voyage that would take him around the world. He made it almost to Australia before the invisible force once again compelled him to return to San Francisco . . . to even more journeys of evil and death . . . and to the sense of waiting that had lived within him from the moment he had arrived in San Francisco ten years before.

Waiting for what? Chase didn't know. Perhaps simply for more cases. Perhaps it was his destiny, the only reason he had survived the horrors of his childhood, to share forever his dark gift for sensing evil—even though every time he shared his sinister gift he died a little, dying more the more he gave.

Perhaps the emotionally devastating journeys into evil were all there was, all there would ever be to his life. Somehow Chase had dared to hope for more—*not* that there had ever been anything in the life of the unloved orphan that had promised more than violence and isolation and despair. Still, when at age thirteen he had fled the orphanage in Nice, it had felt like more than simply running away—as if he were running toward a specific destiny, a purpose, *something* that would somehow justify the loneliness and brutality of his childhood.

He was Charles-Phillipe when he fled the orphanage, the name given to him after the priests from the small church in Saint-Jean-Cap-Ferrat had taken him to Nice; but when he reached England, he anglicized his given name to Charles Phillip and added a last name of his own choosing: Carlton. That was the name of the grand hotel in Cannes, of course, the home of the rich and famous when they visited each spring for the renowned Film Festival.

Those weeks in spring were magical for him, inexplicably magical because he had never once even seen a movie. Still, something—the powerful invisible force that he would come to know so well—had compelled him to risk extreme punishment, to sneak out of the orphanage and hitchhike the twenty-two miles from Nice to Cannes. There he would stand on the Boulevard de la Croisette and gaze at the majestic grandeur of the Carlton and watch with breath-held wonder as movie stars and movie moguls swept in and out of the grand hotel, those real-life images somehow far more mesmerizing to him than any make-believe motion picture could ever have been.

The moment Charles Phillip Carlton set foot on British soil, he felt the first sense of belonging he had felt in his entire life. English, not French, was the language he had been born to speak. He mastered it quickly—and beautifully and reverently—losing all traces of his French accent in the process. He read whatever he could, anything and everything, educating himself, preparing himself for his still-unknown—and yet somehow already predestined—future.

Eventually Charles became Chase. He liked the name before he knew what it meant, and when he read its meaning in a dictionary, he knew that it was the name he was meant to have. Years later, when his dark gift for pursuing evil had been discovered, the women who were his lovers would tease that his name should have been Hunter, not Chase. Hunter was a far more dangerous name, they would say, seductive and powerful and predatory—as he was. Wasn't Hunter in fact the *perfect* name for an icy-eyed panther who stalked murderers with merciless resolve?

But by then Chase knew the subtleties of the English language, and he knew that the name he had chosen as a teenager was right for him. Hunter was a name of violence, a name for a man who pursued his prey with the intent to conquer and kill. One *hunted* other men, and innocent creatures, but the things one *chased* were far more illusory and bewitching—rainbows and dreams. Even when Chase's own restless journey brought him only to the doorway of death, something deep within him, a whisper of hope that had somehow survived the horrors of his childhood, clung with brave defiance to the illusion that he was chasing something more, something better, something wonderful.

Chase went to sea at age fifteen. There was such peace at sea; and at nineteen, when he discovered America, there was even more peace, as if he were getting closer and closer to that illusory place called home. Closer and closer, but still not there . . . until at age twenty-four he arrived in San Francisco and the restlessness that had compelled him to keep moving suddenly vanished. He was restless still, still chasing an enchanting yet unfocused dream, but now it was only a restlessness of the heart. The invisible force that had kept him moving for so long now commanded him to journey no farther, to make his home in the magnificent City by the Bay—*and to wait.*

So Chase waited . . . and what came to him were the voices and visions of murder . . . and he chided himself for ever believing that there could have been more for the unloved and unwanted orphan from Saint-Jean-Cap-Ferrat.

Yesterday the Nob Hill Slasher had been caught. Tonight Chase would lose himself in the music of Verdi and the sensual pleasures of the sultry Vanessa, and as soon as possible he would set sail for the South Pacific, to find peace in the warm aquamarine waters that bathed the island paradise of Bora Bora—until the invisible force beckoned to him again, compelling him to return to San Francisco to face death yet another time.

Chase's gray eyes should have been watching as his lean and agile fingers, those of a talented guitarist—and of a talented lover—inserted a pearl stud into the buttonhole of his shirt. But even before the newscaster began to speak, he looked up, suddenly alert, and focused intently on the television screen in *Sea Witch*'s luxurious captain's cabin.

"The extensive sea search for thirty-four-year-old movie mogul Victor C. Kincaid has been officially called off, two days after the grim discovery of his blood-stained sailboat in the ocean west of Catalina Island. Because of physical evidence on the boat, the police have concluded that Kincaid was struck by the boom and knocked overboard. Unless his body is recovered, it will remain unknown whether he died from the blow itself or if he drowned after he fell unconscious into the sea.

"It was less than six weeks ago that Kincaid's latest blockbuster, *Serenade,* swept the Oscars, and just a week ago today that he stood in the winner's circle at Churchill Downs celebrating the Kentucky Derby victory of Schoolteacher, his three-year-old filly. A memorial reception will be held tomorrow in Burbank at Triple Crown Studios, where Victor Kincaid and his cousin Bradford Lancaster together ran the most powerful motion picture studio in Hollywood. A glittering array of stars and celebrities are expected to assemble to remember one of their very brightest, Victor C. Kincaid . . . lost in a tragic accident at thirty-four."

As the newscaster spoke, images appeared on the screen. The first was of Victor C. Kincaid's sailboat, *Sea Goddess,* the pristine white twin of Chase's menacingly black *Sea Witch.* The remainder of the images were of the movie mogul himself. There was a still photograph of a face that spoke of impeccable bloodlines—strong, handsome, aristocratic. Then there was videotaped footage of him accepting the Oscar for Best Picture followed by him accepting the trophy for the first jewel of the Triple Crown. The images were of Victor C. Kincaid, but they were images, too, of Chase Carlton—*identical* to the way that he himself would look if he cut his shoulder-length midnight-black hair and shaved the face that had been hidden beneath matching lustrous black for so many years.

For the first time in the thirty-four years of Chase's tormented and restless life, he felt a sense of calm. This was what he had been chasing. Not a dream, not a rainbow, just, quite simply, the truth. The invisible force that had silently yet powerfully guided his long journey from Nice to San Francisco—and then had insisted that he wait—had destined him to be here, at this precise moment, to see the images of the brother about whom he had known nothing . . . but for whom, perhaps, he had been searching all his life.

The astonishing calm vanished swiftly, the deceptive center of a raging storm, and even the hopefulness of the truth, that there might at last be answers to the questions that had plagued him since he had first learned of his abandonment, was suddenly shattered by the greater truth: Once again his journey had brought him to death.

His brother, his *twin* with whom there could have been such wondrous bonds, was dead.

Chase had never known love, but he had witnessed the anguish of its loss on the faces of those whose loved ones had been brutally stolen from them by the evil whims of murderers. And now, even though he had never known love, he felt the immense pain of its loss. Emotion washed over the raw wounds of Chase's heart—searing, not soothing—and filling all the places within him that had always before been simply empty.

Simply empty. The cold, dark emptiness that had been his constant companion for his entire lonely life would have been almost welcome now; because now, as the empty places filled with the loss of love, the pain Chase felt was far greater than all the pain that had come before.

It was a very long time before Chase was able to move, and longer still until he could trust his voice to follow the surprisingly decisive commands that came from deep within. Finally he turned off the television and dialed the familiar home telephone number of Frank Russell. On any of the Saturday nights during the past three months, Chase would have tried reaching the homicide detective first at the precinct. But now the menace of the Nob Hill Slasher was over. Frank would be at home with his family.

"It's Chase, Frank."

"Chase," Frank echoed as a rush of adrenaline shot through him. Calls from Chase Carlton were calls about murder—always—and even the calm in Chase's voice now did nothing to reassure. Chase's voice was always calm, even when he called with messages of ominous urgency. *He's on the move, Frank. I can feel him. He's going to kill again tonight.* But the terror of the Nob Hill Slasher was over, wasn't it? They *had* apprehended the right man, hadn't they? Yes. There was absolutely no doubt about it. Still, for some reason Chase was calling—and his voice held the solemnness of death. Frank asked uneasily, "What's up?"

"I just saw a news report about a man who was lost in a sailing accident near Los Angeles." *Lost* . . . Chase had believed that he had been in control enough to speak, but emotion was so new to him, so foreign, that he had vastly miscalculated its power, and now it powerfully flooded his throat.

"Kincaid?" Frank asked into the abrupt silence. "The movie mogul?"

"Yes," Chase managed to say. Then he paused again, still struggling to batten down his own storm-tossed emotions—but also wanting to give the very astute Frank Russell a chance to reflect on the report that he had obviously just seen as well. Would Frank make the connection between Chase Carlton and Victor Kincaid? No, Chase assured himself. No one would. He alone knew that hidden beneath his dark black hair was an identical portrait of aristocratic elegance. Finally, he continued evenly, "I'd like to speak with someone at LAPD who's familiar with the case. I assume homicide investigated before ruling it accidental. I thought maybe you could give me a name—and an introduction."

"Sure, although you don't need an introduction. Your name—and reputation—are known. Are you getting vibes about Kincaid?"

Vibes. It sounded so commercial, as if he should open a booth at a carnival and tell fortunes. Chase disliked "vibes," although he hadn't found a better word. There was nothing in the dictionary to describe the sense he had for murder, the darkness in his mind that gave him an entrée into hell through the devil's own private door.

"Call it simple curiosity, Frank."

"Okay. Well, I'll give Jack Shannon a call. He may not have been the one who investigated, but he'll have the facts. Death among the rich and famous is his specialty. He doesn't get vibes, but he has an uncanny instinct for knowing a murderer when he looks one in the eye. It's a very useful talent in a town where everybody's an actor."

"Will you try to reach him tonight?"

"Right now. And I *will* be able to reach him because he's got a serial killer of his own on the loose down there—some psychopath who's strangling beautiful young women using guitar strings as the murder weapon. Jack is going to recognize your name, Chase, and he sure as hell could use your help. He's a master at solving murders with motives—money, passion, revenge—in which the killer and victim know each other. But your specialty, the random and senseless murder of strangers, is a little foreign to him."

"I have to take time between cases, Frank."

"Okay. I'll tell him that up front, then."

As Chase waited for Lieutenant Jack Shannon's call, he thought about Frank's distinction between the murders in which he specialized and the carefully planned murders committed for money or revenge with which Shannon usually dealt—as if the murders committed by serial killers were without motive or calculation, as if the psychopaths had no will or control, as if somehow they could not help what they did.

Chase Carlton knew the truth about the men who killed again and again for no other reason than that they were addicted to the intoxicating pleasure of causing terror. *That* was their motive. And as for calculation and control? Their calculation was chilling, their control pure ice—far more of each than the fiery impulses that resulted in crimes of passion. And were they helpless to stop themselves, destined to murder, unable not to? No, Chase knew. The men in whose minds he had dwelt knew full well the evil of what they did, and they chose to do it, simply, horribly, *because they wanted to.*

The apologists for serial killers contended that the murderers were victims too, compelled to their crimes because of an all-important ingredient that was missing from them: conscience. It had probably been there once, a small seed which with proper nurturing would have taken root in their hearts. But the seed hadn't taken root because the critical earliest years of their lives had been barren of love, filled instead with violence and brutality.

Chase knew all about the unspeakable horrors that could be inflicted on an innocent child. Firsthand. And he knew all about the rage.

And he knew that what one did with that rage was a matter of choice.

Chapter Two

"This is Jack Shannon," the resonant male voice identified itself twenty minutes after Chase's conversation with Frank. "I understand that you are interested in the death of Victor Kincaid. Do you think he was murdered?"

The blunt question caught Chase off guard. But from the standpoint of the homicide lieutenant, why else *would* he be interested? And, Chase realized suddenly, maybe that was precisely what had compelled him to place the call to Frank. Had he simply wanted to find out about the life of his twin brother—his life not his death—he would be on his way to Los Angeles at this very moment to attend tomorrow's star-studded memorial reception. His appearance, the mirror image of his movie-mogul twin, would cause gasps of astonishment amid the sea of rich and famous. The gasping sea would part, of course, permitting him to approach the parents who could have given him a life of safety and happiness and love but had chosen instead to abandon him, to destine him to a life fit only for a killer.

Until this instant Chase hadn't even considered staging the real-life drama that would far eclipse anything even Hollywood's best screenwriters might script. Had the idea of attending the reception been rejected by his subconscious before it even had a chance to surface? Somewhere amid all the unfamiliar emotions had there been the familiar whisper of death, the inexplicable yet confident knowledge that a murder had been committed? Chase didn't know. He knew only that something had compelled him to find out about his twin's death before making his own stunning appearance in L.A.

"Do you think he was murdered, Lieutenant?"

"Yes, I do," Jack replied solemnly. "That's what I think, what I believe, but it's a feeling that I can't substantiate with fact. Murder or no murder, the body probably will never be found and the death has already been officially ruled accidental."

"The investigation is over?"

"Unless I can come up with something new—like you. Victor Kincaid was very well liked and respected. There's a great deal of resistance to shrouding his death in unnecessary scandal. Given your reputation, however, if you felt strongly that a murder had been committed, I think I'd be able to persuade the police commissioner to let me pursue it further. So . . . may I tell you what we have and what troubles me?"

"Sure," Chase agreed, as he had agreed so many times to listen to a police officer's description of a crime. Now, as he forced his mind to listen to the grim details of this most important of all crimes, he steeled his heart to hear the words he did not want to hear.

"Okay. He left Marina del Rey late Tuesday night. No one saw him leave, but we have witnesses who are positive that his sailboat was still in the marina at ten-thirty but gone by midnight. The boat was spotted drifting west of Catalina at noon on Thursday. The sails were furled, the fuel tank was empty, and the automatic pilot was set for a course that would have taken it from the marina into open ocean without running into land." Jack paused, then continued solemnly. "He was struck by the boom and either died of the head injury itself or drowned when he fell overboard. There's more than enough physical evidence to support the theory of a lethal head injury—although not an instantly lethal one. Because of the amount of blood on the deck, the presumption is that he staggered, dazed and bleeding, before falling overboard." Jack paused again, then asked, "You're a sailor, aren't you? Frank told me that I would be reaching you on your sailboat."

"Yes." I'm a sailor. *We both were.*

"Well, I'm not, but here's what bothers me. He was an expert sailor. He had even crewed for Dennis Conner in the America's Cup. Last Tuesday night there was a dense off-shore fog, flat-calm ocean, and absolutely no wind."

"Sailors like to be at sea," Chase offered quietly. "Wind or no wind."

"I understand that, but—short of colliding with another boat in the fog—this should have been the safest sailing voyage ever. He wasn't struggling with sails in the midst of a gale and the boat wasn't being tossed by waves. So how could he have been struck by a boom with enough force to kill him? And if what the large amount of blood on the deck tells us is that he staggered for a while before falling overboard, why didn't he just lie down on the deck? Isn't that what a sailor as experienced as he would have instinctively done?"

"Yes, but . . ." As Chase listened to Jack's concerns, reason battled with emotion. Chase did not want death for the twin he had never known, and even more, he did not want murder—not that the lieutenant's concerns necessarily pointed to murder. True, it was quite surprising for an expert sailor to be struck by a boom, and even if dazed and staggering a man who had spent as much time at sea as Victor Kincaid should have known to seek sanctuary on the deck. But his brother might have been so lost in thought, or so awed by the mystical splendor of the fog-misted sea, that for a critical instant he forgot the danger that was there always, even when the ocean was at its most docile. Even in midst of a most deep and peaceful sleep, the sighs and stirrings of the slumbering water came with immense power, more than enough to cause the boom to crash with deadly force—and more than enough, too, to spill a gravely injured man overboard and into its vast dark depths.

His twin's death could have been an accident, and that was the fervent plea made by Chase's heart; but the mind that was so very experienced with violent calculated death compelled him to ask, "How do you think the murderer got off the boat?"

"By swimming ashore. Given the maturity of the bloodstains, the coroner believes that the head injury may have occurred as early as midnight Tuesday. If so, if the murder was committed shortly after the boat left the marina, it wouldn't have been much of a swim. There was a large assortment of scuba gear on the boat. No one can tell me if any equipment is missing, but the number of wet suits is the same as the number of weight belts, which raises the possibility that the murderer wore one of the suits—and put its weight belt on the victim."

Chase closed his eyes at the image of his brother's weighted body sinking—lost forever—into a watery grave; but as the horrifying image only intensified in the darkness, the turbulent gray opened again.

"There's more," Jack continued quietly. "It's even shakier than the physical and circumstantial evidence I've already told you about. However, maybe you of all people will understand."

"Yes?"

"I think his wife is guilty as hell."

Frank Russell had said that Lieutenant Jack Shannon's instincts for murder among the rich and famous were as uncanny as Chase's inexplicable connections with killers who murdered strangers for pleasure—and now those instincts not only sensed that a murder had been committed, they identified the murderer.

"His wife?" Chase echoed softly. "What makes you think that?"

"Well, in addition to the fact that she's clearly hiding something very important about what happened Tuesday night, her behavior for the thirty-six hours during which he was missing was distinctly unusual. Jillian Kincaid is a schoolteacher, with a virtually flawless record of attendance, but she called in sick on both Wednesday and Thursday. She spoke to no one else during those two days, not even the police."

"She didn't report that her husband was missing? What reason does she give for that?"

"That she didn't believe he was missing. Her claim is that it wasn't terribly unusual for him to leave for what was intended to be a short sail and be away for several days."

How often that had happened to Chase himself. He would become lost in the peace and magic and solitude of the sea, and for that enchanted time even the strident screams of his heart would be silenced by the gentle sounds of the wind and the waves. Chase sailed for escape, a brief respite from the land-bound monsters that dwelled in the shadows of his wounded heart. Had his twin's heart been wounded too? Had he too sought solace and sanctuary in the sea?

"What about at the studio? Wasn't he missed there?"

"He would have been missed on Friday, but not until then. Unless meetings were scheduled or he was actively overseeing the production of a film, he frequently worked at home."

Chase had a sudden image of his twin, standing on deck, lost in the misty magic that surrounded him. It was an image of pure tranquillity—until the sea took a sleepy yawn and the boom swung. Then the image became frantic, a gasping, desperate, lonely death as he was swallowed by the cold, dark waters. Victor Kincaid had died sometime Tuesday night. But he hadn't been missed, not by anyone. It was the kind of solitary, unnoticed death that Chase had always envisioned for himself.

Had his brother sent a silent dying cry for help *to him?* Chase didn't know. On Tuesday night he had been so immersed in murder in San Francisco that a more distant anguished cry, even from his twin, would have been only the softest of whispers, unheard amid the violence of the nearby thunder.

But Chase Carlton had missed his twin on Tuesday night—just as he had missed him every second of his lonely and desolate life. Until now his brother's absence had been simply an inexplicable ache in his deeply wounded heart. But now the absence was known, and now it was forever, and as Chase mourned his twin's death, and all that might have been and now would never be, he realized that like the many grieving families he had met he was resolutely fighting the possibility that the death had been a murder. If his brother had to be dead, Chase wanted it to be accidental, the careless sigh of the sea they both loved, not the willful design of a woman who should have loved him—but hadn't.

The image of his twin standing alone on deck and lost in the magic of the sea had been a forced image, Chase knew, a wishful thought, not a vivid memory. Now he forced the peaceful image away and returned to the words of the lieutenant who specialized in murders of greed and passion—and could look into the eyes of a murderer *and know*—and whose calm yet resolute voice communicated with great clarity his deep conviction that Victor Kincaid had been murdered.

"You said his wife is hiding something important about that night?"

"Yes. She says that they had a pleasant dinner together at Clairmont, their estate in Bel Air, and that he left about eight-thirty to go for the sail. Something tells me the dinner wasn't pleasant at all, and I'm skeptical about the time she gave us as well. At that time of night the drive to the marina takes about thirty minutes, and we know he didn't arrive until sometime after ten-thirty. I'm confident that Jillian Kincaid is lying about the details of that night, and it wouldn't surprise me if she's lying about the rest of the things she maintains with equal conviction."

"Such as?"

"Such as that their nearly six-year marriage was perfect."

"Surely other people might know if the marriage was in trouble."

"If anyone knows, they aren't talking. Jillian's family is fiercely protective of her. Her father, Edward Montgomery, is a highly respected attorney. He barely tolerated my questions while the case was open. Now that it's officially closed, he'll object loudly and legally if I continue to pursue my theory."

"He knows that you think his daughter might have murdered her husband?"

"Sure he knows. Why not? Jillian knows it too. Let's face it, she had a sensational motive. Since they had no children, on her husband's death she inherits a fortune—including, but by no means limited to, one half of Hollywood's most profitable studio."

"How does she react to the accusation that she might have killed him?"

"Serenely—and silently. Her stepmother is a surgeon, as highly respected in medical circles as her husband is in legal ones. According to Dr. Claudia Montgomery, her stepdaughter's reaction is shock, pure and simple."

"Maybe it is. Maybe the marriage was perfect," Chase murmured, wanting that for his twin, wanting at least one of them to have found happiness and love.

"Maybe," Jack echoed quietly. "To be honest, I would be delighted to be wrong about my instincts in this case. It's tragic enough to have died at age thirty-four. I'd like to think that the years Chase had were happy ones."

"Chase?"

"Yes. The same as you. It was his middle name, his mother's family name. The public knew him as Victor, but he preferred Chase. That's who he was to his family and friends."

His family name. He preferred Chase. After a whirling moment Chase Carlton asked of the man who had just referred to Victor Chase Kincaid by his preferred name and whose voice had filled with solemn sincerity as he expressed the hope that his twin's thirty-four years of life had been happy ones, "You knew him?"

"We were in high school together. I was from the wrong side of the tracks, a dirt-poor street kid, but I had excelled academically and was a scholarship student at Duncan, an exclusive prep school in Beverly Hills. I was an obvious outsider and it might have been very unpleasant for me had it not been for Chase Kincaid. He made me feel welcome." Jack hesitated a moment and then added, "I don't know why he welcomed me, but I always thought that in a way he and I were kindred spirits. Even though Chase—and his cousin Brad—were at the very center of a circle of wealth and privilege, I got the distinct impression that deep down Chase felt like an outsider . . . a misfit . . . like me."

And like me, Chase thought. He had spent his life on the outside, isolated from others by the demons of his own past and the invisible forces that compelled him restlessly toward his future. Had his brother battled demons of his own? Had he, too, been plagued by a restless searching for an illusory dream?

"For whatever reason, Chase Kincaid was kind to me. He was a friend." After a slight pause Jack added with quiet passion, "If he was murdered, I want to make damn sure that his death doesn't go unavenged."

"So do I."

"Does that mean you sense that he was murdered?"

"I sense something," Chase replied truthfully. But whatever it was, it was quite unfamiliar, a chaotic storm of emotions in which there might never be the calm, detached clarity with which he could diagnose the murder of other people's loved ones with such stunning accuracy. This death did not belong to other people. This was his twin. And for all Chase knew, the powerful storm of unfamiliar emotions he felt now was, quite simply, love. "But I'm not sure yet what it is. I'll need more information, all the police files and whatever personal data you can get about him."

"Such as?"

Everything, Chase thought swiftly, greedy for any detail of his brother's life.

From the standpoint of trying to determine if a murder had been committed, Chase Carlton needed nothing beyond the police photographs of the sailboat. His psychic link had always—and only—been with the murderer, never with the victim. But Jack Shannon didn't know that. No one did. With each case Chase had always accepted everything the police gathered for him, including packages lovingly assembled by grieving families in hope that in some way the treasured mementos of their loved one might help catch the monster; and even though it had never helped he carefully studied the smiling photographs, locks of baby hair, and girlhood diaries; and when the case was over and he returned the mementos, he always implied that they had been helpful indeed.

Chase knew that no package would be lovingly assembled for him by the serenely silent woman who Jack Shannon believed had murdered his twin. But the lieutenant who had once been his brother's friend was obviously eager to provide anything that might be of help in avenging Victor Chase Kincaid's untimely death.

"Photographs, medical records, interviews, videotapes. I assume the local television stations and newspapers would have files on him?"

"Sure. Okay," Jack agreed. "Anything else?"

"Would you mind telling me whatever else you knew about him?"

"I wouldn't mind at all." Jack took a few moments to shift his thoughts from a tragic death to an extraordinary life. When he finally spoke, his voice was solemn still, but laced now with obvious admiration and respect. "He was really quite remarkable. He was only twenty-one when he took over creative control of Triple Crown, the studio founded by his maternal grandfather, Bradford Barrington Chase. Triple Crown was one of the top studios then, but in the past thirteen years it has become *the* top, a feat accomplished by producing exclusively hopeful and uplifting films. Happy endings only."

"That's a Triple Crown trademark?" *I had a grandfather who believed in happy endings only?*

"It is now, but it wasn't before Chase took over. Early on, he made the rather risky decision never to produce films about death or violence. He even passed on optioning *The Silence of the Lambs."* After a brief pause Jack added thoughtfully, "I suppose what Chase Kincaid had was a gift for dreams."

A gift for dreams. Jack's words echoed in Chase's mind. Thirty-four years ago twin boys had been separated at birth. One had a gift for dreams, the other a gift for murder. One had spent his adult life journeying into the minds of serial killers, and the other had refused even to make films about such monsters.

"A man of principle."

"Yes. And a man with instincts that were pure gold. He became famous for turning down scripts that were considered hot properties by all the insiders—and subsequently flopped—and made box office blockbusters from ones that were rejected by everyone else. The Midas touch wasn't limited to his decisions at Triple Crown, either. Chase was a talented musician, a guitarist. During high school, simply as a lark, he created advertising jingles—ones you'd recognize."

As Chase listened, his gray eyes drifted to his own guitar. He, too, was a talented musician; although for him music wasn't a lark but a necessity, its rhythms as necessary to his sanity as the primal rhythms of the sea.

"And," Jack continued, "the horse that just won the Kentucky Derby was a filly no one else wanted. Chase had never bought a racehorse before, and now she's the odds-on favorite to win the Triple Crown." A note of bitterness crept into his voice as Jack added, "He bought the horse for his wife and named her Schoolteacher in honor of Jillian's noble career."

"Had you met Jillian before this week?"

"No. I didn't see Chase again after the day we graduated from high school. He and Brad went to Stanford and I moved to Boston for college and then law school. I practiced law there for a few years before deciding to become a cop. In the four years since I've been back in L.A. I've run into Brad a few times, but never Chase."

"What about Brad? Were he and Chase close?"

"Like brothers. By the way, Brad is appropriately troubled about my concerns that Chase's death might have been foul

play, but he's as adamant as Jillian's parents that she could not
have been involved."

Chase let the last observation settle for a moment, then
prompted, "They were like brothers?"

"Like twins, actually. They were born within a few minutes
of each other, and since their mothers were identical twins—
and their fathers looked like they could have been brothers—
the resemblance between them was striking. Neither Brad nor
Chase had other siblings, so they spent a great deal of time
together."

"And got along well?"

"Very well, even though their personalities were quite different. Despite his immense talents, there was an uncertainty
about Chase. Brad, by contrast, has always had unwavering
confidence and charm. Maybe it was their differences that allowed them to be as close as they were. Brad is really very
devastated by Chase's death."

"What about the rest of the family? Chase's parents?" *Are they
devastated, too, by the loss of their golden son?* Do they ever even
wonder what happened to the other twin? Or did they somehow
know when they gazed at the newborn infants that one possessed gifts of gold and dreams and the other gifts of darkness
and evil? Is that why they abandoned me?

"Brad is Chase's only living blood relative. Both sets of parents—along with Bradford Chase—were killed in a fire thirteen
years ago."

"A fire?" Chase echoed as a shiver swept through him.

Was the sudden chill simply a reflex learned from years of
practicing his own sinister gift? In the macabre world of serial
killers, a childhood fascination with fire, like a history of cruelty
to animals, was a blazing clue pointing toward future destruction and violence.

Or was the iciness he now felt something far more personal,
the final dance of a ghost deep inside, a tormenting phantom
that had taunted him with the thought of one day looking into

the eyes of his parents and demanding to know why they had done to him what they had done?

Or was it the swan song of yet another ghost, smaller and less bold, one that had held on to the defiant hope that one day he would look into their eyes and see love? Another even deeper shiver consumed him as he realized that perhaps he had already gazed into the eyes of his parents. Surely they had been among the dazzling couples who descended on Cannes for the Film Festival. Undoubtedly they had stayed in the lavish suites at the Carlton, the grand hotel to which he had been so inexplicably drawn and for which he had named himself. Had their eyes ever fallen on the unloved waif who stood boldly on the boulevard, gazing with unconcealed wonder at the magical images he saw? They would have recognized him, of course, the mirror image of their golden son. And when—if—they had ever seen him, had they moved hurriedly away, rejecting him yet again?

The painful image of his parents sweeping past him in the sun-drenched splendor of Cannes was suddenly superceded by the vividly blazing image of their fiery death.

"What happened?" he asked.

"They were all spending Thanksgiving at a private lodge at Lake Tahoe. It was a wooden structure, quickly engulfed in the flames which were apparently ignited by a spark from the fire-place. Brad and Chase were at a casino at the time, but both sets of parents and the grandfather were asleep in the lodge." Jack hesitated a moment, and when he spoke again, his voice was very quiet. "I told you that I never saw Chase again after we graduated from Duncan, but I did hear from him. Three weeks after his parents died in the fire at Lake Tahoe, my own parents were killed. They'd been Christmas shopping and were having lunch in a restaurant when a gunman walked in and opened fire. He killed thirteen people before turning the gun on himself. I was at school in Boston then and hadn't even heard about the death of Chase's parents until he wrote to me. It was a letter of sympathy and understanding, and it meant a lot. We exchanged a few letters after that, but eventually the correspondence stopped."

"I'm sorry about your parents," Chase offered solemnly. "That must have influenced your decision to become a cop."

"It did, although it's not something I've ever mentioned." In fact, Jack had told no one about the murder of his parents, not his professors at Harvard when it happened, and no one since. It was a private truth, a private tragedy, one that the press would surely have sensationalized had they known. At last the mystery would be solved, the grim explanation for the passion and dedication with which the sexy-attorney-turned-homicide-lieu-tenant approached his work. Now Jack had shared the carefully concealed truth with Chase Carlton, and he wasn't sure why he had done so, but a deep instinct told him that his very private secret was safe still. "I imagine the death of Chase's parents influenced his decision to make movies without violence—with happy endings only."

"I imagine so," Chase agreed softly as Jack's words echoed: the death of Chase's parents . . . the death of *my* parents. From the instant Chase had seen the news report, there hadn't been the slightest doubt in his heart that he and Victor Kincaid were twins, and as he listened to Jack talk about his brother, he became ever more certain. But where was the proof? Chase's incisive mind suddenly wanted more than two thirty-four-year-old men with identical faces, shared passions for music and the sea, and complementary gifts for good and evil. "Were Chase's parents French by any chance?"

"Whatever it is you have, you really do have it, don't you? I suppose the term 'vibes' is a little too facile—"

"His parents *were* French?"

"No. But he was born in France."

"That information would be useful to me," Chase said as calmly as he could. "The date and place of his birth."

"I have that right here, on the cover sheet of his file. Let's see. He was born in Saint-Jean-Cap-Ferrat on November eleventh, nineteen fifty-nine."

"November eleventh?" Chase echoed, hoping the shakiness he felt wasn't detectable in his voice. His mind was satisfied now, but with the proof, old wounds were opened in his heart; and they threatened to weep their ancient anguish into his voice.

After promising Jack that he would begin reviewing the information as soon as it arrived, Chase abruptly ended the conversation. He didn't feel the relief in the bloodless hand as it released its viselike grip of the receiver, nor did he make a conscious decision to permit his body to sit on the edge of his bed. His thoughts were far away from *Sea Witch*'s luxurious captain's cabin, and it would be a long time before he would be able to concentrate coherently on the extraordinary idea that was dancing in a far corner of his mind. Right now coherent thought was not possible. He was wholly consumed by the truth that echoed throughout his entire being, causing round after round of pain as it ricocheted, opening wounds he had believed had long since been scarred far beyond further pain.

Victor Chase Kincaid had been born on November eleventh, the same date on which he himself had been found just before dawn near the altar of the small church. Chase had always assumed that his actual birthday was the tenth—or perhaps even the ninth. He had always imagined, always *hoped,* that he had been at least a day old when his parents left him, that they had agonized—at least for a little while—over the decision to give him away.

But now he knew the truth. He had been only a few hours old when he had been abandoned.

It had taken his parents almost no time at all to decide that he wasn't worth keeping . . . or loving.

Chapter Three

"You bastard."

Chase looked up in response to Vanessa's soft hiss, met her beautiful, angry eyes, and considered her words. He had spent his entire life believing that he was indeed a bastard—both literally and figuratively.

As a boy, he had created an orphan's fantasy about his missing parents. The people who spent holidays in the secluded villas of Cap Ferrat were wealthy, famous, and aristocratic. Never once did Chase's imagination place himself among them. He decided, without a flicker of regret, that he was of far humbler stock. His parents were young lovers who lived in Saint-Jean, the busy fishing village nestled in a cove in the rocky peninsula. His mother was a barmaid, or a flower girl, and his father was a fisherman. They were in love, *deeply in love,* and one day they would marry . . . but that wonderful day never came. Instead came the day when his father's tiny fishing boat didn't return from the sea. His mother was young, and poor, and grieving, and afraid. Who could blame her for leaving him in the small church in the middle of the night? She knew he would be found there, and cared for, and . . .

And then the fantasy that permitted the abandoned and

unloved orphan to love his missing parents became even more wondrous. His father hadn't really been lost forever at sea; he had only been misplaced for a while. On his return to Saint-Jean, within moments of his reunion with the woman he loved, the two of them rushed to the orphanage to rescue their beloved son.

The fantasy that one day he would be rescued by his loving parents was what had enabled Chase to survive the brutality of his childhood. He would wait for them forever, he vowed bravely, and sometimes it was only the vow itself that kept him alive. But with each passing year, the reality of his life became more harsh, and the joyous hope of his fantasy became more faded, and when he was thirteen it became physically and emotionally impossible for him to wait any longer to be rescued. He had to save himself, what little was left, so he ran away, leaving the hope and the fantasy far behind.

Many times a beautiful woman had softly hissed "You bastard" to Chase Carlton. Until now he had believed it to be entirely true. But now he knew that it was only a half-truth, an accurate portrait of his coolly—most said cruelly—indifferent heart, but not of his pedigree. He was a purebred, not a mongrel, the legitimate son of rich and privileged parents who could have kept him . . . but had chosen not to.

The storm that raged within him now didn't reach his gray eyes. Chase wouldn't permit it to. Instead, with glacial calm he appraised the angry vision who stood before him, provocatively dressed in shimmering gold lamé. He had failed to meet Vanessa at the Opera House as promised. That was obvious. But Chase had no idea how long he had been lost in the swirl of memory, truth, and pain. To his heart it felt like a lifetime.

"What time is it?"

"Almost eleven. I waited until the second intermission before giving up on you."

Chase stood up from the bed, and with the powerful grace of a panther, he began moving toward her, gesturing casually to the tuxedo trousers and partially buttoned dress shirt as he did.

"As you can see, my intentions were good," he said, his voice soft, seductive, and without a trace of apology. Now his gray eyes glittered messages of ice and fire: the chilling command that she abandon her petulance . . . and the smoky promise of the smoldering passion that awaited her when she did.

"I hate you," Vanessa whispered to the eyes that both mocked and beckoned, eloquently reminding her that he would not be tamed or controlled, not ever, and reminding her, too, what his talented lips and hands and body could do . . . if she would let him. She felt the promise of his caress, the wonderful rushes of her own desire, even before his strong, lean fingers touched her face. She repeated, more tremble now than hiss, "I hate you."

"I know," Chase answered as his demanding lips found hers. An anguished thought threatened—I am deserving of hatred—but he forced it away. Right now what he needed was escape from all thought.

Tonight he would lose himself in pleasure. And tomorrow?

Tomorrow he'd begin the agonizing wait for the information that would arrive from Jack Shannon. And when it did, he would learn by heart, for his heart, every detail there was to learn about his twin. And four weeks from tonight he would walk out of the sea as Victor Kincaid . . . and into the arms of a murderess.

As he felt Vanessa's fury melt beneath his expert caresses, Chase wondered about the next rich and beautiful woman to whom he would make love. Jillian Kincaid would *have* to make love to him, of course. He would be her beloved husband, miraculously risen from his watery grave, and he would have only shadowy memories of his past life—and no memory whatsoever of what had happened the night he disappeared.

He would make love to his brother's wife, watching her eyes as he did, searching for proof of her treachery. Would the serenely silent murderess be able to hide her terror when she met the intense gray gaze of the man she believed she had murdered? Would her skin turn to trembling ice as she felt the skilled caresses of a passionate ghost?

Chase would make love to his brother's wife, his brother's killer, making her tremble with fear—*and with desire*—as he seduced from her a confession of murder. But could he really conceal his own rage well enough and long enough to lure from her the deadly confession?

Yes, of course he could. Chase Carlton had spent his lifetime controlling his rage, after all, an entire lifetime during which he had trained his gray eyes to be as opaque and unyielding as the misty fog in which his twin brother had met his death.

He would control his rage, and he would masterfully seduce, and Jillian Kincaid, trembling with desire and terror, would confess her most evil secret to him.

The Tiffany clock in Clairmont's elegant living room gently chimed eleven. It was a soft intrusion into the silence that had lingered this time for almost thirty minutes. The vigil for Chase Kincaid had begun at noon on Thursday, and now it was Saturday night and he was lost forever. But the anxious vigil continued still . . . for his wife.

Jillian Kincaid wasn't alone in the living room of her Bel Air home, but the invisible wall of pain surrounding her was quite impenetrable, even to the immense love of those who sat in silence with her: Brad, who had always been more brother than cousin to Chase; and Edward, the father she had never really known until tragedy had struck once before; and Claudia, the stepmother who had rescued her from living forever in the memories of that distant tragedy.

Now tragedy had struck again, and Jillian had retreated into tormented silence, and even though for the past two days and nights Brad and Edward and Claudia had taken turns gently speaking words of love to her, they had no idea whether any of their words had been heard. But as the Tiffany clock finished its soft chiming, Jillian lifted her auburn head, and as the luxuriant mane that had veiled her emerald eyes parted, they saw remarkable clarity. And when she spoke, both her words and her voice were astonishingly clear.

"It's time for you all to go home."

"It's time for bed, darling," Claudia countered gently. "But why don't Edward and I stay here with you again tonight?"

"No," Jillian answered. "Thank you. I'll be fine."

"Jillian . . ."

"I'll be fine, Dad," she repeated firmly. Then, seeing the fatigue and strain on the handsome face of her beloved father, she added softly, "You need a good night's sleep in your own bed."

"We all need a good night's sleep," Claudia said, her light blue eyes lovingly caressing first her husband and then her stepdaughter. After a brief hesitation she asked Jillian, "Do you remember that there's a memorial reception tomorrow at the studio?"

"At four. Yes, I remember."

"You don't have to be there, Jillian."

"Yes, Dad, I do."

"Why don't I stay here tonight?" Brad suggested. "I've spent enough nights here that the guest room bed is very familiar to me."

The last was said quietly, a wistful reminder of a time that would never be again. Brad would come over to screen Triple Crown's latest offering, and they would celebrate with champagne, and then Chase and Jillian would insist that he spend the night at Clairmont rather than venture down the winding road that led from their hilltop estate.

As an expression of gentle apology touched Brad's handsome face, Jillian thought how fortunate it was that she was able to meet his gaze without the additional anguish of seeing Chase. The cousins looked alike, everyone said, and that was true from a distance. Striding together, tall and dark and handsome and powerful, they did indeed seem a matched set. But at closer range, zoom-lensed, to her the differences were far more dramatic than the similarities. Brad's eyes were a dark blue that was almost black, not Chase's gray; and at rest Brad's lips were slightly amused, not intensely serious; and he always seemed more at ease than the man she loved, more confident, more comfortable, less restless.

Because Jillian didn't see the striking similarities others saw, it was possible now for her to meet the dark eyes of Chase's cousin, and to acknowledge with a soft smile the many happy memories the three of them had shared, and to remind him, too, how grateful she was for his friendship. Once Brad's dark eyes gently told her that he understood the silent messages of her smile, Jillian's expression became solemn again—and determined.

"No, Brad. Thank you, but it really is time for me to be alone. And besides, I won't truly be alone. Annie's here." At the sound of her name, the golden retriever who lay curled in warm sympathy at Jillian's feet raised her head. Jillian affectionately stroked Annie's soft fur, and then, smiling bravely at the beloved and worried faces that surrounded her, she assured them: "I'll be all right."

After they left, Jillian walked outside with Annie and stood in the fragrant garden of roses beneath the glittering ceiling of stars. In the distance lay the ocean, vast, dark, and so very cold.

Oh, Chase, her heart cried as her mind filled with the memory of Tuesday night. His image was crystal-clear: the handsome face that had been so stricken by her words, so disbelieving at first; the gray eyes that had blazed with anger when he had realized how resolute she was; and then the so-familiar restlessness that had compelled him to leave her even then, even when they might have shared all the painful truths and secrets of their hearts—at last.

"Give me another chance, Jill."

"How can I?" she had asked, hoping, *hoping* that he would help her find a way.

But he had only answered her soft plea with one of his own.

"Think about this, *please,* just a little longer." And then, before she could even answer, the restlessness she knew so well, and hated so much, had come between them again, taking him away from her. Jillian felt its invisible power even before she saw it in his eyes and heard its urgency in his voice. "I have to go now."

"Where?" she demanded, even though she knew. Chase was going to his boat, of course, to sail, to escape—as always.

"I have to go," he repeated, his gray eyes restless and stormy. "But will you wait for me? Please? Will you wait until I return? We'll talk then, *really* talk. I promise. Jill? Jillian?"

She had answered Chase's almost desperate plea with a silence born of her own anger and hurt . . . and finally, with no answer but that angry silence, he had left.

And now, as her emerald eyes glistened with starlit tears, Jillian whispered to the vast blackness beneath the twinkling stars, "I *was* waiting for you, Chase. Oh, how I hope that somehow you knew that . . . and that you died knowing that despite everything I loved you *so much.*"

"I'm afraid for her, Claudia," Edward confessed quietly.

They were in their own bed in their home in Brentwood, and she was cradled in his arms.

"I think she's a lot stronger than we know."

"Because of him." Edward's bitterness toward his son-in-law was unconcealed. "She's needed to be strong to live with him for the past six years. I suppose it would be a mistake for me to simply point out to her that she's much better off without him?"

"A big mistake," Claudia agreed softly as wave upon wave of grief swept through her for her son, for all that might have been and was now lost forever.

Claudia knew she needed to hide her grief from the man who was holding her with such tenderness. She had told Edward many truths about the very bright, unloved orphan girl she once had been. But she had never told him about the twin sons she had borne for Rachel and Victor Kincaid, not even when Jillian had astonishingly met and fallen in love with the twin who had survived that secret birth.

As Claudia lay in the arms of the man she loved and felt the tension in his body as he recalled the great unhappiness that *her* son had caused *his* daughter, her own mind drifted to more distant memories—the long-ago day when the glorious November dawn had greeted her just-born son with a golden promise of happiness and love. On that day Claudia had reassured Victor Kincaid of the solemn promise she herself had made, that she would never attempt to be part of her son's life. It was a promise she had kept, even when her marriage to Edward had brought her to Los Angeles.

She read all the articles about the brilliant young filmmaker, of course; and she studied the photographs of the man whose dark handsomeness was so like his father's; and she marveled with joyful pride at the wondrous gifts he gave the world, his magnificent movies of hope and love. But she kept her solemn promise. She had no wish to shatter the illusions of her son's life, nor to undermine or tarnish his loving memories of the parents who had died so tragically in a Thanksgiving blaze at Lake Tahoe.

Claudia vowed never to reveal the truth to her son, but she found herself wishing that one day she might at least meet him. It wasn't an entirely fanciful wish. There were quite plausible scenarios that might logically bring together the movie mogul and the doctor. Claudia was a plastic surgeon. Instead of specializing in cosmetic surgery for the stars, however, she performed hope-giving surgeries for children whose faces had been misshapen from birth or had been tragically damaged by trauma. Someday, at one of Hollywood's many black-tie charity benefits, Victor Chase Kincaid and Claudia Green Montgomery might meet. That scenario was at least plausible.

What was entirely implausible was that the shy and lovely young woman who was her stepdaughter, and who was planning to devote her life to teaching underprivileged children, would ever meet Southern California's most eligible bachelor—much less marry him.

But on a sparkling sapphire day in June, six years before,

Jillian had called to say that there was someone she very much wanted them to meet. Claudia and Edward had waited hopefully, expectantly, because the soft voice had filled with a happiness that they had never heard before.

Then Victor Chase Kincaid was there, in the living room of their Brentwood home, and Claudia's heart stood still as she waited to be told that he knew the truth about his birth. But this surprise wasn't about the reunion of a mother and a son. It was instead about the love of an innocent twenty-three-year-old schoolteacher and a dazzlingly successful and powerful twenty-eight-year-old man. Jillian and Chase had met only a week before, quite by chance, and already they knew that they would marry as soon as possible.

The pure joy in Jillian's shimmering emerald eyes had been mirrored by the sensuous gray; and there had been joy, too, in Claudia's own light blue—joy, and tears, as she first hugged the young woman she loved as a daughter, and then the man, the son she had never before even held.

The marriage of Chase and Jillian Kincaid began with such love and such joy that it seemed their happiness would last forever . . . but it didn't. *Because of Chase,* because of his moods, his restlessness, his dark, brooding silences. Claudia Green's son had inherited his stunning handsomeness from his father, as well as Victor's creative genius.

But, she wondered sadly, fearfully, had the ghosts of loneliness that had haunted her own unloved young heart during her pregnancy somehow cast dark shadows on Chase's as well? The ghosts could be banished, Claudia knew. She herself had been rescued by Edward's love. If only Chase would allow Jillian's boundless love to rescue him . . . but instead he squandered that magnificent love, and sometimes the destruction seemed almost purposeful, as if he were compelled to prove to Jillian his unworthiness of her.

There had been times of great happiness for Jillian and Chase. It came in dazzling brilliance, like the sun magically appearing from behind the darkest of clouds; but then, just as swiftly and as unpredictably, it would vanish.

And now Chase was gone, and in time, please, Jillian would allow herself to bravely find a new and happier love. But for Victor Chase Kincaid there would be no other love, no other happiness. For him, forever, there would be only darkness.

"Claudia?" Edward asked softly into the lingering silence. Was she appalled by his cruel and heartless words, the not-so-subtle implication that his son-in-law's tragic death had been for the best? No, he decided when he moved to see her eyes. She didn't look appalled. She looked only sad—and strangely fearful. "What is it, darling?"

Claudia wondered what Edward would do if she answered his question with the truth, that she was the mother of the man who in life had caused his lovely daughter such sadness and who in his tragic death had plunged Jillian into memories of a tragedy which had devastated her once before. It was that distant tragedy that had brought Edward and Claudia together, and even after all these years the tormenting worry dwelled within her that Edward's love for her was mostly gratitude for what she had done for Jillian.

The woman who had spent her life, until Edward, believing without question that she was undeserving of love was afraid now to test the strength of that love. If she told him the truth, would he conquer his lingering anger toward Chase and join her in mourning the loss of the son whose life should have been so happy and golden—and yet wasn't? Or would the revelation of her extraordinary secret signal the end of their love?

Claudia didn't know.

She knew only that it was a risk she couldn't take.

"I guess I just need to be held," she finally told the concerned and loving eyes.

Edward drew her even closer, cradling and protecting her. But even in the sanctuary of that wondrous closeness, Claudia felt the ominous presence of her secret lying between them, invisible yet so powerful, threatening to destroy.

Chapter Four

"Lieutenant Jack Shannon is here to see you, Ms. Windsor," the security guard announced through the intercom.

Even across the thirty-two floors of wiring between the condominium's marble foyer and her lavish penthouse, Stephanie heard the guard's excitement. The handsome homicide lieutenant was very well known. The streetwise kid who had graduated at the top of his class at Harvard Law School had become a legend in this town of legends, a brilliantly shining star in the glittering galaxy. In fact, to many the real-life drama of the attorney who for some mysterious reason had abandoned his lucrative Beacon Hill practice to become a cop was far more intriguing than most of Hollywood's fictional offerings.

Jack Shannon had a sixth sense for murder, it was said, and he was relentless and totally without compromise in his pursuit of criminals. He was, it was also said, just as relentless and uncompromising when it came to women. Oh, yes, the sexy lieutenant was interested in women; but so far neither Hollywood's most glamorous stars nor the Platinum Triangle's most wealthy heiresses had been able to lure him into lasting commitment. Not that they hadn't tried. But, it seemed, as tireless—and breathtaking—as his passion was in bed, it paled in comparison to the tirelessness of his passion for his work. The man who with compulsive patience pursued even the tiniest of clues in a homicide investigation didn't begin to have such patience when it came to relationships.

Lieutenant Jack Shannon was committed to capturing criminals, and he did so magnificently. But, apparently, he had no intention whatsoever to be captured himself.

Now the man who apprehended murderers and broke hearts with equal icy ease was here to see her, and Stephanie knew why, but still she felt a rush of annoyance that he had intruded without warning—especially now, when she needed to be so focused, rehearsing again and again the words she would say to Jillian.

"Ms. Windsor?" the security guard pressed.

"Yes. All right. Please send him up."

As she waited for Jack Shannon's arrival, Stephanie forced herself to clear her mind of thoughts of the woman who had once been her friend—the only true friend she had ever had—and to recall the already carefully rehearsed lines that she would speak to him. She had delivered the lines once before, to the officer who had interviewed her shortly after she had called the precinct. The lieutenant *himself* would probably want to talk to her, the officer had predicted with reverent awe. So Stephanie had made a point of remembering the already scripted words.

And now the "lieutenant himself" was on his way up, not even bothering to call in advance to see if this was a convenient time for her. How Stephanie wished that when she opened the door to him she could simply gaze at his arrogant face and tell him that he would have to return at another time—ideally, for his sake, at a prearranged time, since she might turn him away if he presumed to appear again without warning.

But Stephanie didn't dare attempt to utter such a defiant pronouncement. It would be laced with emotion, and emotion was her greatest enemy, the greatest threat to her secret shame.

So when the doorbell rang she greeted him with a polite but cool "Lieutenant Shannon," then allowed her expressive sap-

phire-blue eyes to eloquently convey her annoyance as she
appraised him with what she hoped looked like pure disdain.

The disdain in Stephanie's eyes could only be for the lieutenant's arrogant presumptuousness, not for his appearance. Jack
Shannon was as handsome as any leading man in Hollywood,
and he was even more alluring because he was taller than most
leading men, a commanding presence, life-size and yet somehow larger than life. The face beneath the dark brown hair was
a chiseled sculpture of strength, and pride, and intelligence; and
the seductive dark blue eyes were as uncompromising as he
was, and as relentlessly intense; and he was dressed impeccably
in a timelessly elegant ensemble of navy and gray, a perfectly
tailored Ivy League look that was a legacy of his years spent
practicing law on Beacon Hill.

"Ms. Windsor," Jack replied with matching politeness.

There was nothing in his ice-blue eyes or his languid, sexy
smile that revealed to her that he was a fan. But he was. He
watched *Corpus Delicti* without fail, programming his VCR to
record the top-rated dramatic series whenever he knew he
wouldn't be home at ten P.M. on Thursday night. Stephanie
Windsor played homicide lieutenant Cassandra Ballinger, a fictional female counterpart of the real-life Jack Shannon, as beautiful as he was handsome, and as tough too, and as dedicated
and intelligent—and human. For Stephanie it was an Emmy-
award-winning role, but for Jack it was his life, and in the
beginning he had watched *Corpus Delicti* simply to dismiss
Hollywood's latest implausible vehicle for one of its most glamorous actresses.

But Lieutenant Cassandra Ballinger had gotten to him. That
he had found himself actually liking the fictional homicide lieutenant had been a big surprise. Jack anticipated no such surprises about his feelings for the actress who portrayed her.
Stephanie Samantha Windsor was an heiress, after all, which in
Jack's not insignificant experience eventually and inevitably
translated into petulant demands that he *care;* and Stephanie
Samantha Windsor was also an actress, which meant that she

had paved her golden path to stardom with her ability to pretend and to deceive.

Lieutenant Jack Shannon might play for a while with a beautiful heiress-actress; but he was quite certain that he would never actually like or trust one.

The heiress-actress in question stood before him with graceful elegance. And, Jack realized, she was even more beautiful in person. Her hair, like his, was dark brown; but unlike his, which was further darkened by strands that were almost black, there was pure gold in her lustrous sable, the soft golden glitter of moonbeams. Her beautiful face held intelligence and pride, as did his, and a defiance that Jack read as haughtiness; and her eyes, like his, were blue, but the brilliant sapphire of a summer sky, not, as his were, the deep dark blue of the ocean.

As the haughty blue met his, appraising and disdainful, there was a shadow of vulnerability, an improbable cloud in the bright sapphire sky. Jack had seen such surprising clouds in the eyes of Lieutenant Cassandra Ballinger. For the fictional homicide lieutenant they were wonderful embellishments, compelling, Emmy-winning glimpses of humanity. But in the actress-heiress he found the falseness most annoying. Stephanie Samantha Windsor was trying to disarm him by casting surprising and intriguing shadows of vulnerability in her beautiful eyes.

Jack wasn't disarmed. He was simply annoyed. But he concealed his annoyance and offered pleasantly, "I apologize for not calling first. I was in the area and stopped on impulse. I appreciate your willingness to see me."

"You're welcome," Stephanie murmured reflexively and safely. It was one of the mechanical phrases that she could speak swiftly, without thought or rehearsal, and which gave her time to carefully prepare her next words. "I already told the officer everything I know."

"Yes," Jack answered, feeling a rush of renewed annoyance at the haughty stiffness of her measured, inflectionless speech. He allowed the annoyance to surface just a little, deceptively cloaked in a smile that became even sexier as he reminded her that he, too, was a celebrity in this town of stars. "But I thought you might be disappointed if I didn't interview you in person."

Jack expected his pleasantly delivered taunt to disarm—or at least to provoke. But Stephanie didn't bristle. Instead, the brilliant sapphire eyes sparkled, *twinkled,* and a lovely smile touched her beautiful lips—and it was he who was disarmed.

As Jack waited for her to embellish her suddenly vibrant expression with a lively reply, he found himself looking forward to what she would say, anticipating with pleasure a dance of words with her, a *pas de deux* of clever repartée. But as his dark blue eyes gazed intently at her sapphire ones, the dazzling sparkle vanished and the vulnerability returned—and he was suddenly left feeling as confused and uncertain as she appeared. Could the shadows of vulnerability possibly be authentic?

Releasing her from his intense—and obviously discomforting—gaze, his eyes drifted for a moment to the beautifully tailored black-and-white linen dress she wore, an outfit as solemn and formal as his own.

"Is this a bad time?" he asked, meeting her eyes again. "Were you on your way out?"

His questions seemed neither difficult, nor overly intrusive, but it was still several moments before Stephanie answered.

"I need to leave in about thirty minutes," she said with measured care. "But it's fine to talk until then."

"Okay. Good." Jack smiled, gently not mockingly, amazed by his inexplicable yet powerful urge to reassure her. "Thank you."

"You're welcome," Stephanie murmured reflexively.

Then she turned and led the way to the living room, a luxurious place that sent a peach-and-cream message of warmth and welcome and offered a panoramic view to the west—to Santa Monica and the ocean beyond. Jack waited for her to be seated, then he sat too and removed from his jacket pocket a small notebook. In it, carefully transcribed by him, were the salient features of the statement Stephanie had given to the officer on Thursday afternoon, eighteen hours after the slain body of Janine Raleigh, the Guitar String Strangler's latest victim, had been discovered and forty hours after what the coroner had determined to be the approximate time of her brutal murder, between nine and ten P.M. Tuesday evening. When Stephanie called the police station on Thursday to report that she'd had dinner with Janine Tuesday evening, her call was taken by one of Jack's assistants; only moments before Jack himself had left for Marina del Rey to begin to investigate the disappearance of Victor Chase Kincaid.

"Let's see," Jack began, glancing at his notes even though he knew their contents by heart. "You and Ms. Raleigh had dinner together at the Chart House in Malibu." He looked up from the notes to the slightly apprehensive eyes and asked, "Why?"

"Why?" Stephanie echoed. Echoing was another technique she used to buy time in which to prepare her next words. The answer to Jack's question came to her quickly, elaborately, and eloquently—because of the ocean, and the gulls that soar with such joyous freedom, and the powerful rhythm of the surf, and the silvery moonlight that shimmers on the rippling black sea. But because she had to, Stephanie condensed the elaborate and eloquent answer into a succinct and manageable reply. "Because of the view of the ocean."

Jack smiled. He liked the Chart House for the same reason. After a moment he clarified his question. "I meant, why did the two of you have dinner together that night? Were you good friends?"

"Good friends?" she echoed again. When her words were ready, she answered, "No. We were colleagues more than friends."

"Why did you have dinner together on Tuesday?"

"Does it matter?"

"Everything matters when there's been a murder," he offered gently, and then even more gently, "you know that Lieutenant Ballinger."

The beautiful sapphire eyes seemed surprised at his gentleness, then confused, then thoughtful as she considered her answer. Finally she said, "Janine wanted to discuss a role that she had just been offered."

"What role?" Everything mattered in a murder case, but it was Stephanie's hesitancy, the care she took before answering his almost certainly irrelevant questions that piqued Jack's curiosity—and his annoyance. Was she playing with him? Was she pretending that she had potentially significant information that she might *or might not* choose to reveal to him? He repeated solemnly and not gently, "Everything matters in murder." And then, pointedly, he added, "And, Ms. Windsor, you were the last person to see Janine Raleigh alive."

The taunt caused a sudden sapphire storm, a tumultuous fury of anger, frustration, and uncertainty. Jack waited, wanting to hear the honest words that matched the honest brilliant-blue emotion.

But although the storm clouds lingered, Stephanie calmed the fury before she amended quietly, "I was the second to last person to see her alive, Lieutenant."

Jack was impressed. His remark had been intentionally provocative—and she *had* been provoked—but instead of allowing incautious words to flow to her beautiful and impeccably well-bred lips on a river of righteous indignation, she had subdued her emotions before speaking. The provocation had been intended to make her more swiftly forthcoming with the details of her dinner with Janine—not because she herself was a suspect. True, the victims of the Guitar String Strangler weren't raped; but still, despite the absence of overt sexual violence, the belief was that the monster was, as virtually all serial killers were, a male. Besides, Jack knew, because he was compulsive and had checked, Stephanie Windsor had an airtight alibi—the all-night filming of the season finale of *Corpus Delicti*—for at least one of the five Tuesday nights on which the killer had prowled and strangled.

Now he smiled at the beautiful woman who had been provoked by his comment, provoked *yet so under control,* and agreed easily, "The second to last—yes. So, what role?"

"The lead in *Journeys of the Heart.*"

Jack's dark blue eyes narrowed at the coincidence. *Journeys of the Heart* wasn't scheduled to go into production until next spring, but already it had gotten a great deal of ink in the Hollywood press, proclaimed with surprising unanimity by insiders as the film destined to be Triple Crown's most stunning yet. Those who had read the extraordinary screenplay by first-time writer A. K. Smith heralded it as—at long last—a richly emotional and deeply compelling story *about a woman.* Which made the lead in *Journeys of the Heart* the most coveted role in Hollywood.

"Why did Janine Raleigh want to talk to you about the role?"

"Because I'm the one who recommended her for it."

"To whom did you recommend her?"

"To Brad Lancaster and Chase Kincaid."

Which could only mean that Stephanie herself had been offered the role first and had turned it down. There were many *faux* mysteries in Hollywood, intrigues created by publicists to keep their stars in the headlines, but one of the authentic mysteries was why Stephanie Windsor had never appeared in a feature film. She owned the small screen, and there was absolutely no doubt that she could own the silver one as well—if she so chose. But for reasons known only to the notoriously reclusive actress, she had always said no to movies—including, apparently, to the one that would feature the role of the decade.

Why? Jack wondered. He guessed that she wouldn't tell him. It would be hard to argue that her own career decisions had anything whatsoever to do with the murder of Janine Raleigh, and it was difficult enough getting her to answer the relevant questions. Still, he hoped he could get her to answer at least one that wasn't pertinent at all to the Guitar String Strangler murders, but to the other death—*the other murder*—that had occurred on the same Tuesday night.

"Did you know Chase Kincaid well?"

The question caused turbulence, and something more, something that looked to Jack like sadness.

"No," Stephanie answered softly. "I met him only once, about two months ago."

"When he and Brad offered you the role in *Journeys of the Heart?*"

Stephanie nodded. After a moment she asked, "Did you have other questions about my dinner with Janine?"

"Yes," Jack said. *But I'd also like to know why you're so obviously saddened by the death of a man you say you barely knew.* "According to the notes the officer gave me, you and Janine left the restaurant together at about eight-thirty?"

"Yes," Stephanie replied swiftly and with relief. *At last* he was asking questions for which she had already carefully prepared the answers. "There was very little traffic on the Pacific Coast Highway, so it was before nine when I dropped her off at her apartment building in Santa Monica."

"The notes say that you watched her go inside the building?"

"I watched until the front door closed behind her."

"And you saw no one else either in the foyer or near the building's entrance? Are you very sure?"

Stephanie hesitated, not because she needed time to script her answer, but to once again recall the scene, to be certain she had forgotten nothing. She had done this a hundred times in the past few days, and the memory was always the same. She had watched until the building's glass door had closed. Janine had turned to her then and waved gaily, a final thank-you for recommending her for the role of a lifetime, and for encouraging her to take it, and, with articulate miming, an extravagant thank-you, too, for the unnecessary kindness of watching until she was safely inside the lighted security of her locked building . . . the place where, just minutes later, she would be so brutally murdered.

"I'm very sure." Then, with a thoughtful tilt of moonbeams and sable, Stephanie asked a question that she had rehearsed during the previous interview but hadn't asked. "That means that either the Guitar String Strangler lives in her apartment building . . . or was someone she knew well enough to permit inside . . . doesn't it?"

"I think so. For a variety of reasons, I believe that it was probably the latter. Did she happen to mention any problems she was having with anyone—an estranged boyfriend perhaps, or an angry colleague?"

"No. No angry colleagues of either sex. And," Stephanie added softly, "the only man Janine talked about was her fiancé."

Jack nodded solemnly. It was the fiancé who had discovered the body when he returned from New York Wednesday evening. He had been onstage a continent away at the time of the murder; but even if he had had no alibi, and even though he *was* an actor, Jack had seen his anguish and had no doubt that he was not involved in the brutal slaying of the woman he had so obviously loved.

Janine Raleigh had been murdered by the Guitar String Strangler, not by her fiancé and definitely not by a copycat killer. The deep, merciless grooves where the three guitar strings had dug into her neck had obviously been caused by the same right-handed monster who had caused virtually identical grooves in four other women. There were other grim details, too, known only to the police. All the victims had had pierced ears, and each woman had been wearing earrings at the time of her death. From each the Strangler had taken a souvenir—the left earring—and in its stead he placed an expensive memento: a half-carat diamond stud. The diamond found in the left earlobe of the first victim, murdered the day after Valentine's Day, had been flawless. The quality of the gems found in the next four victims had been very good but not perfect. Except for the flawlessness of the first diamond, there was nothing distinctive about the earrings. Diamonds were common in Los Angeles, as was wealth, as were jewel thieves.

The Strangler's unique signature was a glittering tease, but it provided no real clue to his identity. The murder of Janine Raleigh, however, was significant. By murdering her in the sanctuary of her apartment, the Strangler had departed from his pattern of selecting apparently random victims away from their homes—on the lamplit campus of UCLA near the Sculpture Garden, on the sand beneath the Santa Monica pier, in the alley behind the Mann Theater in Westwood, in the stately shadow of the West Gate entrance to Bel Air.

The Strangler had always been quite bold, murdering in areas where the violence might well have been witnessed; but until now he had behaved like the classic "organized" serial killer, the deliberate stranger who, except during the final terrifying moments of her life, had no relationship with his victim. Now, by murdering in a place to which he had been admitted without force, he had escalated his boldness. It was possible, of course, that he and Janine Raleigh hadn't known each other, that he had used a ruse to gain entry; but if she had known him, it was the first possible break in solving the horror that had repeated itself without fail, and with grim precision, between nine and ten P.M. every third Tuesday since February fifteenth.

"She mentioned no men other than her fiancé?"

Stephanie bought time with a beautiful smile. That was a technique too. Usually the men at whom she smiled such a smile didn't care about the words she prepared, or if she spoke them at all. But the intense dark blue eyes that waited now wanted her answer.

"It's possible for women to go an entire evening without discussing men, Lieutenant."

"Touché." Jack's smile was as provocative as Stephanie's had been. It was a smile that usually made women care as little about his next words as most men cared about Stephanie's—suddenly becoming far more interested in what else his sensuous lips could do.

"If you have no other questions, Lieutenant, I really do need to leave soon."

"Okay. Just one more question. Do you remember what Janine was wearing?"

Yes, Stephanie thought. And I know that the other officer

wrote it down. He even told me that it was the same dress Janine was wearing when she died.

It shouldn't have been necessary for her to repeat the information, but it was so much easier to say it again than to find the words to tell Lieutenant Jack Shannon that he should carefully reread his assistant's notes.

"A turquoise dress with a multicolored scarf at the waist."

"Earrings?" Jack asked casually, knowing full well that she hadn't been asked about them before. Why inadvertently reveal the importance of earrings? the other officer had queried after admitting to Jack that no, he hadn't asked about earrings. Besides, he had added, they knew from the earring that Janine was still wearing in her right ear what the left one looked like, didn't they? Yes . . . but the reason Lieutenant Jack Shannon's record for catching murderers was the best in Los Angeles was because he compulsively double-checked even the most obvious details.

"Earrings?" Stephanie echoed. It took a moment for her to conjure the image in her mind, and a few moments more to put what she saw into words. Finally she said slowly, carefully, "She wore a gold star in her right ear and a silver crescent moon in her left."

Jack nodded, as if she were merely confirming something that he already knew. But in truth he was now in possession of a detail that was known only to himself, to Stephanie, and to the murderer. It was a tiny yet critical detail that would distinguish the real killer from the many impostors who inevitably tried to garner fame by confessing to murders they hadn't committed— or at least playing cat and mouse with the already overworked police department. Now even if descriptions of the five victims' earrings were leaked to the press, only the Strangler would know that the mate of the gold star was a silver crescent moon.

"May I offer you a ride?"

"A ride?"

"From the way you're dressed, I assume that you're going to the reception for Chase Kincaid." Yes, Jack realized from the surprised blue eyes and flushed pink cheeks. He realized, too, that Stephanie was waiting with apprehension for him to say the obvious: even though you met him only once. Jack bypassed the obvious and went directly to its logical follow-up. "Why are you going?"

"Why are you?"

"Because Chase and I knew each other in high school. Admittedly, it was a long time ago . . . but he was a friend. So, what about you? Because of Brad?" he asked. When he saw that the answer was "no," he queried, "Because of Jillian?"

"Yes." Stephanie drew a steadying breath, found more words, and explained. "Like you and Chase, a long time ago Jillian and I were friends."

"A long time ago," Jack repeated quietly, his blue eyes demanding embellishment.

After a moment Stephanie confessed softly, "I haven't seen or spoken to her for fifteen years."

"But you're going to the reception today because of her. Why?"

"Because I know she must be devastated by his death."

"You know that even though you haven't seen or spoken to her for fifteen years?"

"Yes." Brave, unshadowed confidence filled Stephanie's sapphire eyes as they met his skeptical dark blue ones. "Yes."

"Okay. Well. Shall we go?"

"I prefer to go by myself."

"I'll see you there, then." Jack's reply was easy, casual, but his thought was not: And, Stephanie Samantha Windsor, I will watch very closely the reunion between you and your friend . . . because you, like Jillian Kincaid, are obviously hiding very important truths.

Chapter Five

Stephanie didn't ride to the reception at Triple Crown Studios with Lieutenant Jack Shannon, nor did she drive herself. Instead, she traveled across town by limousine, shielded from the outside world by the shaded glass that afforded undistracted privacy for her thoughts. She sat with perfect regal posture, her back straight, her beautiful chin up, her white-gloved hands folded primly on her lap. It was exactly the way she had been sitting twenty years ago, on the sofa in the living room of Jillian Montgomery's home, when they first met . . .

"Hi."

Stephanie hadn't heard the footfalls behind her on the carpet, but at the sound of the voice she turned. The other girl was about her own age—nine—but that was where the similarity ended. Stephanie had been beautiful from the moment she was born, and this girl, despite her huge, startlingly green eyes and luxuriant mane of auburn hair, was decidedly plain. Plain, and smiling, something else that distinguished her from Stephanie; and when she spoke, there was the greatest difference of all: she was very verbal.

"My name is Jillian," she explained, plopping down on the sofa beside Stephanie. "Are you here to see my mom? Are your parents meeting with her now?"

Stephanie answered the bright green eyes the only way that she could—with a solemn nod.

As Jillian gazed at the beautiful yet silent—*and so sad*—girl, her own natural shyness was conquered by her wish to help. "Well," she began gently, her eyes earnest, concerned, and not the least bit disapproving. "Since my mom is a speech therapist, and it doesn't look like you've had surgery on your lips, it seems that, maybe, you have a problem with stuttering. Is that it?"

Stephanie answered with another nod, even more solemn this time, as she silently confessed to the secret that was so shameful for her and so devastating to her parents. She was their golden girl, the only child they would ever have, and she was supposed to be *perfect.* Her looks were quite perfect, as rare and precious as the wealth and privilege to which she had been born. Stephanie Samantha Windsor, heiress to the luxurious Windsor Hotels, was flawlessly beautiful, and she had been meticulously schooled in the manners and demeanor of the very rich. But she could not speak, not one word without stuttering, not even her own beautiful but so difficult name; and the harder she tried, the more desperate she became, making speech even more impossible . . . and making her parents' disappointment in her even greater.

She had been to all the best speech therapists, of course, but her progress had long since been completely blocked by the fear of disappointing even further, of being loved even less than she already was. The past year and a half had been spent in total silence at the mansion in Holmby Hills and in the boarding school to which she had been banished as punishment for the shameful imperfection which, according to her parents, she simply refused to correct.

Now she and her parents were here, and to Stephanie it felt more like a final threat than a last hope. But how much farther away could she be banished than she had already been? How much less could she be loved than she already was? How much greater pain could there be than overhearing her parents bemoan the complicated birth—hers—that had made it impossible for them to have more children, perfect children who would never disappoint?

Meredith Montgomery was their last hope. She had been recommended to the Windsors for years. She could work magic when no one else could, Stephanie's parents had been told; but nonetheless they had resisted bringing their daughter to Meredith until now. Meredith was a specialist, yes, but she worked for the public schools, helping speech-impaired children who had no other source of hope and whose parents could not otherwise afford the best. Since Jillian's birth, Meredith had worked for the public school system still, but her office was in her home in Brentwood. It was a very nice house in a very nice area—because Edward Montgomery was, after all, a partner in a prestigious law firm—a place to which the Windsors felt comfortable venturing from their mansion in the hills.

Meredith Montgomery was Stephanie's last chance. Stephanie had felt the threat, not the hope, but now her young heart raced as she gazed at the green-eyed girl whose hopefulness suddenly seemed so contagious.

"Can you recite poetry without stuttering?" Jillian asked. "Or sing? Or read a passage from a book?"

Yes, Stephanie knew, she could read words that were already written down. The other therapists had urged her over and over to expand on this, to write the words down first in her mind and then speak them as if she were reading from a page. She had tried, oh, how she had tried, but she had always failed. Emotions—desperate fear and desperate hope—would suddenly take over, crashing like unwelcome waves on words written in sand, swiftly erasing all memory of the carefully scripted words and drowning her in an even greater sense of her own worthlessness.

Stephanie knew that she could read words that were written

down . . . and that she couldn't. But still, to the hopeful emerald eyes, she bravely nodded yes.

"Well, then, you're going to be fine." Jillian made the pronouncement with absolute confidence, embellishing her words with an absolutely radiant smile. "My mom will be able to help you. You'll be fine. You'll see."

This time Stephanie answered with hot tears. It had been so long since she had cried. Tears, she had learned, washed away nothing. But these were different tears—hopeful, grateful ones—and as Stephanie's eyes glistened, so too did those of the auburn-haired girl who was so plain . . . and so beautiful.

And then, and it had been so long—ever?—that she had been hugged, Jillian curled her arms around Stephanie and added softly, "My mom will help you, and so will I."

Meredith was true to Jillian's promise, as was Jillian herself. Together they worked magic, and there was even more magic. Stephanie found a best friend, and because Jillian so generously shared her own loving mother, Stephanie found a mother too; and for the first time in her life Stephanie learned of love.

How she wished she could tell Meredith and Jillian how very much she loved them. She could speak now, by writing words in her mind and then reading them. She became expert at it, especially with Meredith and Jillian, and sometimes there was only a heartbeat of silence between the words they spoke to her and the answer she gave in return. With others the delay was always longer, but Stephanie learned to fill in what might otherwise have been awkward silences with mechanical phrases— "Thank you," "You're welcome," "Yes," "No," "Okay," "Well," "I see"—or by simply echoing the last words spoken by the other person.

Stephanie could speak, but she still could not give voice to her emotions. She felt the words of love in her heart, and she could even see them carefully scripted in her mind; but when she tried to speak those most important truths, her emotions blurred the words with invisible tears and she knew that if she tried to speak, she would stutter—and she was so afraid of that, so terribly afraid of the lonely and shameful prison of silence to which she once had been condemned.

The friendship between Stephanie and Jillian survived despite separate schools—Jillian in public schools, Stephanie at the exclusive Westlake—and despite the fact that as the little girls became little women, Stephanie's stunning beauty blossomed even further and Jillian's plainness only became more entrenched. Stephanie never saw her best friend as plain. By any measure of physical beauty, Jillian's brilliant emerald eyes, luxuriant auburn hair, and glowingly radiant smile *were* beautiful, of course; and by the only really important measures of beauty— love and kindness and generosity—Jillian was extraordinary. She greeted the world with joyous hopefulness, marveling with reverent wonder at the bountiful gifts of nature: the exquisite delicacy of flowers, the splendor of sunsets, the welcoming warmth of sun-kissed sand, the magnificent promises of rainbows.

Teenage boys noticed Stephanie, all men did, and they didn't notice Jillian at all; but it didn't matter, because Stephanie and Jillian had more important things to consider than boys— they had dreams. Stephanie's dream was to be an actress. She knew that in her own life she might never be able to articulate her emotions, or to speak the lively thoughts that sometimes leapt into her mind only to be subdued and edited before she spoke them aloud. But she had already discovered in her drama classes at Westlake that through acting, through pretending she was someone else, she could offer a few moments of precious freedom to the powerful emotions and vivacious personality held prisoner still by her own ancient fears.

Stephanie was going to be an actress, and Jillian was going to be a schoolteacher. She would teach English, giving to her young pupils the literacy that she believed was so essential to almost every dream; and during the summer she would write, novels maybe . . . or, maybe, screenplays for her talented best friend.

In January of eighth grade, when they were both fourteen, a tragedy occurred that ended their wonderful friendship. It was a stormy Wednesday evening. The rage of wind and rain had assaulted Los Angeles for over two days.

Just after dusk Meredith arrived at Stephanie's Holmby Hills mansion to retrieve her daughter. Before parting, the best friends promised that they would talk, as always, right after dinner; and Meredith gave her surrogate daughter a loving hug and told her that she would definitely be at opening night of Westlake's production of *Pygmalion,* in which Stephanie was playing Eliza; and then Meredith and Jillian drove off into the storm, the golden glow of their headlights dancing off the raindrops.

Stephanie noticed the dance of headlights and raindrops, because Jillian had taught her to celebrate even the soggy gifts of nature, and she smiled at the glistening gold. But ever after rain would fill her with anger and dread; because that evening, as she drove down the steep hill from the mansion, Meredith Montgomery lost control of the car.

The brakes failed, the police decided, waterlogged perhaps from the relentless rain, or maybe merely because brakes sometimes failed. For whatever reason on that stormy evening the brilliant beam of gold moved faster and ever faster through the raindrops, a too-frantic dance—and a fatal one.

The roomy station wagon that had always seemed so safe, a solid symbol of family, of normalcy, was crushed into a small metal coffin. Jillian and Meredith were trapped inside; and as Jillian watched in helpless despair as her beloved mother died, she died too, a death of hope and spirit and innocence.

Jillian was eventually removed from the car, and because there were devastating physical injuries as well, she was rushed to UCLA Medical Center. Her pelvis was shattered, as was her face, its delicate bones mercilessly crushed, its fair skin pierced and torn by fragments of glass.

While the doctors fought to save Jillian's life, Stephanie Windsor and Edward Montgomery kept their anxious vigil in a small, windowless waiting room. During the six years that Stephanie and Jillian had been best friends, Stephanie had seen Edward only once. He was a virtual phantom in his daughter's life, a brilliant attorney whose star was rising and who devoted far more of his waking hours to his crescendoing legal career than to his daughter or wife. It was a benign neglect, the price of immense success, and at its very core there was great love. The success for which Edward worked so hard was for his family, so that Jillian and Meredith would never want for anything. Jillian deeply loved the father she barely knew; but still, even her own effortless speech came to a shuttering halt in his presence, braked by a mixture of shyness and awe.

With the tragedy Stephanie and Edward were suddenly thrown into an awkward companionship of tormented silence. Stephanie couldn't speak, because emotion hopelessly blurred all words; and the stunningly articulate attorney couldn't speak either, as unable to express emotion as she and as tormented as she by the words of love he hadn't spoken enough to the woman he had loved so much—and the words he didn't even know how to speak to the daughter he scarcely knew.

The doctors repaired Jillian's shattered pelvis as best they could. She would always have a limp, they explained, and, yes, there would probably always be pain if she pushed too hard. Her shattered face remained hidden beneath stark white bandages, haloed by her auburn hair, the starkness further accentuated by the haunted emptiness of her stricken emerald eyes. Jillian was awake, as she had been throughout the entire horror of the accident, but she wouldn't speak, not to Edward, not to the team of doctors and nurses that cared for her, not even to her best friend.

Stephanie wanted desperately to help the friend who had helped her so much. She wanted to tell Jillian how much she loved her and how much she, too, missed the mother Jillian had so generously shared with her. She sent those messages to Jillian in the way she always had, with the expressive blue eyes that could be windows to her heart when she allowed them to be; but even their crystal-clear eloquence wasn't enough to lure her best friend from her resolute and tormented silence.

So, courageously, Stephanie tried to speak the emotional words. But the words stumbled and stuttered, not helping Jillian and plunging Stephanie deeper and ever deeper into her own memories of silent imprisonment and shame. She started hating herself again, as much, no, *more* than she had hated herself as a little girl. She wasn't helping Jillian, and with every faltering word she was destroying herself; but still, day after day, she sat beside her faraway friend and whispered hopelessly fragmented words of love.

At the end of the second week, Jillian's nurse told Stephanie that in three days Jillian would be transferred to a hospital in San Francisco. There was a woman doctor there—Dr. Claudia Green—a plastic surgeon who specialized in severe facial injuries to children. Three days . . . surely she could sit at Jillian's bedside and endure her own pain and self-loathing for just three more days.

But Stephanie didn't return, and by abandoning her best friend because of her own torment, she proved beyond a shadow of a doubt the truths she had learned as a child: she was deeply flawed, destined to disappoint, undeserving of love, of friendship, or of dreams.

By the time Jillian returned to Los Angeles, her plain—and then shattered—face had been replaced by one that was as exquisitely beautiful as the loveliness that had always dwelled within her. Jillian had a new face and a new mother. The gifted plastic surgeon not only brilliantly repaired the devastating injury to Jillian's face; she saved both father and daughter from the massive trauma to their hearts as well.

Stephanie wasn't in Los Angeles when Jillian returned. She had long since banished herself to a finishing school in Switzerland. Emerging impeccably "finished" at eighteen, she spent the following year as a debutante. By year's end she was engaged to a man ten years older than she, with a stunning pedigree that matched her own. She had become the perfect puppet her parents had always wanted her to be. Her speech was perfect, they thought. Perfectly refined and impeccably unemotional words flowed from her lips with measured, regal elegance. Her parents loved her now, of course, now that she neither disappointed nor embarrassed them.

One month before her wedding was to have taken place, Stephanie finally allowed herself to remember the only two people she had ever loved—and who had loved her even though she was undeserving—and who had enthusiastically encouraged her to pursue the dream of becoming an actress that her own parents had viewed only with arch disdain.

Meredith and Jillian Montgomery were gone from her life forever, but the memory of their love would remain with her always. Stephanie wrote two letters. The first was to the parents whose "love" had always been so conditional. The second was to the man who had never even begun to know her, who had never wanted to know more than the perfect beauty he could see—and the perfect body he could possess whenever he wanted, ungentle conquests, not tender caresses of love. Stephanie considered delivering the messages to her parents and her fiancé in person. But she knew her emotions would only stutter her words, and she didn't want to give any of them the satisfaction of feeling relieved to be free of her and her embarrassing imperfection.

Stephanie almost wrote a third letter to the best friend to whom she hadn't spoken since her stumbling whispers of love six years before. It would have been an unselfish letter, a wish that Jillian's life would be filled with love and happiness always. But Stephanie feared that generous Jillian might forgive her unforgivable betrayal; and even though she was terribly lonely, and missed her best friend so very much, Stephanie knew she did not deserve such forgiveness.

Having escaped what would have been a suffocating marriage, Stephanie bravely began to pursue the dream that somehow seemed essential to her very survival—her only chance to
express emotions imprisoned deep inside.

Stephanie wanted to be an actress, but she didn't care at all
about fame. In fact, she didn't want it. With fame would come
scrutiny. There would be reporters who would wonder at the
careful slowness of her answers to their questions, and eventually someone would discover the secret whose greatest shame
of all was her abandonment of her best friend.

Television actresses commanded far less scrutiny than their
feature-film counterparts, Stephanie knew, and within the world
of television, daytime attracted far less attention than prime time.
If she could just land a small part in a daytime soap
opera . . .

It was supposed to be a small part, a beautiful but not
memorable ingenue who would spend a few months in *The
Young and the Restless*'s Genoa City and then disappear. The
character wasn't supposed to have much personality, much less
a sense of humor, but Stephanie gave such sparkle and vitality
to even her most bland lines that the writers responded with
more and better words for her to speak, and the viewers responded with letters expressing hope that she would remain in
Genoa City forever.

Stephanie won the daytime Emmy for Best Supporting Actress three years in a row, and when her character was elevated
to lead-actress status, she won that Emmy as well. Her success
captured attention, but by then she had the full support of her
cast members. They knew no secret truths about Stephanie
Samantha Windsor, of course, but they protected her nonetheless, revealing to the inquiring press what they knew to be true:
that she was a gifted and generous actress and that their great
respect for her talent translated into great respect, too, for the
privacy that seemed so important to her.

By the time she made the transition from daytime to prime
time, the Hollywood press accepted her demure reclusiveness

as well. It was appropriate, somehow, for an heiress. Not that they wouldn't all love to do in-depth interviews; but they respected Stephanie's right to privacy in the same way that, at long last, most of the journalistic world respected the privacy of Jacqueline Kennedy Onassis.

So nonintrusive was the press that it might have been possible for Stephanie to accept one of the many feature-film roles that she was constantly being offered despite her well-known "absolute contentment" with the small screen. But until she read *Journeys of the Heart,* she had never found a role worth the potential risk of increased attention and scrutiny.

It was an extraordinary role, and it seemed as if first-time screenwriter A. K. Smith had written it precisely for her. In one intense and evocative performance Stephanie would be able to reveal the full range of emotions that lived deep within her. Had the script belonged to any studio but Triple Crown, or had Chase Kincaid said anything to imply that his wife knew she was being offered the part, Stephanie would have said yes. But there had been nothing personal; nothing to suggest that Chase knew that she and Jillian had once been friends, nor that Jillian was aware he was offering her the role of a lifetime. There was no reason Jillian *would* have shared their past with Chase, of course; no reason whatsoever that she would have ever mentioned the friend who had never really been a friend at all . . .

Stephanie turned down the magnificent role—because of Jillian. Not that Jillian would have tried to get Chase to change his mind. She was far too generous, too forgiving, for that. Stephanie simply decided that it would be wrong, terribly unfair, to put Jillian in the awkward position of having to pretend to be happy that such a wonderful role had been given to someone as undeserving as she.

Stephanie wanted only authentic happiness for her friend. Two months before, as she had gazed at the stunningly handsome man who Jillian had married, her heart had sent a silent plea: Make her gloriously happy, Chase. Fill her life with joy and love—forever.

But now Chase Kincaid was dead, and once again a tragic accident had plunged Jillian into an anguish she did not deserve. Stephanie wanted to help, at least to offer to help. She knew that Jillian might not want her help, might not trust it, and she planned to make it very easy for Jillian to refuse her offer if she chose.

But as the limousine neared Triple Crown Studios, Stephanie's heart made another silent plea: Oh, Jillian, let me help you this time. Please believe that I won't abandon you again.

Even if I stutter.

Even if the whole world hears me.

Chapter Six

By the time Jack arrived at Triple Crown Studios, the elegant mirrored and marble lobby was already a glittering galaxy of stars, starlets, and Hollywood's behind-the-scenes rich, famous, and powerful. They had all assembled to bid a somber adieu to their gifted favorite son and to offer heartfelt condolences to his beautiful widow.

Jack looked forward to speaking to Jillian Kincaid again, one final time, to see if the remarkable emerald eyes that had seemed so wary—so *guilty*—appeared that way to him still. It would have been nice to have had a chance to speak to her privately, but when he spotted her at the far end of the flower-adorned lobby, he knew that would be impossible. As always, her parents and Brad hovered protectively.

Jack moved unhurriedly toward Jillian and her loyal and loving entourage, the journey through the sea of rich and famous as important perhaps as the destination. In the hushed conversations that filled the lobby with a somber hum he might overhear something of interest about the marriage of Chase and Jillian Kincaid.

But Jack's leisurely journey yielded nothing, not a whisper of scandal, not the tiniest clue that there might have been deadly secrets. Others were offering their condolences to Jillian when he reached her, so Jack patiently waited his turn a few feet away, reflecting on what a shattered reception line this was. The beautiful bride was a widow now, but at least she still had her parents. The devastation on the groom's side was far greater. Only Brad, the best man, had survived. Both sets of parents and the only grandparent had perished in a blazing inferno and the groom himself had drowned in a watery grave.

Finally it was Jack's turn to approach, and as he did he saw Jillian stiffen, her already rigid body steeling itself even more, her emerald eyes searching and anxious.

"Lieutenant Shannon. Have you found Chase?"

"No, Mrs. Kincaid."

The news caused a flicker of something in the brilliant green depths. What was it? Jack wondered. Relief, he decided. Relief that her husband's body hadn't been found . . . because then there could be no proof of a crime—no evidence that more than a single blow had been delivered to the black-haired head, no marks left by a weight belt which had somehow become unfastened by the push and pull of the ocean's deepest currents.

"Then why are you here, Lieutenant?" Edward demanded.

Jack met Edward's challenging gaze briefly but returned to Jillian before answering. There was fear in her beautiful eyes now—fear that he would keep pushing her to reveal the truths she so obviously kept hidden. But even as he watched the fear vanished, replaced by proud defiance.

Jillian Kincaid knew that he couldn't push any further, because her father wouldn't permit it, and as he met her unwavering gaze Jack wondered if, for the first time in his career, he was face-to-face with a murderer who had committed a perfect crime.

Subduing his frustration, he finally said with quiet calm, "I came to offer my condolences."

"That's very thoughtful of you, Jack." The politely pleasant voice belonged to Brad. As he spoke, he moved closer to Jillian,

as if attempting to redirect toward himself the intense assault of
Jack's dark blue eyes.

Brad's voice was pleasant. But his dark eyes were not. He
had listened with solemnity to Jack's concern that Chase had
been murdered and had spent long, patient hours telling Jack
about Chase's rivals, none of whom, to Brad's knowledge, had
been enemies. But Brad's patience had vanished swiftly when
Jack had pointed the finger at Jillian.

Jack saw Brad's outrage now, the unmistakable warning to
leave his cousin's grieving widow alone. After a moment he
returned once again to that widow, the woman whose family
protected her as if she were a delicate porcelain doll that would
shatter into a thousand pieces with even the slightest breath of
harshness. As Jillian met his gaze with unwavering defiance,
Jack thought, You are far stronger than they know, aren't you,
Jillian Kincaid? Somehow you have convinced these people
who love you of your frailty—and of your innocence. Did your
loving husband discover your true strength and treachery too
late?

"Please let me know if you remember anything else about
the evening your husband disappeared, Mrs. Kincaid."

"Why, Lieutenant?" Edward Montgomery asked brusquely.
"It's my understanding that the case has been officially closed."

"Yes," Jack calmly answered the attorney whose resolute
expression promised to cause trouble for him if he continued to
plague his precious daughter without cause. This was Hollywood, the home of Lieutenant Columbo and his clever games
with rich and famous murderers. But the adventures of
Columbo were pure fiction, and the plain fact was that unless
the case was reopened, Lieutenant Jack Shannon had absolutely
no right to question Jillian Kincaid ever again. To do so would
be harassment. Jack knew it, and Edward Montgomery knew it.
But still, as Jack bade farewell to the porcelain doll who had
perhaps committed the perfect murder, he said quietly, "Chase's
death was officially ruled an accident. But you know that I have
my doubts, Mrs. Kincaid. I always will."

Jack wanted to see the effect of his final taunt on the emerald eyes in the stunned moments before her family intervened; but he got only a fleeting glimpse—and what he saw looked far more like pain than anger. The remaining moments were stolen from him by a teary-eyed starlet who arrived to breathlessly express her grief by gushing effusively to Jillian about how very kind Chase had been to her, how he had believed in her talent and had given her her first big break.

Jack withdrew from the stunned emerald, and in just a few long, graceful strides he met flashing sapphire. Stephanie was too far away to have heard the words he had spoken to Jillian Kincaid, but quite obviously she had witnessed Jillian's reaction to the exchange and was angered by what she had seen.

"Ms. Windsor. We meet again."

What did you say to her? the expressive sapphire demanded with crystal-clear eloquence. *How dare you hurt her! You are despicable, Lieutenant Shannon. Despicable and arrogant.*

Jack stared at the blazing eyes, intrigued by the brilliant blue emotion but annoyed by the messages. Stephanie hadn't seen her friend for fifteen years, yet it was abundantly clear that she believed Jillian Kincaid to be innocent of all crimes—whereas he, the presumptuous homicide lieutenant, was apparently guilty of the capital offense of bothering her friend.

"Everything matters in murder," Jack hissed softly at the so very beautiful, and so very impassioned, and so very judgmental sky-blue eyes. And then, with a contempt that equaled hers, he added coldly, "You know that, Lieutenant Ballinger. You know that."

He left her then, his long strides graceful and unhurried still, despite his churning anger. He was twenty feet away from her before he realized that she hadn't said a word. She hadn't needed to. Her remarkable eyes had communicated her thoughts with the dazzling clarity of the most flawless of jewels.

*   *   *

Everything matters in murder. The words swirled in Stephanie's already swirling mind as she watched Jack stride away. What did he mean by that?

She should follow him and confront him. That's what the confident, sassy, and articulate Lieutenant Cassandra Ballinger would do . . . as would any true friend of Jillian Kincaid. But Stephanie knew all too well her own meager abilities—and her own immense limitations.

She was an impostor as a confident, sassy, and articulate woman . . . just as she was an impostor as a true friend.

"Stephanie?"

The voice came from behind her, soft, familiar, and *welcoming.* Stephanie felt a hot mist in her eyes even before she turned. Then she was face-to-face with the woman who as a girl had been her only friend. The exquisitely beautiful face was startlingly different from the face of the girl she had known, but the huge green eyes and the full, generous lips were the same; and now from the icy depths of emerald grief came a flicker of warmth, and the softest whisper of a smile touched the lovely lips.

"Jillian," Stephanie whispered, her heart filling with gratitude and love, filling, flooding, and threatening to erase her carefully rehearsed words. With soft urgency she added, "I want to help you."

"I need your help," Jillian confessed quietly. *And I am so grateful that you are willing to offer it after the unforgivable way I rejected it the last time. How I have missed you. How I have needed my best friend.* "Thank you."

"I hadn't realized you two knew each other," Brad said as he joined them. "Hello, Stephanie."

"Hello, Brad."

"It was a long time ago," Jillian explained. Then, as Edward and Claudia approached, she said, "Dad, you remember Stephanie Windsor."

"Of course." Edward smiled at Stephanie, acknowledging that they had been bonded once before in tragedy. The gentleness of Edward's smile said more: that he had been emotionally unequipped to handle that tragedy, perhaps they both had been; and it sent a promise for both of them: that this time they would do better for Jillian.

"And this is Claudia," Jillian said. She didn't identify Claudia as her stepmother. That title seemed far too distant. The woman who had rescued her from her tormented silence, and had introduced her to the father she had never really known, and had watched with loving pride as she had blossomed into a woman was her mother now, beloved and cherished as Meredith had been.

Stephanie heard the love in Jillian's voice as she made the introduction, and for a magnificent moment she thought she might have heard something more, a generous invitation to share this wonderful mother as Jillian had once been so willing to share the wonderful mother who had died. The invitation was embellished by Claudia herself, her light blue eyes adding their own warmth and welcome.

"Would you be able to come to dinner some night this week, Stephanie?" Jillian asked impulsively, prompted by her sudden awareness of a small group of people waiting patiently to offer their condolences to her.

"Yes. I'd love to. Any night would be fine."

"Shall we say Wednesday, then? I have an adult literacy class to teach Tuesday evening and I'll probably be busy tomorrow night catching up with what's accumulated at school."

"School?" The words, with various inflections of surprise and worry, came in stereo from Brad, Edward, and Claudia.

"I'm going back to work tomorrow morning," Jillian told her family with quiet resolve. *I have to, don't you see? I can't—I won't—allow myself to descend again into the silent madness of my grief.*

Chapter Seven

In the beginning, as they sat in the living room at Clairmont while the casserole heated in the oven, Stephanie and Jillian's conversation focused on Annie—how pretty she was, how soft, how wiggly, how friendly, how loving; and they talked about Jillian's teaching career and Stephanie's role in *Corpus Delicti*. It was a tentative dance of inconsequential words, a necessary prelude to the more important ones that might be spoken. Each woman wanted more words, but each was uncertain too—and fearful.

Finally, because the smiles and glances that had embellished the inconsequential words had given her courage, and because she had always been the more verbal one, it was Jillian who began the brave journey into more important and more dangerous territory: the past.

"What do you think of my new face?" she asked softly, with the honest candor of the shy yet forthright girl she once had been.

Jillian knew that Stephanie had been discreetly studying her face, more revealed now than at the reception, makeup free and unshadowed in the natural light that filtered into the room. Without makeup or shadows, the truths of her new face were

fully exposed. The scars were thin and delicate, pearly, gossamer threads that were just a shade whiter than the fairness of her
skin.

"Very beautiful," Stephanie answered with the heartbeat
swiftness with which she had always been able to talk to her
best friend. The swiftness had returned already, slowed only by
the emotion that accompanied it. Jillian was very beautiful, that
was indisputable, the tiny, thin lines adding interest and detract-
ing nothing from her newfound beauty. But there was suddenly
such uncertainty in the emerald eyes that Stephanie asked
gently, "What do you think?"

"I think that Claudia did a wonderful job . . . maybe too
wonderful."

"What does that mean?"

"It means that if I didn't have this face, Chase would never
have noticed me." Jillian frowned, her expressive eyes thoughtful and sad. "It was love at first sight, for both of us. Chase fell
in love with what he saw, the beautiful cover, not who I really
am."

"Chase Kincaid was a gorgeous man, but you fell in love
with far more than his stunning good looks, Jillian. I know you
did," Stephanie said emphatically to the generous girl who had
never cared at all about covers. Stephanie was absolutely confident that Jillian had fallen in love with the real Chase—with his
heart—but it was obvious that Jillian didn't believe that the
reverse had been true. "What makes you think the same wasn't
true for him?"

"There was just so much that we never told each other, never
shared. I was as guilty as he. I suppose I was afraid that if he
really knew me . . ." Jillian sighed softly. "We should have been
friends as well as lovers—but when Chase was troubled, he
didn't turn to me."

"What troubled him?"

"I don't know."

"Who did he turn to? Brad?"

"No. At least I don't think so. He just turned inward. When

something was bothering him, he would go sailing by himself or stay up all night, playing his guitar. And if I tried to reach out to him, he only withdrew further." *As if he were as afraid of revealing his flaws to me as I was afraid of revealing mine to him.*

"I'm so sorry, Jill."

"Thanks." A grateful smile trembled on Jillian's lovely lips. After a moment she assured her concerned and sympathetic friend, "Chase and I had wonderful times, too, Steph. Everything Chase Kincaid did he did magnificently—including, in breathtakingly romantic moments, marriage."

"You loved him very much."

"Yes. I loved him very much," Jillian confessed softly. Then, and even more softly, she confessed, "That's why it hurts so much that the police officer in charge of the investigation— Lieutenant Jack Shannon—believes that I murdered him."

"What?" As vividly as Stephanie recalled the arrogant lieutenant's softly hissed reminder that everything matters in murder, it hadn't occurred to her that he thought her gentle and loving friend might be involved in such a crime. "How can he possibly think that?"

"He has reasons, good reasons. He's appropriately bothered by the fact that Chase, who was an experienced sailor, could have been careless enough to have been struck by the boom, and he also senses that I didn't tell him the whole truth about what happened that night." Jillian's honest green eyes bravely met the brilliant blue ones that had filled swiftly with righteous indignation—for her. "And he's right, Steph. I told him that Chase and I had had a pleasant dinner together that evening and that afterward he had gone for a sail. The truth is that we had a terrible argument. It was my fault. I started it. Something was troubling him, something deeper and darker than anything that had come before, and it had gone on for almost three months. He had withdrawn completely from me, as if I weren't even there. I felt so desperate, so helpless . . . so worthless." Jillian stopped abruptly. *Just like you must have felt when you tried to help me and I wouldn't even acknowledge that I had heard your words. I just let you stutter and stutter . . .*

"Jill?"

"Anyway, we argued that night. Chase was very upset when he left to go sailing, and . . . Lieutenant Shannon is right. I *am* responsible for Chase's death. Our argument, on top of whatever else it was that had been troubling him, made him so distracted that he wasn't aware of the boom—"

"Oh, Jillian," Stephanie whispered. "Please don't blame yourself. I know you must be tormented by the last words you said to him . . . and by all the words you didn't say." *Just as I have been tormented all these years by the words I didn't— couldn't—say to you.* Stephanie couldn't speak that emotional thought, not now, not yet, but somehow she was able to offer a soft reassurance. "I'm sure Chase knew how much you loved him."

"I hope so." That gentle hope flickered briefly on Jillian's sad and lovely face; but it vanished quickly, replaced by bewildered anguish. "I don't know, Stephanie. Maybe I should tell Lieutenant Shannon everything. The case is officially closed, and my father has let him know in no uncertain terms that he won't tolerate any more questions, but it still bothers me that he believes Chase could have been murdered."

"And that you could have been a murderer."

"That doesn't bother me for me, only for Chase. Chase and Jack Shannon once were friends. I want him to know that Chase didn't marry a woman who was capable of murder."

"Why don't I tell Jack?" Stephanie suggested impulsively.

"You know him?"

"We've met." It was obvious that Jillian hadn't witnessed her glowering encounter with the arrogant lieutenant at the reception, so now Stephanie smiled beautifully, as if her past meetings with Jack Shannon had been entirely pleasant ones. "It would be much easier for me to tell him than for you to."

Easy? The word itself taunted. No, Stephanie knew, it would not be easy at all. But, she realized as she saw her friend's sudden hope, this is so important to Jillian . . . and miraculously she trusts me still . . . and she's willing to give me a second chance to prove my friendship. I don't deserve a second chance, but Jillian is willing to give me one. I can do it. I will. Somehow.

The somehow came to Stephanie then. It was something she had never tried before, but it would work, wouldn't it? Stephanie Windsor couldn't speak fluidly, compellingly, emotionally to the intense ocean-blue eyes. But confident, sassy, and articulate Cassandra Ballinger could. She would talk to Jack Shannon in character—homicide lieutenant to homicide lieutenant.

"Let me do this, Jill."

"All right," Jillian agreed with obvious gratitude. "Thank you."

"You're welcome," Stephanie countered, grateful as well. Thank you for trusting me, Jillian. I won't let you down this time. I *won't*.

The phone rang then, and as Stephanie watched her friend's eyes fill with sudden apprehension, she realized that as long as Chase was still missing, Jillian held on to the fragile hope that he was alive, that he would return, that at any moment he would walk through the front door.

The call was from Brad, not the police, and as soon as Jillian's obvious relief told her that Brad wasn't calling with the news that Chase's body had been found, Stephanie left to check on the casserole and replenish their lemonade.

By the time she returned, Jillian was off the phone, seated on the couch, her auburn head bent, her slender body very still.

"What is it, Jill?"

The auburn head lifted, revealing an expression of deep sadness. "Brad just told me about Janine Raleigh, that she was killed Tuesday night by the Guitar String Strangler."

"You didn't know?"

"No. After Chase left that night, I just waited here for him to return. In the two days before the police arrived to tell me that his sailboat had been found, I didn't listen to the radio, or read the newspaper, or watch television." *I just waited, as he asked me to. Annie and I just waited in absolute silence, listening for the sound of his car on the gravel.* "I didn't know that the Strangler had struck again."

"Why on earth did Brad tell you now?" Stephanie asked, her annoyance unconcealed. Why was Brad burdening Jillian with another inexplicable tragedy, especially one that had occurred just hours before Chase had sailed to his death?

"Because," Jillian said softly, "when I told him that you were here, he wanted me to ask you to reconsider accepting the lead role in *Journeys of the Heart.*"

"You knew that I had been offered the role?"

"Yes," Jillian answered, surprised—and a little hopeful. "It was my idea."

"Your idea?" Stephanie echoed, needing to, needing time. "Neither Brad nor Chase ever mentioned that."

"No." Both Brad and Chase had known how much Jillian wanted Stephanie to accept the role, how perfect she was for it, but . . . "Neither of them knew of our friendship."

Friendship. Jillian shivered at the word, at her own betrayal of it and her memories of that betrayal. She had heard Stephanie's desperate whispers. She had heard the stuttering words of love, and the great pain those brave utterances had caused her friend, and she had willfully allowed Stephanie to suffer. No, *worse,* she had wanted Stephanie to suffer as she was suffering.

Fifteen years ago, when their friendship ended, it had been Stephanie who had stuttered. Now, as perhaps, maybe, please, their friendship was getting a second chance, it was Jillian who spoke with halting emotion.

"I . . . it . . . was my idea. The role seemed . . . right . . . for your eight-octave talent."

"Eight-octave," Stephanie murmured. It had been their favorite description as teenagers, eight-octave talents, eight-octave dreams, eight-octave careers, eight-octave romances. They were going to experience the full range of life, they had decided. They were going to bravely sample every note on the scale, fearlessly embracing both the sharps and the flats, the harmony and the discord, the entire magnificent eight-octave symphony.

Jillian drew a steadying breath before admitting quietly, "I'm A. K. Smith, Stephanie. I wrote the role of Elizabeth in *Journeys of the Heart* for you."

For me? Even though I betrayed you? Even though I abandoned you when you needed me the most?

There had been a time, when they had been best friends, that Stephanie and Jillian had been able to perfectly read each other's thoughts. That was what had always made it so easy, so effortless for Stephanie to speak . . . because the words scripted in her own mind were already scripted in her friend's as well.

But now both the emerald and sapphire eyes were clouded, their messages undecipherable to each other . . . even though their hidden thoughts were remarkably the same.

I wish I had the courage to apologize for what I did to you—to us. But I'm not strong enough, not now, not yet, and I need your friendship too much now to risk losing it again. Someday I will tell you though. Someday I will apologize.

After a few moments, and at precisely the same moment, the clouds vanished. The blue and green were crystal-clear again, as were the messages, clear, and hopeful—and identical.

I want to be your friend again. And I promise—oh, how I promise—this time I will not let you down.

Chapter Eight

"There's a Lieutenant Ballinger on line one, Jack."

"Thanks. I'll take it in my office."

Jack smiled as he walked toward the relative privacy of his glass-walled but soundproofed and bulletproofed office. In the four days since the memorial reception for Chase Kincaid, he had been thinking about Stephanie. A lot. She was an intriguing blend of fire and ice; impassioned sapphire blazing amid chillingly patrician manners and coolly elegant speech.

Jack thought about Stephanie, and he worried about her. She had, after all, been very near the Guitar String Strangler. Had the monster been watching that night when she dropped Janine off? Had his evil eyes filled with bloodlust *for her?* With the five victims to date, the psychopath had shown a clear preference for beautiful women with darker shades of hair—luxuriant manes of auburn, brown, and black, not the glittering golds of the California blonde. Stephanie's dark, rich sable would undoubtedly appeal to the killer. But, Jack thought, her lustrous hair was laced with moonbeams, and might even shimmer pure gold beneath the moon itself. Would the ribbons of spun gold warn the Strangler away? Or would they, shining as one, merely serve as a magnificent beacon to him?

With vivid and horrifying clarity Jack could see Stephanie's terror as the Strangler approached her, and he could sense the deep inner strength that would compel her to struggle with courageous defiance. But what filled Jack with his own private terror was the memory of her cool and dignified elegance. Would the perfectly bred Stephanie Samantha Windsor scream, even to save her life? Her control was so great, her manners so impeccable . . .

Jack thought about Stephanie, and worried about her, and very much wanted to see her again. But he knew that he couldn't call her, not without what she might fairly perceive as an ulterior motive, until the issue of Chase Kincaid's death had been put to rest one way or the other. Chase Carlton had received the box of information on Tuesday, and today was Thursday, and the man who had a gift for sensing murder had promised his verdict on Saturday—following the running of the Preakness.

Jack's instincts about Chase Kincaid's death were very strong, and his track record of pinpoint accuracy rivaled that of Chase Carlton; but nonetheless Jack found himself hoping that this time he was totally wrong. It was a hope for all of them: for the memory of Victor Chase Kincaid, and for his beautiful young widow, and for that widow's loyal and intriguing friend—a woman who Jack very much wanted to get to know better.

And if Chase Carlton sensed that a murder had been committed?

Then it would be a long, long time before Lieutenant Jack Shannon could call Stephanie Windsor.

But now she was calling him, and she undoubtedly had an ulterior motive of her own, and it was obvious that she, as Lieutenant Cassandra Ballinger, was planning to play with him.

Well. So be it. Jack was a life master at playing seductive games with beautiful women.

He would play for now, if that's what she wanted, but someday . . .

Jack pressed the first blinking light on his desk phone and greeted pleasantly, "Lieutenant Ballinger."

"Lieutenant Shannon," Stephanie replied swiftly, pleasantly too. She had carefully scripted, rehearsed, and memorized an array of possible words to say, and she was in character now, speaking with the voice that belonged to the ever-confident and always provocative Cassandra. "I wondered if we might discuss a case."

"Certainly. Let me guess. The tragic death of Chase Kincaid?"

He was mocking her. Fine, Stephanie thought. I am, after all, mocking him as well.

Jack Shannon had every right to be annoyed by her presumptuousness, the fictional homicide lieutenant approaching the authentic one as if they were equals. But it was the only way she could do this without faltering. And she had to do this, without faltering, for Jillian.

"Yes," she answered smoothly. "The tragic death of Chase Kincaid. I understand you are concerned that his death was actually murder and that you regard his widow as a prime suspect."

"*The* prime suspect," Jack clarified quietly. They were playing, but this was very interesting. Obviously Jillian Kincaid had told her friend the truth about his suspicions, and obviously, too, the serene widow had been sufficiently worried about those suspicions that she had persuaded her friend to call him. To what end? Jack wondered. To find out if he was pursuing the case still? To convince him of her innocence? The smart move for Jillian Kincaid would have been no move at all. But that was why perfect crimes were so rare. Criminals became nervous, impatient, and they began making critical mistakes. Jack felt his heart set a new—and suddenly impatient—pace, but he forced calm and asked with casual nonchalance, "Has she confessed to you, Lieutenant Ballinger?"

"She's innocent, Lieutenant Shannon."

"I see. That wasn't my impression. Would you care to try to convince me that I'm wrong?"

"Yes. Is this a good time?"

"Not really. Besides, I think this is something that should be discussed in person, don't you?"

Stephanie drew a soft breath. It had been a foolish hope that she would be able to accomplish this over the phone. Sternly reminding herself that she was the clever and capable Cassandra Ballinger, for whom everything was easy and possible, she answered, "Yes, of course. Shall we find a time tomorrow—at your convenience—when I can come to your office?"

"What would be convenient for me, Lieutenant, would be dinner tonight."

Stephanie felt the power of the uncompromising blue eyes at the other end of the phone. Jack Shannon knew she was committed to having this discussion with him, and that knowledge put him in the driver's seat. He was willing to play this game with her, to permit her to give him Jillian's message, but they were going to play by his rules.

Dinner tonight with the dangerously sexy man who caught murderers and broke hearts with equal icy ease? *Sure.* She, Cassandra Ballinger, could do that. It was only four o'clock now, plenty of time to drive to the studio and borrow from wardrobe one of the provocative homicide lieutenant's most provocative cocktail dresses.

"Dinner tonight would be fine," she answered finally, and with Cassandra breeziness.

"Good. Why don't we go to the Chart House? I'll make reservations for eight, so I'll be by to pick you up at seven-fifteen."

"I think it would be best if I just met you there," Stephanie countered, breezily still, Cassandra still. The busy lieutenant who would be out investigating her own murder case until just moments before she would arrive—dressed dazzlingly—for her sunset dinner with a fellow lieutenant.

Jack guessed that he could demand that she allow him to drive, and that she would accede to his wish, but with a pleasantness that didn't betray the annoyance he truly felt, he simply said, "Fine. I'll see you at the Chart House at eight."

Jack recognized the cocktail dress at once, a memorable, seductive sparkle of gold sequins that she had worn in *Corpus Delicti*'s cliff-hanger season finale. And Jack recognized too, at once, that she was in character.

Cassandra Ballinger had the perfect disciplined posture of Stephanie Windsor, but in Cassandra it was less stiff, more confident, the poised and graceful elegance of a cat instead of a princess. The two women had the same lustrous moon-kissed hair, of course, but like the posture, Cassandra's hairstyle was more relaxed and confident, a luxuriant cascade of soft curls instead of the severe chignon Stephanie had worn to the memorial reception. And the remarkable sapphire eyes shared by both? They were focused outward now, allowing no glimpses into their luminous depths, looking directly at him but focused slightly beyond . . . as if gazing at an invisible TelePrompTer just behind his head.

"Jillian knows that you know that she's been concealing something from you," Stephanie began as soon as they had ordered. "The truth is, she and Chase argued on the night of the accident."

"About what?"

"I don't know the details, but they don't really matter. Even happily married couples argue from time to time, don't they?"

"I wouldn't know," Jack said quietly, staring at her, commanding with his intense blue eyes that she meet his gaze. When she followed that silent yet powerful command, he asked very gently, "Would you?"

Stephanie frowned at the gentleness, the intimacy. Then, forcing her focus beyond him once again, she said evenly, "Surely you know that all relationships have problems."

"Yes, I do know that, and I also know that sometimes such problems become lethal ones."

"Jillian didn't kill Chase."

"She did, however, conceal the fact of the argument from me. For what reason, Lieutenant Ballinger?"

"Because she's very private . . . and because she wanted to protect Chase's privacy too."

"Maybe what she wanted to protect was a marriage that was in deep trouble. Such a marriage, especially when the wife stands to win twice as much with her husband's death as she would in a divorce, is one terrific motive for murder. Surely *you* know that."

Stephanie quivered inside at his mocking tone, but still Cassandra managed to say with compelling conviction, "Jillian did not kill Chase. She couldn't kill anyone."

"You seem so sure, Stephanie," Jack said softly, speaking to her, not to Cassandra, to the suddenly and so genuinely impassioned sapphire eyes. "To me Jillian's serenity, her calm acceptance of Chase's death, is very incriminating. Convince me otherwise."

Stephanie drew a steadying breath. She had mentally prepared pages and pages of possible script, and she had also anticipated his skepticism; but even though she had accurately remembered the intensity of his dark blue eyes, she had been unable to adequately prepare for their power . . . or for their powerful effect on her. Jack Shannon knew that she was playing Cassandra, and he was tolerating the charade for the moment because it amused him.

The handsome homicide lieutenant was very dangerous when he was amused. Stephanie shivered at the thought of what Lieutenant Jack Shannon would be like if he were angry, or if he no longer found her presumptuous game amusing.

You are Cassandra Ballinger, Stephanie urgently reminded her racing heart. You are strong and tough and confident. Your heart doesn't race with fear—or desire!—even when you are being appraised by mocking, and yet somehow so approving, seductive blue eyes. You know your lines perfectly. *Now say them.*

"When Jillian was fourteen, she and her mother were in a car accident. The car was crushed and they were trapped inside. By the time the rescuers got them out, Jillian's mother had died. You may have noticed that Jillian walks with a slight limp."

"Yes."

"Well, the accident is why she has the limp, and it also explains why she has what you call her incriminating calm."

"How's that?"

"Despite her own almost fatal injuries, Jillian never lost consciousness. She was awake the entire time, watching helplessly as her mother died. After that she withdrew completely. She was silent, and I suppose it might have been interpreted as calm by someone who didn't really know her, but it was really severe shock."

"That's how her stepmother explains it now."

"Well, Claudia should know. It was she who finally got Jillian to speak again."

"Not you?" Jack asked, his words crashing through the brilliant blue façade, shattering the outwardly focused sapphire into glittering storm-tossed shards. "I got the impression that you were there too."

I was there, but what I had to offer wasn't enough. Now I have a second chance to help my best friend, and you're undermining me, making it too personal, too close to Stephanie and too far from Cassandra. And worse, there is such gentleness in your eyes, such intimacy, as if you might actually care. Stop, please, *stop!* "I was there then, yes, but that's hardly relevant to what we're discussing now."

But it *is* relevant to you, Jack decided as he gazed at her. Relevant, and terribly important. He wanted to know why. And he would—sometime. But right now, because it was obviously so troubling to her, he agreed casually, "Not relevant at all. So, Jillian Kincaid's reaction to this tragic accident is the same as to the accident fifteen years ago: shock."

"Yes," Stephanie said, relieved, so very relieved, that they had returned to the script.

"And the reason she didn't tell me about the argument was to protect her privacy."

"His privacy."

"Okay. And what is it that has made her decide to have you tell me all of this now?"

"She knows that you and Chase were friends. She doesn't want you to believe he married a woman who would have murdered him. It's for Chase, for his memory, not for her."

"Admirable," Jack offered. It was admirable, of course, admirable and loving, and Jack found himself hoping it was true.

"Jillian loved Chase very much. She is devastated by his death."

As Jack listened to her impassioned words, he was convinced of one thing: Stephanie truly believed that her friend was innocent of everything except the most generous of loves.

"So?" Stephanie asked hopefully as she saw the sudden gentleness in his dark blue eyes. "Can you let it go? Can you believe that Chase's death was accidental?"

The emotion, set in expressive sapphire, was now pure Stephanie. Out of loyalty and love, she had enacted this elaborate charade for her friend, and she was obviously very hopeful that it had been a success. Jack felt a powerful desire to tell her yes, she had succeeded brilliantly. But he couldn't. His own impression that Chase Kincaid had been murdered was too strong, and had only been further strengthened by the out-of-the-blue phone call from murder-maven Chase Carlton.

"I'll tell you the truth, Stephanie," Jack said finally. "I am pursuing one final lead. I realize that you may tell Jillian this, which will prompt calls from her father to the commissioner to stop me, but by then I'll have the answer I'm waiting for."

"And if the lead doesn't confirm your suspicions?"

"Then I will believe in your friend's innocence."

"When will you know?"

"This Saturday afternoon, right after the running of the Preakness."

After a long, thoughtful silence, Stephanie said quietly, "I'm not going to mention to Jillian that you're pursuing this final lead. But will you let me know the result?"

"Of course," Jack agreed. "I'll tell you over dinner Saturday night."

They hadn't even finished their cocktails yet—her Diet Pepsi, his Scotch rocks—and the business discussion was concluded for now . . . and somehow she had to get through the rest of this evening without a script . . . and now he was suggesting that they do this again on Saturday . . . and she had to, for Jillian, so that she could tell Jillian once and for all that Lieutenant Jack Shannon's suspicions had been put to rest.

"Oh," she murmured finally. "Sure."

"Good. So," Jack said softly, commanding her blue eyes to follow his. "Tell me what you think of the sunset . . ."

If Cassandra Ballinger's gold-sequined cocktail dress had conferred a magical confidence—and it *had* as they'd discussed Chase Kincaid's tragic death—its magical spell was shattered the moment Lieutenant Jack Shannon expertly guided the conversation into personal, emotional, unscripted territory. That was where Jack wanted to be, asking questions that were answered elaborately and eloquently in brilliant sapphire . . . and haltingly and sparingly in words.

She wanted to talk to him! In the beginning, as the springtime sun had set on Cassandra Ballinger and the full golden moon had risen on Stephanie Windsor, there had been such gentleness in his dark blue eyes, and such interest; and there had been an entirely new magic as she found herself actually believing that if—by some even greater magic—she could actually articulate the lively and honest thoughts that came to her, he would welcome them. He would laugh appreciatively at her clever, irreverent humor, and his handsome face would soften with tenderness at her honest emotional confessions.

But she couldn't talk, of course, and as the evening wore on and her own crescendoing frustration and fear inhibited her even more, she saw impatience—and frustration—in the dark, demanding blue . . .

Her car was parked in a remote corner of the Chart House's oceanside parking lot. Their path was softly illuminated by the golden moon, their conspicuous silence somehow augmented by the rhythmic whispers of the waves.

I'm sorry, I'm sorry, I'm sorry, Stephanie thought miserably. How she wished she could say that—even that! But she knew it was impossible. He would logically demand further explanation of her words, emotional explanations that she could not give without faltering.

Still, when they reached her car and she looked up at him to say good night, those were the words in her eyes, a sad and eloquent apology drenched in moonlight.

It was an apology to which Lieutenant Jack Shannon responded by gently, so very gently, cupping her face in his hands. And then, even more gently, and tenderly and unhurriedly, he began to kiss her.

Stephanie had never been kissed like this, for what Jack did was to kiss her face, her *face,* not simply her lush and lovely lips. With great care, as if he truly cherished her, he placed kisses on her temples, her eyelids, her nose, her cheeks. As if he cherished her . . . as if he wanted to know every inch of her . . . as if, maybe, by this gentle and thorough exploration he hoped to find a secret passageway to her heart.

All men before Jack Shannon, including her fiancé, especially her fiancé, had cared only about Stephanie's beautiful lips. Swiftly and roughly, the men before Jack had claimed her lips, conquering, possessing, invading even deeper. And then, swiftly and roughly, they had wanted even more of her.

No man had ever tenderly caressed Stephanie's face, just as no man had ever cared about her pleasure—or her pain.

Stephanie felt pleasure now, small, brave whispers of a most wondrous desire; and then, as if Jack knew that she was ready to welcome him, that she wanted to, his lips found hers at last. And, as she welcomed him, there was neither possession nor invasion, only shared pleasure . . . and rushing warmth . . . and compelling hunger . . . and soft sighs of pure joy.

And when Jack suddenly stopped the kiss, Stephanie saw the desires of her own moonlit eyes wondrously mirrored in his; and the brave whispers deep within her joyfully murmured, Yes, yes, *yes.*

"Do you know what I would like?" he asked softly.

Yes. You would like me to invite you to my bed—and no man has ever even bothered to ask before, only demanded—and even though there is so much more danger with you . . . yes, *yes,* you are invited.

"What would you like?" she echoed with matching softness.

For a moment Jack's resolve faltered. The invitation in her shimmering blue eyes was so clear, so wonderful; but he wanted so much more from Stephanie Windsor than the pleasures of her beautiful body. He wanted her heart. It was something that Jack Shannon had never wanted before, and had himself never given; but it was something for which he was now willing to take great risks.

"What I would like, Stephanie, is for you to tell me your thoughts, your *real* thoughts, before you so carefully edit them." Jack saw surprise. No, it was amazement . . . amazement that he even knew she edited her thoughts, and even greater amazement that he cared. Amazement—and for a magnificent moment what looked like joy—and then, suddenly, shatteringly, it vanished, replaced by pure apprehension. "Don't worry, Stephanie. I won't be horrified by your unedited thoughts. I promise."

Oh, but you would be so horrified if I tried to speak them.

No man's touch had ever before caused her to tremble, and no man had ever before cared about her thoughts or ever believed that there was anything beyond her flawless beauty that might be worth knowing.

Stephanie wanted to make love with Jack Shannon, to share

with him the bold desires she had never shared before. For her, that brave and unedited intimacy would have taken immense courage, and it would have been very dangerous for the lonely heart that had never been cherished or loved; but she had been willing to take the risk for one night, for *just one night* of tenderness.

Such bold physical intimacy wasn't enough for Lieutenant Jack Shannon, though. He wanted more . . . so much more . . . too much.

"Stephanie?" Jack saw the sapphire storm, the sudden immense pain, and he wanted to cradle her against him and love it away. And he would. But now he found a patience he hadn't known existed within him, not for anything except murder, and as he waited for her to speak, he encouraged her with the gentlest of smiles and then the most tender of voices. "Talk to me, Stephanie."

I c-c-c-can't. Even her thought stuttered! Ice-cold waves of fear—and shame—swept through her, chilling her, drowning her.

Stephanie couldn't speak. She could only answer with her head and with her eyes. As shame compelled her to shake a stiff no in response to Jack's gentle and impossible command, the icy chill of her fear filled the sapphire, transforming the moonlit blue from lovely and vulnerable to haughty and distant.

Jack saw both the haughtiness and the fear.

Why fear? he wondered. Was it perhaps the fear of risking one's heart? Was such a terrifying risk as new to her as it was to him?

Jack wanted to know, but he saw in her wary sapphire eyes that now was not the time to push. Smiling gently, he touched her flushed cheeks with exquisite tenderness and said softly, "I'll call you after the Preakness to finalize plans for dinner."

Chapter Nine

Marina Yacht Club
San Francisco
May 21, 1994

Chase Carlton's winter-gray eyes focused intently on the television screen in *Sea Witch*'s luxurious forward cabin. Just moments before Schoolteacher had won the Preakness, and now Brad Lancaster was standing in the winner's circle, speaking to the television cameras.

The emotion Brad felt was obvious in his voice. "I accept this trophy in loving memory of my cousin, Victor Chase Kincaid. I hope, I *know*, that he is watching today. I also accept this trophy for Jillian Kincaid, the remarkable schoolteacher in whose honor the remarkable filly was named—and the true jewel of Triple Crown Studios."

Moments later the production credits began to roll, over an elegant image of the victorious strawberry roan draped in the traditional mantle of black-eyed Susans, but Chase's gaze remained intently focused until ABC left the racetrack at Pimlico altogether, electronically transporting its viewers to a plush golf course in South Carolina. Only then did he move, first turning off the television and then depressing the rewind button on the VCR.

Chase was disappointed that the recording he had just made contained no new footage of Jillian Kincaid. She had been mentioned, of course, in the hour-long pre-race coverage. Indeed, much had been said about the tragedy that had befallen the owner of the odds-on-favorite filly, and about his courageous wife. Despite the loss of her beloved husband, the dedicated schoolteacher had already returned to her third-grade classroom in one of Los Angeles's most disadvantaged areas. She had declined all interviews, and because it would have been indefensible for the press to have prevented the grieving but valiant widow from her noble mission of bestowing the immeasurable gift of literacy on needy children, they had been forced not to ambush her as she made her way in and out of the school.

The footage of Jillian Kincaid shown during the pre-race coverage of the Preakness had been nothing more than what Chase had already received from Jack Shannon and already knew by heart: the videotape taken two weeks earlier at the Kentucky Derby. Jillian had stood beside her husband that day, her auburn hair swept off her beautiful face into a luxuriant ponytail adorned with scarves that were the same teal and forest as the silks worn by Schoolteacher's jockey. Serene and elegant and patrician, she had seemed as regal, as demure, as bred to win as the auburn-coated Thoroughbred that had been named in her honor. Even in the winner's circle the only clue to her jubilance at the victory had been her soft smile and the even softer glow in her brilliant emerald eyes.

Chase had hoped that the broadcast of the Preakness would provide additional glimpses of his brother's beautiful wife. But it hadn't, and now the race was over, and so was the waiting. It was time to put into action his careful plans. And, if all went as planned, three weeks from today, shortly after Schoolteacher galloped to the Triple Crown triumph at Belmont that everyone was predicting—the odds-on-favorite filly now the sentimental one as well—there would be a miracle: a dead husband returned from his watery grave.

There were no obstacles to Chase's plan to become his twin. He knew that now; but he remembered the racing of his heart when he had first opened the box from Jack Shannon and had hurriedly searched its contents to find his brother's medical records. Chase Carlton and Chase Kincaid needed to be physically identical . . . and they were.

Neither twin had ever had major surgery. The movie mogul had no history even of broken bones, and the stalker of murderers had only the skull fracture from the fall in Denver. But the bony evidence of a serious head injury was precisely what Chase Carlton needed: compelling proof that he had been struck by a boom with enough force to cause significant amnesia. Chase knew that his body, like his heart, bore many more scars than that of his pampered twin; but even the most deep and vicious of his scars could be explained by his four-and-a-half-week ordeal at sea.

The two boys born thirty-four years before in Saint-Jean-Cap-Ferrat were physically identical, not just the mirror images so often seen in twins. The fingerprints taken from *Sea Goddess*'s blood-splattered deck were identical to his own, and from the videotapes Chase discovered that they were both right-handed and that their speech was virtually identical as well. Chase himself had long since lost his British accent, but the legacy of the elegant and proper English he had taught himself was indistinguishable from the refined speech his brother had learned at the exclusive private schools to which he had been sent.

It was his destiny to become his twin, Chase decided. It was his destiny to avenge the death of the brother he had never known but had always missed. The seemingly random events of his life suddenly fell into place, including the near-lethal fall in Denver. Had he not sustained that serious head injury, Chase Carlton would not have known precisely how to feign amnesia, nor would he have known its mysterious and varied manifestations. When he had awakened from his own coma, Chase had no memory of the events leading up to the injury—and never would—and he had only the most fleeting, shadowy glimpses of his own life. But even though his personal history was hidden in shadows, his knowledge of the world in which he lived was remarkably intact; and he had been able to speak, and read, and drive, and sail without any relearning whatsoever.

Such a selective amnesia seemed improbable, and indeed all the neurologists concurred that it was quite a rare presentation. But it did happen, they said. Whether the suppression of virtually all personal memories was from physical or emotional trauma they couldn't say. But when all the brutal memories of his life eventually returned, and Chase was forced to live anew the immense emotional horror, he knew without question that his selective amnesia had been purely physical. Otherwise, surely, had it been able to, his mind would have forever banished those personal memories to the merciful darkness.

Victor Chase Kincaid would return from the sea with a selective amnesia for personal memories that was identical to what Chase Carlton had experienced years before—a convincing amnesia, medically quite authentic, perfectly feigned by someone who had lived through it.

It was Chase's destiny to become his twin, and the invisible force that had so restlessly and relentlessly compelled him toward an unknown destination was now strangely calm, *content.* He needed no more invisible guidance. His course from here on was crystal-clear.

Chase had already told the marina's security guard that he was sailing for the South Seas—Bora Bora to be exact—and that he imagined he would return in four to six months. And if he didn't return? Chase didn't address that possibility with the guard. But he knew that in eight months, when the marina's annual fees were due, someone would try to track him down. It would take no time to discover that *Sea Witch* had never reached the tropical waters of French Polynesia, and eventually it would occur to someone to open the trunk of his car—an easy task, since, as always, he was leaving the keys with the guard.

In the trunk Chase had placed a box of documents, records of his financial holdings and a letter addressed to Lieutenant Jack Shannon in which he had detailed his plan and which concluded with the ominous observation that had Chase Kincaid miraculously reappeared—only to die yet a second time—that his death, both the deaths, had indeed been murder.

The letter that Chase had locked in his car contained information that Jack Shannon would have only in the event of his death. For now the message he would give the homicide lieutenant was an entirely different one. As they had arranged when they'd spoken Tuesday afternoon, Chase reached Jack in his office at the precinct.

"I've carefully reviewed everything you sent me," Chase began truthfully.

"And?"

And now the lies begin. "And I believe that Chase Kincaid is still alive."

"What?"

"That must have been the reason I felt the need to speak to you in the first place. I sensed there was something wrong when I saw the news report. I realize now that it wasn't that I sensed that the accidental death was really a murder, but that he wasn't dead at all."

"Where the hell is he?"

"Somewhere dark . . . and at sea," Chase answered slowly, as if he were actually envisioning the shadowy place he described. He didn't possess that type of psychic power, of course, but Jack Shannon didn't know that. "In the hold of a boat, I think."

"Rescued by someone who wouldn't instantly take him into the nearest port," Jack offered quietly, knowing that he didn't need to elaborate on possible scenarios with Chase. The man who helped the police track serial killers didn't need to be told that the world wasn't filled entirely with Good Samaritans. Drug smugglers wouldn't rush a rescued man to a safe haven, nor would someone who realized they had found a treasure at sea—a wealthy man whose family would pay dearly for his return.

"I guess so," Chase agreed solemnly. "I sense that he's quite confused. He probably has no idea who he is, and neither does whoever has him." This time it was Chase who didn't elaborate. He didn't need to remind Jack that Victor Chase Kincaid's wallet had been found on the varnished table in *Sea Goddess*'s galley.

"Is he going to survive?"

"I don't know. I can't predict the future. At this point, though, I think it would be unfair to give his wife that hope."

"I take it you don't sense that she tried to murder him."

"No. I don't sense that at all."

That was the "truth" Chase wanted Jack to believe. He wanted the lieutenant to leave Jillian Kincaid alone, to allow her to believe—if indeed she was a murderess—that she had committed the perfect crime. The real truth was that Chase sensed nothing at all about his brother's beautiful wife. He had forced himself to stare endlessly at the photographs of the sailboat splattered with his twin's blood, hoping to at least sense whether he was gazing at the scene of a crime—or the scene of an accident.

But his heart and mind had been hopelessly blurred by his own emotions, and there was no clarity beyond the chilling one: his twin was dead. Chase knew that with absolute and excruciatingly painful certainty. In the past week he had come to realize that throughout his lonely life he had somehow felt the invisible presence of his missing brother, and had been comforted by it. That comforting presence was gone now, leaving him feeling more isolated, more empty, more cold than he had ever felt before.

His twin was dead. That was a painful certainty. As Chase had spent anguished hours staring at photographs of shining varnish splattered with the blood of the twin with the gift for dreams, he had desperately hoped for some proof of his own more sinister gift. Finally there had been something, a vague impression of violence. But were those mindprints left by a murderess at the scene of a crime? Or was the violence he felt merely his own rage at the careless yawn of a slumbering sea which had so whimsically stolen his brother from him?

Chase had no idea if Jillian Kincaid was a murderess. He knew only that it was his destiny to become his twin, and to gaze into the brilliant emerald eyes of his brother's wife—and to learn the truth.

"So . . . Chase Kincaid is alive and Jillian Kincaid is innocent of all treachery." Jack spoke into the silence, succinctly summarizing Chase Carlton's astonishing revelations. "Are you really certain about this?"

"As certain as I can be. No one has ever been able to explain what it is that I have—least of all me," Chase confessed. After a moment he added quietly, "But in the past my feelings have been quite accurate."

"And you're as confident of this feeling as you have been about others that have proven to be right?"

"I feel more confident of this than I've ever felt before."

"Okay. Well, then, thanks. I appreciate your taking the time to review this for me. Nothing would make me happier than to have Chase Kincaid suddenly reappear."

Nothing would make me happier either, Chase thought. But I know it isn't going to happen—not really.

Five minutes after his conversation with Chase Carlton ended, Jack dialed the number to Stephanie's penthouse.

"It's going to be a stunning sunset. Shall we try the Chart House again?"

"Oh, hi." As Stephanie spoke the two mechanical words, and felt the battle between her voice and her lungs for precious air, she realized that she hadn't been breathing normally—hardly breathing at all—since the end of the race. She had been anxiously waiting, knowing he was going to call, trying to prepare her words, her heart, her hopes.

"Hi. Is Jillian there?"

"No." Jillian had asked her to watch the Preakness with her and Edward and Claudia—a solemn memorial, not a party—

but because she needed to be at home for Jack's call, Stephanie had declined. "Did you get the result of your final lead?"

"Yes." And then, because he didn't want to play, because what he wanted with Stephanie Windsor went far beyond playing, Jack said, "I guess I was wrong."

"Really?"

"Really. So maybe since the case is closed you'll have champagne tonight instead of Diet Pepsi?"

No. Stephanie had tried champagne once, by herself, to see if it would ever be safe for her to drink in the company of others. She had very much liked the warm, floating feeling that had so magically blurred her memories and softened her pain. But she knew that she could never allow her mind to be that blurred in a setting in which she might have to speak, and she sensed, because it was so very appealing, that it would be unwise to permit herself to drink alone. So she drank nothing—ever.

Having a glass of champagne with Lieutenant Jack Shannon, whose tender caresses made even her thoughts tremble, would be impossible, far too dangerous . . . just as being with him at all would be too dangerous. He wanted far more from her than she could give, and he would be so very disappointed if he knew the truth.

"Stephanie?"

"I can't have dinner with you tonight," she said slowly, carefully, coolly.

"Tomorrow night?" Jack asked pleasantly even though powerful rushes of anger began to pulse within him.

"No."

"Never?" he pressed, his voice cold, mocking, laced with contempt. He had wanted more than games, and despite the sapphire fear he had seen—no, *because of it*—he had believed that she wanted more too. But Stephanie Samantha Windsor was a gifted actress. She had played her role to perfection, beyond perfection, involving him emotionally to ensure her success. And now her triumph was complete, her friend was in the clear . . . and it was time for the final curtain to come crashing down. "Mission accomplished?"

"I . . ." No, don't think that! I want to see you, but I *c-c-c-can't.*

"You what?" Jack urged, his voice suddenly soft, because in just the whispered "I" he had heard what sounded like despair, hadn't he? How he wished he could see the impassioned sapphire eyes that embellished that single syllable. How he wished he could hold her lovely face and gently convince her that it was safe to speak to him the secrets so carefully hidden in the vulnerable blue shadows. "You what, Stephanie?"

"Nothing," she whispered to the voice that was as soft and as cherishing as his kisses had been. *I'm* nothing. I have nothing to offer you, nothing to cherish. "I have to go now. Good-bye, Jack."

Twenty minutes after his phone call to Jack Shannon had ended, Chase cast off the lines and steered *Sea Witch* toward the Golden Gate Bridge—and the journey beyond.

It was a journey in which Chase Carlton would disappear entirely. Once he was safely at sea, he would shave his beard and cut his hair, and over the next three weeks, as he fasted to become the gaunt and ravaged Chase Kincaid who would rise from the sea, he would indelibly etch in his mind everything Jack had sent him about his brother. It would be those authentic details which would appear in tantalizing glimpses from the shadows of his shattered memory.

In the almost endless days and nights between the discovery that he was a twin and the arrival of the information from Jack, Chase had read all he could find on the subject of twins. He now knew of the intriguing mysteries, myths, and legends; the extraordinary psychic bonds they were said to share, and the amusing tricks played by them on the unsuspecting world.

Had he and his brother been raised together, they might have—no, they *would* have—been best friends. They would have shared hopes and dreams, and secrets and laughter. As lively schoolboys they would have delighted in confounding parents and teachers with their identical looks; and as teenagers they might even have tried to confuse the girls they dated.

Chase was planning to cause confusion now with a grown wife, not a teenage girlfriend, and his plan bore no resemblance whatsoever to any lively or amusing trick.

But it was a date of sorts, Chase mused. The ultimate date . . . with an emerald-eyed murderess.

PART TWO

Chapter Ten

Puerto Vallarta, Mexico
June 9, 1994

It was time: midnight on the second Thursday in June. The tropical night was warm, a soft memory of the harsh heat of the day, and the sky sparkled with an infinity of stars, their dazzling glitter unmuted by the lights of nearby humanity or the glow of the moon.

It was time to bid adieu to *Sea Witch*.

How simple it was to destroy a dream, Chase thought as he disabled the bilge pump and disconnected the intake hoses. In moments his beloved boat began to take on water, and in a few moments more she would be swallowed whole by the night-black sea. Chase knew exactly where he was, the depth of the water and the soft sandiness of the ocean floor below. Someday, after he had seduced a confession from a murderess, he would return to this isolated place and resurrect his drowned sailboat.

For now it was necessary for *Sea Witch* to vanish, just as Chase Carlton had himself vanished over the past three weeks. He was his twin now, the handsome Kincaid face hidden beneath a newly grown beard, his strong, lean body gaunt from lack of food and water, his winter-gray eyes clouded from starvation—and searching, desperately searching, for clarity in the dark fog of his memory.

Chase had decided to sink *Sea Witch* under the dark cover of the moonless night even though in broad daylight there would have been no witnesses in this remote area north of Puerto Vallarta. The nearby islands were uninhabited, as was the stretch of coastline along which he would journey on foot for the next two days. Sometime Saturday he would reach civilization, staggering toward a group of sunbathers perhaps, exhausted and starving and battered by the tropical sun. The sunbathers would want to rush him to the nearest hospital, but he would insist that all he needed was something for his parched throat and a plane ticket to Los Angeles. A dream was waiting for him there, he would whisper, the dream of loving emerald eyes that had nurtured him throughout his ordeal.

Chase wore an old denim workshirt and a pair of faded jeans. Given to him by his "captors," he would explain, explaining, too, that they must have stolen his solid gold wedding ring. The pale band of skin on his finger where his wedding ring had shadowed it from the sun for the past six years would logically be gone now, darkened by the tropical sun during the days—or was it weeks?—that he had spent on the uninhabited islands, recovering from his ordeal, eating the fruit he could find when he was strong enough to search . . . and every day gazing toward the land to which he would swim as soon as he was able, the distant shoreline which he prayed would be the beginning of his journey home.

The actual swim Chase had left for himself was about a mile and a half, a distance he could manage easily in the warm offshore waters.

Or so he thought. Within moments of diving from the deck of his sinking sailboat into the tropical sea, Chase felt chilled. It was an icy warning to him of how truly debilitated he was, how his sleek, lean body had become totally depleted of even the thinnest protective layer of fat. For the past three weeks he had allowed himself as little food and water as he would have been able to find during the days when he had been strong enough to search on the deserted island.

Very realistic, he thought, fighting a quiver of panic as he swam just far enough away from *Sea Witch* that he wouldn't be sucked under as she sank. When he reached the safe distance, he treaded water and looked back toward her. A deep instinct warned him not to squander his limited energy by treading water, to begin instead his slow but determined swim to the closest point of shore. But Chase's starved mind was floating now, and something else—his heart perhaps—wouldn't let him turn his back on the sailboat he loved as she sank into the sea.

So he treaded water, his energy drained further by the shivers that began to ripple through his body, and watched with solemn reverence as with extraordinary grace and dignity *Sea Witch* succumbed to the weight of the seawater that filled her hull. She struggled a bit, resisting with proud elegance, her mast a straight and tall silhouette against the sky of stars; but finally, and with astonishing silence, without so much as an undignified splash, she listed and then vanished into the blackness.

I'll come back for you, Chase's floating mind promised. I'll resurrect you from your watery grave . . . just as I am resurrecting my brother.

Then he turned, his eyes searching the distant shadow of land until they found its closest reach, a rocky point that stretched like a skeletal finger from the white sand beach into sea. As he had gazed at the shoreline during the light of day, his energy untested from his safe perch on *Sea Witch*'s varnished deck, he had planned to swim toward the sand. But now that seemed too far. He would emerge from the chilly water at the rocky point instead. He would rest there for a while and by dawn he would be strong enough to begin his two-day walk along the palm-shaded beach.

The water was so cold, and so heavy, and it seemed to be fighting him, resisting with all its might the efforts of the weak and shivering body that struggled to move ever closer to land. Surely he was making progress, but the rocky shadow was still far away and with every stroke the effort became even more difficult. The ocean was calm, breathing its deep, gentle breaths of slumber as it had on the night his twin had been lost. But there was a tidal asymmetry to the breaths, the inhale greater than the exhale as the ebbing tide pulled water from the shore, creating a gentle undertow that was suddenly a monumental opponent in his own desperate battle toward land.

Chase had always been a strong swimmer, and when he had swum before, the sea had always been an ally, just as it had always been when he had skimmed along its surface. But now the sea was his enemy, threatening to claim him as it had claimed his twin.

No, his mind protested, defiantly fueling his weak limbs with pure will. Everything will not end here. There is too much to be learned . . . too much to be avenged.

But don't you want to meet your long-lost twin? the watery depths whispered seductively. You knew each other so well long ago, when you lived together in the watery sea of your mother's womb, and you have spent your entire life in a restless search to find again that sanctuary and that peace. Your brother is here, waiting for you to join him again . . . for eternity. Come. He is waiting for you. Join him, *join him.*

Chase battled the seductive whispers of the sea and the alluring promise of a forever peace with the images his mind had conjured up in the past weeks: the disbelieving horror on the face of his brother as he realized that the wife he loved had so brutally betrayed him . . . the fountain of blood that had gushed from his wounded head as he had staggered on the deck of his boat . . . his frantic cries as he pleaded for help, for mercy, swallowing seawater instead, gasping, drowning, with no one to save him . . . his death witnessed with evil satisfaction by the woman he had trusted and loved.

Chase was gasping and drowning now, and there were no witnesses, and he had never trusted or loved. But he had been betrayed—oh, how he had been betrayed—from the moment he had left the peaceful sanctuary he had once shared with his twin.

It's not going to end here, Chase told the body that now shivered from both cold and fatigue. I am going to learn the truth about my brother's death. And I am going to learn, too, the truth about what was done to me, and why, all those years ago.

There had been times before in Chase's life when he had been very near to death—as a small child, punished with brutal and near-lethal violence; and as a teenager, cold and starving as he bravely fled the horrors of the orphanage; and as a man, in hand-to-knife combat with a monster who had killed often and was addicted to that evil pleasure. At those times, even—*especially*—as a small child, Chase had accepted the possibility of his own death with a sense of calm, of relief, and with no sense whatsoever of sadness or loss. But now, as he was close once again to death, Chase felt neither calm nor relief.

My life isn't going to end here. There is more to do . . . more that I must do . . . answers that I must have before I die.

Finally the shadow of rocks began to loom larger, extending its stony hand to him as if in greeting and welcome. The rocks were willing to receive him, to offer him a safe haven; but as Chase neared them, he was suddenly caught in the midst of an angry and ancient battle, the primordial war between land and sea. The bony finger of rock extended defiantly into the water, and the sea yielded that territory with begrudging anger, churning and swirling as it tried to force the rocky invader out of its watery domain. Chase was in the midst of the ancient battle, an innocent victim crashed against the rocks like a sacrificial offering. The sea revoked its human offering before the rocks could offer a firm hold, and he was pulled back into the swirling water, only to be offered, and revoked, again and again.

Even though he was strangely numb to the pain, strangely disembodied, Chase heard the cracking of his own ribs; and he felt the sudden and surprising layer of warmth where before there had been none. It wasn't that the cold sea had suddenly become warm, he realized vaguely. The warmth was his own blood, spilling freely, a gushing crimson beacon of color and scent to the sharks that prowled the tropical waters, their sleekly stylish bodies moving toward blood with the same lustful pleasure as the serial killers he had known.

It was in the midst of swirling thoughts of sharks and death that a surprisingly comforting thought surfaced, floating above the turbulence like a soft, fleecy cloud above a storm. If he survived, the thought promised, he wouldn't need to explain his own scars after all. The fresh layers of vicious wounds would conceal the vestiges of the old ones, and they would be even more dramatic proof of the ordeal endured by Victor Chase Kincaid.

If he survived . . .

Chapter Eleven

Clairmont Estate
Bel Air, California
June 11, 1994

Thirty minutes after Schoolteacher crossed the finish line at Belmont, and Brad Lancaster had accepted the Triple Crown trophy for Jillian, in loving memory of her husband, the doorbell at Clairmont sounded. Annie remained where she was, pressed against Jillian, but her golden body went on alert, quivering far more with excitement than ferocity.

Jillian and Stephanie went on alert too.

"Reporters," Stephanie offered.

"I suppose so," Jillian agreed as she left the living room couch and moved to the nearby closed-circuit monitor to look at the image of whoever was at the front door. After a moment she said softly, "No. It's Lieutenant Shannon."

Jillian's walk from the living room to the front door was a journey of dread. After almost five weeks of waiting and hoping, the wait and the hope were over. Chase's body had been found. With a sudden and ominous jolt Jillian realized how much the hope for a miracle had been sustaining her, allowing her to deny the truth and avoid dealing with what had really happened.

But now Lieutenant Shannon was here. The hope, the delusions, had come to an end.

"I have some news, Mrs. Kincaid," Jack said as soon as she

opened the door. He extended a hand to Annie, who instantly diagnosed him as friend not foe, but his eyes never left the anxious emerald ones. I have no sense that Jillian Kincaid tried to murder her husband, Chase Carlton had said moments after making the pronouncement that Chase Kincaid was still alive. Now that astonishing pronouncement had come true, and Jack wanted to believe all the words Chase Carlton had spoken, but still he needed to see Jillian's eyes when he told her. "I just received a call from the police in Puerto Vallarta. They believe that Chase is a patient in a hospital there."

At his words, the remarkable green filled with disbelief. But, Jack decided, it wasn't the skeptical disbelief of a murderess who knew with absolute certainty that what he was saying was wrong. It was instead that of a loving wife who desperately wanted what he was saying to be true and yet was fearful that it might not be. Jack felt a sudden urge to reassure Jillian, but at that moment his attention was wholly distracted by the appearance of Stephanie.

There was such joy in her beautiful blue eyes, pure, unselfish, radiant joy, as if she had wished for this happiness for her friend more than she had ever wished for anything in her own life. The joyous sapphire met Jack's intense gaze briefly, enough to cause a whisper of pink in her lovely cheeks, then Stephanie focused on her friend, and after a moment Jack did too.

"Chase was found last evening on a beach north of Puerto Vallarta," he explained gently to the still-disbelieving and yet now so hopeful emerald. "He was semiconscious—suffering from exposure, dehydration, and infection—but he kept saying your name."

"My name?" Jillian echoed softly.

"Just your first name. It didn't mean anything to the tourists who found him, but this morning Dr. Carl Peters, a neurologist from UCLA who is also on vacation there, overheard the story, remembered from the news reports that your name was Jillian, and began to wonder. He went to the hospital to offer his theory as well as his medical expertise. By the time he arrived, Chase had already whispered your full name as well as his own. The doctors notified the Mexican police, who called me."

"I need to get to him," Jillian said urgently. Had she been able to get to Chase by walking—by running—she would have dashed past Jack right then and started that joyous journey. But she couldn't simply run to him. Forcing her mind to focus, she murmured, "Brad has the jet in New York, but I can charter—"

"I've already made arrangements," Jack interjected quietly. "A plane is waiting for us at the Santa Monica airport."

"Us?" Stephanie spoke for the first time, finding a word to echo and embellishing it with indignant and fiercely loyal sapphire eyes.

"Chase's appearance reopens our files," Jack explained truthfully but gently, hoping to convey with his gentleness that he wasn't planning to pursue his theory of attempted murder. He did need to investigate though, enough to put a final and accurate closure on the case.

The gentleness in Jack's voice didn't soften Stephanie's indignant glare; but Jillian, whose eyes now glittered with such obvious hope, and such radiant innocence, offered swiftly, "It's okay, Stephanie. Thank you for arranging for the plane, Lieutenant."

Other arrangements were made quickly. Of course she would be happy to stay with Annie, Stephanie agreed with a nod; and she nodded, too, when Jillian asked if she would explain everything to Edward and Claudia, away for the weekend at a medical meeting in Seattle, when they called; and yes, she smiled bravely, she would tell Brad everything as well, even if he called before Jillian actually left, while she was hastily packing a small suitcase for herself and Chase.

But when the phone rang shortly after Jillian had gone upstairs to pack, just as Stephanie and Jack had moved in silence into the living room, Stephanie gazed at it with such sudden apprehension that Jack offered, "Shall I answer it?"

"Yes . . . please," Stephanie said, her worried expression clearly conveying the truth: the caller was undoubtedly Brad, and the message was so wonderful, and yet so emotional, that she would be grateful if an outsider gave it.

It was Brad, and after Jack had given him the astounding news, and had listened in thoughtful silence to Brad's reply, he said, "I'm as sure as I can be long distance, Brad." Brad's cautious skepticism didn't surprise Jack, of course; and, he realized, had Chase Carlton not suggested to him that Chase Kincaid was still alive, he would have viewed the news far more skeptically than he had. "The clothes he was wearing weren't what Jillian described the night he disappeared, and his wedding ring is missing, but—except for a dramatic weight loss—the physical description fits. The skull X ray they took shows a healed fracture that is entirely consistent with the head injury he would have gotten from the boom. I'm not positive that it's Chase, Brad, but I think there's every reason to hope that it is."

The conversation ended moments later, with Brad's assertion that as soon as Schoolteacher was safely en route back to Barrington Farm, he would board Triple Crown's jet and meet them at the hospital in Puerto Vallarta.

"Thank you," Stephanie said when Jack replaced the receiver and turned his intense blue eyes to her. "Would you like some lemonade?"

"No, thank you. I'm fine," he replied, following her gaze to the pitcher and glasses on the coffee table. She and Jillian had obviously been drinking lemonade, not champagne, as they had watched Schoolteacher become only the twelfth horse in racing history to win the coveted Triple Crown.

"Well, please have a seat, then," Stephanie murmured, gesturing gracefully to the living room couch.

It was obvious that Jack wouldn't sit until she had, so Stephanie settled first, in a plush chair across from the couch. The chair was plush, but she sat rigidly, back straight, head bent, eyes cast downward, intently focused on the hands that were folded politely—tightly—in her lap.

"I'm very happy about this, you know," Jack said finally, gently, hoping to reach with gentleness the sapphire eyes that were hidden behind the luxuriant veil of moonbeams and sable. "I'm very happy that Chase is alive."

His voice was as gentle and tender as the cherishing caresses she would never forget—and it was demanding too, *commanding.*

Without her permission, Stephanie's golden brown head lifted and her eyes bravely met his.

"And you're happy that Chase and Jillian will have a second chance?" she asked softly.

"Yes. I believe in second chances," Jack answered with matching softness. "Don't you?"

Yes, her sapphire eyes answered swiftly, with brilliant clarity and without her permission. I believe in second chances for Jillian and Chase . . . and maybe even for Jillian and me.

But not for you and Jack, a harsh voice reminded. You *c-c-c-can't,* remember?

As Jack watched the lovely hopefulness fade to fear, his dark blue eyes sent a gentle, caressing plea. Don't be afraid, Stephanie, not of us, and especially not of me. I would never harm you. Don't you know that?

Her fearfulness relented then, as if in bold reply; but it wasn't replaced by shimmering hope. Instead, Jack saw sadness, the same wistful sadness he had seen in moonlight at the Chart House. "Stephanie?"

I'm sorry, Jack. I'm sorry.

Before Jack could find the words to say next, to gently lure to her lips the anguish which she kept so silent, Jillian reappeared in the living room and it was time to leave.

Jack didn't say good-bye to Stephanie. He simply smiled a smile filled with promise—to which, for a wondrous surprised moment, her sky-blue eyes answered yes . . . before filling anew with sadness.

Chapter Twelve

Puerto Vallarta
June 13, 1994

It was a dream. The soft musical voice whispered words of love to him, and he felt the splendor of that love on his fevered brow as trembling fingers caressed his skin with the exquisite delicacy of whispered kisses.

"You're going to be fine, Chase," the soft voice promised. "Everything is going to be fine."

Her words and her touch were magnificent promises, balming the fiery pain that seared through him with every breath, soothing the gasping images of blood and death and drowning that haunted his mind. But he was drowning still, immersed in a blurry world that was hot this time, not chilled like the sea. He struggled to surface, to open his eyes to the soft voice, but . . .

"I've missed you so much. Please wake up, Chase, please come back to me."

It was the almost desperate plea of her heart that finally compelled his heavy lids to yield to the wishes of his own, and when they did, what Chase saw was a dream still, of loving emerald eyes, and a smile as soft as her voice, and a luxuriant tangle of auburn silk tousled from a night and a day and a night again at his bedside.

Chase's carefully laid plan had been to arrive on her doorstep at Clairmont, a gaunt and ravaged surprise, in hope of seeing pure terror when she first beheld the man she knew to be a ghost. But that carefully laid plan had been irrevocably shattered the moment he himself had been so mercilessly shattered against the bony peninsula of rock.

Jillian Kincaid had now had ample time to adjust to his miraculous return; and what Chase saw in the shimmering emerald—all that he saw—was radiant hope and joyous welcome.

Never, not once in his entire life, had Chase Carlton been greeted with a look of such happiness . . . and for a wondrous moment he felt the boundless magnificence of being loved. But the wondrous—and so foolish—moment was swiftly conquered as his bright and quickly awakening mind sent an urgent warning, Beware! She is a black widow, a most treacherous one, because already she has discovered your greatest weakness—your never-loved heart—and she is preying on it. She is seducing you into her web, and it is such a clever seduction, such an enchanting disguise: the hopeful and joyous innocence of a bride.

"Jillian."

"Hi," she answered softly, smiling still, even though her heart was breaking. There had been such happiness—a greater happiness than she had ever seen—when his eyes had first opened to her. A breathtaking happiness, soaring, exhilarating, and her own heart had soared in response. But then, as his gray eyes had so suddenly filled with storm clouds, darker and more turbulent than any she remembered, her soaring heart had lost its wings and had plummeted precipitously to earth. In those first breathtaking moments of happiness had Chase remembered the wondrous beginning of their love? And then swiftly, oh, too swiftly, had he recalled its slow and painful death?

"Hi," Chase echoed, his voice softer than it should have been. Some of her joyous radiance was fading—and even though he knew it was simply a clever disguise, his foolish, never-loved heart didn't want to see it go.

"How are you?"

"I hurt," Chase confessed. "Someone seems to be stabbing hot pokers into my chest and refuses to stop."

"You have fractured ribs as well as deep wounds. The doctors will be able to give you pain medication now that you're awake. They've been holding off because of your delirium."

"I've been delirious?" Chase had a vivid memory of his delirium, the grotesquely horrifying images of blood and death and drowning. What if, in that delirium, he had given voice to his nightmares—or to the truth? "Ranting and raving?"

"You were obviously very tormented," Jillian said gently. Very tormented—as always. "But most of what you said was unintelligible."

"Most?"

"Everything except our names," Jillian clarified, not permitting the frown she felt at the memory. Chase had murmured their names over and over, but the recitation had been distant and formal, not intimate and loving: Jillian Montgomery Kincaid, Victor Chase Kincaid.

"That was all?" Chase pressed as casually as possible, but watching her intently. Did I, in my delirium, whisper the word "twin" or "Carlton" or "murderess"?

"That was all that I could understand."

Her magnificent emerald eyes were clear and unflickering . . . and so enchanting that Chase felt the wonderful seduction beginning again. Abruptly he looked away, breaking the black widow's magical spell, and concentrated on surveying his surroundings. He was obviously in a hospital, but the view was unusual, a lush, brilliant tableau of mauve and lavender bougainvilleas with the sparkling azure sea beyond.

Chase remembered clearly his midnight swim toward shore, and the sudden warmth as his shredded flesh bled into the sea, but he remembered nothing else until the delirium of his nightmares . . . and then, most recently, most wonderfully, the dream of the soft voice and delicate touches that had compelled him to awaken.

"Where am I?"

"A hospital in Puerto Vallarta. Three nights ago a group of tourists taking a sunset sail spotted you lying on a beach about fifteen miles north of here. Do you remember how you got there?"

"I remember swimming toward shore, toward a rocky peninsula. The currents were strong, or maybe I was just very weak. I clearly remember being swept against the rocks, but I don't remember getting to the beach."

"And what about before that, Chase? Where were you swimming from? Do you remember?"

"From an island. I'd been there for a while, resting, trying to get strong enough to swim toward land. Before that I was on a boat, a fishing boat, I think. I was very ill, very confused, but eventually I decided that I wasn't safe on that boat. The people who were caring for me seemed . . . sinister. One night, when I could see a shadow of land—the island—in the distance, I managed to slip overboard and swim to it. I lost track of time after that, but I suppose I was there for several weeks before I felt strong enough to attempt the swim to the mainland."

Chase paused then, wanting her to ask the next logical question, needing to watch her eyes and hear her voice as she did. And what he saw—and what he heard—was concern . . . and perhaps fear.

"What about before the fishing boat, Chase? What do you remember?"

He looked at her for several moments before answering. Then, very quietly, he said, "Nothing. I remember nothing."

"But you remember going for a sail on *Sea Goddess,* don't you, and being struck by the boom?"

"*Sea Goddess.* That name is familiar, but . . ." Chase narrowed his gray eyes at the still-uncomprehending green ones. She didn't yet understand the magnitude of his amnesia. He saw her fear that he would remember that night; and soon, he realized with a rush of awakening rage, he would see her relief, that of a murderess, when she discovered that he didn't. Fighting to control his now-crescendoing rage, he asked evenly, "Did you say I was struck by a boom? That sounds . . . careless . . . improbable. Is that really what happened, Jillian?"

"I think so."

"Don't you know? Weren't you there?"

"No." *I wasn't there, but you were probably thinking about me, about the terrible things I had said to you—and that's why you almost died.* "What do you remember about that night, Chase?"

The emerald fear was there still, and now Chase saw such immense sadness that something deep within him felt an astonishing wish to reassure.

You want to reassure the murderess? his mind taunted. Well, don't worry, the feeling won't last. As soon as you see her incriminating relief that you remember nothing about that night, you'll want to kill her, not reassure her. Go ahead. Tell her. And watch what happens to her beautiful green eyes when you do.

"I remember nothing at all about that night."

There it was: *relief.* But it was just a flicker, and what came next wasn't triumphant confidence—the perfect crime perfect still—but what looked like worry and love—*for him.*

Jillian Kincaid was hiding an important secret about the night his brother had died. Lieutenant Jack Shannon had known it, and now Chase Carlton knew it too.

But was the secret kept by Jillian Kincaid a lethal one? The question came from his heart, Chase realized, that lonely, gravely wounded thing that had been chasing an illusory dream all its life . . . and now had awakened to one . . . and was seduced.

Just as your twin was seduced, his mind warned. Maybe that was his brother's weakness, too, a fatal susceptibility to love, to the *look* of love in radiant emerald eyes.

"You'll have to tell me about that night, Jillian. In fact, you'll have to tell me a lot of things. The truth is that I remember being very ill on a fishing boat, but before that I remember . . . nothing."

"You remembered me."

"Your name, yes, and your face." The weak—and gentle and yearning—place in his heart was gone now, replaced by the cold, empty strength Chase knew so well. "I know that we are both Kincaids, but I don't know who you are, or how we're related to each other. Are you my sister?"

You are so cruel, Chase Carlton. It was an accusation that Chase had heard often from the beautiful women who had been his lovers. They never accused him of physical cruelty, of course, *au contraire;* but, except in bed, he was so cold, they raged, so uncaring. Chase's lovers responded to his cruel indifference with rage, not with hurt, because they knew by deep instinct how dangerous he was; and although they entrusted their most intimate passions and desires to him, they were smart enough not to put their hearts in jeopardy.

But now his cruel words caused pain, not rage—bewildered, excruciating anguish—and the unfamiliar gentleness within him wanted to comfort.

Don't be fooled, his mind said harshly to his rebellious heart. Don't be fooled by her.

"Jillian? Who are you?"

The magnificent auburn head bent under the weight of his cruelty, and Chase followed the suddenly veiled gaze downward to her beautiful hands, to her left hand. A wedding band adorned that hand, a traditional ring of solid gold crowned by a delicate cluster of diamonds and emeralds.

Eventually the unadorned right hand curled over the bejeweled left one, and finally, slowly, the auburn lifted, and what Chase saw were tormented green eyes filled with soft apology as she confessed quietly, "Your wife, Chase. I'm your wife."

Chapter Thirteen

Claudia, Edward, Brad, and Jack were all in the waiting room when Jillian appeared with the news.

"He's awake," she announced quietly.

"Really awake? Not delirious or confused?"

"Yes, really awake. But . . ."

"But?"

Jillian drew a steadying breath. "He recognized me, and knew me by name, but he didn't remember his relationship to me."

"What?"

"There's more, Brad," Jillian said to the disbelieving dark eyes. "He really doesn't remember anything except being in the hold of a fishing boat and then on an island. He doesn't remember the accident—or anything that came before." Then she turned to her stepmother and asked, "But he *will* remember, won't he, Claudia?"

"Darling, he just woke up," Claudia answered with reassuring calm. "We know that he had a very serious head injury on the night of the accident and now there are electrolyte disturbances and fever and pain compounding everything else—all of which means it's simply far too soon to make any predictions.

With a head injury as severe as his was, there's often what's called retrograde amnesia—a lasting amnesia for the acute event as well as for minutes, hours, or even days preceding it."

"But not for an entire lifetime."

"I think that would be very unusual."

"And very terrifying," Jillian added softly as her emerald eyes bravely met the dark blue ones of Lieutenant Jack Shannon. "Please don't add to his terror by telling him your theory, Lieutenant."

"I hadn't planned to." Admittedly, Jack had hoped to hear Chase Kincaid's account of what had happened that foggy night on *Sea Goddess,* but he had interviewed enough victims with head injuries to know all about retrograde amnesia, and to know that what Claudia said was undoubtedly correct. Chase's memory of that night was likely to be lost forever. "Does Chase seem terrified?"

"No . . . not yet. But—"

"He needs time to recover, darling," Claudia interjected gently. "For weeks his mind and body have been focused solely on survival. He needs time, safe, peaceful, quiet time to allow the memories to resurface. Now that he's awake, why don't I call Carl and ask him to see him again? As a neurologist, he's an expert in amnesia."

"Hello." Jack greeted the older and dramatically gaunt and ravaged version of the Chase Kincaid he had last seen sixteen years before. "My name is Jack—"

Chase stopped Jack's words by raising a thin yet commanding hand. "Wait, please, just a moment." Chase had guessed by the age, and the graceful stealth with which Jack had entered the room, and the shrewd intelligence of the dark blue eyes, that this was the homicide lieutenant to whom he had spoken but had never seen. But he had waited to hear the first name to be certain. Now his gray eyes gazed searchingly at Jack, and after a moment they closed, as if searching for other images in the shadows of his mind. When he decided he had struggled long enough to be convincing, he opened his eyes again and said, "Jack . . . Shannon."

"Yes."

"We knew each other a long time ago," Chase continued. "When we were kids . . . no . . . in high school."

"That's right," Jack said. "And that's good. Your memory is already coming back."

"Not really. Not enough. Not fast enough. I can place us in high school together . . . and we were friends . . . but nothing after that."

"There really hasn't been anything after that," Jack said, deciding not to share now the memory of the letters they had exchanged following the deaths of their parents. "We went our separate ways after high school."

"But you're here now."

"As a friend . . . and as a cop. I'm with the Los Angeles Police Department. I was the one who investigated when you disappeared. Jillian says you don't remember anything about that night?"

"Nothing," Chase confirmed, impressed by Jack's inscrutable calm. It was obvious that the lieutenant had no intention of planting in the mind of a man who had no memory the deeply disturbing worry that, perhaps, his wife had wanted him dead. Jack Shannon had been, and obviously still was, a true friend to Chase Kincaid. "I don't remember much, and I have no idea if what I'm remembering is real or imagined. I keep getting fleeting images, like glimpses of dreams."

"Such as?"

"Such as an image of fire . . . and snow." Chase frowned, an authentic frown of anguish and loss, and added truthfully, "The image comes with a feeling of great sadness."

"Your parents—and your aunt and uncle and grandfather—died in a fire at Lake Tahoe. It happened in November, at Thanksgiving, so I imagine there was snow on the ground."

"I was there?"

"In Tahoe, yes, but you were at a casino at the time of the blaze."

"What the hell are you doing in here, Shannon?" Brad demanded angrily as he entered the room. "We agreed that you could see Chase after the rest of us had—not before. You said you were going to make a call to your office, but instead you came in here."

"I did make the call to my office," Jack replied evenly. "The doctors were just coming out of Chase's room as I was passing by, so—"

"Hey, Brad, relax," Chase intervened, his voice easy and teasing, a tone he hoped his twin had used for years when speaking with his cousin—*their* cousin. As he gazed at the now-smiling dark eyes of the man who had been a brother to his brother—and was his own and only living blood relative—Chase felt a rush of emotion. When he spoke again, the emotion made his voice waver. "Hello, Brad."

"Hello, Chase," Brad echoed, emotional too. "Welcome back."

"I'm a long way from back."

"But you recognize me."

"Yes. You're my brother . . . no, my cousin."

"Right. And?"

"And we're good friends."

"Damn right. And together we run the most powerful motion picture studio in the world."

Chase shook his head with carefully planned disbelief. He had no intention of stepping into his twin's role at Triple Crown. Chase Kincaid's amnesia for work would be total, his golden gift for dreams hidden in the darker shadows of his lost memory. Chase Carlton was here to do what he did best: catch a murderer.

As soon as he could travel, he would insist on going to Clairmont. There, in his brother's home, he would hope to find invisible messages—of danger perhaps, and of love. The mindprints left by a murderess . . . and the heartprints and soulprints left by a twin. He would become Jillian's constant companion, a long, dark shadow that clung tenaciously, even in the harshest midday sun; and perhaps in that bright relentless glare the brilliant emerald would be unable to conceal its fatal flaws.

"Are you telling me that you don't remember anything about Triple Crown?" Brad pressed.

"Triple Crown," Chase echoed. "Something to do with horse racing . . . ?"

"May we come in?" Jillian's beautiful face held the same uncertainty as her voice.

"Of course." It was Brad who answered, smiling gentle reassurance at her. "He remembers who I am and that we're cousins."

"Oh, good," Jillian whispered. I'm glad he remembers you, Brad. I just wish he remembered me. Chiding herself for the selfishness of her wish, Jillian smiled bravely at Chase and said, "These are my parents, Chase. Edward and Claudia Montgomery."

Chase greeted Jillian's parents politely but without a flicker of recognition. Jack had told him what they were—a highly respected attorney and an equally prominent plastic surgeon—but no photographs of either of them had been included in the information Jack had sent.

Edward Montgomery's greeting was reserved, Chase thought, the appraising and almost skeptical caution of an attorney rather than the relief of a father-in-law who had grieved over the loss of a much beloved son-in-law. But the quiet greeting from Jillian's stepmother glowed with gentle welcome and embracing warmth.

"Hello, Chase," Claudia said softly to her son. And then, as she stood in the small room with the bright, tropical view that was so very like the view from the room in which he had been born, she thought, You have another chance at happiness, Chase, another chance at love.

And, she promised, I will do whatever I can to help you.

*   *   *

Dr. Carl Peters confirmed what Claudia had suggested about Chase's amnesia. Given the severity of the head injury as evidenced by the healed skull fracture, it was most likely that Chase would have permanent and total amnesia for the accident itself, as well as for events that occurred hours, perhaps even days, before it.

And as for the rest of Chase's memories? How much would return was unpredictable, but it was quite possible, Dr. Peters reassured, that in time he would remember everything. For the near term he predicted that the memories would come randomly, dreamlike glimpses of images, each of which was a tiny piece of the vast jigsaw puzzle of his forgotten life. The glimpses of memory would be random, but they might be triggered, as memories often were, by the potent remembrances of the senses—by sights and sounds, and tastes and fragrances, and textures and touch.

Chase would need a tour guide, someone who knew the once-familiar but now foreign territory of his past and could help interpret and translate the memories for him, embellishing the fleeting glimpses so that the tiny and undecipherable pieces could begin to interlock and finally coalesce into a clear and vivid portrait.

Chase needed a patient and devoted tour guide to travel with him on his frustrating journey through shadows. And, Dr. Peters advised, it would be ideal for him to make that journey in a place that was safe and familiar to him. After giving his prognosis, and his offer to follow Chase's progress on his return to Los Angeles, Carl Peters left—as did Jack. Now that Chase's complete and permanent amnesia for the accident had been confirmed, he needed to make arrangements for his own flight back to L.A.

"I can't wait to get Chase home," Jillian told her parents and Brad as soon as the four of them were alone.

"Why doesn't he stay with me?" Brad suggested quietly.

"What?" Jillian asked with surprise—and pain. True, Chase remembered his relationship to Brad, and had no such memories of her, but still. . . . "You heard Dr. Peters, Brad. Chase needs to be in familiar surroundings. That means Clairmont, his home, our home."

"I'll move in there, then."

"Thank you, Brad, but it's not necessary. Chase will need your help, of course. There are all the childhood memories that you know and I don't. But you have a studio to run, after all, and now that school's out, I have nothing to do but help him."

"You have a little studio work to do yourself," Brad reminded her. *"Journeys of the Heart,* remember? Now that Stephanie has agreed to play the lead and Peter Dalton has agreed to direct, we really need to get going on preproduction." After a moment his handsome face grew solemn and he clarified, "What I was thinking, Jillian, when I suggested that I move into Clairmont, was that you move out. You could stay with Claudia and Edward, or at my place, or find someplace new."

"What?"

"You don't owe Chase anything."

"He's my husband!"

"He wasn't a very good husband." Brad's eyes left the stunned emerald ones and glanced briefly at Jillian's parents. He saw solemn support from Edward, and surprising defiance from Claudia, but nonetheless he added gently but emphatically, "We all know that."

"That's right, darling," Edward concurred with a gentleness that matched Brad's.

"What are you saying, Dad?"

"Just the truth, Jill. Chase made you unhappy. In the weeks since his accident you've been adjusting to spending the rest of your life without him. Maybe it would be best if you just—"

"No," Jillian interjected softly. No, I haven't spent the past few weeks adjusting to my life without Chase, she thought. I've spent them waiting for him, as he asked me to wait, and now, as he promised, he's returned . . . and we're going to talk, really talk . . . and we're going to share the secret truths and torments of our hearts . . . and our love will be what it always should have been.

"Be reasonable, Jillian," Brad urged. "Yes, Dr. Peters said that once the memories start to coalesce they might flood back quite quickly. But he also admitted that it was totally unpredictable. It might be years before Chase's memory fully returns—if it ever does."

"I'm willing to spend those years helping him, Brad. He's my husband."

"For better or worse?"

"Yes!"

"Oh, no," Brad said quietly as the realization hit him. "You see this as a second chance, don't you? You've always been such a romantic."

"Is that so terrible? Isn't that the reason you liked *Journeys of the Heart* so much?"

"Of course. And it's why I like you so much too. But be reasonable, Jillian, please. Memories or no memories, the man Chase is inside hasn't changed. Don't you think that eventually the same history—the same *unhappy* history—that you've lived for the past six years will repeat itself?"

"I don't know, Brad," Jillian confessed. Was it inevitable, no matter what she did, no matter how honestly and courageously she approached their love this time, that she and Chase were destined to travel to the same horrible destination that they had reached on the night of his accident? It was a question that could be answered only with time, and it might be years; but it was a risk she was willing to take despite the obvious disapproval of her father and Brad. Turning to the person who had remained silent so far, she asked softly, "What do you think, Claudia?"

Claudia drew a steadying breath as she looked from her hopeful stepdaughter to her solemn husband. Oh, Edward, I love you so . . . and I know you want what's best for Jillian . . . and so do I. She's my daughter too, and Chase is my son, and . . .

Returning to Jillian, she replied with quiet passion, "I think, my darling, that believing in second chances is as important as believing in dreams."

"Hi," Jillian greeted softly when she returned to Chase's room.

He was awake, gazing outside toward the golden ball of fire that was falling slowly but relentlessly toward the sea. He had been thinking about her, how to behave with her, how to control both his enchantment and his rage.

A man with no memory who returned to a wife as loving as Jillian seemed to be would himself be gentle, grateful, hopeful. But if, lurking in the shadows of that man's hidden memory, there was a vague and ominous whisper of murder, that darkness might surface from time to time, mightn't it? Yes. Which meant that he could, and should, act unpredictably toward Jillian Kincaid, sometimes gentle, sometimes glacial, sometimes kind, sometimes cruel.

Before awakening to the welcoming green eyes, Chase would have believed with absolute confidence that gentleness would have been the most difficult for him. But, he realized anew as his eyes left the setting sun and met the shy yet smiling Jillian, gentleness wouldn't be difficult at all.

"Hi."

"Did Dr. Peters talk to you about your amnesia?"

"Yes." And his words had been almost identical to the words Chase had heard from the neurologist in Denver. "Mixed metaphors about glimpses of dreams and pieces of jigsaw puzzles and journeys through shadows."

"For which you'll need a dream interpreter . . . and a piece fitter . . . and a tour guide," Jillian said softly. "Brad has offered, and you have known him all your life, and I know that you have stronger memories of him than of me, and it's obviously your choice, but . . ."

"But what, Jillian?"

"Well, I just want you to know that I would like to be the one who helps you remember. I'm a schoolteacher, I don't know if you remember that, but it means that I have lots of experience explaining things."

"And lots of patience?" Chase asked of the uncertain emerald eyes.

It was such a soft sell, such a modest recounting of her credentials—her experience as a teacher, not her rights as a wife—that Chase couldn't be sure what she really wanted. The murderess was quite safe, of course. Dr. Peters had surely told her that a clear and vivid memory of "the accident" would never surface. But wouldn't even a confident murderess want to control the memories still, to carefully orchestrate, manipulate, the ones that did return? And if Jillian weren't a murderess, but merely a loving wife, then wouldn't she do everything in her power to help her husband rediscover their wondrous love?

Chase couldn't tell what Jillian Kincaid wanted. But did she know, he wondered, how enchanting it was to him that her offer of help was made with such lovely uncertainty?

Of course she knows, his mind answered. She knows precisely. The black widow who had seduced his twin into her silken web of treachery and deceit surely knew the most clever way to his heart—their hearts.

Oh, yes, he was enchanted by this shy and beautiful woman who had enchanted his brother. And even though he felt a surprising wish for her innocence, and even though there was a part of him that wanted to believe in the magnificence of the love he saw in her eyes, the ice-cold hardness of Chase's heart was not in great danger of melting. But, he decided, it was very helpful to see, and to feel with such surprising and powerful clarity, exactly how Jillian Kincaid had bewitched his twin.

Finally, as gently as his brother would have, Chase answered. "I'd like you to help me, Jillian. And I'd like to go home with you as soon as possible."

Chapter Fourteen

Clairmont Estate
June 19, 1994

At Jillian's insistence, Edward, Claudia,, and Brad returned to Los Angeles two days after Chase awakened from his delirium.

"We'll be fine," Jillian assured her family as her heart filled with hope. Chase wanted to be with her. Surely that meant that somewhere deep in the shadows was a happy memory of their love, of what it could be.

They might have all returned to Los Angeles, transferring Chase from the small resort-town hospital in Puerto Vallarta to the state-of-the-art medical center at UCLA, but both Claudia and Carl Peters confirmed that Chase was receiving excellent care right where he was, in the place that usually specialized in diseases of tourists—serious sunburns from overzealous sunbathing, Montezuma's revenge from injudicious consumption of local produce, sprains and bruises from out-of-shape vacationers suddenly at play. Chase was the most critically ill patient admitted to the small hospital in a very long time, but his fluid and electrolyte management—as well as the care of his broken ribs and infected chest wounds—could not have been better anywhere.

The transfer would have been an exhausting ordeal for him, and Chase himself expressed a surprisingly strong preference for remaining exactly where he was. He would sleep almost constantly, after all, a sleep induced by pain medication and the powerful demands of his convalescing body for rest; and when he awakened, what could be more tranquil and idyllic than the cheerful view of flowers and sky and sea?

The doctors, including Claudia and Carl, predicted that it might be another two weeks before Chase would be ready to comfortably fly home. But by late Sunday afternoon, only eight days after word of his miraculous reappearance first reached Los Angeles, the infection in the deep chest wounds had resolved so dramatically and the electrolyte imbalance had improved so markedly that all the intravenous lines were removed.

Chase was still very weak, and every breath still caused flickers of fire as the sharp points of his shattered ribs stabbed the surface of his lungs, but nonetheless as soon as the lines were removed, he announced that he wanted to go home— immediately. The doctors acquiesced to the steely resolve in the dark gray eyes, and while Jillian made arrangements for the flight home, Chase finally relented to the doctor's firm insistence that he receive a shot of Demerol for the flight.

He knew that it was the last dose of pain medication he would take. The Demerol numbed the pain, yes, and helped him get the rest that was so necessary to his recovery; but, too, it blurred his mind. In the hospital in Puerto Vallarta Chase dealt with the blurriness by avoiding all but the most superficial exchanges with Jillian. But once he was alone with her, in the house that had been his twin's, his mind needed to be sharp, alert, and wary.

Jillian wanted their homecoming to be private—and it would be. "I'll be long gone by then," Stephanie had instantly announced when Jillian had called from Puerto Vallarta to tell her that she and Chase would be arriving home at about nine P.M. Jillian hadn't called her parents or Brad. The only other call she made was to arrange for one of Triple Crown's fleet of limousines to meet them at the airport.

Chase wanted their homecoming to be private as well, Jillian realized with a rush of hope when they stood in Clairmont's white gravel driveway and he took the small suitcase from the limousine driver rather than having him carry it inside. Now the limousine was pulling away from the hilltop estate, and she and Chase were alone on the front porch.

Would the sight of their beautiful home cause a sudden flood of hidden memories? Jillian wondered as her delicate fingers inserted the key into the front door lock. And if so, would the memories that flooded first, the ones most desperate to be remembered, be the happiest ones?

She hoped so . . . oh, how she hoped so.

Chase felt a deep cold shiver as he watched Jillian unlock the door. The trembling chill was partly physical, of course, an angry rebellion of the still-needing-to-heal body that had been so precipitously taken from its sickbed; and it was emotional also, a deep shiver of anticipation. Would he feel invisible memories left by his twin the moment he entered his brother's home? And if so, would they be memories of happiness and love—or of violence and betrayal?

Then the door was open, and then he was standing in the white marble foyer, and then he was following Jillian into the spacious teal and cream living room, and then his gray eyes were marveling at the magnificent panorama of lawn and flowers and ocean and sky.

Chase felt no invisible messages from his twin, but he felt something in the twilight stillness, something unexpected and extraordinary and rare. Peace. A sense of belonging. As if, at last, in this idyllic place, he was home. This idyllic place . . . with Jillian.

Before Chase could conquer the intoxicating feeling of peace with vivid images of his dying twin pleading for mercy, the stillness was disrupted by nearby sounds of soft, eager barking and rapidly prancing paws.

"We have a dog?"

"Yes. Her name is Annie. She's in the kitchen. Shall I get her?"

"Sure."

As he waited, Chase realized that he was about to learn from Annie's reaction to him if he and his brother had shared a kindness to animals. He hoped so. To Chase, animals were fellow orphans, as helpless and innocent as the abandoned child he once had been, making no demands, hoping only to be loved. It was unimaginable to Chase that anyone could be cruel to such harmless and gentle creatures, but his own experience with serial killers had taught him that animals were frequently the earliest victims of their cruelty.

Chase's thoughts were interrupted by the sound of rapidly approaching thuds on the plush carpet. He had planned to extend his hands, to let her inhale what would surely be his familiar scent, but long before she reached him, Annie's acute nose had already identified him, and her ears had heard his familiar voice. She bounded to him, a wriggling bundle of golden fur, and upon reaching him, she remained tethered to earth only by her hind feet as she greeted his bearded face with warm pink lappings of welcome.

She nearly knocked him over, and the impact of her excited body hurling against his chest caused painful flares of fire, but Chase welcomed her with gentle hands, marveling at the greeting of pure happiness that was being bestowed on him. Annie's enthusiasm was for his twin, of course, the brother who had obviously been very kind to her, but still Chase allowed himself to savor it.

"She missed you," Jillian said softly. "If you sit on the sofa and pat the spot beside you, she'll curl up next to you."

"Okay," Chase agreed, wondering if Jillian sensed how weak he was, how the inside of his chest was an inferno of flames, how much he needed to sit.

In moments he was seated, and Annie was curled as close as she could be, her body still trembling with excitement, her golden head resting on his lap. As Chase stroked the soft head, he thought about the loyal and trusting creature he hadn't even known existed. Had Chase and Jillian Kincaid had a child, a son or daughter left fatherless by the death at sea, Chase would have found a different way of solving the mystery of that night. Posing as a miraculously alive husband was unkind—yes, cruel—if the wife were innocent of all crimes; but posing as a child's missing father was a pretense that Chase would not have used, not even to catch a murderess. He knew far too well, and far too painfully, the fragile sensitivities of children.

Chase hadn't known about Annie, and since the few revelations he had made after first awakening in the hospital in Puerto Vallarta, he had purposefully withheld any further fleeting glimpses of memory. He wanted, needed, to wait until his ravaged body was strong again, and his mind was unblurred by drugs, and he had absolute control of the foolish place in his heart that was far too susceptible to the uncertain yet radiant joy that greeted him every time Jillian saw him anew.

Now he and Jillian were at Clairmont, and the final shot of Demerol had long since lost both its pain-numbing and mind-blurring potency, and even though the fiery weakness of his body would command him to rest soon, he lifted his eyes from the golden head to Jillian and asked, "Will you tell me about Annie? She's a golden retriever?"

"Yes, and we think she's a purebred. You and Annie and I all met on the same day. You two met first. You were on your way from here to a wedding reception at the Beverly Wilshire when you saw her in the middle of the street, staggering amid the busy traffic. She was just a puppy, and you thought she had probably been hit by a car. You were afraid that she might run away when you tried to catch her, to help her, but the moment you called to her, she came. You realized as soon as you held her that she hadn't been hit, at least not by a car. She had been abused though, badly mistreated, and was suffering from malnutrition. It was a Saturday afternoon, but you found a veterinary hospital that was open for emergencies. Do you remember any of this?"

"No." I have no memory of rescuing this orphaned and abused animal; but I know from personal experience of a pure-bred baby who was abandoned—and mistreated. And now rescued? Chase wondered. His twin had once rescued an or-phaned puppy. Was that same generous twin, with his gift for dreams, by his own death rescuing yet another orphan? Was the golden brother giving his dark twin a chance to find answers to the questions that had tormented him all his life, a chance perhaps even for happiness and love? After several long, thoughtful moments, Chase repeated, "No, I'm sorry, I don't remember."

"The veterinarian told you that it would be a few hours before he had enough data to make a decision about what course of action would be best. During that time, you went to the wedding reception."

"And that's where you were?"

"Yes. It was June, exactly six years ago last Saturday." Jillian shrugged softly, hopefully, at the coincidence. She and Chase had met—and swiftly and wondrously fallen in love—on Satur-day, June 11, 1988; and it had been on Saturday, June 11, 1994 that he had returned to her from the sea. "I was living in a house in Westwood with three other women, one of whom was a model who was dating Brad. She was supposed to accompany him to the wedding reception, but she got delayed at a shoot in Palm Springs. She couldn't reach him by phone, and had to get back to work, so she called to ask if I would keep trying for her. When I gave Brad the message, he insisted that I go to the reception with him in her place."

"So you and Brad were already good friends when you and I met?"

Jillian hesitated before answering. From the very beginning of their relationship, she had bravely portrayed herself to Chase as far more confident than she truly was—a confidence and experience and sophistication to match her beautiful face. But the truth was that she had been innocent, inexperienced, and uncertain. And why had she never confessed to the man she loved the truth of her innocence? Because she feared that Hollywood's most dashing bachelor would desire her less if he knew that beneath the beautiful façade she was really the shy and unglamorous girl she had always been?

That was part of it, Jillian knew, but there was something else too, a reluctance to burden Chase with the immense responsibility of caring for all the wounded places in her heart. On that very first day, when she had seen the deep gray flickers of sadness for the puppy he had just rescued, she realized how sensitive Chase was, how he felt in his own heart the anguished torments of the world.

Jillian had spared Chase her own deepest wounds, and there was so much, too, that he had never shared with her—and it had been that silence, those secrets, that had driven them apart.

But now she and Chase were beginning again, weren't they? And now she was a gifted screenwriter, and she could rewrite their script, just a little, just enough to give them a second chance . . . couldn't she?

"I guess that even then Brad was like an older brother," she answered finally. "Fond of his little sister, but teasing. He told me I was destined to become an old maid schoolteacher. He said this in the nicest possible way, and I didn't take offense, because my dream had always been to teach."

"So you weren't dating anyone at the time?"

"No."

"Were you recovering from a disastrous love affair?"

"No. I hadn't really ever dated anyone, not seriously." Bravely, so bravely, she met the interested—and surprised—gray eyes. "I've never told you that before, Chase. We decided that it was pointless to discuss our past relationships anyway, but I let you imagine that there had been other men—even though there hadn't."

She suddenly looked younger, perhaps as she had looked

on that June day when his twin had fallen in love with her, and so very innocent.

"I didn't know that you were a virgin?" Chase heard a voice—his?—ask with what sounded like tenderness.

"No," she confessed, courageous still even as her cheeks flushed pink.

Why not? Chase wondered. Why had Jillian never had a serious relationship? And why had she hidden that truth, and the truth of her innocence, from Chase Kincaid? As the questions about Jillian's secret virginity swirled in his mind, his thoughts drifted to how sexually experienced his twenty-eight-year-old twin had undoubtedly been . . .

Seeing the sudden concern in Chase's dark gray eyes, Jillian assured him softly, "You were very gentle." Her assurance caused a flicker of relief. But not, Jillian realized, even the faintest glimmer of what was for her such a wondrous and unforgettable memory. It was painfully obvious that Chase didn't remember the first time—or any time—they had made love. She was discussing the most private of all intimacies with a man who was a stranger. Hurriedly returning the conversation to other, less intimate history, she said, "So, anyway, on that day in June, Brad insisted that I accompany him to what was going to be one of Hollywood's most dazzling wedding receptions."

"And were you dazzled?"

The truth, Jillian reminded herself. This time you are going to tell him the truth. As the pink in her cheeks deepened to a lovely rose, she answered quietly, "Only by you."

"And I was dazzled by you," Chase echoed, a statement not a question, because he knew his brother must have been dazzled by the emerald and auburn vision of innocence amid all the glamour and glitz.

"Well . . ." Jillian smiled softly. "Yes, you were. You told me that later. At the time it seemed to me that you were just grateful that I didn't tease you about rescuing Annie—or about the telltale puppy hairs on your jacket."

"Who teased me? Brad?"

"Brad and others—all very fondly, of course."

"But you didn't."

"No. I thought what you had done was wonderful, and I thought it was even more wonderful that you weren't afraid to admit it—or to show your anger that she had been mistreated. When you called the vet and learned that it would be safe to take her home, you asked me if I wanted to go with you, to hold her during the drive." Her emerald eyes glowed with a golden light from deep within as she added, "We were married seventeen days later."

"At the Beverly Wilshire?"

"No, right here, in the rose garden—the hastily planted rose garden. This property had belonged to your parents, and even though there had never been a house here before, the estate already had been named Clairmont. For the first seven years following your parents' death you lived on your sailboat in the marina. But you finally decided that you needed more space— and a screening room. You designed this house yourself and had moved in just three days before we met. The finishing touches weren't complete until after we returned from our honeymoon."

"Which was where?"

"Bora Bora." Her soft answer was filled with hope. If only he could remember their honeymoon at the Hotel Bora Bora. Her heart set a new pace as she saw that Bora Bora did mean something to him, did ignite some memory . . .

Bora Bora. The coincidence danced inside him. Of all the places on earth, Chase Kincaid had chosen to travel to Bora Bora for his romantic honeymoon with his innocent bride. The tropical paradise chosen for a honeymoon by the twin with the gift for dreams was the same faraway island where the twin with the gift for evil would have been right now, a solitary escape from recent memories of murder to the more familiar memories of loneliness had it not been for a newscast . . . and the uncanny instincts of a homicide lieutenant . . . and the death of a brother.

Now he was here instead of Bora Bora, sitting in a living

room the color of the sea, with a loyal and loving dog curled against him, gazing at a beautiful woman with hopeful emerald eyes . . . and to Chase Carlton this felt like paradise.

But it may well be hell, his mind warned harshly. Chase's wary mind had been conspicuously silent during the romantic stroll down memory lane, allowing his heart—his twin's heart—to feel again the enchantment of falling in love with Jillian. But now it was time for his mind to intervene. This may be hell, not paradise. She may be a clever, cold-blooded murderess.

"I'm very tired," Chase said abruptly. "I think I'd better go to bed."

"Yes, of course," Jillian agreed, as she struggled to conceal her disappointment. She had been so hopeful that the mention of Bora Bora would spark memories of love, and for a few wonderful moments it seemed as if it had; but then, quite suddenly, the gray of his eyes had become ice cold, and very hard. "I'll show you the way to the master bedroom."

"I wonder . . ."

"Yes?"

"Because of my rib fractures, my sleep will probably be restless. Maybe I should sleep in a guest room."

"I've been sleeping in the upstairs guest room," Jillian said quietly. "I'm already settled there. And besides, all your things are in the master bedroom."

As Jillian spoke, she realized that Chase undoubtedly thought she had moved out of their bedroom after he disappeared because it had been too difficult, too painful, for her to sleep in their bed. But in fact she had been sleeping in the guest bedroom since early March, two months before he vanished.

The decision to sleep apart then, as it was now, was by mutual consent, and then as now the reason Chase gave was probably not the real one, even though it was the same: because the restlessness of his sleep might disturb hers. The reason now was the smoldering pain from his shattered ribs; and in March it had been the nightmares that had shattered his sleep.

Chase had always had nightmares, but the ones that had begun quite abruptly in the middle of February had been far worse than all those that had come before, driving him with gasping terror from a sleep to which he usually chose not to return, leaving the bed to play his guitar until dawn—or to sail. Bravely, so bravely, Jillian had tried to get him to share with her the dark and troubling images that seemed to linger even in the brightness of day. But at the brave suggestion, he had withdrawn further into his dark moodiness and eventually he had announced his plan to move into the upstairs guest room.

No, she had countered swiftly. That room had always been her study. It was she who would move.

Restless, tormented sleep. That was the reason, then and now, that Chase gave for why they should sleep apart. But then as now the real reason was far more painful: they were strangers to each other.

Jillian stood up. Chase followed suit, gently dislodging Annie first. She spilled to the floor in a graceful flow of golden fur, then trotted close beside him as Jillian led the way from the cream and teal living room to the wide staircase that swept up to the second floor. When they reached the foot of the staircase, Annie stopped and sat.

"This is as far as she goes," Jillian explained, patting Annie as she gestured with her auburn head to the well-used plush pillow that lay nearby on the floor. "We decided early on that it would be less complicated—or at least less chaotic—not to have this lively ball of fluff sleep with us."

"She doesn't look too unhappy about the arrangement," Chase observed. Annie seemed untroubled. It was he, he realized, who was a little disappointed that the affectionate animal wouldn't be curled near him as he slept.

"No. I think because she's never known anything else, because we've never once broken the rule, it's been easy and unconfusing for her." It had been just as well, Jillian thought, because there would have been confusion for Annie when she and Chase had started sleeping separately. Many times in the weeks since Chase's disappearance Jillian had thought about breaking the rule, allowing Annie upstairs to sleep with her because she so desperately needed the companionship. But she hadn't. Because, she had told herself, Chase is going to return.

When Chase and Jillian reached the top of the staircase, Jillian gestured to an open doorway to their right.

"That's where I'll be," she explained before leading the way to the left, down the wide plushly carpeted hallway to the double doors at the end.

The doors opened to the spacious master suite. It was as luxurious as the living room below, and like the living room, had a sunset view of the ocean. From the living room the vista had included sweeping emerald lawn and bountiful gardens of roses; but from here, because of its second-floor perch, the land fell away and the water seemed very close, creating the magnificent illusion of being at sea.

"Does it look familiar?" Jillian asked when she saw the faint smile that touched Chase's lips.

"Maybe." It was the truth. Maybe this room was familiar, part of a faraway dream that had been forgotten, lost in the glaring realities of his life, until now.

"Everything is exactly the way you left it." Jillian shrugged softly. "Your pajamas are in the top drawer of that dresser."

Pajamas were a refinement, an inhibition, with which Chase Carlton had never bothered. But now he would. Nodding at the dresser to which she had gracefully gestured, he answered, "All right."

"Can I get you something to eat or drink before you go to sleep?"

"No. Thank you. All I need is sleep."

"Okay. Well. Good night, then. Sleep well, Chase . . . and welcome home."

"Thank you. Sleep well, Jillian."

Chase walked back to the doorway with her. As he watched

her walk away, he noticed her limp for the first time. Until today he had seen her walk only the few steps that could be walked in his small hospital room, and today, until now, she had been so close to him that he hadn't detected the unevenness of her gait.

Chase watched until Jillian disappeared down the staircase and then lingered still, waiting for the words, if any, that would greet Annie when she reached the first floor. There were words, soft, loving words that made his heart ache with a longing that was as wonderful—and as impossible—as the forgotten dream.

"Oh, Annie," the soft voice said. "You're so glad he's home, aren't you? So very glad . . ."

Chapter Fifteen

Chase awakened at dawn. His sleep in his twin's bed had been deep, dreamless, and remarkably peaceful. As he focused on his surroundings, his gaze fell on the nightstand to which sometime during the night had been added a water pitcher, a glass, and his pills.

Jillian had been there, standing at his bedside, staring down at him in the moonlit shadows. A shiver passed through Chase as he realized how vulnerable he had been, lost in a deep sleep, having no idea that she was there. Nothing had warned him of her presence; no inner alarm of danger had sounded to awaken him.

Because he was safe? he wondered. Or because, despite the lifetime wariness of his heart and mind, he was already hopelessly trapped in her silken web, bewitched by her just as his twin had been? What expression had been on her beautiful face as she studied him in the shadows? The almost shy joy that she wore when she knew he was watching? Or had her magnificent emerald eyes filled with cold fury as she stared at the man who had miraculously returned from the watery grave to which she had destined him?

There was a note on the nightstand too:

Chase, I forgot about the evening dose of antibiotics until after you were asleep. I spoke with Claudia, who said it wasn't necessary to wake you, but please take them if you do awaken. Jillian.

Chase frowned as he read the note. Her handwriting was round and unglamorous, like an unaffected schoolgirl's, and he marveled at her choice of words—"I forgot about"—as if his pills were her responsibility.

Chase took the antibiotics, but not the Demerol. His mind was clear now, and refreshed from his deep sleep, and he would do nothing to obscure the welcome clarity, which also meant he would do nothing to subdue the fire in his chest. It was there still, a smoldering heat that threatened to burst into flames with a deep breath or a sudden twist.

But, Chase realized, there had been remarkable healing during the deep, peaceful sleep in his brother's bed.

After a long, hot shower, Chase studied his reflection in the bathroom mirror with dispassionate detachment. His lean, strong body was gaunt now, and pale, and freshly scarred. Well, he had been all three of those things many times before in his life. After a moment his gray eyes lifted to appraise the ravages of this most recent ordeal on his face. The scraggly beard that had appeared in the past three weeks of starvation was a far cry from the healthy one he had removed at the beginning of his voyage to Mexico; but even had the newly grown beard been luxuriant, Chase would have shaved it off. Soon, he knew, the press would want photographs. He couldn't run the risk of someone who had known him as Chase Carlton making the connection when he—or more likely she—saw a photograph of a bearded Chase Kincaid.

And his hair? It needed to be cut, but not urgently. The coal black that fell toward his eyes and curled sensuously over his ears was longer now than the style his twin had worn in any of the photographs Chase had seen; but it was still much shorter than the way he himself had worn it for years.

After he finished shaving, as he was selecting an Oxford shirt from his brother's neatly ordered closet, he felt it. It, whatever *it* was: the ominous, invisible messenger of death he knew so well. It invaded him without warning, as always, a violent invasion of ice that stole his breath and drained him of all warmth and even froze his limbs.

Chase Carlton was a victim of his own gift. He could not control it, or conjure it, or conquer it. It came when it wanted, and when it did it was in complete control, mercilessly compelling him to heed its lethal messages.

What was it saying to him now? Chase couldn't tell. His mind was well rested and free of Demerol, but still the message was hopelessly blurred. And who was responsible for sending it? A green-eyed murderess? The ghost of his twin? Chase couldn't tell that either.

Then it was gone, as quickly and mysteriously as it had come, and as it released its icy grip, Chase took a gasping breath that caused an inferno within. Dressing quickly despite the blaze in his chest, he left his bedroom for Jillian's. He would stand outside her room, he decided, and perhaps he would detect that the chilling invasion of evil had been sent from within.

But Chase didn't need to stand outside the bedroom where Jillian slept. The door was wide open, welcoming, and he didn't hesitate even for a moment before going in. He needed to get as close as possible as soon as possible—in case some invisible whisper of ice lingered still in the air.

And if she awakened as he hovered overhead? It would not be so unusual for a man with a forgotten past to stare at the sleeping vision of his once-beloved wife in hope that such an intimate image would lure the hidden memories from their shadows, would it? No, Chase decided as he approached, his footfalls virtually soundless on the plush carpet. In fact, it would be unusual for such a desperate man not to.

If Jillian awakened, his presence could be easily explained. But would she awaken? Chase wondered. Would a deep and ever-vigilant instinct suddenly warn her that from her murderous dreams she had unwittingly sent a message of death, and that now she was being intently gazed upon by a pale, gaunt, freshly scarred ghost?

Jillian didn't stir, and there were no icy vestiges of evil in the air. In fact, Chase realized as he cast his eyes about the room, there was a warmth here, glowing, golden, and very peaceful. The golden warmth was from the awakening dawn, its soft yellow light bathing the room through the skylight overhead. And the sense of peace? From the soothing lavender of the carpet and drapes, perhaps, or from the hand-painted meadow of springtime flowers that blossomed on the walls. Or maybe it was a glorious promise of peace, not an ominous message of evil, which drifted gently, invisibly, from Jillian as she dreamed.

His brother's wife was very beautiful, Chase thought as he returned to her sleeping face. An angelic portrait of innocence framed by a tangled auburn halo. Jillian's magnificent emerald eyes were hidden now, behind long lashes that rested on her cheeks like the most delicate of fans. When she was awake the startling green commanded all attention, but now Chase focused on her other lovely features: the pretty nose, the full and generous lips, softly smiling, wonderfully welcoming, even in sleep—and for the first time he noticed the tiny lines. They were virtually hidden when she was awake, lost in the animation of her expressive face. But in the motionlessness of sleep, the pure white scars, the gossamer threads that surely indicated surgery, were clearly visible.

Why had Jillian Kincaid had surgery on her beautiful face? She was only twenty-nine. Was she so obsessed with youth and beauty that already she had a plastic surgeon reverse the first gentle tugs of nature? Chase suddenly found himself hoping that Jillian wasn't that vain, believing that she wasn't—and just as suddenly he reminded himself of the reason that he was now standing at her bedside.

He left her bedroom then. As he did, leaving her, the golden warmth, and the gentle peace, Chase felt as if he were trudging through heavy snow; and he realized that even without pain pills it was going to be very difficult to keep his mind clear. Jillian Kincaid blurred everything. Just as, perhaps, she had blurred the mind of his twin, making him believe in her magical spell.

When Chase reached the bottom of the staircase he was greeted exuberantly by wriggling golden fur, another magical and blurring spell for a man who had never been missed. After a flurry of petting, Annie led the way to the kitchen.

Once there, she sat expectantly in front of the door that opened to the outside—even though in the lower half of the expensive wood a smaller door had obviously been inserted for her. Chase opened the kitchen door, and Annie bounded out without a backward glance. She didn't expect him to accompany her, Chase realized. But, he thought, she would have quite specific expectations on her return.

Without stopping to think about where dog food might logically be kept—in a distant pantry far away from the food for humans—he simply opened the cupboard nearest the sink, and there it was.

How had he known? He hadn't, he told his racing heart, nor had his hand been invisibly guided by the ghost of his twin. In this household where Annie was obviously so important, it simply made sense that her food would be kept in a prominent place.

By the time Annie returned, Chase had read the label on one of the cans and decided that an entire can was a reasonable amount to give her. Reasonable—and probably correct, he thought as he watched her approach her bowl with full approval and not a wiggle of surprise.

*   *   *

"Good morning."

"Good morning," Chase echoed as he turned from the stove in the direction of the soft, shy voice.

"Did you sleep well?"

"Surprisingly well. I gave Annie a can of dog food and was just making some oatmeal. Would you like some?"

"Sure. Thank you." Hopefulness filled her emerald eyes as she added, "You remembered."

"What did I remember?" How much food to feed Annie? That my twin—like myself—liked oatmeal, even on a summer day?

"You remembered to use the back burner. We've always done that because of Annie. She's never actually reached up to the stove, but we've always worried that if she did, her paws could touch the front burners."

It was instinct, not memory, of course. In *Sea Witch*'s galley, where by himself, and only for himself, Chase cooked oatmeal almost every day, he always used the front burner. But here, where this golden-haired animal sat at his feet as he stood by the stove, he had without conscious thought used the back burners, safely away from the trusting and eager paws.

"I'm not sure if it was memory or simply instinct," he said with gentle apology. "I do know that I have no memory of why she doesn't use her dog door."

"We don't know why. When we had it installed and tried to teach her, she seemed very frightened by it. We decided it must have triggered memories of when she was mistreated. She's never used it—and obviously we haven't pushed." Jillian smiled with amused affection at the golden animal who seemed to know, because they both kept looking at her as they spoke, that she was the topic of this gentle conversation. Tilting her auburn head at the golden one that cocked back at her, Jillian teased lightly, "Besides, it's much more fun, much more attention, to have human beings open doors for you, isn't it?" Lifting her smiling eyes to Chase, she said with a soft laugh, "Annie has us right where she wants us—very well trained."

Chase answered with a smile, but it faded as Jillian's expression suddenly became worried.

"What?" he prompted.

"You shaved."

"Yes." He watched her carefully, to see if she was searching for proof that he wasn't a ghost after all, just an impostor. But there was neither discovery nor triumph on her thoughtful face. There was only loving concern.

"You've lost so much weight."

So have you, Chase realized. Jillian was far thinner, far more frail, than the sleekly elegant woman he had seen in the videotapes of the Kentucky Derby. Gaunt and pale, as he was, as if the past few weeks had been a terrible ordeal that she, like he, had barely survived.

"I'll gain it back." *We both will.* It was a gentle promise from the hopelessly blurred, hopelessly enchanted place in his heart. "And I'll also get my hair cut."

"Oh."

"Oh? Don't you want me to cut it?"

"Well . . . it's up to you, of course." Jillian shrugged softly. "I like it this length."

"Then this is how I'll wear it."

As a flush of pink colored her cheeks and she seemed so pleased, shyly not triumphantly, that he would wear his hair to her liking, the gentle and never loved *and so foolish* place in Chase's heart wondered, Would you like it even longer, Jillian? Would you, perhaps, like it exactly the way Chase Carlton has always worn it?

"What would you like to do today?" Jillian asked after they had finished their oatmeal and were drinking second cups of coffee.

She was like a gracious hostess, Chase thought. He was the out-of-town visitor, someone she really didn't know but who was a good friend of a good friend, and now she was asking her guest what he would like to do, what sights he would like to see.

There were sights Chase needed to see, but all but one—*Sea Goddess*—were right here, in this remarkable house designed by his twin. After feeding Annie and before beginning the oatmeal, he had taken a brief tour. By Bel Air standards, he supposed, the house was more cottage than mansion. To him the graceful lines and economical yet creative use of space combined with the impeccable craftsmanship of the woodworking made the house feel like a beautifully and lovingly crafted yacht . . . a house he himself might have designed . . . a place on land where he might have felt the peace of the sea.

"I've already done a little wandering around the house and I thought I'd do more," he said in answer to Jillian's gracious question. "I also thought if there are photo albums, it might be helpful for me to look through them. And . . ."

"Yes?"

"Did I keep a journal?"

"I don't know. I don't think so. But if you did, it would be in your study. The albums are there too."

"Okay. I'll start there, then." It was where Chase had planned to spend the morning anyway, in the wood-paneled room with the view of the sea, surrounded by shelves of books and the golden trophies that symbolized the immense successes of his twin's golden life—glittering statues of Oscar and a shining replica of the America's Cup.

"What about you, Jillian? What would you like to do today?"

"I have a few things I need to do—grocery shopping mainly, and a load or two of wash." Jillian stopped with a frown.

"What?"

"Just before we left Puerto Vallarta the nurses gave me the jeans that you were wearing when you were found. I guess there had been a shirt, too, but it was so badly torn that they threw it out. Anyway, they aren't your jeans, but . . ."

"But why don't we keep them?" Chase suggested, feeling a

surprising rush of sentiment for the faded, well-worn jeans that had been Chase Carlton's favorite pair.

"Okay, I'll wash them, then." Jillian stopped abruptly again, stopped this time because she thought he was about to speak . . . no, to object to what she had said. "Is that all right with you? Would you prefer that I didn't wash them?"

"No, it's fine," Chase said, adjusting, remembering who he was supposed to be: a man who had a wife who did things for him, who seemed to *want* to do things for him—putting his pills beside his bed, buying his groceries, washing his clothes. "Thank you."

"You're welcome." Surprise flickered, and then, encouraged by the gentleness she saw in his face, Jillian offered bravely, "Other than doing a little grocery shopping and laundry, what I'd like to do today is help you . . . if I can."

"Do you know much about my childhood?"

"No, I'm sorry, I don't." Jillian's voice filled with soft apology that his first specific request for help was something for which she had so little to offer. "But Brad does, of course, and I know how much he wants to help. I called him last night to let him know we were home. He hadn't expected us back this soon, and had already scheduled meetings all day today and tomorrow, but I know he'd be very happy to cancel them."

"It's not necessary, Jillian. I do want to talk to Brad, of course, but I think that looking through the albums by myself first would be most useful." After a moment, he added quietly, "I'd also like to talk to Jack Shannon."

"To find out more about the accident?"

"The accident?" No, Chase thought as he looked at her suddenly anxious eyes. *You're going to tell me about that.* "Isn't that the least important of the memories I've lost?"

"Yes," Jillian agreed. "I think it is. You want to see Jack because you once were friends?"

"And because I recognized him so quickly. I thought that seeing him again might trigger even more memories."

"Why don't I see if he's free for dinner some evening this

week? If it's all right with you, I could invite Stephanie Windsor to join us."

"Stephanie Windsor?" Chase echoed. And then, because he guessed that Jillian had seen surprise and perhaps even recognition on his face, he added, "That name is familiar."

"She's an actress. You've only actually met her once—in late March of this year—but she and I were friends as girls." Answering the obvious question in his interested gray eyes, Jillian explained. "She and I hadn't seen each other for a long time, but in the weeks since your disappearance, we've spent quite a bit of time together. It was she who stayed here with Annie while we were in Puerto Vallarta. Anyway, she knows Jack, so I thought . . ."

"That would be fine."

By ten A.M. the weather had changed dramatically. The summer day was warm still, but the blue skies had surrendered to a swift and powerful invasion of clouds that wept a torrent of raindrops and showed no sign of abating.

"Hi." Jillian stood in the open doorway of his study. "I'm sorry to bother you."

"That's okay. I was just about to take a break."

"Nothing?" she asked quietly as she saw what looked like sadness—and such loss—in his stormy gray eyes.

"Not really," Chase lied. Just an excruciating collage of painful images: how very much I look like my father . . . how pretty—and how fragile—my mother was . . . how the photographs stopped shortly before my, *our,* twenty-first birthday, because almost certainly the film from that celebration was in the camera still two weeks later—at Thanksgiving—and was destroyed with my parents during the tragic holiday blaze.

The images of his parents and his grandfather caused great anguish; but the photographs that caused the greatest pain, and the greatest confusion, were the photographs of his twin. In the many pictures taken of Victor C. Kincaid as a boy, his face had always been smiling. But to Chase it seemed that in virtually every photograph his twin was looking beyond the camera, as if searching for something more, something that was missing.

Until the wedding pictures. Those were portraits of pure joy. In the gray eyes that gazed into the emerald ones, Chase saw peace, as if the restless searching at last was over, as if his brother had finally found what had been missing—the illusory and wondrous dream that had been beckoning to him from beyond the horizon.

The wedding pictures were pure joy, complete with the lively golden retriever puppy, and the honeymoon photographs taken in Bora Bora were beyond joy, and there were many other happy photographs taken in the past six years. But with each passing year the number taken—or at least the number carefully mounted in the album—had declined.

Focusing on the woman who had been the dream at the end of his twin's restless search, Chase asked, "Are you off to the grocery store?"

As Jillian nodded yes, her eyes drifted toward the window, to the rainstorm, with what looked to Chase almost like dread.

"It's not really an emergency to go to the store now, is it?" he asked. "I know for a fact that we have enough oatmeal to last for days."

"Yes, but . . ." *But I want to prepare your favorite dishes.* I want to recreate the tastes and textures that will spark the happiest memories . . . the beginning . . . when we used to dine together no matter how late you got home. As Jillian had been finding the almost forgotten recipes, and making the long shopping list, the weather had undergone its dramatic and soggy change. It wasn't supposed to rain like this in June. But despite the rain, she was going to go shopping—*now.* She wasn't going to let ancient fears wash away her plans to resurrect the lost memories of love. "There are things I want to get."

"Why don't I go with you?" Chase suggested. And then, in response to her obvious surprise, he said, "I take it I didn't usually accompany you to the store."

"Not usually," she answered with a soft smile. Then, bravely, because she had promised her heart that she would say brave things to him this time, she added, "In the beginning, you did. In the beginning, we were together as much as possible."

"Do you mind if I go with you now?"

"Of course not."

"Good. I'll just go upstairs and get my wallet."

"Are you going to drive?"

Chase saw the sudden flicker of hope and wished that he could say yes. But it was too dangerous for him to drive, especially down the steep, unfamiliar road in the pouring rain.

"I hadn't planned to. I think that until my ribs—and maybe my reflexes—are a little more healed, it would be best for me not to."

There were two cars in the carport, a midnight-blue Legend and a fire-red Ferrari. Chase had read about the Ferrari in one of the articles Jack had sent him about his twin. It was a 1965 250 Le Mans, one of only thirty in the world, and it was valued at over two million dollars. Despite its immense value, his brother had driven it often.

Chase knew about the fire-red Ferrari, but still, as he looked at the cars in the carport, he asked, "Mine and yours?"

"Yours and ours," Jillian said. "The Ferrari was your father's, the prize of his collection, given to you on your twenty-first birthday."

"And it's drivable?"

"Oh, yes. You drive it all the time when you're driving by yourself."

"And when we're together?"

"We take the Legend."

"You don't drive the Ferrari?"

"No." A lovely frown touched her lovely face.

Why not? Chase wondered. Had Chase Kincaid forbidden his wife to drive his precious car? That kind of intense privacy, and cruel distrust, seemed far more like Chase Carlton than like the golden twin with the gift for dreams.

"Would you like to drive it?"

"No," Jillian answered quietly. "No."

Chapter Sixteen

Within moments of leaving Clairmont's white gravel driveway, and despite the treachery of the rain and the limitations of his own fiery pain, Chase was tempted to offer to drive. Not that Jillian wasn't driving well. She was driving very well, very cautiously, but with great fear.

It has nothing to do with my brother, Chase decided, somewhat relieved that her obvious tension wasn't attributable to years of driving with a hypercritical husband. No, it was something else, something deeper, something that made her forget his presence altogether.

Jillian's graceful hands clutched the steering wheel, her knuckles white and bloodless, the delicate lavender veins stretched taut. Her face was taut too, and drained of all color, as white now as the gossamer-thin surgical scars. And her eyes had lost their radiant glow, ice-green and fearful, straining for clarity amid the pelting rain as she cautiously guided the car down the steep and winding road.

The taut, ashen tension abated slightly when they reached the end of the first series of treacherous turns and traveled for a while along a plateau . . . but it returned in full force as they neared what Chase recalled from the day before would be the second—and last—steeply curving descent before they reached the flat stretch of road that led to the entrance of Bel Air.

It was only when they had reached that flat stretch, and a soft pinkness had returned to her scar-white cheeks, and relief had replaced fear in the luminous emerald, that Chase spoke.

"Why don't we go somewhere and get a cup of coffee?"

There were booths in the Old World Restaurant in Westwood, high-backed wooden booths that were illuminated by tabletop candles and afforded complete privacy for intimate conversation.

"You were terrified driving down the hill," Chase said quietly. "Tell me why."

"I wasn't terrified . . ." Jillian faltered. She had never been good at lying, and she had promised herself that this time she would tell Chase all the truths.

"Yes, you were," he countered softly. "Is this something you've told me before? Or something new?"

"Both. You know—you knew—about my accident, but you never knew that I was afraid of driving down the hill from Clairmont." Seeing the sudden apology in his gray eyes, she assured him swiftly, "I'm not always afraid, Chase, just on days like today, when it's raining this hard. There haven't been many days like this in the past six years." *Just today, on your first day home, when we are beginning again.*

"Tell me about your accident."

"It happened when I was fourteen. Stephanie and I were best friends then—my mother and Stephanie and I. Stephanie lived in Holmby Hills, at the top of a hill very much like ours. One evening, in the midst of a rainstorm, my mother came to pick me up. As we were driving home, the brakes failed. The road was slick and steep and . . . we crashed." Jillian drew a breath and then said very quietly, "My mother fought *so hard* to stay alive . . . but she couldn't."

The green eyes were far away. *There,* Chase realized, inside the car on that stormy night, seeing it all over again, reliving the terror. After several silent moments he asked gently, "You remember every detail of the accident, don't you?"

"Yes. I was quite seriously injured, but I never lost consciousness."

"Was your mother able to speak to you?"

Her nod was almost imperceptible. The only clue was a ripple of candlelight shimmering softly through her auburn hair.

"She told me that she loved me. That's all she said, over and over."

"Oh, Jillian." And then, because he couldn't help it, because he had to comfort her if he possibly could, Chase reached across the table to touch her lovely, anguished face. At his touch, her tears began to spill, splashing like hot raindrops onto the lean, strong fingers that caressed her so gently. "I'm so sorry."

He would have cradled her face forever, until her heart had wept all its tears, but after several silent moments it was she who suddenly, abruptly, pulled away.

Was it the sudden revulsion of a woman who knew that the hands that touched her belonged to a ghost? No, Chase decided as he gazed at her glistening emerald eyes. He saw embarrassment not terror, embarrassment perhaps that she had shared such emotional intimacy with a man who had no memory of their love.

"Thank you," she whispered.

"You're welcome." Chase watched another magnificent dance of candlelight as she tilted her head thoughtfully, obviously debating whether to speak aloud the thought. Wanting her to, he offered gently, "There's more."

"Yes."

"Tell me."

Her long lashes fluttered down at his command, and Chase expected that when she showed him again her beautiful eyes, her secrets would be carefully hidden, the impulse to share even more intimacy with him completely vanquished.

But he was wrong. When Jillian's eyes lifted again to his, Chase saw brave green candor.

"I blame myself for my mother's death."

"What?" he asked, stunned. Then, very softly, "Why?"

"Because if it weren't for me, for my selfishness in asking her to take me to Stephanie's that afternoon, despite how rainy it was, and then asking her to pick me up—"

"Did she object when you asked her?"

"No," Jillian admitted. "She never objected to anything that made me happy."

"She loved you. Do you think she would blame you for what happened?"

"Oh, no." Jillian's soft voice was filled with remembrance and love. "She wouldn't have been surprised that I blamed myself though. She always teased me about how serious I was, how even as a little girl I assumed responsibility for the world— not in a depressing way, just wanting to make things better."

"Just wanting to help."

"I guess . . . yes."

"You must know that you can't possibly be responsible for a rainstorm, or for brakes that failed, or for a tragic whim of fate."

"I know that now. But at the time I truly believed that I was responsible for what happened. It was a belief that had very important consequences."

"Such as?"

"My relationship with Stephanie. After the accident she came to see me at the hospital, hours and hours every day, trying to get me to talk to her. But I didn't. I couldn't." Jillian paused and then admitted quietly, "No, that's wrong. The truth is that I *wouldn't* talk to her. I suppose the guilt I felt was too much for me to bear alone, so I emotionally shifted some of the blame to Stephanie, wanting her to suffer too, as if it were her fault for living at the top of a hill and having a mother who was herself too selfish to offer to drive me home."

"You told Stephanie that?"

"No. I wouldn't speak to her at all. I hurt her, Chase, and I knew I was hurting her, but I let her hurt anyway—her and my father. I wouldn't talk to either of them. It was cruel of me, terribly cruel."

No, Chase thought. He was the master of cruelty, after all, and he knew that what fourteen-year-old Jillian had done wasn't cruel. It was in fact quite understandable for a lovely young girl whose life had been so tragically shattered.

"You're talking to both of them now," he offered gently.

"Because of Claudia." The candlelight danced again. "I'm not sure what would have happened without her. I had serious injuries to the bones in my back and pelvis—I suppose you've noticed my limp?"

"It's barely noticeable."

"Well, anyway, in addition to those fractures, my face was also very badly damaged. The doctors at UCLA recommended Claudia. She was working in San Francisco at the time, specializing in plastic surgery for children, correcting congenital anomalies as well as repairing facial trauma. It was a specialty she'd had ever since returning from Vietnam."

"Vietnam?"

"She was a surgeon during the war. She didn't need to go. She hadn't attended medical school on a military scholarship. She simply volunteered because she knew that well-trained trauma surgeons were so desperately needed."

"Remarkable woman," Chase said quietly, recalling the light blue eyes that had greeted him with such warmth and welcome in Puerto Vallarta. "And it was she who convinced you to talk. How?"

"By needing me to talk, by needing me to tell her about my mother."

"Needing? Why?"

"Because Claudia herself was an orphan. She never knew her parents at all. As a newborn infant she was simply left on the doorstep of an orphanage. The very first thing she said to me was that she had never had the privilege of having a mother.

Then she told me that she understood from my father that my mother had been wonderful, and that she and I had been best friends, and that she would love to hear all about her. I suppose it sounds like simple child psychology, and I guess in many ways it was, but I think there was more to it. Claudia's own childhood had been terribly sad, and lonely, and without love. I think she really did want to hear about my mother."

Yes, Chase thought, I'm sure she did. It was, he supposed, a dream that all orphans shared, a hope that there was love and safety—and happy childhoods and wonderful mothers—somewhere. How astonishing, he mused, that he and Jillian's stepmother shared that same lonely dream.

"So you told Claudia about your mother," Chase said. "Did you also tell her that you blamed yourself for your mother's death?"

"No. I've never told anyone that before."

"Not even me?"

"No."

"Why are you telling me now?" Chase asked. Why are you trusting me, of all people?

"Because," Jillian confessed bravely, "I hope that this time we'll both tell each other things we should have said before . . . but didn't."

"What didn't I tell you before?"

Jillian answered with a soft smile. "I don't know. You never told me. There were just times—many times—when you were troubled and might have shared your worries with me but instead you became silent—and then restless."

"And I would go sailing?"

"Yes . . . or play your guitar."

Yes, he thought, or play my guitar. Chase knew the tormenting restlessness that drove him to escape to his music and the sea, and in the photographs of his twin as a boy he had seen a similar restlessness. But for Chase Kincaid, that restless searching had seemed to end with the discovery of Jillian. What then had driven his brother away from that rescuing love? Was it a deep, uneasy sense of her impending betrayal? Or was it simply that the golden gift for dreams carried with it worries as weighty and tormenting as those that plagued the dark gift for evil?

"I guess I can't tell you what things troubled me until my memory returns."

"No, I guess not. But in the meantime, if it's all right with you, I'll tell you things I should have told you before. I suppose that won't really be helpful from the standpoint of triggering your memories, but . . ."

"I want you to tell me everything, Jillian. Just tell me when it's something I've never heard before."

"All right," Jillian agreed. Then, encouraged by his gentleness, she said bravely, "There's something else you don't know about the accident. You've seen how handsome my father is, and my mother was very beautiful, but I was really quite plain. It didn't bother me. My looks fit perfectly with who I was, who I was going to be. Because of the way my bones had been crushed, though, and the way my skin had been torn, Claudia couldn't reconstruct my old face. She had to give me this new one."

"Is this why I didn't find any of your girlhood photo albums in the study?"

"Yes."

"But there are some, somewhere. At Edward and Claudia's?" In response to the glittering auburn nod, Chase continued. "It's Monday, isn't it? I imagine they're both at work."

"You want to see pictures of me as a little girl?"

"Don't you want me to?"

"Yes, I want you to," Jillian answered softly. She could have put it off, but she had promised herself—and now him—that she would reveal everything . . . and so far his gray eyes had been so very gentle. "We can go to their house now, if you want. I should call Claudia first, just to let her know, but I have a key."

* * *

"Do they have a key to our house?" Chase asked twenty minutes later as they neared the front porch of the stately colonial in Brentwood.

"Yes, and so does Brad."

Because families have keys to each other's homes, Chase realized. Never in his life had he entrusted a key to the place where he lived to anyone. True, the keys to his car were now in the possession of the Marina Yacht Club's security guard; but that wasn't a sacred trust. That was only a prudent way of ensuring easy access to his trunk, and to the letter to Lieutenant Jack Shannon should he not return, if in fact the sensitive and loving little girl he had just learned about had somehow grown into a beautiful, cold-blooded monster.

The photo album was in the wood-paneled library on the first floor. The only way to look at it together was to sit side by side on the couch, and the only way for Chase to have time to really study the photographs was to touch her hand with his whenever she reached to turn the page too quickly.

Slowly, very slowly, they moved from baby pictures to toddler pictures to little-girl pictures. Until earlier today, in his brother's study at Clairmont, Chase had never looked through a family photo album. And until now, he had assumed the number of boyhood pictures taken of his twin to be quite extraordinary; but even that vast number paled in comparison to what Edward and Meredith Montgomery had taken of their plain—and so lovely—daughter. Unlike his twin, whose searching gray eyes had seemed to gaze far beyond the camera, the huge brilliant green ones had always smiled directly into the lens. It wasn't flirtation or vanity, of course, only an honest and unaffected exuberance for life—and an honest and obvious love for whichever parent was taking the photograph of her.

"Oh, look at Stephanie," Jillian exclaimed softly, breaking what had been a lingering silence when they reached the first page that began to chronicle the friendship of the two girls. "We were only nine, but look how beautiful she was even then."

"I think you both were beautiful," Chase said quietly. "I like the way you looked."

In the restaurant, the luminous glow had come from the candles; but now the radiance that lighted Jillian's eyes and pinkened her cheeks came from something wondrous deep within. "Oh. Well, thank you. I was very comfortable with the way I looked. It was who I was . . . who I was going to be. I wasn't really destined to become the glamorous and sophisticated wife of a movie mogul."

"Was that a terribly difficult adjustment?"

"No," she answered as her glowing green eyes eloquently embellished, *It wasn't difficult at all . . . because of you.*

It was a bold and clear confession of love, and as Chase gazed at her, he felt pure enchantment. Then, with a jolt, he realized what Jillian was doing. She was seducing him. The realization might have come to him sooner, but Chase Carlton was on unfamiliar ground. Jillian Kincaid was seducing him with something he had never known: love.

Chase didn't know love, but he was a master at seduction. As he met her glowing eyes, his own sensuous gray filled with desire, seducing, enchanting in return, just as he had planned to do until she was so vulnerable that she would make a trembling confession of evil to him.

Jillian was vulnerable now, and trembling. She had shared her girlhood secrets with him, and her emerald eyes were now so hopeful, and even though it was all coldly calculated, Chase very much wanted to kiss her, to lose himself in her welcoming warmth, to allow her gentleness to balm the painful wounds of his heart.

Just like my twin, he thought. When I look at her, it feels as if all my restless searching, all my desperate chasing of illusions and rainbows, is over. I am found. She is the dream.

And the nightmare.

Chase didn't kiss her. His smoky eyes simply smoldered with promises of passion as he filled his mind with icy memories of the twin who was dead and the messages of death that had visited him this morning.

And when she was seduced, expecting his kiss, and so hopeful and so vulnerable, Chase Carlton said with excruciatingly cruel softness, "I'd really like to see the sailboat."

"Oh!" The pink deepened in her cheeks, and the radiant emerald glow faded from surprised to confused to embarrassed to hurt, *terribly* hurt . . . but then, recovering swiftly, bravely, she became once again the womanly version of the responsible little girl who had always been so willing to help. "Of course. Today?"

"Right now. It looks as if the rain is relenting, but if you prefer, I'll drive."

"No, it's fine." Jillian closed the album and stood up. "We probably should leave now if we want to make the round trip before the afternoon rush."

"Shall I wait here?" Jillian asked as she turned off the ignition when they reached Marina del Rey.

"No. I'd like you to come with me."

As they neared *Sea Goddess,* the majestic white twin of the now-drowned *Sea Witch,* Chase steeled his heart to see the crimson stains left by his brother's blood, the graphic evidence of death that had been so terribly difficult to look at even in the police photographs.

But the bloodstains were gone. The boom had been repainted and the teak deck had been sanded and polished and oiled. At whose behest had the grim traces of violence and death been removed? Jillian's? Brad's? Perhaps even Jack Shannon's?

The stains were gone, but Chase knew precisely where they had been, precisely where his twin had been standing when the boom had cracked his skull and precisely where he had staggered and then fallen onto the deck. He moved to the place where his brother had been standing and started to turn toward Jillian, to beckon her to join him at that fateful spot.

Then it happened. And *it* was far more potent than it had been this morning, than it had ever been, its invisible messages of violence, and danger, and death alarmingly clear. The warning was pure evil, and it filled his heart and his soul, killing small pieces of those places in the process, the invasion itself causing immense damage.

As Chase felt the evil fill him, more powerfully than ever before, a faraway corner of his mind wondered if this time the invasion would be fatal, if the invisible fingers of ice would freeze his breath and still his heart for too long . . . forever.

"Chase!"

It was the same soft voice that had come to him in the darkness in Puerto Vallarta. And now as then he desperately wanted to awaken to it. But he couldn't.

"Chase, please!"

She was touching him now, her delicate fingers first gently caressing his cheeks, and then with frantic urgency her slender arms wrapping tightly around his waist, her soft warm body pressing against his hard frozen one. It was as if she were trying to transfer her warmth to him, as if she were courageously offering the fragile delicacy of her own body as a shield against whatever it was that was threatening to kill his.

You can't shield me, Jillian, Chase thought vaguely. It's inside me, and it's going to kill me this time. Nothing can shield me from it . . . and nothing can make it go away unless—and until—it chooses.

Nothing—except for Jillian Kincaid.

Miraculously, miraculously, he felt the monstrous glacier of evil begin to recede. The withdrawal was slow, begrudging, scraping and tearing and causing great harm as its deepest reaches of ice reluctantly relinquished their almost lethal grip.

But it *was* leaving.

Why? Chase wondered. Because the malevolent force which had invaded him belonged to Jillian, was under her command and control? Or was it because of her goodness, some intrinsic

loveliness whose gentleness could conquer even the most powerful of evil?

"Thank God," Jillian whispered as she felt him breathe—at
last. Releasing her tight and desperate grasp, she looked up at
him. "Chase, please talk to me!"

He couldn't talk, it was still too soon, but he looked down
at her searching—and so worried—green eyes, and her trembling—and so generous—lips.

"What happened, Chase?" she pleaded. "Did you remember
something? You looked so . . ."

"So what?" he managed to say.

"So terrified. As if you were seeing something unspeakably
horrible." The lovely emerald eyes filled with a terror of their
own as she added with soft disbelief, "Chase, I couldn't hear
your heart!"

Jillian was asking him what he had seen, what had frozen his
heart, and Chase didn't know. It was different this time from
ever before, stronger, more powerful, more evil. Was it perhaps
that today, in this place, what had come to him was the anguished cry of death from the man who had been his twin? Or
maybe it had been death itself, wanting the other half of the
heart and soul it had so whimsically drowned in the vast, dark
sea.

Chase didn't know, and yet he suddenly felt himself believing that there was something in his brother's death beyond the
lazy yet lethal yawn of a slumbering sea. And whatever it was
seemed alive still . . . and so evil . . . and so dangerous.

Dangerous to whom? he wondered. To him? To Jillian? *To
both of them?* Or was this lovely woman who seemed so genuinely frightened for him really the blackest of all widows?

Chase simply didn't know.

"Let's go to Bora Bora."

"What?"

"You said we were married seventeen days after we met, so
that means our wedding anniversary is on the twenty-eighth, a
week from tomorrow. Let's go to Bora Bora then, just like we

did six years ago." Chase looked at the surprised—and worried—green eyes and asked softly, "Or would you rather not?"

"No. I'd like to. But will you feel strong enough to travel that far that soon?"

"Sure." His seductive smile didn't seduce the worry from her eyes. "What, Jillian?"

"Will you please tell me what you remembered that terrified you so much?"

In the past few hours Jillian had told him brave truths about herself, the bravest of which had perhaps been her confession that she and his twin hadn't shared the deepest secrets and torments of their hearts. Now she was asking him to share, and Chase saw such uncertainty in the request—and such courage.

"I didn't remember anything, Jillian. I just felt. Has anything like this ever happened to me before?"

"No, not that I know of. What did you feel, Chase?"

"Danger . . . and evil."

"Danger? Evil? What does that mean?"

"I don't know, Jillian. I honestly don't know."

That's why I want to go to Bora Bora with you, to see if we can leave whatever it is behind . . . or if the treacherous whispers will travel with us—with you.

Chapter Seventeen

Drive carefully, Chase. The words echoed in his mind as he drove the short distance from Clairmont to the Bel Air Hunt Club. It was Wednesday and he was meeting Brad for lunch. No one had ever told Chase Carlton to drive carefully, or to sail carefully, or to take care of himself in any way. Oh, yes, there had been provocative teases from women who wanted him to protect the body that gave them such pleasure; but those were selfish requests, for them, for their desires—not for him. Jillian's admonishment to drive carefully had been about him, not about her, as if she wanted him to be safe always, even if he never remembered her or their love.

During the two days since they had stood on the deck of *Sea Goddess,* Chase and Jillian had been at Clairmont. There had been no intrusions of any kind, no visits from the outside world and no further invasions, either, from the icy world of evil. Chase had never shared his living space with a woman before, had never shared anything except the pleasures of passion; and when the passion was spent, as soon as it was spent, he had always been restless for solitude and privacy.

But for the past two days with Jillian, he had felt great peace—and great confusion.

Chase Carlton had never been in love. But if he had, he would have clung fiercely to that rare and precious treasure; and if the treasure had ever been misplaced, doomed by some trauma to the darkness of shadows, he would have done anything and everything to seduce those memories from their hiding place. Had the woman he loved been miraculously returned from the dead, he would have held her gently, but so tightly; and he would have pleaded, he would have demanded, Remember me, remember us, *remember our love.*

Jillian Kincaid didn't have the bold and demanding confidence of a lover. Yes, she smiled at him with radiant joy every time she saw him anew. And yes, it seemed as if she were trying very hard to trigger his memories. She prepared wonderful meals for him, undoubtedly his twin's favorites, meals that might spark shadowed memories of fragrance and taste—and memories, too, of the care she had taken to make them nutritious, as if she had wanted his brother's heart to live forever. But she hadn't touched him again, not since the afternoon on *Sea Goddess* when she had so courageously tried to shield his body with her own.

Jillian should have been in complete control, helping him only with the memories she chose, changing the truths if she wanted to. But Jillian didn't act like a woman who was in control. She acted like someone who was waiting to know if she would be wanted still when his memory returned . . . someone who wanted him to drive carefully, to be safe, for himself—whether or not he returned to their love.

Brad was standing outside, waiting for him, when Chase arrived at the Bel Air Hunt Club.

"I was expecting to see you pull up in the Ferrari."

"My rib cage isn't ready to drive it yet—at least not to enjoy driving it."

They walked in silence to the elegant dining room overlooking the redbrick terrace and lush gardens of lilacs and roses.

When they were seated at what was certainly the best table in the room, a secluded glass alcove framed in lavender wisteria, Brad finally spoke.

"We inherited this table from our fathers. We've eaten here hundreds of times. Do you remember?"

"No, I'm sorry, I don't."

"What *do* you remember, Chase? Anything?"

The edge of impatience and frustration in his cousin's voice—and in his dark eyes—was quite unconcealed. And entirely understandable, Chase thought as he met Brad's obviously annoyed countenance with calm apology. Of course Brad resented being almost entirely forgotten by the man who had been more brother than cousin. It was the kind of frustrated resentment that Jillian should have felt, but didn't—as if she weren't surprised that her husband's memories of her weren't strong enough or important enough to find their way out of the shadows.

Bradford Barrington Lancaster quite obviously felt that he should be remembered.

For a fleeting moment Chase considered telling his cousin the truth. But Chase Carlton had spent a lifetime trusting no one but himself. Instead, smiling a conciliatory smile at the man with whom he hoped to forge an enduring relationship after the masquerade was over, he said quietly, "I'm sorry, Brad. I really haven't had any more memories since that first day in Puerto Vallarta."

"Surely you could come up with something," Brad countered, his voice now holding an unmistakable note of skepticism.

Is it possible that he suspects I might be an impostor? Chase wondered. Or is there some reason for him to think that I might be feigning the extent of the amnesia?

"I'm trying, Brad, but I can't will the memories to return. I can only expose myself to people and places that might trigger them. Okay?"

"Sure," Brad agreed with an easy shrug. "Tell me what I can do to help with the triggering."

"Well. I've spent a lot of time looking at family photo albums. I know the names and the faces, but I'd appreciate it if you would tell me about the people."

"No problem. Let's see . . . it's really a bloodline more than a family. Our grandfather was a horseman from Kentucky. He spent the first half of his life trying to breed a Triple Crown winner, and when that didn't succeed as planned, he moved here and founded the studio. He had far more success with filmmaking than Thoroughbred racing, but he never gave up the dream of the Triple Crown triumph." A wry smile touched Brad's lips. "I wish he'd been alive to see Schoolteacher cross the finish line at Belmont."

The wryness in Brad's smile and the slight edginess in his voice didn't make his wish seem like the heartfelt wish of a loving grandson for a beloved grandfather.

"It sounds like you really don't mean that."

"Oh, but I do. It would have absolutely killed him that the grandson who never had any interest in horse racing whatsoever had the horse that had always eluded him, especially given the fact that Schoolteacher's bloodlines were far from dazzling." Brad paused. "Don't look so surprised. You knew, everyone knew, that I wasn't terribly fond of our grandfather—not many people in Hollywood were."

"Why not?"

"Aside from the fact that he was a tyrant? Well, then how about the fact that the only reason that I was born—that *we* were born—was because of one of his decrees?"

"Meaning?"

"Meaning that our beloved grandfather's idea of a twenty-first birthday present to his identical twin daughters was to announce to all of Hollywood that on his own sixtieth birthday he would give each twin half of Triple Crown Studios, providing that by that time each had given him a grandchild."

"Just one grandchild?" Chase asked quietly. Was that the

reason he had been abandoned? Because one grandchild from each daughter was all that Bradford Barrington Chase had decreed? By abandoning him, were his parents acceding to Bradford's tyrannical wish? Or was the choice theirs because they needed only the heir—and not the spare—so why bother to keep him?

"At least one," Brad said. "I'm sure that Grandfather would have been delighted to have more than two grandchildren to manipulate."

"But neither of us had siblings."

"No. I was an only child because even having one was an almost unbearable imposition for my vain mother. I think your parents—your mother at least—might have wanted other children, but for whatever reasons they didn't have them."

"Was I close to my parents?"

"You were neither close nor 'not close' to your parents—or to Grandfather. You managed to keep emotionally detached from the psychological politics of the family."

"Psychological politics?"

"Everything was a horse race for Grandfather. Given two people—our mothers, our fathers, us—only one could be a winner. Everyone in the family was forced into constant competition. But you outfoxed the fox. You simply refused to compete. And when the going got really tough, you went sailing."

Chase couldn't read his cousin's dark eyes. Did Brad regard his twin's unwillingness to compete as laudable or contemptuous, a mature detachment or an immature impulse to escape? Was Brad frustrated, as Jillian was, by Chase Kincaid's tendency to vanish to the sea whenever he was troubled?

"You and I weren't competitive?"

"No, not at all, despite Grandfather's impressive efforts."

"We were friends."

Brad smiled warmly. "Yes, we were very good friends."

Their Caesar salads arrived and for several gourmet bites they ate in silence. Then Chase set down his fork and asked, "Will you tell me about what happened at Lake Tahoe?"

Somehow Chase hadn't expected to see such sadness in his cousin's eyes, but he was relieved to see that it was there. And, as if Brad had read his mind, he spoke quietly to that relief.

"Our grandfather was a son of a bitch, and my mother was impossibly vain, and my father was obsessed with power, but I *did* love them all. I was devastated by their deaths—and by the deaths of your parents, whom I also loved."

"Was I devastated?"

Brad's handsome face grew even more solemn. "We both were. We'd been close all our lives, but that tragedy made us even closer. It happened only two weeks after our twenty-first birthday. Suddenly we went from carefree college students with the stable security of our families to orphans who were responsible for carrying on the tradition of excellence established at the studio by our fathers and grandfather."

"Did you say *our* twenty-first birthday?"

"Yes. Technically I was born on November tenth and you were born on the eleventh. But I was born in Los Angeles at four P.M. and you were born in France just after midnight, which means, given the eight-hour time difference, that we arrived on the planet within a few minutes of each other."

Like twins, Chase thought. Maybe that's why he'd been left in Cap Ferrat—because his brother already had a twin.

With quiet solemnity Brad told Chase about the fire at Lake Tahoe, the inferno touched off by a spark from the fireplace that had caused such devastation. Then, for the rest of the meal, he chronicled the history of Triple Crown Studios over the thirteen years that the cousins had run it. By the time they parted, with the smiling assertion that they were looking forward to seeing each other again on Saturday evening—at a family dinner party at Edward and Claudia's—Chase felt that Brad's frustration and skepticism had vanished.

But as he drove the short distance between the Hunt Club and Clairmont, Chase realized that nothing his cousin had told him had been truly personal, nothing that would have been known only to them. Even his outspoken opinion about their grandfather was surely common knowledge in Hollywood, an opinion undoubtedly shared by many.

Indeed, he decided, there was absolutely nothing in what Brad Lancaster had shared with him that he couldn't have learned just as easily from virtually any Hollywood insider.

On his return, Chase found Jillian in the master bedroom, his bedroom. Neat piles of folded clothes were on the chaise longue, and she herself was bent over an open dresser drawer, her face concealed by a shining veil of luxuriant auburn.

"Hi."

"Oh, hi," she murmured, startled. Closing the dresser drawer quickly, her face flushed as she turned to meet him. "How was lunch?"

"I think it angers him that I don't really remember our relationship."

"I imagine that Brad doesn't like to think of himself as forgettable," Jillian offered with a soft smile of fondness for her husband's cousin. "Was he able to tell you anything that triggered your memory?"

"Not really," Chase answered, but he thought, *Able?* Yes, but not willing. Then gently, so that Jillian didn't misinterpret his question as criticism, he asked, "What are you doing?"

"Beginning to think about what to take to Bora Bora . . . if you still want to go."

"I still want to," Chase assured. "I thought you'd already made the reservations."

"Yes, I have. The travel agent called while you were out to say that the Hotel Bora Bora will give us the same overwater bungalow that we had last time."

"Good." Chase left her hopeful emerald eyes to look at the neatly folded clothes on the chaise longue. "There's probably a ritual for how we pack when we travel together. You'll have to tell me what it is."

"Well . . . you would always lay out the things you wanted

to take and I would do the packing. But if you'd rather do it another way . . ."

"No," Chase said. "Let's do it the way we always have."

Chase was amazed at how untroubled he was by the prospect of her packing for him, or of her mingling their clothes together in the same suitcase. It seemed so intimate, an intimacy far beyond what he had ever shared with a woman, far beyond the purely physical intimacies of passion and pleasure that he had experienced so often—and without emotion.

"I wondered," Jillian began haltingly.

"Yes?"

"If you don't need the car, I have an errand I'd like to run."

"Something last minute for dinner tonight?"

"No . . . something else."

"Shall I drive you?"

"No, thank you." Her emerald eyes sent a clear yet apologetic message that whatever her mission was, she wanted to do it alone.

Before he met Jillian Kincaid, Chase's plan had been to force his presence on her at all times, a long, dark shadow even in the harshest sunshine, in hope of shattering her coolly elegant façade. But that was before he met her.

Chase knew that he could insist on accompanying her on her mysterious errand, and that she would generously comply with his wish. But now, smiling gentle reassurance to the woman who seemed so apologetic for wanting even this rare moment of privacy, he said, "I'll hold down the fort here, then. What time are Jack and Stephanie arriving?"

"At seven. I'll be back long before that."

"Okay." Then, as she turned to leave, Chase heard himself say, "Drive carefully, Jillian."

Drive carefully, Jillian. I want you to return safely.

As soon as she was gone, Chase fought the surprising sentimentality by crossing to the dresser to open the drawer that she had hastily closed when he had startled her. What secret was hidden there? What was it that she so obviously hadn't wanted him to see?

Jillian's secret was a white satin nightgown, embroidered with pale pink roses. Pure, bridal, virginal, it was undoubtedly the nightgown she had worn on her honeymoon. She must have been debating whether to take it to Bora Bora this time—a silent deliberation which had been cut short by his arrival.

What would she decide? he wondered. In Bora Bora, but not before, they would share the same bedroom . . . the same bed. Would she wear the gown of provocative innocence there, in paradise, where she and his twin had almost certainly first made love? Surely she knew that the evocative sensuality of lovemaking would be a most powerful way of luring memories from their shadows.

Yes, she knew that, Chase realized. That was why she had been looking at the gown.

But what he didn't know, and wouldn't know until they arrived in Bora Bora, was whether shy and modest Jillian Kincaid would boldly wear such a gown for a man who was a stranger, who had no memory at all of her or of their love.

Chapter Eighteen

Jack knew that he was going to phone Stephanie, but he waited to make the call until two hours before they were both expected for dinner at Clairmont.

"I'll give you a ride." His voice was unstrained, deceptively casual given the gnawing memory that twice before she had refused such an offer. Into the lingering silence that greeted him, he finally teased, "This is your golden opportunity to prove how public-spirited you really are."

By participating in the share-a-ride-with-a-cop program? Stephanie would have teased lightly in return—had she been able to. Instead, eventually, she simply echoed, "Public-spirited?"

"Conservation of gas, minimalization of air pollution, not to mention our little contribution to the unsnarling of traffic," Jack elaborated easily. Then seriously, and with gentle but firm finality, he said, "I'll be at your place at six-thirty."

Jack didn't pressure her to talk during the short drive from her penthouse on Wilshire to the hilltop estate in Bel Air, but Stephanie felt pressured nonetheless. When he smiled his gentle, seductive smile at her, she remembered his cherishing kisses, and the compelling desire in his dangerous eyes and his most compellingly dangerous desire of all: to know her, the real, unedited Stephanie.

She knew that she could not speak without extensive editing and careful rehearsal to the man who made even her thoughts stutter, and she knew something even worse: if by some miracle, honest words and feelings could flow effortlessly from her lips, Jack Shannon would be terribly disappointed. The man whose distant friendship with Chase Kincaid had driven him to compulsively pursue every possible avenue to be certain that his one-time friend hadn't been murdered, his death unavenged, knew all about the solemn commitments and responsibilities of true friendship.

What would he think of someone whose own selfish and shameful fear of stuttering had allowed her to abandon her best friend when that friend had needed her the most?

Stephanie knew exactly what Lieutenant Jack Shannon would think. It was what she herself thought—that her behavior had been despicable, proof positive of how unworthy she was of friendship, of love, of being kissed with tender, cherishing caresses.

Fifteen years before, Stephanie had failed to keep the solemn commitments and responsibilities of true friendship. But she wouldn't fail again. This time, no matter what, she would not abandon Jillian—which was why she had agreed to this dinner despite her own heart-racing apprehension about seeing Jack again. It had obviously been very important to Jillian that she be there tonight, to make the evening a social gathering of friends, not the professional visit of the homicide lieutenant who had once had grave concerns about Chase's disappearance.

"How is Chase's memory?" Jack asked as they turned into Clairmont's white gravel driveway.

"He hasn't really remembered anything since that first day in Puerto Vallarta."

Jack glanced at her thoughtful sapphire eyes and suggested gently, "That must be very difficult for Jillian."

"Yes," Stephanie agreed softly as she remembered the quiet despair in Jillian's voice. It was a despair, Stephanie was certain, that Jillian kept very carefully concealed from Chase.

There was no hint of despair in the brilliant emerald that greeted them moments later. There was only the smiling radiance of a gracious hostess welcoming her dinner guests. And, Stephanie thought, Chase seemed untroubled too. She had seen him only once before, but he seemed different from what she remembered—more relaxed somehow, more calm . . . more happy.

After warm greetings all around and the reintroduction of Stephanie to Chase, Stephanie gazed for a moment at Jillian, her eyes at first thoughtful and then sparkling. Finally she uttered a simple command, "Turn around."

Jillian laughed softly as she followed her friend's command, revealing with a twirl what Stephanie already had guessed: the auburn hair had been rolled to the nape of her neck before being captured by a gold barrette into a casually elegant ponytail. As soon as Stephanie saw the back of Jillian's auburn head, she spun to reveal her own. The lustrous sable with its silky golden moonbeams had been identically styled.

After a moment Stephanie turned back to face her friend. Her sapphire eyes sparkled still, but there was a deeper luster, a solemn wonder in the jewel-bright blue.

"That wasn't planned?" Jack asked.

"No," Jillian answered, her green eyes smiling, like her friend's, and, like her friend's, thoughtful too.

"Quite a coincidence."

"Yes," Jillian agreed, and when she saw from Stephanie's expression the permission to reveal a truth from their shared past, she elaborated, "It was a coincidence that happened often when we were girls. It was remarkable really, because once we discovered that we seemed to be wearing our hair the same way with amazing frequency, we began to test what we decided were mysterious and wonderful psychic powers by creating ever more exotic—or at least ever more imaginative—hairstyles."

"And?" Chase urged, very interested in the two girls who weren't related but seemed to share the kind of psychic bonds that were shared by twins.

"And it happened still."

"And is still happening," Jack observed. "Did either of you ever cut it all off?"

"The ultimate test? Oh, no," Jillian laughed. "We teased each other that someday we might, but . . ."

Jillian faltered then, because as she remembered the distant reason that neither of them had ever cut her long, flowing hair, she realized that recently, subconsciously until this moment, she had been planning to cut her own auburn mane. When Chase . . . when Chase's body . . . was found.

"But?" Chase asked softly.

It was Stephanie who answered, rescuing her suddenly silent friend. "But we decided that short hair seemed far too grown-up."

"And being grown-up was bad?"

The question was Jack's, and it was asked of Stephanie with such gentleness, and such interest, that now it was Jillian's turn to be the rescuer.

She did so quietly, in a faraway voice. "It seemed to us then, as little girls, that being grown-up was the end of romance . . . and of dreams."

The evening was an easy flow of pleasant conversation embellished by wonderful food. Chase had to keep reminding himself that the magnificent portrait of domestic bliss was merely an illusion. That Chase Carlton would ever feel anything but trapped and restless in such a scene—with one woman, married to her, graciously entertaining friends in a landlocked home—seemed beyond imagination.

But now he was living the unimaginable, and the fantasy

was so seductively enchanting that it wasn't until after dinner, over coffee in the living room, that he forced himself to begin to guide the conversation toward the reason he had suggested dinner with Jack in the first place: a discussion of the night his twin had disappeared. Chase wanted to see how Jillian responded to that topic in the presence of the police lieutenant who had believed, until Chase Carlton had convinced him otherwise, that she was responsible for her husband's death.

Chase hadn't known until this afternoon as he glanced through the day's newspaper while Jillian was off on her mysterious errand exactly how he would guide the conversation to that all-important night. But there had been a long article which would suit his purposes perfectly. It was about the Guitar String Strangler, a comprehensive review of all the murders, the places and dates, as well as the names and photographs of the five beautiful dark-haired victims.

The appearance of the article in the *Los Angeles Times*'s edition for Wednesday, June 22, had not been accidental—as of ten P.M. the night before the Strangler, who had struck with haunting regularity between nine and ten P.M. on every third Tuesday between February 15 and May 10, had for the second cycle in a row remained hidden. Tuesday, May 10, was the last time he had claimed a victim. That was also the date on which Chase Kincaid had vanished forever.

After reading the article, Chase decided that it would be quite easy, quite logical, for him to ask casually in the midst of a discussion about the Strangler, May tenth? Wasn't that the date of my accident?

"I saw your name in today's paper, Jack."

"The article on the Guitar String Strangler."

"Yes. I'm sure you're very relieved that it's been six weeks since his last attack."

"I'd be more relieved if I knew why."

"I hope he's dead," Stephanie said. Her soft words had been spoken to the Limoges coffee cup, and her eyes remained on the hand-painted china as she carefully scripted and rehearsed what would come next. When the words were ready, she looked up to Jack and added, "I read the article too. It quoted you as saying you thought it was possible that he was dead."

"It's one of the possibilities," Jack agreed quietly, his blue eyes gently reassuring her that he didn't regard her hope for death for the monster who had so brutally murdered five young women—one of whom she had known—as bloodthirsty in the least. "He's dead, or in jail for some other crime, or no longer in the area."

"Mightn't he have just stopped?" Jillian asked.

"I think that's unlikely, unless there was some hidden purpose in claiming precisely five victims."

"You think serial killers are purposeful, Jack?" Chase asked, abandoning for the moment his own purpose in bringing up the topic and joining the discussion of a subject with which Chase Carlton was intimately and chillingly familiar.

"I think so," Jack replied. "Admittedly, I'm far from an authority, but because of this case I've talked to a number of experts and have read quite extensively about them."

"If he knew what he was doing," Jillian offered thoughtfully, "if he realized the anguish he was causing, maybe he killed himself."

"Unfortunately, serial killers don't kill themselves," Jack said. "They don't seem to feel remorse or guilt about the crimes they commit."

A lovely frown crossed Jillian's face. "But I thought . . . I'm sure I've read about people who have opened fire on college campuses or in shopping malls and when the police arrived have turned the guns on themselves."

"Yes, you have," Jack agreed quietly. "But those people are classified as mass murderers—not serial killers." Even more quietly, he added, "Mass murderers usually do kill themselves."

Chase heard the quiet in Jack's voice, and knew the reason for it, and felt a sudden jolt of regret for having raised the topic of the Strangler. It was supposed to have been an easy segue to the night of May 10, but it had digressed into an area that held emotionally painful memories of Jack's own brutally murdered parents. Chase would have shifted away from the subject entirely now, abandoning even the discussion of the night of his twin's disappearance, but Jillian was staring at him, her green eyes searching—and troubled.

"What is it, Jillian?"

"It seemed, just then, that you suddenly remembered something."

Yes, I remembered about the tragedy of Jack's parents, Chase thought. But you don't know that. You think I've remembered something else, something that obviously worries you. "What do you think it is that I've remembered, Jillian?"

"I thought, maybe, you were remembering something about serial killers. You had been doing quite a bit of reading about them."

Chase's mind swirled at the revelation but somehow he managed the logical question. "Why was I interested in reading about serial killers?"

"I don't know," Jillian confessed. "It was a new interest, though, something that had begun in the months just before your accident."

Why? Chase wondered. The twin with the gift for dreams had refused even to make movies about serial killers. So what had prompted his brother's sudden interest in them? It was likely, of course, that his interest had simply been piqued, as much of the city's probably was, by the ominous terror of the Strangler in their midst.

But what if it was something else? What if Chase Kincaid had been searching *for him?* Had he sensed that somewhere in the dark, sinister world of murder was a dark—yet innocent—heart that missed its golden twin? Had his brother not met with death at sea might they one day have found each other?

"Chase?" Jillian asked gently of the suddenly darkly shadowed dark gray eyes.

It wasn't Chase who answered.

It was Jack.

"That's not what you remembered, is it, Chase?" he asked quietly. "You remembered about me . . . about my parents."

"Yes," Chase said. "I'm sorry."

"It's all right," Jack assured, stunned at the truth of his words. For years he had carefully guarded the secret of his parents' brutal murder. His emotions were private, not for public consumption or invasion. A few weeks ago he had surprised himself by revealing the truth to Chase Carlton. It had seemed safe somehow, a trust that wouldn't be violated. And, Jack realized, he felt that same sense of safety now—especially with Stephanie, the woman with whom one day he hoped to share all secrets, all emotions, all dreams.

It was she who was looking at him now, concerned about him as she echoed softly, "Your parents?"

"They were killed, thirteen years ago, by a mass murderer. A gunman walked into a restaurant and opened fire. It happened a few weeks after Chase's parents died in the fire at Lake Tahoe. Despite his own recent loss, Chase wrote to me about mine."

"Oh," Jillian whispered. "I'm so sorry."

Her lovely eyes embellished her words as she looked at Jack, but after several moments they drifted to Chase, for whom she had messages as well.

They were messages of love and pride, and Chase read them quite clearly, because he had felt them, too, when Jack had told him about the eloquent letter of sympathy and understanding written by his grieving yet so generous twenty-one-year-old twin.

As Jillian's eyes met his, Chase was enchanted anew by the magnificent illusion, and he was reminded anew of how terribly false it was. Even if she was as lovely as she appeared, without pretense or treachery of any kind, Chase Carlton was still nothing more than smoke and mirrors—the mirror image of his golden twin, but himself pure smoke, cruel, shadowed, smoldering with rage . . . and most assuredly nothing for which any eyes should fill with loving pride.

"I'm sorry, too, Jack," Stephanie said. Her voice was soft,

wavering with emotion, and there were more emotional words, impossible to say, except through her eyes. I care, the shimmering sapphire told him. I care about your sadness, your anger, *you.*

I care too, Jack's dark blue eyes replied. I care about your sadness—and I think there is anger deep within you as well. Will you tell me about it, Stephanie? Will you trust *me?*

The silence that had suddenly fallen over the teal and cream living room awakened Annie. She had been sleeping contentedly at Chase's feet, comforted by the chorus of voices that hummed above her. But when the comforting chorus suddenly stopped, she awakened, on alert, her golden head tilted and curious.

The silence had fallen because of Jack, and now it was he who spoke, lightening the mood as he did, "It's quiet, isn't it, Annie? Too quiet."

"I told her to wake up when she thought it was time for more coffee," Jillian said with a smile.

Stephanie accompanied Jillian to the kitchen to get the coffee. After the kitchen door swung closed behind them, she asked gently, "Are you okay, Jill?"

"Okay."

"But . . ."

"But very worried. As grim as the subject was, I hoped that the discussion of serial killers might trigger a recent memory. The only memories that have come back—even the memory tonight about Jack's parents—have been long-ago ones." Jillian gave a defeated shake of her auburn head. "Sometimes it seems so hopeless. Chase remembers *nothing* about us."

"I think he does," Stephanie began slowly. "I think that even though it may not be a conscious memory, he knows that this is his home, the place where he belongs."

"What makes you say that?"

"He just seems so comfortable here, so unfrightened by his

loss of memory." Stephanie smiled gently at the surprised and hopeful eyes and asked, "And what about the way he looks at you, Jill?"

"What way?"

"Maybe you don't see it." Stephanie frowned thoughtfully. "It does seem that it happens more when he's looking at you from a distance—when he thinks that no one is watching. But I've been watching, and what I see is a man who is searching, wanting desperately to remember his relationship with you, because he knows it was wonderful. Chase loves you, Jill. His mind may not remember, not yet, but his heart does. He loves you. I know he does."

How Jillian wanted to believe her friend's reassuring words. But how could she? She and Chase were strangers. Yes, they were polite with each other, careful and respectful; and yes, in the past few days Chase had shown her glimpses of the gentleness and sensitivity that she had always known existed but which before he had always kept hidden from her.

But Jillian knew that she had to face the truth that Chase might never remember her—them; and she had to face the even more painful truth that one day this more gentle and loving Chase might leave her to begin his life anew, to find someone with whom he could share the secrets he had never been willing to share with her.

Chase is alive, Jillian reminded herself. Whether or not he and I have a second chance at our love, whether he leaves me to find happiness with someone else, he is alive. And that's all that matters.

Finding a smile, Jillian said to her beautiful friend, "I think that the description of a man who is searching for something he knows he wants applies rather nicely to Jack when he looks at you. As does," she added softly, "the description of a man who is very obviously in love."

Chapter Nineteen

His seductive and persuasive dark blue eyes had caressed her throughout the evening, and the sparkling sapphire had responded with shy yet brave messages of desire and joy. At midnight, when he drove her back to her penthouse, Stephanie invited him inside.

"Would you like something?" she asked when the mirrored elevator had transported them to the privacy of her penthouse. "Coffee? A drink?"

"You," Jack said softly. "I would like you."

Jack wanted her, and for this wonderful enchanted night, Stephanie would simply banish the truth. Jack didn't want her, not *her*, not really; but her own need was so desperate that she was willing to pretend. She needed his gentleness, the wondrous illusion that she was desired and cherished. She knew it would only be for tonight, but it would be a magnificent memory of tenderness that she would treasure forever.

Jack cradled her face in his hands, his strong fingers weaving gently into her silky, moon-kissed hair. For a very long time he simply marveled at the vision of loveliness that he beheld. Her brilliant blue eyes shimmered with a shy yet courageous invitation that seemed almost innocent; and the warm cheeks beneath his fingers flushed a delicate pink; and her lovely lips trembled, welcoming too, shy too, courageous too; and when at last his lips touched the warm satin of her skin, he inhaled the intoxicating fragrance of *Promise,* the romantic and hopeful perfume inspired by a meadow of wildflowers.

They would have made love in darkness, but when they reached her bedroom, before he began undressing her, Jack found the antique porcelain lamp on the dresser and illuminated the room in a golden mist, their own private moon.

"I want to see your eyes," he explained softly.

From any other man the words would have terrified her: because with any other man she knew that her eyes would have been filled with fear, and confusion, and a desire for privacy not for passion. Look at my perfect body instead, she would have purred, carefully rehearsed words to which any other man she had known would have willingly complied.

But not Jack Shannon. He wanted to see her eyes. And bravely, so bravely, on this night of love Stephanie would show him their honest messages of desire and joy, not confusion and fear.

Jack made love to Stephanie the way he had kissed her beneath the moonlight, tenderly caressing every place on her beautiful body, cherishing all places with equal care—and equal passion—as if each patch of trembling satin might be the secret passageway to the most precious treasure of all—her heart.

Stephanie gave Jack all that was hers to give, every lovely gift of her lovely body, and when it was time, for both of them, to become one, when they both needed that exquisite joy almost desperately, her eyes glowed with brilliant blue wonder.

Had Jack been able to speak at that moment, he would have whispered the astonishing truth that had been singing in his heart all evening, long before they made love, a confident chorus of joy. I love you, Stephanie. *I love you.*

But Jack didn't speak aloud the joyous love song of his heart; and after, as he held her, he realized that their loving had been virtually silent. Yes, there had been the lovely soft sighs of her passion, and the deep sighs of his; and yes, her expressive eyes had told him with unashamed candor of her desire. And yes, *yes,* he believed he had seen even more: that in the shimmering sapphire there had been shimmering love.

For Jack their loving had been emotional, intimate, a wondrous union of their hearts. But what if, for Stephanie, it had been a sharing of bodies only, a passionate alliance of pleasure without any emotional intimacy at all? Jack needed to know. He was in love with the woman he believed Stephanie to be . . . a woman in whom sapphire shadows spoke so eloquently of vulnerability and kindness—and in whom the unshadowed sapphire had, as they had made love, sent crystal-clear messages of joy.

But what if he was misreading all the brilliant blue messages, even the ones that seemed most clear? Or worse, what if he was reading them precisely as she wanted him to, words from a script performed by a gifted actress? Stephanie had played with him the night she had dined in character as Lieutenant Cassandra Ballinger. What if she was playing, pretending, still?

The man who had always believed that he would spend his entire life playing with women, never wanting more than the provocative games, wanted to play no more. He couldn't. Jack Shannon had dedicated his life to protecting innocent lives from brutal murders; he owed his own heart, innocent of love until now, the same protection from lethal harm.

"Talk to me, Stephanie."

"Talk to you?" she echoed as her heart cried, Please don't let it all be over so soon! She had known that eventually Jack would make demands of her which she could not fulfill. But as he held her, and as she valiantly struggled to hold on to the memory of feeling so safe, and so wanted, and so loved, she had desperately hoped that he wouldn't make those demands of her to-night. But now he was. "Talk to you about what?"

"About you." Jack moved so that he could see her eyes, gently parting the love-tangled silk that curtained them. When he could see the lamplit sapphire without its veil of sable and moonbeams, he said quietly, "I want to know what you're thinking and feeling right now—and what you were thinking and feeling while we were making love."

While they had made love, Jack had seen wonder and courage and desire in the brilliant blue; and despite the extraordinary power of their passion—and his impression that although technically experienced, she was quite innocent—he hadn't seen a flicker of fear. But there was fear now, heart-stopping dread, and Jack's own heart froze with a fear of its own as he awaited the truth: *I felt nothing, Jack, nothing emotional, that is. You're a masterful lover, of course, the rumors about you are all true. It was wonderful. You were wonderful. I hope we can do it again and again.*

"Stephanie?" Even his whisper was frozen, a soft hiss of ice. "Talk to me."

I c-c-c-can't. She couldn't talk, and she couldn't turn away from him. His dark blue eyes wouldn't allow it, nor would the strong hands that could caress with such tenderness. They imprisoned her now, gentle still, but unyielding.

Jack saw Stephanie's fear . . . and the hopelessness where before there had been such hope . . . and because he loved her, most of him wanted to cradle her close to him and simply reassure. He fought the powerful impulse to protect her with the harsh reminder that it was he who needed protection, he who was vulnerable.

"You're playing with me, Stephanie—and I don't want to play. I won't play, not with you."

He waited for words, but there was only more silence—and more fear. Finally she withdrew from his glare the only way she could, but just before her eyelids fluttered closed, the frightened blue misted with immense sadness.

Jack waited still. But when neither her eyes nor her lips would open for him, he left her. It was a move which required monumental effort. Jack felt as if, in leaving her, he was tearing himself in half.

Stephanie felt torn in half, too, as he took his warmth and strength and tenderness from her. He was a magnet to her still, forcing her to open her eyes and then to sit upright in the bed, the sheets clutched modestly over her beautiful breasts as she watched with hopeless despair while he dressed.

Jack's back was toward her, but she saw in the graceful movements of his strong body what was surely on his face. Anger. Taut. Carefully controlled. And very powerful.

You wouldn't be angry if you knew the truth about me, Jack! You would only be relieved. As soon as you're gone, I'm going to write the truth to you, and when you read my letter, you will be so very glad that you left me.

Stephanie didn't expect to see his dark blue eyes ever again, and she especially could not imagine seeing again the exquisite tenderness with which he had gazed at her. But when he finished dressing, Jack turned to her. His eyes met hers with surprise—and then with that wondrous tenderness—as he whispered with quiet, impassioned emotion, "I really cared about you, Stephanie Windsor. I really cared."

Then he turned away, and in a few long, graceful strides he had reached the doorway, and in another moment he would vanish from her life forever. Stephanie's desperate thoughts stuttered and stumbled in the hopeless chaos of her mind. D-don't g-go! P-please, p-p-please, *p-p-p-p* . . .

"I love you, Jack!"

The words that came without warning from her lips startled Stephanie as much as they startled Jack. As he turned to face her again, her delicate fingers flew to those lips, traitors to her mind, but loyal—so very loyal—to her heart.

Stephanie's mind would never have scripted such words, nor would it have ever permitted the scripting of such foolish thoughts had they ever dared to dance there. But the words had come from her heart; and they hadn't needed careful scripting at all, because they had been there always, engraved in a delicate, hopeful place; and they had waited so patiently, an entire lifetime, to be spoken.

Now the joyful words had flowed from her heart, and they were the most honest words she had ever spoken . . . and the most foolish . . . and the most futile.

As Jack moved from the shadows near the doorway back toward the lamp's golden mist, Stephanie awaited with humiliation and horror the expression she would surely see on his handsome face. Yes, he had admitted that he cared about her, but this extraordinary confession of her heart would surely be greeted with amusement, perhaps even mockery at its presumptuousness.

But as the golden lamplight illuminated Jack's face, Stephanie saw only the gentlest of smiles—and what looked like pure happiness in the dark, seductive blue.

Her heart soared—and then crashed. Amusement and mockery would have been better, because now Jack was going to learn the truth—and she would be forced to see his disappointment when he did.

"Well," he said softly as he sat beside her on the bed and gently cradled her lovely face. "I love you too, Stephanie."

His loving confession brought a flood of tears to her eyes, anguished tears, not the joyous ones they should have been.

"What is it, darling?" Then, wanting a smile, wanting only happiness for her, Jack teased gently, "Is it such a terrible tragedy to have fallen in love with a cop? Somewhere I have a diploma from a fairly reputable law school. I could have it framed for you."

His words brought a brief trembling smile, but it vanished quickly, with a despondent shake of her head, a shimmering but hopeless dance of moonbeams.

"Tell me, Stephanie. Please tell me."

She couldn't think. Even the stumbling thoughts had disappeared, swept away by the flood of emotions within.

But once again, astonishingly, words flowed from her lips.

"I stutter," she confessed without a stutter.

Jack understood everything then—the great care with which she always spoke, the hesitation before speaking, the controlled diction when the words finally came. At Harvard he'd had a classmate who had been a "reformed" stutterer. His cautious style of speech, Jack realized, had been quite similar to Stephanie's.

Reformed. What a terrible description, Jack thought as he gazed at lovely sky-blue eyes now clouded with shame. Reformed, as in a reformed murderer, as if the stuttering had been a crime, or as in a reformed drug addict, as if her stumbling speech had been an indulgence which—at long last—she had finally abandoned.

"Oh, Stephanie," Jack said softly. "I care that your stuttering has obviously caused you such great sadness. But, my love, it won't ever bother me. I've waited all my life to find you. Waiting to hear the words of the woman I love is a luxury I never believed I would have."

Tears spilled still from her cloudy eyes, necessary raindrops, nurturing ones. As Jack tenderly kissed her falling tears, he whispered, "I want to hear your words, Stephanie. I want to hear them all."

She told him every shame, every disappointment, every truth. The words flowed to her lips without rehearsal, and when she spoke they neither stumbled nor fell.

Why not? Stephanie wondered with astonishment.

Because he loves you, her heart answered. And if you do happen to trip and fall, he will be there to caress your bruises, and dust you off, and hold you until you are ready again to dance and twirl and fly. It is Jack's love that is giving your words—and you—permission to be free *at last*.

Jack loved the little girl who had been imprisoned by shame in a lonely world of silence, and he hated the parents who had so cruelly condemned her to that solitary torment, and he felt immense gratitude to Jillian Montgomery, the nine-year-old whose generosity and kindness had rescued Stephanie from her isolation.

"She was my friend, Jack, my first friend, my only friend, my best friend."

"Until me."

"Until you," Stephanie echoed, an honest echo, not a technique. "But I betrayed Jillian's friendship. She was always there for me, *always,* and when she finally needed me, I abandoned her."

Jack now knew that for Stephanie the greatest shame of all was her abandonment of Jillian. "You were only a girl then, Stephanie," he gently reminded. "You were devastated by Meredith's death, and you were very afraid. Jillian obviously understands what happened and has forgiven you. You're good friends again now, aren't you?"

"Yes, but only because Jillian is so generous. I haven't even apologized to her for what I did." Stephanie frowned and then vowed solemnly, "I need to apologize though, and someday I will."

It was a sacred promise, and it shimmered with apprehension.

"Do you doubt your courage?"

"I guess . . . yes."

"Well, don't. You've already proven both your friendship and your courage by going to the memorial reception for Chase and offering your help . . . and by meeting with me because it was so important to Jillian that I not believe Chase had married a murderess. That wasn't easy for you, was it?"

"No," Stephanie admitted to the ocean-blue eyes that had heard all her shameful truths and had become only more tender with each word . . . each *unstumbling* word . . . every bold syllable that danced forward without faltering, a joyous symbol of her trust and of her love. "Jack? Will you make love to me again?"

"Again and again," he whispered, his talented lips softly grazing her temple. "I will make love to you forever—with one proviso. You have to talk to me the entire time."

"The entire time?"

Jack laughed softly as his lips found hers. "Well, some of the time . . ."

Chapter Twenty

"Chase and I are going to Bora Bora."

Jillian had purposely waited to give the news to her father and Brad until this precise moment—Saturday evening, when they were all assembled for a pleasant family dinner at Edward and Claudia's. They were on the secluded wisteria-cloaked veranda, enveloped by balmy, gardenia-fragrant air.

But with Jillian's words the warm air seemed to chill. The cool surprise she saw on her father's face was mirrored on Brad's, and when Brad spoke, there was a chill in his voice.

"You're what?"

"We're going to Bora Bora." Jillian met Brad's eyes with defiance. "We're leaving on Tuesday night."

"Have you forgotten about *Journeys of the Heart?* It's *your* movie, remember? If we're going to start filming on schedule next spring—and you're still planning to teach this fall—we have to devote the summer to preproduction. Have you forgotten our meeting with Peter Dalton a week from Friday? He's excited about the project, and I think he'll agree to direct, but he's a very busy man. It took weeks simply to arrange this meeting."

"I know all that, Brad, and I haven't forgotten anything.

Chase and I will be back from Bora Bora on Thursday evening."

"Did you know about this?" The question Edward's, and it was directed to his wife.

"Yes," Claudia confessed. "Jillian asked if we would take Annie for the week."

"When was that?"

"Two days ago." Claudia had agreed, very reluctantly, not to tell Edward about Jillian and Chase's trip to paradise. Jillian wanted to tell her father herself. It was a small secret for Claudia to keep, quite trivial compared to the others she had hidden from Edward all these years. She saw now on her husband's solemn face how terribly upset he would be if ever those shattering secrets were revealed. After a steadying breath, she said calmly, soothingly, "Bora Bora is where Jillian and Chase went on their honeymoon, remember? It seems an ideal place to go in hope of sparking memories."

Chase observed the conversation with silent and somewhat amazed interest. Quite obviously both Edward and Brad had strong objections to the trip to Bora Bora. And also quite obviously Jillian had anticipated those objections and had chosen a time that was supposed to have been a pleasant family gathering in which to inform them, so that, Chase imagined, the occasion or his presence or both would subdue their disapproval.

But their disapproval hadn't been subdued in the least. Chase Kincaid's cousin and father-in-law both very much disliked the idea of Jillian being alone with him on the faraway tropical island.

Why?

"What's your problem with this, Brad?" Chase asked, calmly directing the question to the man whose objection had seemed the strongest—at least the most vocal. He saw his cousin's hesitation, the obvious silent debate, and finally commanded, "The truth, Brad."

"The truth? Well . . . okay." Brad paused, using the silence to meet Chase's steady gaze with matching steadiness. "The truth is that I simply don't believe that you are Chase Kincaid."

"Brad!" Jillian exclaimed. "What are you saying?"

"What I am saying," Brad said evenly, "is that I believe this man is an impostor. Yes, he looks remarkably like Chase, and he knows a few facts about Chase's life, but the truth is that with a minimum of research any stranger could know as much."

"He's had a very serious head injury."

"How convenient."

"It's not convenient for him, Brad—it's terrible!"

"Jillian," Chase interjected softly. He wanted to look at her, but his eyes were still locked in a duel with his cousin's. "Let Brad speak his piece. Go ahead, Brad. You believe that I'm an impostor."

"I believe that you *could* be," Brad clarified. "You could be someone who realized the potential significance of his uncanny resemblance to one of Hollywood's richest and most powerful men and who then devised a murderous plot to steal his identity and his fortune." Brad heard Jillian's soft gasp at his accusation, and after pausing a few beats, making it abundantly clear that he was *choosing* to leave Chase's dark gray eyes, he looked at her and reminded very gently, "We both know how very troubled Chase was in the months before his disappearance."

"Yes, but . . ."

"What if he were getting disturbing phone calls—death threats, perhaps? You know that's something he would have hidden from us, not wanting us to worry." Brad paused, allowing his words to settle until he saw her acknowledgement that yes, had he been getting death threats, Chase surely would have kept the fact concealed. Then he continued, "But he also would have wanted to resolve the issue. So, had the mysterious caller suggested it, he would have agreed to meet with him alone, on *Sea Goddess,* late at night. You know that Jack Shannon has grave concerns about what actually happened that night—"

"Brad, please," Jillian interjected, her tone sending an urgent reminder that they had all promised in Puerto Vallarta not to trouble Chase with the disturbing suspicions that the homicide lieutenant once had held.

"Okay. But, Jillian, what I'm suggesting *is* possible. Everyone has a twin somewhere, isn't that what they say? And surely in this era of plastic surgery what nature didn't make identical could be perfected by a talented surgeon." Turning to the gifted plastic surgeon of the family for support, Brad asked, "Isn't that right, Claudia?"

Somehow his voice registered, and Claudia realized vaguely that his question was for her, but her mind was still reeling in response to his earlier words: Everyone has a twin, isn't that what they say? Her son had had a twin . . . who had died moments after his birth . . . *hadn't he?*

"Claudia?"

"I'm sorry, Brad, what did you ask?"

"I asked if, in this era of plastic surgery, what nature didn't make identical could be perfected by a talented surgeon?"

"Oh, yes, I suppose." *Assuming it wasn't identical to begin with.*

"You're wearing your hair longer than Chase Kincaid ever did," Brad continued as he returned to the dark gray eyes. "I've been wondering if that might be to conceal surgical scars."

"No," Jillian said emphatically. "He's wearing his hair longer now because I like it this way."

Brad arched a surprised and skeptical dark eyebrow. "That doesn't mean it isn't concealing scars, Jill."

"It's not," Jillian said. "He doesn't have any scars from plastic surgery."

Chase fought to conceal his own surprise—and concern—at Jillian's confident pronouncement. Had she searched his face for tiny scars? he wondered. Had the delicate fingers that had touched his brow and woven so tenderly into his long coal-black hair in the hospital in Puerto Vallarta, luring him with their gentleness from delirium to consciousness, actually been the hands of a disbelieving murderess examining him for evidence of surgery that would prove he wasn't a ghost after all?

Jillian Kincaid didn't look like a murderess now. She looked like a loving wife defending her husband against this accusation as bravely as a few days before she had defended him against the near-lethal invasion of evil. Somehow on *Sea Goddess* Jillian had melted the ice that was threatening to destroy; and here, now, she was holding up admirably against Brad's dark and chilling glare. But she needed help.

Because, Chase thought, she's fighting a courageous but ultimately hopeless battle against the truth. Because Brad is right. I *am* an impostor.

"What would you like me to do, Brad?" Chase asked finally. "As much as I want to, it's obvious that I can't force my memory to return."

"How about physical proof, then?"

"Blood tests? Fingerprints?"

"I'm sure that the police have samples of both."

Yes, Chase thought. I know they do. And I know that the DNA in my cells and the swirls on my fingers are identical to those of my twin.

Chase met his cousin's challenging gaze calmly, and after a solemn moment he extended his strong, lean arms, palms up, in one gesture offering both the prints from his fingers and the blood from his veins.

"Be my guest, Brad." Chase paused, allowing his words to settle, searching for his cousin's reaction. But Brad's dark eyes were as unrevealing as his own. "I've made no claims whatsoever about who I am—because I don't know. Until now I've believed what you all have told me—that I'm Chase Kincaid—but if I'm not, there's no one who wants to know that truth more than I."

"No," Jillian said, moving to Chase and curling her delicate hands around his bare forearm. "He's Chase, Brad. He's *our* Chase."

"Even though he doesn't look exactly like our Chase?"

"He's thinner."

"More than that."

"Yes," Jillian conceded. "Because of the ordeal he's been through, his features seem harder, I suppose, more rugged. But,

Brad, his eyes and his hands are the same. Eyes and hands are unique. Eyes and hands . . . and heart." She drew a soft breath and added quietly, "I know that because that's all I had left of who I was after my accident."

Brad hesitated a moment, his dark eyes softening for her. Then, with exquisite gentleness, he asked, "Are you saying that he has Chase's heart, Jillian? How can you be so sure? You've always said that you didn't really know——"

"Enough," Edward intervened. "This discussion has gone on long enough."

Jillian cast a grateful glance at her father, and then looked up at Chase.

"You are Chase. I know you are. It's an unspeakable indignity to ask you to prove it." Her cheeks flushed pink as the intense gray eyes met hers, and she suddenly became so aware of her bold grasp on his bare forearm that she promptly let go, but her determination didn't waver as she looked at the man who had made the astonishing accusation. "I won't allow that indignity, Brad. I mean it."

"I want Chase back as much as you do, Jillian."

"He *is* back, and three days from now he and I are going to Bora Bora."

"Okay." Brad smiled at her and shrugged his hands in a gesture of willing defeat. "Okay." Then, smiling still, as if the preceding conversation had never happened, he turned to Chase and asked, "Are you planning to join us for the meeting with Peter Dalton?"

"Yes, if you don't mind. As an observer only, of course, unless my memory has returned by then."

"I don't mind at all. Have you read *Journeys of the Heart?*"

"I assume so," Chase answered evenly. "However, since I have no memory of that reading, I plan to read it again while we're on Bora Bora."

"Good. Hopefully reading the best script we've ever planned to produce will trigger some memories." Brad's smile drifted from Chase to Jillian, picking up gentleness as his gaze fell on

the still-defiant and angry green eyes of the author of the extraordinary screenplay. "I said what I needed to say, Jillian. Now
that I have, let's put it behind us. Please?"

"Maybe cocktails and crab puffs would help," Claudia suggested, preempting what threatened to be an awkward silence
as it became obvious that Jillian wasn't ready to so easily forgive
or forget. "I'll get the crab puffs while Edward pours the
drinks—assuming we're still going to have a nice family dinner
party tonight?"

"We still are as far as I'm concerned," Chase said. Smiling
reassurance to Jillian, he added, "I'm honestly not offended by
what Brad said. He's simply trying to protect me . . . you . . . all
of us."

Jillian's emerald eyes softened slightly at his reassurance and,
sensing that she and Brad might more quickly reach a rap-
prochement if he weren't there, Chase turned to the woman
who was also obviously hoping for harmony and offered, "I'll
help you with the crab puffs, Claudia."

Claudia needed to be alone. She needed time and privacy to
calm her trembling heart and focus her trembling mind on that
faraway November night. "There's a second baby," the doctor
had said moments before the anesthetic had thrust her into
darkness. "He is dead," Victor Kincaid had told her hours later.
Those vivid memories had come as she stood on the veranda,
reeling at Brad's casual allusion to twins, but she wanted to
plumb the depths of those memories, to conjure the images and
search for something never before seen in Victor's dark eyes,
some clue that his words might not have been true.

But Claudia wasn't alone, because Chase had chosen to
accompany her to the kitchen. And now, instead of concentrating on that faraway night in the past, she was going to learn
what the present had in store. Would he appraise her with the
same warrior-noble solemnity with which he had withstood
Brad's astonishing attack? And then would he quietly utter the

shattering words, Hello, Mother. It's me, the son you left for dead.

The woman surgeon who had served so valiantly in Vietnam, and who had become a minor legend there for nerves of steel wrapped in a deceptively delicate package, couldn't find those nerves now—at least not enough to bravely meet her son's steel-gray eyes. Instead, she turned away from him, moved to take the hot crab puffs from the oven, and opened the door before she realized she wasn't wearing oven mitts.

"Where are they?" Chase asked.

"In the top drawer beside the sink," she told the deep voice that seemed helpful, not accusatory.

Chase found the mitts, removed the hors d'oeuvres from the oven for her, and in response to her silent gesture placed them on the tile countertop. Then, as he watched her transfer them to a serving platter, he said, "I take it you think it's not the end of the world for Jillian and me to go to Bora Bora."

"No," Claudia answered. She rested her hand on the counter for support, a buttressing that was far less casual than it appeared, and at last turned to face him. Smiling, she elaborated, "I don't think it's the end of the world at all. I think it will be good for both of you."

I hope it will be, she thought. I hope with all my heart that you are Chase Kincaid . . . and that you will remember your love for Jillian . . . and that this time you will treasure that love.

"I guess that means you don't think I'm an impostor," Chase pressed. His tone was gentle, but he was pressing her. *Why?* he wondered. Why was he questioning the allegiance of the one family member who, beginning with her warm welcome in Puerto Vallarta, had seemed to be genuinely on his side? Because, he realized, something he had seen in her eyes during Brad's attack made him wonder if it was actually Claudia who had the greatest doubts of all about who he really was.

"That's what it means," Claudia answered quietly, holding her son's intense gaze as she did and smiling, even though what she saw filled her with dread.

It was what she had seen in Puerto Vallarta. He had been delirious then, and only semiconscious, but his eyes had fluttered open briefly. The gray had been confused, disoriented—and yet there had been clarity too, a clear and haunting message of despair.

Claudia had never seen such hopelessness in the eyes of Chase Kincaid; but it was something she recognized, something she herself had known very well. The legacy of despair from her own loveless childhood had dwelled in her heart and haunted her eyes until she was rescued by Edward's love. Claudia had seen the dark shadows of despair in Chase's eyes in Puerto Vallarta, and she saw them again now.

No, she told herself. He *is* Chase Kincaid. My other son died at birth. The shadows I see now are new ones, because of the ordeal he has just survived and the confusion of his amnesia. They are not because he, as I, lived the loveless and anguished childhood of an orphan.

How she wished she could know with certainty that the assurance she gave herself was true. How she wished—such a grim wish—that she could send an investigator to Saint-Jean-Cap-Ferrat to find the tiny grave where her other son had lain in peace for the past thirty-four years. But there would be no such small grave in Cap Ferrat. "Where is he?" she had asked Victor Kincaid when she had learned that one of her infant sons had died. "With us," Victor had answered without even a heartbeat's delay. Then he had assured her, "Rachel and I will find a beautiful and peaceful place for him."

Claudia knew that her son didn't lie in the marble crypt in Los Angeles with Rachel and Victor Kincaid. She had gone there one day, searching for her baby, to bid him farewell at last—and to bid farewell, too, to the man and woman who had been parents to the twin who had survived. But the unnamed infant who Victor Kincaid had told her had died in Cap Ferrat wasn't there. Claudia hadn't been terribly surprised. Victor and Rachel had obviously wanted to spare their son the sadness of knowing he had a brother who had died. Her other son was buried elsewhere, in the pastoral tranquillity of the Loire Valley, perhaps; and he had been buried in that peaceful place for the past thirty-four years, *hadn't he?*

Chapter Twenty-One

Memories of the dinner party swirled in Chase's mind, raising troubling questions, evoking powerful emotions, and preventing sleep still, three hours after he and Jillian had politely bade each other good night and retired to their separate bedrooms.

As, in his wakefulness, he relived Jillian's defiant indignation at Brad's suggestion that he was an impostor, Chase recalled as well his distinct impression that she very much *wanted* him to be her husband, and now, hours later, he felt still, actually felt, the sensation of her delicate fingers curled over his bare forearm. There were many reasons that a cold-blooded murderess would want an impostor to believe that she had been fooled by him, his mind reminded, harshly countering the enchanting memories of his heart.

Eventually Chase's mind and heart simply had to call an exhausted truce on the subject of Jillian, and he left the memories of her to reflect on the reactions of Edward and Brad.

Edward Montgomery had clearly disapproved of the trip to Bora Bora, but the precise reason for his disapproval had never been clearly expressed. Perhaps it was simply fatherly worry for a beloved child, an instinctive parental protectiveness of which the orphan Chase Carlton had no personal knowledge but for which he felt respect and, even after all these years, a sense of longing.

Chase didn't begrudge Edward his fatherly concern, neither was he angered by Brad's suspicions. His cousin had boldly and with a minimum of apology laid his provocative cards faceup on the table. Chase admired his candor. And, like Edward, Brad was motivated by a loving protectiveness of Jillian, of Triple Crown, and of Chase Kincaid himself.

Chase knew nothing of the dynamics of family, but he would have found the outspoken honesty of his cousin and Jillian's father strangely appealing had it not been for the underlying message: they did not want him. Chase felt sadness, but not surprise, at the revelation. Even disguised as his golden twin, the reactions he evoked were the ones he had known throughout his thirty-four years as Chase Carlton. He was an outsider, as always. The sinister darkness that dwelled within him caused apprehension and wariness, not the welcoming joy that had surely always greeted his twin. Even the man who had been like a brother to Chase Kincaid, and who was his cousin too, did not want to claim him.

At three A.M. Chase left his bed. Sleep was obviously not going to come, and the thoughts that prevented it had begun to burrow into the deepest and most painful wounds of his heart.

Had he been on *Sea Witch,* Chase would have set sail into the night's darkness. Such escape to the sea was unavailable to him now, but there was still music. More than once he had gazed lingeringly at the guitar in his brother's study.

Dressing hurriedly, Chase left the master bedroom, walking quietly past the guest room where Jillian slept. On his first night at Clairmont, Jillian had left the door to her room wide open. The door was open still, but now just ajar, a little more shy, a little less bold in its invitation. Had the door been fully opened, Chase realized that he would have walked into the room of springtime flowers to look for a moment at the sleeping face haloed by shimmering auburn.

At the foot of the sweeping staircase Chase was greeted by a sleepy—and then quickly lively and eager—Annie. She padded beside him with her jaunty prance as they walked together to the study. Once there, as if the two of them had gone through this late-night ritual a thousand times, she waited expectantly while he removed the guitar from its case, then curled at his feet when he sat to play.

The music flowed over him and within him, drowning thought, bathing wounds, transporting him to a place that felt almost like peace . . .

Chase had no idea how long he had been playing when he looked up and saw her standing in the open doorway. Her fluffy bathrobe was cinched tightly at her slender waist, and her sleep-tangled auburn hair spilled in soft cascades over her shoulders, and the expression she wore was shy . . . and brave.

Chase stopped playing the moment he saw her. "Hi. Did I awaken you?"

"Hi. No." Jillian knew from years of experience that the sounds of music from his study didn't travel upstairs. She hadn't been awakened by sounds, but something *had* awakened her. Some invisible hand had shaken her from sleep and then compelled her to him. "I'm not sure why I awoke. I just did." With a gentle tilt of the tangled auburn, she added softly, "You remember how to play."

"I guess I do. Music and lyrics seem to be coming to me."

"The song you were just playing, Simon and Garfunkel's 'The Sound of Silence,' is one of your favorites."

Yes, it is, Chase thought. "The Sound of Silence" was a favorite of Chase Carlton, at least it was a song that he played often, its lyrics of solitude and loneliness having special meaning to him. But why had such a song been a favorite of Chase Kincaid? Was it possible that the golden twin had sensed the dark twin's solitude, had somehow heard the sounds of silence from his brother's lonely heart?

"Well." Jillian's tentative word was punctuated with a soft shrug of shimmering auburn. "I didn't mean to intrude."

"You're not intruding," Chase countered swiftly, surprised by the sudden confidence of his words. The women who had visited *Sea Witch* had, of course, noticed his guitar; but he had resolutely declined their provocative pleas that he serenade them with love songs. Now he heard himself asking, "Do you have a request, a favorite? I can't guarantee that I'll remember how to play it, but I'll try."

Jillian hesitated. There were wonderfully romantic songs that he had once sung for her. But there was another song . . .

"Do you remember 'Bridge Over Troubled Water'? It's another Simon and Garfunkel." I never had the courage to ask you to play it for me . . . but it's all about us . . . what we might have been . . . the closeness we might have had if you had ever let me help you with your pain. Jillian realized with sudden apprehension that her request was far more presumptuous—and far more intimate and revealing—than a request for a love song would have been. I would have been your bridge over troubled water had you let me . . . but when you were the most troubled you always ran away.

Chase knew the song very well. If "The Sound of Silence" was the theme song of his lonely and solitary life, then "Bridge Over Troubled Water" was the ballad of his dreams—faraway, impossible dreams of someone who would care about the deep wounds and vicious scars of his heart.

As Chase began to play the familiar song, he gazed at Jillian and was magically transported to a place where impossible dreams weren't so impossible after all. She was there with him, her face aglow with love and her emerald eyes promising to caress his pain as gently as hours earlier her delicate fingers had caressed his skin.

Chase had never sung to anyone before, but now he sang to Jillian, and even though her lovely lips remained silent, there was a rich and vibrant harmony, as if she were singing too . . . as if their hearts were singing together.

A string broke then, shattering the perfect harmony with what felt to Chase like an ominous warning: Don't believe in dreams. Nothing—*nothing*—in your life has ever promised you that such wondrous imaginings can come true. Chase chose not to heed the warning. It would take only a few moments for his expert hands to replace the broken guitar string. Then swiftly, swiftly, he and Jillian would return to the music, the magic, the dream.

"I must have some extra strings around here somewhere," he said softly.

"Yes," Jillian answered with matching softness. She wanted what he wanted, to return to the magnificent place they just had been. It was a place as unfamiliar to her as it was to him. Despite all the prayers and wishes of her heart, she and Chase had never journeyed there before. Her hand trembled slightly as, with elegant grace, she gestured to an antique table. "There, beside you, in the top drawer."

As Chase withdrew a string from one of the already opened packets, his eyes fell on a small gold object in a far corner of the drawer.

"It looks like one of your earrings is in here too."

"Oh?" Then, smiling, she added, "Good."

Good . . . more than good. She had searched frantically for the missing earring, half of the pair that Chase had given her on their first wedding anniversary. The earrings were diamonds, brilliant cut stones of a half-carat each, and they were identical, with flaws or color—except for the sparkles of fire that danced within the ice. Jillian had worn them often, in good times and bad, but just before Valentine's Day one glittering twin had mysteriously disappeared from its pink satin nest in her jewelry box.

The beautiful diamond hadn't mysteriously disappeared after all, Jillian realized now. It had simply become dislodged, by her hand or his, and it had fallen into the plush carpet of his study. The realization came with relief—and then sadness. Chase had obviously found the missing earring, but instead of returning it to her, instead of knowing that she would have missed it and been searching for it, he had simply put it into the drawer.

That careless gesture, and his obvious lack of understanding of how upsetting its loss would have been to her, was an eloquently painful reminder of how distracted he had been in the months before his disappearance—and a painful reminder, too, of how far he had withdrawn from her and her love.

But now Chase had returned from the sea, and there was a new gentleness in his gray eyes, and a new softness in his voice, and just moments before she had seen such longing, such desire . . .

A soft, lovely smile touched Jillian's face as she watched Chase retrieve the missing earring from the depths of the drawer; but its hopefulness faded swiftly when she saw the piece of jewelry he withdrew. The earring wasn't hers, neither the precious lost diamond nor the missing half of a less cherished pair. The swirls of gold belonged to another woman.

Had she been here, in their home, listening to Chase sing, caressed by the deep longing in his voice and the smoldering passion in his seductive gray eyes? Had the golden earring been dislodged by talented fingers that had left the magic they had strummed on the guitar to create even more magic as they entwined in her hair?

"Jillian?"

She willed her fingers not to tremble as she took the other woman's earring, but she could not meet the searching, demanding gray. She had vowed to be truthful to him, and to help him find the hidden memories, but was it so very wrong to have hoped that the memories that would return first would be the happiest and most hopeful ones? Was it so selfish, and too foolish, to believe that if Chase remembered first the wonder of their love—and if she enhanced those memories with secret truths they should have shared before—that the anguish of what had become of that love would no longer matter?

Yes, it was selfish, and perhaps terribly foolish, but . . . but the Chase who had miraculously returned to her from the sea was more gentle, more sensitive, more loving than the old Chase had been—and that meant that everything could be different this time . . . *didn't it?*

Yes, her heart answered. I can't, I *won't* tell him what became of our wonderful love—not yet, not until he remembers how it began . . . and not until he decides how he wants it to be this time.

The magical spell was shattered now, its brilliance as irretrievably destroyed as even the dazzling fire of the most perfect of diamonds could vanish with a precise, splintering blow. Jillian needed to get away from the searching gray eyes—and from this room, where for a wondrous moment there had dwelled a dream, but which now belonged to another woman, one to whom Chase had also sung the secrets and passions of his heart.

"I guess I'd better go put this in my jewelry box," she murmured finally.

"Okay," Chase agreed with quiet reluctance.

What had happened? he wondered. It was as if Jillian had been suddenly invaded by images of ice, of death, just as he had been on the deck of *Sea Goddess.* On that afternoon, because Jillian had feared that he was going to die, she had curled her soft, warm body against his frozen one, warming him, shielding him . . . and now he should have done the same. He wanted to, *was going to,* but as suddenly as it had come, the icy moment passed. Jillian was alive, breathing, and obviously very eager to flee from him.

For that breathless moment of ice, her stricken emerald eyes had seen death, Chase was sure of it. But what vision of death had been triggered by the golden earring? The death of his twin? Or was it, perhaps, the death of her beloved mother? Perhaps the lost—and now found—golden earring had belonged to

Meredith Montgomery, and seeing it again had recalled to Jillian the horrifying images of that witnessed death.

Chase hated the anguish of that tragedy for her.

But he hated even more the idea that what had caused Jillian's glowing green eyes to suddenly chill was the remembered image of the foggy night when she had murdered his twin.

Chapter Twenty-Two

The scheduled departure time of Qantas Airlines' Tuesday evening flight from Los Angeles to Papeete was 9:45 P.M. That nine-hour journey into night, Jillian explained to Chase, was only the first part of the long voyage from Bel Air to Bora Bora.

Qantas Flight 104 would arrive just before four A.M. at Faaa Airport on Tahiti. There, as dawn broke over the South Pacific, they would await their early morning Air Tahiti flight to Bora Bora. Forty-five minutes after departing Faaa they would touch down on Bora Bora, on the landing strip that was located on a motu within the island's coral reef. The islet location of Bora Bora's airport meant that the next part of their journey would be by boat, to Vaitape village on the main island. Once docked, they would be met by "Le Truck" and fifteen minutes later they would at last, at about nine A.M. local time, arrive at the destination that made the long trip well worth the effort—the enchanting and secluded Hotel Bora Bora.

Jillian's detailed description of the journey that would begin that evening was given to Chase over oatmeal on Tuesday morning. The description was, he realized, a preamble to what came next: the suggestion that since neither she nor his twin slept well on planes, perhaps they should try to rest Tuesday afternoon before beginning their long nocturnal voyage.

It was Jillian who suggested the afternoon naps, but as soon as they returned from taking Annie to Edward and Claudia's, and just after Chase announced that he was going to try to sleep, she said that she was going out for a while—a last-minute errand.

Chase didn't nap, of course. The only reason he had even said that he was going to try was so that she would. And now she was gone on a mysterious errand and he wandered from room to room, totally alone in the house—without either Jillian or Annie—for the first time ever.

Totally alone? Mightn't there be ghosts here, too, phantoms of good and evil that had been patiently waiting for this rare moment of absolute privacy? As he wandered, Chase willed all conscious thoughts away from his mind, clearing it of all clutter, freeing it to hear even the faintest of whispers, the softest of heartprints.

Come to me, he silently commanded the ghost of his twin. Talk to me. Let me know if what I'm doing is right—or if I am merely intruding where I don't belong. Tell me, *please.*

Chase Carlton had never been able to command the invisible voices of murderers to speak to him. The icy whispers of death came at their own pleasure, on their own sinister whim, defying him whenever he tried to conjure them, enveloping him with their evil at times when he most desperately needed peace.

Chase could not summon the evil voices of murderers . . . nor, it seemed, could he summon the gentle voice of his twin.

Finally he gave up, settling in the living room with the copy of *Journeys of the Heart* that he had planned to take to Bora Bora with him. He would begin reading the script now, he decided, while he waited for Jillian to return.

Jillian had told Chase that she had written *Journeys of the Heart* for Stephanie, to showcase her best friend's eight-octave talent and in hope of healing the wounds of their shattered friendship; and he had heard Brad describe the screenplay as a "work of art"; and he knew from Jack Shannon that under his twin's golden guidance Triple Crown Studios had only produced movies with happy endings.

Chase expected a beautifully written story with a happy ending, but he was quite unprepared for what *Journeys of the Heart* really was: a love letter to his twin, a journey of love that began in soft despair and courageously traveled to hopeful joy.

Chase Kincaid had obviously shared Brad Lancaster's enthusiasm for the commercial potential of Jillian's screenplay. But had the man with the gift for dreams realized that the blockbuster tour de force was in fact a most private—and shy and brave—plea to him for greater intimacies of the heart?

Chase had read the screenplay once and was beginning to read it again when Jillian returned.

"This is extraordinary," he told the emerald eyes that had become apprehensive as she realized what he was reading.

"Oh! Thank you."

"Did I tell you that before?" Did I—did *he*—understand?

"You said 'terrific' and 'wonderful'—never 'extraordinary.' " *And your voice was never this gentle.*

"Did I tell you that I was deeply moved by it?" *Did he hold you as close as he could and ask you to share with him all the desperate wishes that were so carefully written between the lines?*

"No, you didn't tell me that," Jillian said quietly. After a moment she added, "I'm hopeful that with Stephanie playing the lead, audiences will be moved as well."

"I'm sure they will be." His gaze followed hers downward to the two paper sacks that were held—clutched—by her delicate fingers. "Successful shopping trip?"

"I hope so." Uncertainty flickered in her green eyes as a rush of pink filled her cheeks. "I saw this, and since you don't have one this color—the color of your eyes—on impulse I decided to get it for you."

As Chase took the sack she offered him, the larger of the two, he asked, "Something for Bora Bora?"

"No, it's not really tropical enough. I thought just for wearing around here—or for sailing."

What Jillian had bought for him was a shirt, a short-sleeved cotton tennis shirt exactly like the ones that Chase Carlton wore with jeans—and Chase Kincaid wore with khaki slacks.

The color of your eyes, Jillian had said. Which meant that the shirt should have been some shade of gray: the shimmering silver of smoke, or the hard glint of steel, or the ominous darkness of a winter storm.

But the shirt that Jillian had bought for him wasn't gray at all. It was a light, bright blue.

"You see my eyes as blue?" Chase asked gently as his gray eyes journeyed to her lovely, hopeful, and surely color-blind emerald ones.

"Yes, sometimes . . . when you're happy. The gray becomes blue then—the same light blue as the shirt."

"It does?" Chase asked with unconcealed amazement. No one had ever told him that his eyes were sometimes blue—no one, not ever. Of course not, he thought. Because no one, not ever, had seen happiness in his eyes. Had *she?* "Have you seen the blue since my return?"

"Yes," Jillian said softly. It had been such a welcome sight. The blue of happiness had been in hiding for so long, lost in the clouds that were a symbol of his torment; but the blue had miraculously returned with him from the sea. It had been there in those first wondrous moments in Puerto Vallarta when he had at last opened his eyes to her gentle pleas; and she had seen it again when he had looked at the photographs of her as a plain little girl; and again during the magical time when he had sung to her.

And now, as he smiled his thank-you for the gift, the blue was there again—and it gave her the courage she needed to offer the smaller sack to him.

"I got this for you too. I thought maybe it might help spark memories."

The sack itself was beautiful, awash with the rich, luxurious colors of a rainbow. Written in elegant script atop the vibrant colors were the words Castille Jewelers, and below, in gold script too, were inscribed the locations of the Castille boutiques: Beverly Hills, New York, Dallas, Paris, London, Rome—and L'île des Arcs-en-ciel.

The piece of jewelry within the sack wasn't gift-wrapped. It was simply nestled in pure white tissue paper which, when Chase unfolded it, revealed a shiny new wedding band.

"You bought my engagement ring at Castille, and that's where we got our wedding bands, so I bought this one there as well." Jillian's explanation was hurried, breathless, and apprehensive. "The inscription is the same as it was on the ring you lost."

Chase left her uncertain emerald eyes long enough to read the words carved in gold: *Chase and Jillian, June 28, 1988— and always.* When he returned to her anxious gaze, he said gently, "This was your mysterious errand last Wednesday."

"Yes. You don't have to wear it if you don't want to."

"Why wouldn't I want to?"

"Because . . ."

"Because?"

"Because you don't remember us—our marriage." *Our love.*

"But we are married, Jillian," Chase Carlton heard himself say. They were remarkable words, and they they came with remarkable emotion, a defiant rush of hope from a heart that despite everything still wanted to believe in dreams. Chase's mind struggled to clamp down on the foolish—and so dangerous—emotion by sending urgent reminders of death, *of murder.* But his defiant heart, in enchanting collaboration with the now glowing emerald eyes, filled his own eyes with bright blue; and with exquisite tenderness, he repeated the impossible wish, "We *are* married."

PART THREE

Chapter Twenty-Three

Bora Bora, French Polynesia
June 1994

Jillian had told him that his twin had never been able to sleep on planes, but Chase had no idea if that was also true for him. Most of the journeys of his life had been by sea, and the few times he had flown—to pursue killers or to meet with other experts in murder at the FBI—the flights had occurred during the day.

Once settled into the luxurious comfort of the first class cabin of Qantas's night flight to Papeete, Chase decided that it would have been quite possible for him to sleep on the plane . . . but that would have meant abandoning the obviously frightened—no, terrified—Jillian.

It was presumptuous of man to dare to fly, of course, and tonight nature attacked that arrogant boldness with a punishing vengeance. The journey of the plane through the storm-ravaged skies didn't frighten Chase in the least—quite the contrary. It was that same reckless defiance, after all, that compelled him to sail into even the most threatening of seas. The heavens were angry tonight, a fury of powerful wind and pummeling rain, tossing the heavy plane as if it were the lightest of feathers.

As Chase gazed at the beautiful ashen face beside him and saw the stark fear in her emerald eyes and the delicate hands that curled almost viciously into bloodless knots in her lap, he wondered if, perhaps, she was reminded of another stormy night, when her mother's car had become a metal coffin . . .

The strong, warm hand that covered both of hers startled her. For a moment Jillian stared at it, feeling the comforting warmth and focusing on the shining gold band that now encircled one of the long fingers.

"Did I ever know how much flying frightened you?"

"No," she confessed softly, turning then to the gentle voice and even gentler gray eyes. "It usually doesn't."

"But tonight it feels like the night of your accident."

"Yes. I just need to get lost in the book that I brought," she murmured.

But instead of reaching for the book, her hands unclasped a little, just enough to allow his hand to fall between them, and once there her delicate fingers intertwined with his. Chase's hand was gently imprisoned by hers, and Chase would have been more than content to spend the entire flight precisely like this, hands entwined as he sought to reassure her that every dip and skitter of the jet would not be its last.

But quickly, too quickly, Jillian became self-conscious about the intimacy.

"I guess I should start reading my book," she said suddenly, releasing the hand that had been captured with such brazen boldness by hers.

"Do I—did I—know any card games?" Chase asked impulsively.

"You were always very good at gin rummy." Jillian smiled. "This flight was quite turbulent six years ago too." Her smile held because even though a troubling thought taunted—*he didn't notice then how frightened you were*—it was vanquished by what had happened now: he had noticed . . . and he had cared. "We played gin rummy and sipped champagne all night."

"Then why don't I find some cards and champagne?"

* * *

When they deplaned at dawn in Tahiti, they were greeted by a golden just-born sun and a warm, tropical cocoon of intoxicating fragrance. They were tired, but it was a floating fatigue on which they gently drifted through the remainder of the journey. The Air Tahiti flight from Papeete to Bora Bora was faultlessly smooth, and the boat trip from the airport to Vaitape was through mirror-calm aquamarine waters.

Paradise, Chase thought as his gray eyes surveyed the grandeur of the tropics that unfolded before him. He saw in the panorama of sky and sea shades of blue he had never before seen, and rich new shades of green in the lush forests; and as he and Jillian were escorted from the open-air lobby to their overwater bungalow at the Hotel Bora Bora, he discovered in the luxuriant gardens of hibiscus and plumeria unique shades of crimson, mauve, fuchsia, and lavender.

For years Chase Carlton had been planning a sea voyage to Bora Bora, a solitary, lonely journey to paradise. Now he was here, with his twin's beautiful bride, in a romantic honeymoon bungalow that was caressed by balmy breezes and serenaded by the songs of the sea.

"This is spectacular," he said after the escort had deposited their luggage inside the bungalow and then discreetly withdrawn.

"Yes," Jillian agreed. "Do you want to explore the hotel now?"

"I think we'll both feel more like exploring after a nap, don't you?" Chase asked gently of the exhausted green eyes. "Why don't you go ahead and shower and change while I unpack?" When his suggestion caused obvious surprise, he teased softly, "I wasn't usually the one who unpacked?"

"No."

"Well, let me give it my best shot."

"Okay. I just need to get my nightgown and robe out of the small suitcase."

Had she packed the white silk negligee? Chase wondered, not for the first time, as he watched her move to the suitcase. No, he discovered. The nightgown Jillian had brought on this trip to paradise was cotton, and very modest, a quaint and pretty bouquet of violets embroidered on cream. The gown was as innocent and as virginal as the white silk, but it was crafted for sleep—not for seduction.

Chase had finished unpacking their neatly folded clothes by the time Jillian emerged from the bathroom. She was a vision of innocence and purity, her lovely, freshly scrubbed face framed in glistening auburn, her tired emerald eyes shy, hopeful—and uncertain.

"Sleep well," Chase said softly. It was the bedtime wish that he had said to her, that they had said to each other, every night before retiring to their separate rooms.

Now there was only one room—romantically caressed by a fragrant tropical breeze.

And now there was only one bed—large enough for them to sleep quite separately still, of course, but a dramatic change nonetheless.

Jillian seemed a little relieved by his words, Chase decided. Relieved that he would make no demands for greater intimacy? That he understood that even though they were in this honeymoon bungalow, they were strangers still?

Jillian felt relief, and Chase felt inexplicable disappointment; but just before she turned away from him, he wondered if he saw a shadow of disappointment, too, cross her lovely face.

The slow, rhythmic rise and fall of her shoulders told Chase that Jillian was already asleep by the time he finished showering. He couldn't see her face. She was turned away from him, her slender body on the farthest edge of the bed, draped by a veil of damp auburn that glittered with all the brilliant colors of fire.

Chase Carlton had never slept, simply and only slept, with a woman; nor had he, on the occasions when he had joined an already sleeping lover in bed, taken any care whatsoever not to awaken her; nor had he ever been clothed. But now he wore a pair of his twin's cotton pajamas, and now, as he moved to join Jillian Kincaid in bed, he took great care not to disturb a sleep that he hoped was peaceful, untormented by the painful memories that had been evoked by their dark, stormy voyage five miles above earth.

As he eased himself between the cool sheets, Chase realized the full measure of his own fatigue. The exhaustion was far more emotional than physical, his energy sapped from worrying about Jillian during the turbulent flight, not from lack of sleep. To Chase, sleep had always been merely a necessity, never a welcome luxury, a haunting journey of violent nightmares to which he submitted warily—and only when he absolutely had to.

He was exhausted now, but still he resisted the pull of slumber. Lying awake, listening to the lapping of water and the calls of seabirds, and to the delicate ebb and flow of Jillian's gentle breathing, was far more peaceful than sleep. Why fall asleep to nightmares when he could lie here, wide awake, in the midst of a most wonderful dream?

This is a wonderful dream? Lying beside a sleeping murderess?

The silent voice came suddenly, harshly, a merciless taunt that shattered the fragile peace and stridently reminded him of his mission.

But his mission had changed. Since the afternoon on *Sea Goddess,* everything had changed. Yes, on that afternoon he had felt the unmistakable presence of evil—and death and violence and danger—but the danger had seemed *for* her, perhaps for both of them, not *because* of her.

In the past ten days Chase's impression—or was it merely a wish?—of Jillian's innocence had only become stronger. So much so that his impulsive decision to take her to Bora Bora, away from the comfort of her domain, her silken web, had hardly seemed necessary.

Chase could have, of course, canceled their trip to paradise. But he hadn't wanted to.

And now he lay in the same bed with her.

And now she was waking, a gentle stirring, and a moment later she turned toward him and her eyes fluttered open.

Her luminous emerald eyes seemed to be focused on him, but Chase wondered if Jillian really knew where she was and who she was with. Here. In bed, in paradise, with a stranger. With him . . . not his twin.

Jillian had awakened from dreams, and even though Chase saw such brilliant clarity, she was surely lost in a dream still. Or perhaps what filled her eyes with such hopefulness was the memory of six years before, in this same bed, when she had made love for the first time with his brother.

Before he met her, Chase assumed that Jillian would be like the women he had always known. He had planned to seduce her as he had seduced them, to entice her with his masterful sensuality until she pleaded with him to satisfy the powerful desires he had awakened. And then, at her moment of greatest vulnerability, when he had absolute control, he would seduce the confession of murder from her.

Yes, Chase, yes, I tried to kill you! But I failed, didn't I? And I'm so happy that I did, so happy that we are here together again and that your talented hands and lips are caressing me . . .

But Jillian Kincaid was not like any other woman Chase had ever known. He had expected confidence, and selfishness, and defiance. But from the very beginning she had been only uncertain, and generous, and kind.

And if her enchanting innocence was all merely a ruse, the most clever of traps? Then it was she who had won, she who had so masterfully seduced—and he who was the most vulnerable.

Jillian was lost in a wondrous dream, or a magnificent memory, but with glowing green eyes and softly trembling lips she invited him to join her in the dream, to make new memories with her, now, *now.*

As Chase's lips greeted hers, he thought, This would drive even the most shadowed memory into glorious sunlight. If memories were recalled most vividly when they had been recorded by the senses, then the extraordinary sensations of touching the smooth satin of her skin, and tasting the warm sweetness of her mouth, and inhaling the intoxicating fragrances of gardenia and coconut in her freshly shampooed hair, and hearing her soft sighs of desire, and seeing that desire mirrored in her radiant emerald eyes would surely awaken even the most quiescent memory.

No matter how dark the shadows, the wonder of kissing Jillian, simply kissing her, would instantly and joyously heal whatever trauma had driven them into hiding. Kissing Jillian sparked no memories for Chase Carlton, of course, but as her generous mouth greeted his, welcoming him with passion and joy, Chase felt a healing too . . . a miraculous soothing of the wounds of his heart, seemingly incurable wounds from immeasurable trauma, balmed now, healing now, bathed in a goodness that came from within her and overflowed to him.

If this was a dream, he wished never to awaken. If this was a cruel treachery, then he wanted to be trapped in the enchanting web forever.

Forever. Chase wanted to make love to her slowly, forever, but his own desire *and hers* were compelling them swiftly to greater closeness. Her delicate fingers found his chest beneath his pajamas, and his lean hands began to search with trembling wonder the secrets of satin hidden beneath her modest cotton gown.

And then she stiffened.

"What?" he asked softly.

"I didn't bring my diaphragm."

Her eyes filled with apology at her confession, and her passion-flushed cheeks became even rosier. Chase had known from the moment that she had withdrawn cotton not silk from the suitcase that Jillian had not planned to seduce him. She had spent the past ten days preparing his favorite meals in hope that the wonderful and once-familiar tastes and fragrances would spark memories; but she had not *planned* to offer him the greatest sensuous feast of all.

Why not? Chase knew the answer: because she didn't have the confidence of a seductress, nor the confident belief of a wife that the memory of making love to her would be the most powerful memory of all. Jillian wasn't confident of her allure, or its memory, and there was more: the plain little girl who had become beautiful through tragedy—but who had still planned a life dedicated to her students and her books—didn't make love casually, not with a stranger, not even when that stranger looked exactly like the man she had loved.

Jillian hadn't planned to make love with him in Bora Bora. She had packed neither the provocative negligee nor her diaphragm. But as she had awakened from her dreams, Chase had awakened her desire . . . and he saw that desire still in the eyes that now filled with soft apology.

Jillian wanted to make love with the tall, dark stranger who had brought her to paradise—but she wouldn't make love without protection.

Why not? Chase didn't know, but he saw clues to the answer, worrisome clues, as the apology in her eyes transformed to sadness and pain—and fear.

Oh, no, his heart whispered in silent protest. Were there deadly secrets after all? Was his twin's marriage actually so deeply troubled that the bride refused to bear his children even now, even when her husband had been miraculously returned to her from a watery grave?

Oh, Jillian, am I wrong about your innocence? Have you so artfully blurred every instinct for perceiving evil that I ever possessed? Is your shy and generous loveliness merely a magnificent act, the most treacherously clever of all disguises?

"Would it be such a tragedy for you to get pregnant?" he demanded finally. All softness was gone from his voice, and the blue in his eyes—the brightest blue Jillian had ever seen—was now lost in dark, opaque, and angry gray. The coldness of his demand caused a mist of tears in her anguished eyes. Conquering a sudden powerful urge to comfort her, Chase commanded with even more chilling harshness, "Tell me, Jillian."

"You didn't want children, Chase."

"*I* didn't?"

"No." Tell him everything, Jillian's heart pleaded. Tell him how you felt about what he did to you. Even though his eyes are so very angry now, give him a chance to be gentle, to understand the pain he caused you. Allow him to explain if he can. "In the first few years of our marriage, you made it a point to attend all the pageants at the school where I teach. You were so wonderful with the children there. You even arranged field trips for them to the studio. You seemed to have a natural gift with children, an ability to sense what was important to them. Do you remember that?"

I know about children, Chase thought. I know how sensitive and fragile they are, even the ones that seem so tough. And I know what is important to them: to be safe, to be loved.

Somehow the twin who had been safe and loved knew that too. Chase answered finally, quietly, "Maybe . . . vaguely."

"Well, you really were wonderful with them. Which is why I assumed that you would want children of your own." Jillian drew a soft breath and gazed steadily at the dark gray eyes. "But when you learned that I was pregnant, you became very angry."

"Angry? Why?"

"I don't know why, Chase. You never told me."

As Chase saw in her eyes that she was searching still for the answer, he felt a rush of anger toward his brother. Since the discovery that he had been a twin, the emptiness and horror of his own life had at long last been explained. Chase Carlton's life had been loveless and brutal so that the life of Chase Kincaid could be good, happy, *perfect*. Chase Carlton had been the dark twin, his heart cruelly indifferent to the women with whom he shared the pleasures of passion; and his brother had been golden, his heart filled with everything the dark twin didn't possess—kindness, generosity, and love.

They were the tarnished twin and the glittering twin, and Chase had accepted without bitterness that it had been his destiny to live a lonely life of horror so that at least one of them could live a life of dreams. But was he now about to learn that his golden twin, too, had been tarnished?

Chase Kincaid should not have been cruel to the lovely little girl whose life had been irrevocably changed by a tragic car accident. The man with the gift for dreams should not have issued a dream-shattering command to his bride. Even cruel and heartless Chase Carlton—*especially* Chase Carlton—would never have given such a devastating order.

"You had an abortion."

"No, and you never suggested that I have one."

"No?" The flicker of relief Chase felt vanished swiftly. There was no baby, which meant—what? That his twin had abandoned his newborn in a cold, dark church? "What happened?"

"Even though you never told me why you were so upset about my pregnancy, you eventually apologized for your anger—and sometimes you even seemed happy about the baby." Jillian paused. Then, with immense sadness, she said quietly, "At the beginning of the fifth month, I miscarried our baby, our daughter. You were in Africa at the time overseeing the filming of *Savanna.*"

"But I came home right away." *He came home to be with you, to comfort you, to share the loss with you.*

"No. You were in a remote part of Kenya. It took Brad almost two days even to reach you. When he suggested that you fly home, you asked him what would be the point."

No! Chase's heart protested. My twin could not have been so cruel. All cruelties—both given and received—belong to me, not to him.

"But you wanted me to come home."

"I wanted that very much."

"And Brad told me that you wanted me to be with you?"

"Yes. He even offered to fly to Africa to take your place."

"You're absolutely certain that he told me?"

"Why wouldn't he?"

"I don't know," Chase murmured. *I'm just searching for a way to preserve my shining image of my golden twin, a way not to hate the brother I never knew but want to love.* "When did I come home?"

"Six weeks later. We didn't talk about my miscarriage then, or ever, and you never mentioned it in the letters you wrote to me from Africa. It was as if the pregnancy had never happened, which was what you wanted from the beginning. We never talked about having children after that, but you were always very careful to make certain that we used birth control."

No wonder Jillian's family was so protective of her. No wonder he had sensed such ambivalence about his miraculous reappearance in her life. Chase's heart pounded with sudden fury at the golden twin who was supposed to have been everything the dark twin wasn't but whose callous treatment of his wife far surpassed the worst Chase Carlton would ever offer; and he felt angry, too, with himself for his own cruelty to Jillian, for pushing her, for making her cry.

Why was he so angry? Jillian wondered as she saw the black rage in his eyes, its immense power rippling the strong muscles of his neck and jaw. Was it because of how he had behaved in a lifetime he couldn't even remember? Or because she had revealed those unhappy memories to him? Or was his dark anger caused by all the memories of their love suddenly coming out of the shadows—the most vivid memory being the last one—the devastating words she had spoken to him the night he disappeared?

Jillian didn't know what had caused his anger, but the restless torment she saw was terribly, painfully familiar. She realized then that what Brad had said was true. Even though the Chase who had returned to her seemed far gentler than the one who had disappeared, his *essence* wouldn't change. He would remain the man he had always been—the man who kept the most important truths of his heart hidden from her.

In another moment, without another word, after hurriedly

exchanging his cotton pajamas for his swim trunks, he would leave. Chase knew where the swim trunks were, of course, exactly which drawer of the bamboo chest, and now his surprising and so nice offer to unpack for them became simply a means for him to make his swift escape.

Chase would change his clothes and leave, escaping from her, not trusting her to help him with his torment. He would dive from the porch of the romantic bungalow into the warm aquamarine waters, swimming as far as he could—and then even further; and when at last he returned, they wouldn't speak again of the restless rage that had driven him away.

And it would begin again, the carefully concealed truths that once before had created a wedge between them, a dark and depthless abyss which all her love could not bridge. With the realization Jillian felt a sharp, familiar pain. Knife-like and piercing, it cut her heart in two and severed her foolish hope that she and Chase might have had a second chance.

Right on cue, Chase left the bed and strode swiftly to the chest of drawers. But instead of opening the drawer that held his neatly folded swim trunks, he simply stood, his back to her, stiff, taut, and very still. Even beneath the loose cotton of the pajamas, Jillian saw the tension in his strong, lean body . . . a body on the very verge of explosion . . . a noble animal mercilessly caged and desperate for his freedom.

Explode at me, Chase! Find freedom by talking to me. Please. *Please.* It was a silent prayer that Jillian had prayed a thousand times, and now in this second—and last—chance with him, she struggled for the courage to whisper the words aloud.

But her courage was gone. Crushed by the heavy weight of memories, Jillian's energy was now already focused on the immense task of steeling her wounded heart, preparing herself to smile bravely when he returned . . . to hide her own pain . . . to forgive him for not sharing his . . . and, as always, to go on.

In her mind, Chase had already left the bungalow, and she was concentrating on the future, when he would return.

But then Chase turned toward her, and his jaw rippled still with barely controlled rage, and his handsome face held an expression of anguished nobility, but there was exquisite gentleness in the gray eyes as he approached, and then sat beside her on the bed, and then, so tenderly, touched her tear-dampened cheeks.

"I'm so sorry," he whispered, his voice hoarse with emotion. "I'm so sorry that you were hurt then—and now."

"Chase," Jillian whispered. "Thank you."

"Don't thank me," he countered swiftly, harshly. And then, because the harshness clouded the magnificent hope he had seen in her surprised emerald eyes he asked gently, "Why in the world would you thank me?"

"Because even now, even after all this time, it helps me to hear that you are sorry."

"How long ago was it?"

"It will be three years in October—the seventh." Jillian tilted her auburn head and asked quietly, "You've apologized, and I can tell that you mean it, but you don't remember any of it, do you?"

"No."

Jillian's expression didn't waver at that truth, grateful still for his apology, however belated. But she should have received it three years before, and it should have been an impassioned plea to be forgiven for the unforgivable. Chase's anger at his brother's cruelty returned in a powerful rush, compelling impulsive words to his lips, "Why did you stay with him after that?"

Him. It was a monumental slip. Chase's heart had made it happen, of course, an emotional wish to dissociate himself from the man who had hurt her so deeply. As he waited for Jillian to react to his words, his renegade—and so foolish—heart pounded with even more wishes. Tell her all your truths, and about the kind of man *you* are: a lonely man who despite the horrors and lovelessness of his own life would never have hurt her as he did.

"Because I loved him . . . you," Jillian answered quietly.

Then, smiling softly at his surprised gray eyes, she explained, "Sometimes I think of you—of the you who you were then—as 'him' too."

"You do? At the party at your parents' you seemed so confident of who I am. Was that only because of the way I look?"

"No. In fact, sometimes you look very different from the way I remember you." Jillian shrugged softly. "But I know it's you because of what's inside. I'd seen only glimpses of your gentleness before. I don't know why you hid it from me, but you did. Anyway, I knew it was there. I knew how tender and gentle and kind you were."

"And you've seen glimpses of that since my return?" Glimpses of tenderness? Gentleness? Kindness? In *me?*

"Oh, yes, and much more than glimpses," Jillian answered, seeing the gentleness now with brilliant clarity in the gray—no, the wondrously blue, blue eyes. "I know you don't remember about the baby we lost, but I think that the sadness you feel in hearing about her now is what you must have felt then, even though you never shared it with me."

"I'm sure that's what he, what *I,* felt."

"Do you have any idea why he . . . why you . . . didn't want to have children?"

Chase hesitated a moment, and when he answered it was for himself, truths from the wounded heart of Chase Carlton.

"Maybe I was afraid of the enormous responsibility. Maybe I didn't believe I had enough to offer and that no matter how hard I tried, I couldn't be certain of protecting a child from life's sadnesses and tragedies."

"You did seem afraid when I first told you," Jillian said, remembering now the dark gray fear that had preceded by several heartbeats the smoky anger. "But I was afraid too, Chase. The thought of my child, my daughter, grieving for me the way I grieved for my mother terrified me. But I'd decided that together we did have enough to give, and that one of us would always be there to love her and cherish her and protect her. My pregnancy wasn't an accident. I know I should have told you that I was trying to get pregnant, but I thought it would be a wonderful surprise, something I could give you that would make you so happy."

But Chase Kincaid had been angry, not happy, and he had so cruelly refused even to share his wife's grief when the pregnancy she had wanted so much ended in miscarriage.

So what if, right now, Jillian Kincaid confessed to Chase Carlton that the hurt inflicted on her by his twin had festered, a deep and aching wound which had finally erupted in an explosion of frustration and pain on a fog-misted night in the midst of a slumbering sea? What if she admitted that on sudden impulse she had thrust the boom at him, not to kill him, but yes—*yes!*—to hurt him, and to get his attention at last? And what if she added further that when she saw the extent of the injury she had caused, she decided to let him sleep forever in the sea he loved more than her?

Would he blame her? Chase wondered. Would he see that she spent the rest of her life in prison when all she wanted—a dream they both shared—was to be loved? No, he realized, he wouldn't blame her at all.

Chase should have told her the truth, all of it, right then, because even if Jillian Kincaid had killed his brother, *she was innocent.* The dangerous chill of evil that he had felt on the deck of *Sea Goddess,* the ice that had seemed to come almost from within, was his twin's heartprint after all, and his impression that the danger was *for* Jillian, not because of her, was right too—for the great harm the golden twin had caused her heart.

Chase should have told Jillian Kincaid all those truths then.

And after he was done, he should have left her forever.

But Jillian spoke first.

"I wanted you to kiss me, Chase," she said softly, bravely. "But . . . I guess . . . maybe it was a little too soon. Maybe we need to learn more about each other first."

Learn more about each other. The words made Chase's heart race with hope. Learn more about each other, Jillian said, *not* learn more about the past. As if the past no longer existed. As if what was important now was the present and the future. As if what truly mattered were Jillian Kincaid and Chase Carlton— the woman who had once loved a man who had hidden his gentleness from her . . . and the man who had never known gentleness in his life until now.

Without another word Chase offered her his hand, and she gently imprisoned it between both of hers, and that was the way they slept, hands entwined, a peaceful sleep filled with dreams and hope.

Chapter Twenty-Four

For that week in paradise Jillian and Chase lived only in the present, sharing with reverent wonder the splendor that surrounded them: the red-orange brilliance of the fire trees against the azure sky . . . the breathtaking sunsets of mauve and pink and purple and gold . . . the magnificent treasures that lived in the warm aquamarine waters.

They spent hours snorkling in the lagoon, marveling at the sea's silent yet vibrant world of color and activity. Since her accident, Jillian had been unable to run, or jog, or even walk for long distances without pain. But she could swim. Indeed, Jillian Kincaid was a very strong swimmer.

Strong enough to easily swim ashore from a fog-shrouded sailboat. The unwelcome thought came without warning. Chase banished it swiftly, ferociously.

Jillian and Chase talked about the sea and the flowers and the sunsets and the stars, and with those honest words about their reverence for nature, and with the smiles and glances that embellished the words, they learned a great deal about each other. Jillian learned that Chase was all she had always believed him to be—and more: more sensitive, more thoughtful, more gentle than she had ever dared to imagine. And Chase learned, for the first time in his entire life, what happiness felt like, what peace felt like, what love felt like.

Chase and Jillian had both known great loneliness. For Chase it had been a lifetime companion, relentless and ever present. For Jillian the loneliness visited only intermittently, when she had lost her mother, and then her best friend, and for the past six years, when she had loved so desperately and with such futility. During their week in paradise Jillian and Chase didn't talk about the loneliness they each had known; but if they had, it would have been a conversation about something that had existed in the past, a dark, heavy cloak they both had once worn but which now was gone.

They touched often that week, their caresses as natural and gentle, and as intoxicating and warm, as the balmy sea breezes that caressed their skin. Sometimes neither remembered quite when or how their fingers became entwined, but once discovered, the realization was welcomed with soft smiles, not sudden self-consciousness. Fingers became entwined; and salty drops that spilled onto cheeks and lashes from sea-dampened hair were affectionately dabbed away; and beneath the starlit heavens, as they marveled at the twinkling of an infinity of suns, his arms curled around her slender waist; and when they slept, such peaceful sleep, they touched always.

They kissed too, kisses that were delicate and innocent and chaste; whispered kisses that seemed to say that there were wonders enough in paradise, the magnificent discoveries of their hearts and souls. They would leisurely savor those wonders for now, treasuring each one and postponing the joyous discovery of their passion until later.

Later . . . when they returned from paradise to reality. When they left the uncluttered magic of the present and reentered the world filled with the shadowy secrets of the past and the great uncertainties of the future. For the week in Bora Bora Chase had been himself, a gentle and loving self he had never before known. The quiet truths spoken from his heart had been welcomed by hers, and the love in her radiant eyes had been for him, not for his golden twin . . . hadn't it?

Yes, his heart answered. She cares about you, *you.*

And how are you rewarding that care? a voice taunted. By deceiving her. The deception had been justifiable once, a necessary ploy to entrap a murderess, but now it was purely selfish, the greediness of a starving and lonely heart.

It was true, of course. If he could stay in paradise with Jillian forever, basking in the warmth of her loveliness, living this magnificent deception, he would. And she would too, he bravely told the taunting voice. Her eyes had been so joyful here, so free of uncertainty.

But Chase Carlton and Jillian Kincaid couldn't live in this magical paradise forever, and Chase knew that Jillian deserved all the truths. He would tell her, he promised the taunting voice. On their return to Los Angeles, after he stood once again on the deck of *Sea Goddess* and confronted anew the dangerous ghost of his twin, he would tell her everything.

And if he didn't survive the confrontation with his brother's ghost? If, even from his watery grave, the golden twin refused to share any of his treasures, especially the greatest treasure of all?

Then he would have had this week in paradise with Jillian. It was already far more happiness than Chase Carlton had ever imagined.

He gave her the earrings just after they boarded Qantas's Thursday morning flight from Papeete to Los Angeles. They were Tahitian pearls, lustrous, luminous, and perfectly matched.

"Each pearl has its own tiny rainbows," Jillian marveled as she gazed at the play of color in the iridescent white. "Thank you, Chase. I love them." *I love you.*

Qantas Flight 103 from Papeete arrived at LAX exactly on time—at 6:45 P.M. On the way to Clairmont, Jillian and Chase stopped briefly in Brentwood to pick up Annie at Claudia and

Edward's. Then they were home, and it felt like paradise still, as if all the magic had traveled with them.

Tonight Jillian and I will sleep in the same bed here, Chase thought. And tomorrow afternoon, after Jillian and Brad and I have had our luncheon meeting with Peter Dalton, I'll go—by myself—to *Sea Goddess*. And tomorrow night I will tell her all the truths.

And if she forgave him? If her emerald eyes welcomed him still? Then Chase Carlton and Jillian Kincaid would resume their own bold journeys of the heart.

They spent a quiet evening watching the summer sun set over the Pacific, and playing with a lively Annie, and smiling, and touching, and making silent promises to make the magic feel so welcome here, so comfortable, that it would never leave.

"Probably Brad," Jillian said softly as a ringing phone intruded but didn't shatter the magic.

"Probably," Chase agreed as he watched Jillian move toward the phone. Undoubtedly, he amended silently and with a rush of annoyance. Brad would be calling under the pretext of making certain that they had arrived home as scheduled and hadn't forgotten the one o'clock luncheon meeting with Peter Dalton at the Hotel Bel-Air, but he would also be calling, Chase knew, to see if there had been any major breakthroughs in his extraordinarily recalcitrant memory. Chase knew that his annoyance with Brad was irrational. It was both natural and loving for Brad to hope that his cousin's memories of the past would return. Brad had no way of knowing that *this* cousin wished to live only in the present . . . and the future.

The smile of affection that had touched Jillian's lips as she anticipated speaking to Brad vanished as soon as she heard the caller's voice. Her smile faded, and the color drained from her cheeks, and when she turned to Chase, her delicate hand wrapped tightly over the receiver, he saw that the radiant glow that had lighted her brilliant emerald eyes for the past week was gone as well.

"It's Nicole Haviland."

Chase recognized the name at once. Nicole Haviland was one of Hollywood's top stars, a ravishingly beautiful embodiment of talent and confidence and glamour. Had the life—and hope—not drained from Jillian's face, Chase would have assumed that Nicole was calling about studio business.

But there was death in Jillian's lovely face, and her teeth tugged mercilessly at her lower lip as if trying to prevent herself from uttering aloud the words she did not want to say, the memories she did not want to reveal.

Chase knew the words just moments before her soft voice finally spoke them.

"She was . . . is . . . your mistress."

I'm so sorry, his gray eyes gently told her. I'm so very sorry that he betrayed your love—again.

Chase did not want to speak to the Academy Award-winning actress. He wanted only to hold Jillian, to comfort and love her. But Nicole Haviland was waiting, an undeniable presence on the other end of the phone that Jillian held in her hand.

Jillian's eyes fell away from Chase's gaze as he took the receiver, and the fingers that had found his so often—and with such brave wonder—during the past week managed now to avoid even the slightest brush.

Then she left, to give him privacy in which to speak to his mistress, and Annie, who might otherwise have stayed with him, padded along in a somber effort to comfort Jillian as they vanished into the kitchen.

Within a breathlessly seductive syllable, Nicole Haviland was familiar to Chase. She was like all the other confident, demanding, beautiful women who had been his lovers, women with whom he had shared every intimacy—except love.

"I can't believe that you haven't called me, Chase!" Nicole's sexy voice both purred and growled, and Chase could easily envision the petulant and seductive pout on her famous face. "I've been on location in Spain and I didn't even know that you were *alive* until my return last week. By then you'd already left for Bora Bora."

"How did you know about Bora Bora?"

"Brad, of course."

"He told you when I was returning too?"

"Naturally, and I've been counting the seconds."

And you didn't let many seconds pass between my arrival home and your call, did you? Chase thought angrily. His anger, he realized, was more with Brad than with Nicole. True, since learning about his twin's unforgivable treatment of Jillian after her miscarriage, Chase had a heightened understanding of Brad's protectiveness of her. But telling Nicole precisely when he was due home from Bora Bora, and knowing full well that she would call, revealed just how far Brad's protectiveness of Jillian went. It was abundantly clear that Brad Lancaster had decided that the relationship between Jillian and Chase Kincaid should not be given a second chance.

Chase fought the anger he felt toward his cousin with the truth: on the topic of Jillian and Chase Kincaid, he and Brad were, in fact, in complete accord. Even before this call from his brother's mistress, Chase too had decided that his twin's betrayal of Jillian's love was unforgivable. The golden twin did not deserve a second chance with Jillian Kincaid . . . but what about the dark twin? What about the twin with the gift for evil who, because of Jillian, had discovered the gift of love as well?

"I'm sure that Brad also told you that I remember virtually nothing of the past thirty-four years."

"Of course he told me." Nicole's voice held the same note of skepticism that Chase had heard in Brad's voice about the remarkable extent of his memory loss. Then, purring softly, seductively, she promised, "I can make you remember me, *us,* Chase. Come over here right now and I guarantee that I can cure your amnesia—at least for the most memorable aspects of your past."

Nicole's offer was made with absolute confidence, the certain knowledge that the sensual pleasures of making love with her were quite unforgettable. It was such a contrast to Jillian, who had made no such provocative offer, not even shyly, as if she knew that she was forgettable—as if his twin had convinced her of that.

"Come *now,* Chase," Nicole urged. "I'm wearing the black silk teddy you've always—"

"No," he answered harshly. "I'm not coming over, not now, not ever."

"You bastard," Nicole whispered.

The softly hissed epithet from a beautiful woman was very familiar to Chase Carlton, and now he heard in Nicole's confident proclamation that the heartless indifference that had sparked such a comment to him aptly characterized his brother as well.

"Some things don't change, Nicole."

"I guess not. Your loss, Chase."

Nicole severed the connection with a petulant slam. Chase replaced the receiver slowly, steeling his heart to meet the wounded emerald eyes . . . if she would even look at him.

Jillian was seated at the kitchen table, head bent, back stiff. When she sensed his presence, her back stiffened even more.

"I'm sorry," Chase said.

"I know."

In Bora Bora, when he had apologized for his twin's inexplicable refusal to share with her the loss of their baby, Jillian had accepted his apology with gratitude. It was an apology she had always needed and never before heard. But now, as Chase apologized for his twin's infidelity, Jillian's answer told him that this was an apology she knew very well.

"Will you look at me?"

In response to his gentle plea, the auburn head lifted slowly, regally, an immense effort against the heavy weight of sadness that bent it.

"It meant nothing . . . she meant nothing." Chase saw that these words, too, were familiar. "I've told you that before?"

"Yes."

"When?" Chase pressed as he saw sudden shadows of fear. "When did I tell you, Jillian?"

"On the night of your accident."

"We talked about my affair with Nicole on that night?"

"About your affair, yes. I didn't know until after your disappearance that the woman was Nicole."

"How did you find out?" *Did Brad tell you?* Did he think it would make the loss of your unfaithful husband more bearable, not a loss at all?

"She came to see me a few days after the police suspended the search. I guess it was important for her to have me know how you felt about her." Jillian shrugged softly, a small, ineffectual gesture against the enormous weight of even more painful memories. "She told me that you loved her and that you were planning to leave me and marry her. She wasn't your first mistress, Chase, both she and I knew that. But she said she was different from the others, that your feelings about her were different."

"But they weren't, she wasn't," Chase countered. *You are the one who is so very different.* "I wasn't going to leave you for her. You knew that. You just said that I told you on the night of the accident that she meant nothing to me. Did you believe me?"

"Yes, I believed you," Jillian said quietly. *You weren't going to leave me, Chase, but I was going to leave you. I had to, I was dying, you were killing me.*

Jillian tried to prevent the memory of that night from showing in her eyes, but she knew that the searching gray saw something—her fear perhaps, or perhaps her attempt to hide it.

"Jillian?"

She couldn't talk about that night, not now, not yet, but he was looking at her with the tenderness with which he had gazed at her in paradise, welcoming her, wanting to hear the inner-most secrets and torments of her heart. Jillian couldn't tell Chase the secrets of the night he disappeared, but she bravely asked the tender eyes about another torment that had lived for so long, in anguished silence, deep inside.

"Why did you need other women, Chase? I know you don't remember the details, but you were able to tell me your fears about having children without specifically remembering our baby." Jillian paused, then offered the explanation she had al-ways believed. "I've always thought it was because I was so . . . inexperienced. I thought you must have wanted someone more confident, more provocative and daring—"

"Oh, Jillian, *no,*" Chase whispered hoarsely, stopping her, refusing to permit her to blame herself for her husband's re-peated betrayals. She needed an answer to her question, she deserved one, and after a moment he gave her the only one he could, the truth from his own life of passionate yet meaningless affairs. "Maybe I felt unworthy of you. Maybe I felt such an emptiness in my heart that I didn't believe I could ever love or be loved. Maybe it was easier to live that self-fulfilling prophecy, to prove my unworthiness by betraying you rather than by trying to love you and failing."

His honest words only caused confusion on her lovely face. Of course, Chase thought. What did he expect? The belief that he was unworthy of Jillian's love was surely *not* the reason his golden twin had had affairs. The man whose life had been an overflowing fountain of wishes granted and dreams fulfilled had simply been cavalier with his wife's precious love. To the brother who had everything, Jillian had merely been another jewel in the glittering treasure trove of his life. The twin with the gift for dreams, it seemed, didn't know a dream when he was living it.

Chase Kincaid had been carelessly cruel with Jillian's love, hurting her repeatedly, asking her forgiveness, and confident that she always would forgive. But on a fog-shrouded spring night, had she at last refused to forgive him any longer? Had her deeply wounded heart finally been unable to endure further agony?

To the woman who was so obviously hiding something very important about that night, Chase commanded gently, "Tell me what happened the night I disappeared, Jillian."

Unmistakable fear flickered in her emerald eyes before her head bent again, concealing the apprehensive green behind a thick veil of glittering auburn.

"We . . . argued," she answered finally, speaking to the delicate hands that were curled tightly, bloodlessly, on the table. "And then you left to go sailing."

"You didn't go with me?" *Look at me!* "You weren't on the boat too?"

"No, I was here." Jillian didn't look up, but she stood up. "I'm sorry, Chase, but I'm very tired—and I want to be well rested for the meeting with Peter Dalton tomorrow."

"Okay," he agreed, standing too.

He wanted to touch her face as he had so often in the past week.

But they weren't in paradise any longer.

The past had returned with a vengeance.

And the magic was shattered.

"She looked so happy," Claudia reminded her frowning husband. "They both did. Edward, you saw that!"

"Yes, I did," Edward admitted, smiling then for his wife. "You were right, Claudia. It was good for them to go to Bora Bora."

Claudia's heart raced with hope at his words and at the gentle apology in his eyes. Did that mean Edward had finally forgiven her for not telling him in advance about the trip? Even though he understood that Jillian had asked Claudia to keep it a secret, wanting to make the announcement herself, it had been abundantly clear that Edward believed she should have told him—forwarned him—anyway.

Because, Claudia knew, Edward believed that there should be no secrets between husband and wife—ever. Quickly, too quickly, the heart that raced with hope began to stumble. Trying to rescue it, she asked softly, "Chase and Jillian seem to be starting over, don't you think?"

"Yes," he answered, but with his reply the frown returned to his face. "But what's going to happen when his memory returns?"

"Maybe it never will. Maybe the past is over. Isn't that the way it should be? Shouldn't all that matters be the present and the future?"

"Maybe that's the way it should be, Claudia, but the past is the foundation."

Claudia shivered at the ominous warning in her husband's words, fighting her own fear of what Edward would do if he ever discovered the quicksand of deceit upon which she had built their love.

"Everything's going to be fine for them, Edward. Everything is going to be wonderful."

"You know I hope so." The handsome face became more somber than Claudia had seen it since the first day they met, when Edward had flown to San Francisco to ask her to help his beloved and so damaged daughter. With quiet passion he added, "But for his sake, Chase had better not hurt Jillian ever again."

Chapter Twenty-Five

Jillian had wanted to get a good night's sleep, to be well rested for the day in which the words she had crafted about the brave and treacherous journeys of the heart would begin their own journey toward life on the silver screen.

But the moment she appeared in the kitchen, Chase knew that she hadn't slept at all. Her beautiful dark-circled eyes gave eloquent testimony to her sleeplessness.

Chase hadn't slept either, of course. He had spent the night in his twin's study, playing the guitar, hoping that he would look up and see her in the open doorway.

"Good morning," he said softly. *I'm so sorry that he hurt you . . . that I hurt you.*

"Good morning," Jillian echoed, smiling shyly at the gentle gray eyes that greeted her. Neither refreshing sleep nor wonderful dreams had balmed the wounds that had been reopened. She had been forced to balm them herself, an act of sheer will, blanketing them with protective layers of love and hope. She wanted to keep trying, she had decided. Even though the memories were so painful, she wanted their love still, *more,* because the week in Bora Bora was more wonderful than any other week she and Chase had ever spent together.

"Sit down, Jillian, and I'll make you a bowl of oatmeal."

"I think I'll just have coffee, thanks. I'm a little too nervous—too anxious—to eat."

"Because of the meeting with Peter Dalton?"

Because of that . . . because of us. "In the world of filmmaking, writers are the lowest in the hierarchy and directors are at the top. Peter has won Academy Awards for writing as well as directing, so it's very possible that he'll want to rewrite every word of the screenplay to conform to his vision."

"Surely the people providing the money for making the film have some say over what the director does. Surely Brad will intercede." Surely Brad will protect you—*as always.*

"Brad will defer to Peter. Brad's genius is in the marketing of the finished product, not in its creation."

"And what about me?" Chase asked, even though he already knew the answer. Chase Kincaid had inherited his father's—their father's—creative genius. "Did I make a habit of permitting even the best directors to compromise my vision?"

"No." Jillian laughed softly. "You absolutely never let that happen."

"Then it won't happen this time, Jillian," Chase promised solemnly, seeing her obvious surprise at his pledge of support.

Why wouldn't she be surprised? he asked himself. His golden twin had an impressive history of letting her down.

Chase poured the first cup of coffee for both of them, and Jillian had just gotten up to pour the second when the phone rang. Even though she was closest to it, Chase made a move to answer, to protect her from the sultry voice of yet another mistress.

But he was stopped by her brave smile. She would answer it, the smile told him. Chase smiled in return, even though he felt a rush of anger at his brother: Jillian should not have to dig deep for courage to answer the telephone in her own home.

The relief and affection in her voice told Chase at once that the call was from family. The caller was Brad, and for a moment that could have lasted forever, Chase heard the softness in Jillian's voice as she told his cousin how wonderful Bora Bora had been. The moment passed quickly, the conversation obviously shifted by Brad to a topic that caused surprise, then disappointment, and then, just before the conversation ended, a new smile.

"Peter can't make it to lunch today after all," Jillian explained to Chase after she replaced the receiver. "He's been delayed on a shoot in Alaska. He and Brad have tentatively rescheduled for Tuesday."

How long had Brad known that the luncheon meeting wasn't going to happen? Chase wondered, wondering, too, if part of what had caused Jillian's disappointment had been the same thought that now danced tauntingly in his own mind: We didn't need to come back last night. We could have stayed in paradise four more days.

Jillian's disappointment had eventually given way to a beautiful smile. When she spoke again, Chase learned the reason for it.

"Brad invited us to join him for dinner tonight. He's made seven o'clock reservations at the Hotel Bel-Air and he's invited Dad and Claudia and Stephanie and Jack as well."

Just as Chase was certain that the cancellation of the meeting with Peter Dalton was *not* last-minute, he knew that the Friday evening reservations at one of Los Angeles's most popular restaurants had surely been made long before this morning.

Jillian said softly, "You're scowling, Chase."

"I guess I was just trying to decide if Brad is friend or foe." And if he has even more surprises planned for tonight. Nicole Haviland—or another sultry mistress—dining at a nearby table perhaps?

"Friend," Jillian assured swiftly. "Brad loves you very much."

"And what about us? How does Brad feel about us?"

"He cares about both of us. He wants both of us to be happy."

"But not necessarily together."

"Brad has had an insider's view of our marriage, and some of what he has seen has worried him, but he truly wants what's best for us. We don't have to do dinner tonight, though, if you'd rather not."

"No, it's fine." Chase smiled reassurance. "It should be a very pleasant evening with family and friends."

Chase had planned to return to *Sea Goddess* after the luncheon meeting with Peter Dalton. But he postponed his solitary trip to Marina del Rey, deciding instead to spend the entire day at Clairmont with Jillian and Annie, hoping, *hoping* to erase the uneasy memory of Nicole's phone call and to restore the wondrous memories of Bora Bora.

Chase made oatmeal for Jillian after all, and then they played catch with Annie, and when she had had enough they went through the week's mail, and then unpacked their suitcases, and then watered the roses. They lingered over each event of the quiet day, as if not wanting it to end until they came up with another project to do—together.

After lunch, with gentle reluctance, Chase suggested to the fatigued—but more hopeful?—Jillian that she rest before the dinner party. He could have gone to the marina then, but he remained at Clairmont, a shepherd ever vigilant over his sleeping flock . . . over Annie, who slumbered contentedly at his feet in the living room and Jillian, who slept peacefully upstairs.

During the week in Bora Bora, Chase had seen Jillian in shorts, and in modest one-piece swimsuits, and in brightly colored sundresses, and in the demure cream and violet nightgown. She had worn her hair long and free there, a loose flow of molten lava that glittered in the tropical sunshine and shimmered beneath the starlit sky.

When she appeared fifteen minutes before they were due at

the Hotel Bel-Air, she wore elegant green silk, and her long firelit hair flowed as it had in Bora Bora, but now it was swept softly off her face to reveal the pearl earrings he had given her.

The twin pearls shone with their tiny rainbows, and her emerald eyes were shining too.

"You look wonderful, Jillian."

"Oh! Thank you." Then bravely, almost flirting with her handsome husband, she said, "You look wonderful too."

As he had waited for her, hoping she would be rested and smiling, Chase's eyes had been the color of the impeccably tailored charcoal suit he wore. But when he saw the rainbows in the pearls, and the promises of rainbows in her eyes, the gray had begun to yield to blue . . . and with her words the transformation to pure blue, happy blue, was complete.

"Ready?"

"Ready."

When they reached the carport and Chase moved to open the passenger door of the Legend for her, Jillian hesitated, her expression thoughtful as her gaze drifted to the Ferrari.

Chase knew her thoughts and awaited the results of her silent debate with breath-held hope. One night beneath the stars in Bora Bora he had gently guessed the reason that she avoided riding in the Ferrari: because the small car felt to her like the crushed metal coffin her mother's station wagon had become on that long-ago night of rain and death. Yes, Jillian had confirmed quietly, that was the reason.

Now she was thinking about getting into the car that she so feared, and now Chase sent silent a command, Trust me, Jillian. I will take care of you. I promise.

Jillian answered the silent command with a brave and hopeful smile as she suggested softly, "Why don't we take your car?"

The birthday gift that Victor Kincaid had given his golden son was a dream, another in Chase Kincaid's vast collection of dreams. The vintage Ferrari appeared to be in mint condition, meticulously maintained. But, Chase wondered as he put the key into the ignition, had his brother treated this rare gem as carelessly as he had treated the most precious treasure of all?

No, he decided as the car responded promptly and with the softest of purrs. *This* dream had been carefully tended.

As they glided out of the carport and onto the white-graveled driveway, Chase smiled at the only dream that should have mattered . . . and she smiled in return, trusting him, overcoming her fears and her nightmares, bravely beginning yet again.

Then they were leaving the white gravel of Clairmont, and then turning onto the steep winding road that would take them from their hilltop perch to the Hotel Bel-Air, and then . . .

Then suddenly and horribly they were in the midst of Jillian's nightmare. The scene was mostly different, of course. This was a picture-perfect summer evening, not a rainy winter night, and she was riding in a two-million-dollar Ferrari, not a trusty old station wagon. But in the one grim detail that truly mattered the scene was identical . . .

Jillian sensed the sudden and catastrophic failure of the brakes the instant Chase did, but as his every instinct fought for their survival, her mind floated almost passively to the inevitable.

They would crash.

She would watch him die.

And if she were lucky, *very lucky,* she would die too.

The treacherous curves came faster and ever faster, each one a new and more difficult test for the steel of his nerves, the acuteness of his reflexes, and the craftsmanship of the car. The brakes were gone, and so were the gears, but for the moment the feather-sensitive steering held; and, for the moment, the wheels maintained their precarious relationship to earth.

But soon, Chase knew, the speed at which they were hurtling downward would make negotiating the hairpin turns completely impossible. The wheels would lose their valiant battle against centrifugal force and the car would spin, a spectacular cartwheel of metal and flames, off the road—and into eternity.

Beyond the too rapidly unfolding concrete, his mind's eye visualized their only hope—the short stretch in which the road flattened briefly before spilling down into yet another cascade of twists and turns. It was the plateau on which, as Jillian had driven in the pelting rain on his first morning in Bel Air, her fear had relented slightly.

The plateau was where and when he and Jillian would have to leave the runaway car—if they made it that far. There was an estate on the plateau, on the right-hand side of the road. The mansion itself was surrounded by a redbrick wall, but between the road and the wall was an expanse of thick luxuriant lawn. In the few racing heartbeats between the time the wheels touched the grass and the speeding car crashed into the wall, he and Jillian would jump to safety.

"We're going to have to jump." Chase's eyes remained on the road as he spoke. When his words were greeted by silence, he asked, "Jillian?"

She didn't answer still, and when he risked a fleeting glance at her, Chase saw emerald eyes that were staring straight ahead, strangely mesmerized, as if lost anew in a horror film that she had seen before but which never failed to frighten. Chase saw her terror, and something even more terrifying: her resignation.

Jillian knew what was going to happen.

She had accepted it.

"Jillian? *Jillian.* Listen to me." Chase risked another glance. She was staring straight ahead still, and there was no sign in the ashen face that she had even heard him. When he spoke again, it was with a voice he had never heard before. It was his heart speaking, and its impassioned words came from the restless, lonely place that had spent an entire lifetime chasing dreams and rainbows, a desperate search that he knew now had been for her. "I love you, Jillian. *I love you.*"

When her voice came at last, it was small, a soft whisper above the scream of wheels that clung frantically to earth. But Chase heard it with exquisite clarity.

"Chase?" she asked with hopeful wonder. "You love me?"

"Oh, yes, I love you," he answered softly. Then, urgently, he said, "Let me love you, Jillian. Give me a chance to love you. *Please.*"

Slowly, as if in a dream, Jillian nodded her reply, a shimmering dance of auburn that told him yes, *yes*.

"Unbuckle your seat belt," Chase urged gently, wondering as he did if she was focused enough to follow his instructions. And if she wasn't? If he couldn't get her to jump? Then they would die together, and in those final moments he would tell her again and again of his love.

But Chase heard the unmistakable click of metal as she unbuckled.

"Good," he said softly. "Now unbuckle mine. Okay. Now, when I say 'jump,' we both jump. Jump as far as you can, Jillian, and try to roll when you land. We'll be on grass, but it's going to feel much harder than that."

Chase heard a soft laugh, and then felt the delicate touch of her fingers on his cheek.

"I love you, Jillian," he whispered hoarsely.

"I love you too, Chase."

The car should have spun out of control on the final curve before the plateau.

That it didn't was simply a divine gift of love.

As Chase turned the car onto the lawn, he told her to jump, and a heartbeat later, when he was absolutely certain that she had obeyed his command, he jumped too. Two heartbeats later the Ferrari crashed into the redbrick wall and burst into flames.

The sounds of metal plunging into brick, and gasoline exploding into a blazing inferno, were merely distant thunder to Chase as he stumbled toward Jillian. She was a small, crumpled mound of green silk shrouded in magnificent auburn. Small. Crumpled. Motionless.

Oh, Jillian.

As he neared, the auburn moved, and then he saw her

emerald eyes, anxious and searching, until he was found. And then there was shimmering joy and the promise of an infinity of rainbows.

"Chase!"

She had raised up only to her grass-stained knees by the time he reached her. Chase fell to his own knees in front of her and drew her trembling body close to his.

"Jillian," he whispered, his lips brushing against her tangled auburn hair as his hands, his entire being, reveled in the wonder of holding her. His lips caressed the fragrant silkiness of her hair, and then something not so silky—grass. Laughing softly, he removed the blade of grass from his mouth and pulled away to look again at her eyes.

Chase had seen the lovely emerald illuminated by the sun, and by candles, and by the moon and the stars; but now, illuminated by the inferno that blazed behind him, the green was more radiant than ever. Firelit, like her hair. But, he realized, the glow came from deep within, from Jillian's own inner fire, her passion, her love.

"Are you all right?" he asked as he tenderly cupped her beautiful dirt-smudged face in his trembling hands. "Your hips? Your back?"

"I'm fine," Jillian assured him, ignoring the screams of pain. The pain would subside. It didn't matter. "How about you? Your chest?"

"I'm fine too," Chase said, ignoring, too, the anger in his barely healed and now reinjured ribs. "I think we're both going to have some pretty sore muscles tomorrow."

"It doesn't matter."

"No," Chase agreed, curling her closer. "It doesn't matter at all."

They were an island of love amid a sea of chaos, holding each other, touching with gentle wonder even as the world behind them blazed and the smoky sky filled with the strident screams of sirens. The police, fire fighters, and paramedics all arrived with impressive speed, as did a curious crowd of wealthy and elegant neighbors.

Word of the spectacular crash reached the dining room of the Hotel Bel-Air almost as quickly as the alert went out over the emergency radio frequencies. The five people who had been awaiting the arrival of Jillian and Chase rushed to the scene, not knowing what they would find, guided only by the ominous plume of dark gray smoke that obscured the brilliant azure sky.

Expressions of relief touched all five faces the moment they saw Jillian and Chase. For Jillian's parents and Stephanie the relief was pure, untarnished, embellished only by happiness. For Jack there was immense relief that Jillian and Chase were alive, but it was tainted by deep worry as he gazed at the smoldering carcass of the car.

Jack's ocean-blue eyes were calm, his perusal almost casual, but there was nothing either calm or casual about his thoughts. This was the second near-fatal accident to have befallen Chase Kincaid. Jack didn't like the coincidence at all. His worry became laced with frustration as even from a distance he could tell that the damage done to the car had been massive. Even the best specialists in the department would be hard pressed to find traces of possible treachery amid the wreckage.

But Chase had survived, Jack reminded himself. And for *this* accident Chase Kincaid would be able to provide an eyewitness account.

By the time the five reached Jillian and Chase, Jack had artfully concealed his professional worry. That left only one pair of eyes—Brad's—that weren't filled with pure relief. Indeed, the dark expression that greeted his miraculously alive cousin looked like an unconcealed wish for death.

"You son of a bitch!" Brad hissed. "What the *hell* were you doing?"

Chase had anticipated a possible confrontation with his cousin this evening. In fact, assuming he could find a private moment alone with Brad, he had planned to utter almost the identical words, fueled with comparable fury, to him. You son of a bitch! What the *hell* were you doing telling Nicole Haviland the precise moment when Jillian and I would be returning from Bora Bora?

Chase had anticipated a possible confrontation with Brad. But not now, not moments after he and Jillian had narrowly escaped a death of blazing violence.

"I beg your pardon, Brad?"

"You were obviously driving like a maniac," Brad fumed. "You can do what you want with your own life, but what right do you have to risk Jillian's? She could have been killed."

"We both could have been killed, Brad," Chase amended solemnly. "But not because of my driving. The brakes failed."

"What?" With a dark frown Brad muttered, "That damned car has always been so temperamental." Then, frowning even more darkly, he said, "It probably hasn't been serviced since you disappeared, has it? No, of course not, because you remember *nothing*. The brakes need to be bled every few months." Brad turned to Jillian then, and with a look of gentle apology offered, "I'm sorry, Jill. I should have thought to have it done—or at least to have reminded Chase."

"I should have remembered too," Jillian said. "I should have reminded him."

"No," Chase said quietly but emphatically to the responsible woman who as a responsible and sensitive girl had assumed the crushingly heavy weight of guilt for another tragic accident for which she had not been to blame. "It's not your fault, Jillian." Chase held her gaze until her beautiful green eyes acknowledged his words, and that she would heed them, then he returned to Brad. Smiling wryly, he said, "It's not even *your* fault, Brad. It just happened, that's all. And now it's over."

Chapter Twenty-Six

Claudia and Edward drove Chase and Jillian back up the hill to Clairmont, lingering just long enough to see that they were safely inside the house before driving off.

Once inside, Chase and Jillian were greeted by an exuberant Annie. They lavished affection on the enthusiastic golden-haired creature until she had had enough, and then, without a word and moving into the other's arms at the same moment, they turned the gentle affection to each other.

It was an embrace of reverent wonder, of solemn gratitude, a slow, tender dance to the music of their hearts. Chase's lips gently caressed her tangled auburn hair, and then her grass-stained forehead, and finally, between kisses that created a halo of love around her radiant emerald eyes, he whispered, "You heard what Claudia said. Long, hot showers—as soon as possible—are our only hope for muscles that will be willing to function at all tomorrow."

Jillian smiled. "Long, hot showers it is, then."

"And soup? Hot chocolate? I could heat something while you're showering."

"No, thank you, not for me. Besides," she added gently, "you need your own shower as soon as possible too."

"Okay. Just showers, then—and bed."

"Yes." With a thoughtful tilt of her auburn head, Jillian asked softly, "Chase? Will you sleep with me tonight?"

Chase locked the doors and got Annie settled for the night before going to the master suite to take his shower. Once there, he forced himself to linger beneath the hot spray even though his thoughts kept traveling to Jillian, to holding her as she drifted to sleep . . . and holding her still as she slept.

Chase expected Jillian to be in bed in the master suite by the time he finished showering. But the bed was empty. After dressing in a pair of his twin's pajamas, he walked down the hallway to the room where she had slept since his arrival at Clairmont. The door was wide open, welcoming him into the room of wildflowers lighted now by the pale pink glow of the summer twilight.

Jillian was awake, waiting for him. Freshly shampooed auburn hair framed her face and spilled onto an ivory cotton nightgown. It was embroidered with roses, not violets, but it was as pure, as modest and innocent as the gown she had worn in paradise.

As Chase joined her in bed, the eyes that greeted him filled with dreams. He had seen the look before, when she had awakened from a brief sleep on their first morning in Bora Bora. Then he had believed that the look wasn't for him, instead a faraway memory of love with his twin.

But the eyes that gazed at him now weren't faraway at all, and the only memories of love in the glowing green were the memories still to be made . . . tonight . . . with him.

"Jillian."

"Hi," she whispered to the eyes and voice that spoke with such raw emotion, such unhidden passion, such unconcealed need.

"Hi," Chase echoed as his lips found hers. Hello, my precious love. Hello, *hello.*

The kiss was far hungrier than any of the kisses in Bora Bora, deeper and more confident and more demanding—quickly demanding that there be nothing between them, no distance at all, not even the soft cotton barriers of pajamas and roses. Chase removed the thin layers of fabric that separated them, and then, and for a very long time, he simply held her, marveling at that closeness, feeling her soft, lovely warmth against his lean, powerful strength, listening to the rhythm of her breathing and the joyful music of her heart.

At last he moved, beginning the tender journey of discovery and desire. His gentle and so talented hands began the journey, and his gentle and so talented lips followed, traveling from the glittering auburn silk to the radiant emerald eyes, to the passion-flushed cheeks, to the soft satin of her lovely neck, and the even softer satin of her shoulders.

Suddenly there was tension in her lovely body, and a sigh caught in her throat, and the fingers that had delicately woven into his long black hair tightened. The eyes that met his glistened still with love and desire and dreams, but there was uncertainty too, a dark shadow amid the radiance.

"Jillian?"

"I have scars, Chase, from the accident. They're quite . . . startling. I didn't know if you remembered."

Chase answered her worry with the gentlest of smiles, his eyes blue with love. "I love all of you, Jillian, *all* of you."

"Oh, Chase," she whispered with quiet joy, the shadow of her own worry disappearing quickly—until she saw a sudden dark worry in the loving blue. "Chase?"

"I don't want to hurt you. You've been hiding it admirably . . . but I know that your back was reinjured."

"It doesn't hurt," Jillian answered truthfully, her eyes filling with wonder at that truth. The screams of pain had been miraculously silenced by his love—all the screams of pain. Nothing hurt now, not her back, not her heart, not her soul. All the hurts that had lived within her for so long that they had seemed an essential part of her had simply vanished. "Nothing hurts."

"No," Chase agreed softly, marveling too that the deep wounds that had ached within him for his entire lifetime were gone now, completely healed by her. "Nothing hurts anymore."

They loved, a tender dance of desire and passion. Nothing was hidden, no intimacy shadowed, no treasure of love forbidden, no gift of love denied. And when they were one, Chase met her joyous green eyes as he tenderly kissed the tiny scars that had transformed her from plain to beautiful. Each kiss eloquently told her the most important truth: that he loved the little girl inside, the shy and generous little girl who had always possessed the greatest beauty of all.

"I love you, Jillian." The emotional whisper of love rode on a crest of desire which soon, very soon, would command all words, all breath, all thought.

"I love you too, Chase," she echoed, her emotional whisper, like her crescendoing desire, an exact mirror image of his.

"Jillian . . . *Jillian."*

Their loving had been without shadows, nothing hidden, and after, as Chase held her, when it was at last possible for him to speak again, his first words, gently spoken, were the beginning of the unshadowing of the secrets of their hearts and of their love.

"Will you tell me what happened the night I disappeared? There's something about that night that worries you, something that you haven't wanted to tell me, isn't there?"

Always before, his questions about that night had caused fear. Now Chase saw only relief.

"Yes, there is, and I will tell you," Jillian answered softly. "But I need to tell you first that I didn't move into this bedroom after you disappeared. I moved here two months before. You were having terrible nightmares and you thought it would be best for us to sleep separately. I don't know what the nightmares were about, but whatever it was remained with you even during the day. You were obviously deeply troubled, and I didn't know why, and you wouldn't tell me. You shut me out in all ways—emotionally, physically . . . completely. That was very difficult for me, of course, but I also think it was difficult for you. Your guilt, or whatever, simply added to your torment. Anyway, I made a decision. It was the right decision for me, and I honestly believed that it was right—best—for you too." Jillian drew a steadying breath. Then, bravely, so bravely, she met the loving blue eyes and said quietly, "That night, Chase, I told you that I wanted a divorce."

If Jillian had told him that that night she had willfully murdered the man who had so cruelly betrayed her love, it would have been a far less painful truth to hear than this. This shattering revelation meant that Jillian had wanted the love to end, the hearts to separate, the lives to go on without each other forever. To Chase it seemed a greater death.

Even if Jillian's lovely face hadn't now been solemn with remembrance, Chase would have known that the words she had spoken to his twin had been carefully considered, honest in both their anguish and intent, neither a frivolous nor petulant ultimatum delivered merely to get his brother's attention.

Two months ago Jillian had wanted a divorce from Chase Kincaid. For her own survival she had needed to separate her heart from his forever.

"How did I react?" Chase asked, his own heart feeling such immense pain now that he wondered if he was feeling emotion for both himself and his twin.

"You were upset, angry." Jillian frowned, bewildered still by the reaction. "I guess I thought you might be relieved, but you weren't. You told me you didn't want to lose me. You promised that we would talk—really talk—when you returned. You promised that, and you seemed so sincere, but instead of staying to talk to me then, you left to go sailing. Even then, Chase, even when you told me that you wanted to try to make our love work, you were so restless to get away from me. You asked me to wait for you, to do nothing until you returned."

"And did you agree?"

"I didn't agree or disagree. I was angry—and so confused."

"Because despite what I had said, I was running away from you still."

"Yes," Jillian said, grateful that he understood. Then her eyes filled with pure sadness. "I let you leave without giving you my answer. But I *did* wait, Chase. I waited, and then they found the boat, and . . ."

"And when you learned that I had been struck by the boom, you blamed yourself for causing me to be so distracted that I forgot about its danger," Chase finished softly, seeing now what Jack Shannon had seen: guilt. Once again Jillian had assumed responsibility for a tragic death for which she was not to blame. "Didn't you?"

"Yes."

"Well, don't," he commanded gently, even as a harsh truth taunted him.

If, at this moment, Jillian told him their love was over and he escaped to the sea, his mind would be so wholly consumed by the loss that, like his twin, he would forget completely the dangers of even the most docile of waters. He would be at risk for a blow from a swinging boom; and once stunned and lying on the deck, he might remember his loss, and, like his brother, he might simply choose to fall into the beckoning oblivion of the sea. His death would not be Jillian's fault, just as she was not to blame for what had happened to his twin. It would be his own fault, just as it had been his brother's, for cruelly betraying her most generous love.

Feeling his own impending death, Chase asked very softly, "Do you still want a divorce?"

"No, Chase, of course I don't."

As Jillian looked at him with shimmering love, a monumental realization settled. Until the day he had appeared in Mexico, she had lived with the immense guilt of his twin's death. But then he had appeared, and as Chase Kincaid had promised her, they had talked, really talked . . . and Chase Carlton had saved his brother's marriage.

In the process, he had fallen deeply in love; and on this night of love he had planned to expose all the secrets that shadowed their love, revealing to her his true identity and the twin truth: that the man who had so cruelly betrayed her love was dead.

But now Chase realized that Jillian would only feel great guilt when she learned that Chase Kincaid had died after all. In the past few weeks, she had forgiven her husband everything, every cruelty and betrayal—which meant that it was Chase Carlton, not Chase Kincaid, who had to die.

Such an *easy* death. Chase Carlton would scarcely be missed and certainly not mourned. Yes, there might be lovers who would idly ponder what had become of the talented hands and lips that had given so much pleasure; and yes, the police and FBI might wonder with annoyance what had become of the man with the gift for evil, but . . .

It would be very easy for Chase Carlton to disappear forever. In September, when Jillian was back at school, he would fly to San Francisco, reclaim his car keys from the marina security guard, announcing as he did that he had found moorage for *Sea Witch* elsewhere and planned never to return.

Chase Carlton was dead, and Chase Kincaid had been forgiven, and now he whispered softly, "I love you, Jillian. I want to spend the rest of my life making you happy . . . if I can."

"You can, Chase." A lovely frown touched her lovely face. "I wonder if I can make you happy though."

"You already have, Jillian," he said, kissing away the uncertainty. *You've already given me a lifetime of happiness, erasing thirty-four years of loneliness and pain as if it never existed.* "How long had it been since we had made love?"

"Almost six months." Her eyes filled with brave wonder as she confessed, "But, Chase, we have never made love in this bed before . . . and it was never like this before, never like tonight."

Making love had never been like this before for him either, of course. He had never before made *love* to anyone. Now his heart raced at the confession that it had been different—wondrous—for her as well.

"It will be like this every time, Jillian," he promised. "It will be even better."

"It can't be better . . . can it?"

"Oh, my precious love, I think it can."

Chapter Twenty-Seven

"Are you leaving me, Lieutenant?"

"Never," Jack vowed softly as he walked to the bed. He wove his long fingers into her sleep-tangled moonbeam-ribboned hair and repeated quietly, "Never."

Stephanie's heart raced at the solemnity of his vow, and the tenderness of his dark blue eyes, but she finally offered, "You look awfully dressy for someone who's planning to spend the entire day in bed with me."

"That *is* my plan though." His lips caressed hers promisingly as he spoke. "I just need to check on something at the precinct first. I'd hoped to be back before you even awakened."

"You need to check on Chase's car," Stephanie said to the surprised blue eyes that had tried unsuccessfully to conceal his worries about the accident from her.

They might have talked then about his worry, and that he didn't need to hide it from her. And that might have led to the next: that she hated that he had to see violence, and mutilation, and the strangled corpses of young women, but that she understood why he did what he did and wanted him to share more with her, even *more* of the emotions he felt. She and Jack already shared emotions, and already their closeness was far greater and far more joyous than either had ever before believed was possible.

But before Stephanie could tell him that she hoped there would be intimate conversation amid the other intimacies he had planned for the day, the phone rang.

"Maybe that's the report on the car now."

"Maybe." And maybe, Jack thought, I'll learn that there was nothing sinister in the charred remains at all, simply an accident, and we can all go on with our lives.

A precise diagnosis as to why the brakes of the valuable Ferrari 250 Le Mans had failed could not be made, the officer told Jack. They had found nothing, however, to suggest tampering. Which meant, Jack realized, that this was all they would ever know about the accident. It was probably, most likely, quite simply because the brakes had not been bled on schedule.

Nothing sinister at all.

Except that when the officer spoke again, what Jack learned was far more evil and far more devastating than anything he had imagined.

Stephanie watched Jack's handsome face grow dark with disbelief and concern, becoming darkest of all, most deeply troubled, when he confessed quietly, "I didn't see it. I didn't even *consider* it." He sighed and added, "Okay, I'll take it from here."

Then the call was over, but still Jack glowered at the phone, the powerful muscles in his jaw rippling with silent rage.

"Jack?" Stephanie asked softly. "Was it . . . *did* someone tamper with the brakes?"

"It's much worse than that, Stephanie," he said with quiet apology as he met her anxious eyes. "They couldn't tell about the brakes—the car was too badly damaged—but they found something inside the car, under the driver's seat."

"What, Jack? What did they find?"

"A plastic bag. The plastic was melted by the heat of the fire, but the bag itself was away from the flames so its contents—a number of guitar strings and four earrings—were perfectly preserved." Perfectly preserved, Jack thought grimly, including the blood and skin fragments embedded into the strings by un- speakable violence. Gazing at her beautiful, worried, and still- uncomprehending sapphire eyes, he asked gently, "Do you remember when I wanted to know what earrings Janine Raleigh was wearing the night you had dinner with her, the night she was killed? That was because the Strangler always removed the left earring from his victim and put a diamond stud in its place. We assumed that he kept the earrings as souvenirs."

"Jack?" Stephanie's whisper held a soft note of protest.

His voice was as gentle as possible, but the news Jack had to tell her wasn't the least bit gentle . . . and it signaled the end of so much hope. "Three of the four earrings found in the bag are the exact twins of the earrings found on the victims of the Guitar String Strangler."

"Someone found out about the earrings," Stephanie coun- tered swiftly. "This is a cruel, *horrible* hoax."

"It's not a hoax, Stephanie. The fourth earring found in the bag is a silver crescent moon. Only you and I—and the Stran- gler—knew that Janine was wearing an unmatched pair."

"Chase did *not* murder Janine, Jack. He didn't murder any- one!"

He murdered five women, Jack thought. And there was far more proof than the compelling physical evidence. Stephanie needed to hear that proof, just as he had needed to recall it as his heart, too, had screamed in silent protest when the officer had revealed to him the devastating news.

"Listen to me, Stephanie. I know that this seems . . . impossi- ble, but there's more. When I was investigating Chase's disap- pearance, Jillian said that she usually taught an adult literacy class at her school on Tuesday evenings—every third Tuesday. I realize now that those were the same evenings on which the Strangler attacked."

"But she was home with Chase on the evening Janine was killed."

"Yes, that's right, because that afternoon one of the other

teachers asked her to trade for another evening. She was home with Chase, but as she told you, they argued, after which he left to go sailing. Jillian always maintained that he left Clairmont at about eight-thirty, and we know that his sailboat was still at the marina two hours later . . . and we know, too, that like all the other victims, Janine was murdered between nine and ten. What was unique about Janine's death was that it happened in her apartment—as if she knew her murderer."

Jack stopped, not needing to say the rest. Of course Janine Raleigh knew Chase Kincaid. He had just offered her the role of a lifetime, after all, the lead in *Journeys of the Heart*. Jack didn't need to say that, nor did he need to remind Stephanie that there had been no further murders since May 10, the night on which, just hours after Janine Raleigh's death, Chase Kincaid had mysteriously disappeared.

Jack watched as the woman he loved heard his words—and struggled valiantly against the horrifying revelation. Her brilliant blue eyes blazed with emotion . . . and then quite suddenly became calm, and crystal clear.

"Maybe Chase Kincaid *was* the Guitar String Strangler, but that was a *different* Chase Kincaid. He's dead now and the man who has returned in his place is gentle and loving." Her eyes shimmering with hope, she pleaded softly, "Don't tell them, Jack. Please don't tell Jillian and Chase about the Chase Kincaid who is dead."

"I have no choice."

"But he has no memory of the monster he once was!"

"He *claims* to have no memory," Jack countered solemnly, remembering with grim clarity that it had been Chase who had raised the topic of the Strangler after dinner at Clairmont. Had that been a calculated ploy of a clever murderer, a man whose memory was fully intact and who for his own amusement had decided to play cat and mouse with the homicide lieutenant? Or had the grim topic been prompted by a shadowy memory in the mind of a man who truly did have amnesia—and who, according to Jillian, shortly before his death had become fascinated with serial killers? "Maybe Chase has amnesia, Stephanie, or maybe he's simply decided to begin again, to give himself a second chance."

"Himself *and* Jillian. Jack, you saw them after the accident yesterday. They love each other *so much.* I'm sure Chase has no memory of what he used to be. Can't he—can't they—have that second chance?"

"No," Jack answered with the harshness of a man whose own parents hadn't been given such a luxury. "Five women have been murdered. Five young women who will never have a chance at anything ever again."

Jack saw the turmoil in her beautiful eyes, the lovely wish for happiness at last for the friend whose life had been touched before by inexplicable tragedy and the grim realization that that happiness was about to be brutally shattered *by him.* With that realization came anger.

Jack needed to know if the anger he saw was for him. By shattering her friend's happiness was he committing a crime that Stephanie would never forgive?

Stephanie was angry, *and she was silent,* and Jack needed to hear the honest words of her heart. Stephanie Samantha Windsor hadn't stuttered, not once, since she had told him all her shameful truths. During their wondrous weeks of love, her words had flowed on a river of joy from her heart to her lips. Her heart was full now, flooding with emotion, but she wasn't speaking.

Because she was afraid that she would stutter? Jack wondered. Because her shame—and her pride—were stronger than their love? Because she didn't trust him after all? Stephanie had once abandoned her best friend because of fear. Was she going to abandon their love for the same reason?

No. Jack wouldn't allow it. And if the thoughts that stumbled in her mind now were that she could never forgive him for being the executioner of Jillian's dreams, that she could no longer love him? Then so be it. Jack needed to hear her say the words. He would not allow their love to end with silence.

"Tell me what you're thinking, Stephanie. Do you hate me?"

"Hate you?" she echoed with soft surprise. "No, I hate that this has happened. And I hate what this is going to do to Jillian. But I don't hate *you,* Jack."

"No?"

"No." The breathtaking relief and love that she saw in his sensuous eyes made her tremble, all of her, even her thoughts. Then gently, not knowing if her words would tremble too, not caring if they did, she said, "I love you, Jack."

"And I love you." He drew her to him then, and his lips caressed her temple as he spoke. "And I'm so sorry that this has happened to Jillian."

"But it has," Stephanie murmured quietly. "I know that you have to go to Clairmont and arrest Chase. I'm going with you."

"No, you're not," Jack countered softly. "Chase may remember everything, Stephanie."

Jack's voice was filled with love, but the words themselves carried an ominous truth: the arrest of a serial killer, even a man who had once been a friend, could be extremely dangerous. Stephanie had imagined an emotional scene in which she and Jack would apologetically share with Jillian and Chase what had been found in the Ferrari and in which they would all look at each other with disbelieving sadness.

But Jack was right. That might not be the scene at all. Chase's memory might already be fully intact, or he might suddenly remember everything—and try to flee.

And then Lieutenant Jack Shannon might have to shoot the friend who had become a murderer.

"You're not going by yourself."

"No," Jack assured her. "I'll have backup before I ring the doorbell."

It suddenly occurred to Stephanie that in the meantime, while Jack was arranging for backup and driving to Clairmont, she could simply pick up the phone and tell Chase and Jillian everything, warning them so that they could be long gone by the time the police arrived.

She wouldn't do that, of course, and Jack had known that. Jack had trusted her—and her love.

"Jack?" she asked softly. "Should you have told me this?"

"Probably not. But I needed to tell you, Stephanie." He smiled gently, a smile for her, for them, despite the somberness of the moment. And then, with the tenderness of his most tender caresses, he asked, "Does it make you feel like a wife?"

"Yes."

"Do you like the feeling?"

"Yes." It was a whisper of hope.

Jack's smile became even more gentle as his hands cradled her face. "I know that Jillian will need you now more than she's ever needed you before, and I want you to be with her. But, Stephanie Samantha Windsor, when Jillian is strong again, when you think it's time, will you marry me?"

Everything trembled—her heart, her thoughts, her soul. But there was no stuttering, and there never would be again.

"Oh, yes, Jack, I will marry you."

Chapter Twenty-Eight

"Hi."

"Hi," Chase echoed softly. "I was making breakfast for you. I was going to bring it upstairs."

Breakfast in bed for his love. Only that wonderful plan, and thoughts of a loyal and patient golden retriever, had convinced him to leave her side an hour before.

Now she was here, in the kitchen. Her firelit auburn hair was shower-damp, as was his own midnight-black, and she was wearing, as was he, a gift of their love. Jillian wore the pearl earrings in which glittered the promises of rainbows, and Chase wore the blue shirt that was the color of the happiness in his eyes; but those gifts and promises were trivial compared to the gifts and promises that shimmered in their eyes.

Chase crossed to her, and when he was close enough to touch, it was Jillian who bravely touched first, her delicate fingers reaching for his face. His hands encircled her waist, drawing her closer, and then she tiptoed, to kiss him, and whispered, "Good morning."

"Good morning." Laughing softly as his lips greeted hers, Chase asked, "How are your muscles? Stiff and sore?"

"I feel wonderful, Chase."

"So do I." His hands gently framed her face. "So do I, Jillian."

Annie needed a little affection then from Jillian, and she bent to lovingly run her fingers through the wiggling golden fur.

"It's a glorious day," she murmured to both of them. "What shall we do with it?"

"Annie has already put in a vote for a quiet, sun-soaked day in the rose garden," Chase offered, knowing full well that as wonderful as Jillian said she felt, her muscles, like his, needed a day of rest beneath the warmth of the summer sun.

"That sounds perfect to me." Her fingers lingered in Annie's golden fur as she lifted her eyes to meet his. "Will you sing to us?"

"Always."

The doorbell sounded then, a melodic chime that brought a soft smile to Jillian's face. "A concerned relative, I'm afraid."

The orphan who had always longed for a family had one now. He was going to spend his life convincing Jillian of his love and convincing his family—her parents and his cousin—of his worthiness of her . . . and of them. With quiet emotion he said, "It's nice to have concerned relatives."

"Yes." Jillian's smile faded slightly as she mused, "I suppose it could also be reporters."

As they walked from the kitchen toward the front door, they checked the image on the closed circuit screen in the living room. The early morning visitor was neither a relative nor a reporter, but a friend: Jack.

Jack and four other police officers, they discovered when they opened the door and saw that in addition to Jack's car there were two patrol cars with two officers each standing beside them.

"I have some news," Jack said quietly, the solemnity of his tone eloquently conveying the fact that the news was bad—*very* bad.

"Come in."

While the four officers remained on guard outside, Jillian, Chase, and Jack settled in the living room. Chase and Jillian sat together on one of the couches, with Annie pressed close, and Jack sat directly across from them on the couch's twin.

"It's an update on the Guitar String Strangler," Jack began, watching the intelligent gray eyes carefully. "I'm going to tell you some details that have previously been known only to the police."

"All right," Chase agreed, surprised by Jack's words but even more surprised by the delicate hand that suddenly and almost desperately entwined with his. As he smiled gentle reassurance to Jillian, he fought his own unfocused but crescendoing fear with a mantra of love: We love each other, nothing can hurt us.

The mantra faltered quickly, its soothing promises lost in the thunder of a taunting reminder: Many things can hurt us. The truth can hurt us.

The truth can *hurt* us, Chase's heart conceded. But it cannot destroy us. Nothing can.

But Chase Carlton was about to learn how wrong the defiant wishes of his heart could be.

"As you know," Jack said, "the victims were all strangled with guitar strings. Like most serial killers, the Strangler took a souvenir from each of his victims and also left something behind. What he took was the victim's left earring, and what he left in its place was a diamond one."

It was then that the delicate fingers tightly entwined in Chase's turned to pure ice.

"Jillian?" Chase asked of the suddenly terrified green eyes. Then, because she couldn't or wouldn't speak the unspeakable, he demanded of Jack, "Where is this going, Jack? What's going on?"

He doesn't know, Jack realized. He doesn't remember the monster he once was.

Solemnly, and with the gentleness of a friend, Jack answered Chase's question. "In the Ferrari, hidden under the driver's seat, we found a plastic bag. It contained the guitar strings that had been used as well as the missing earrings from four of the five victims."

"Oh, no," Chase whispered, a soft protest of the heart against the monumental and devastating truth.

As he had begun his journey to Mexico, Chase Carlton had believed that it was his destiny to avenge his twin's murder; and in the past week he had revised his mission to a most magnificent one—to spend his life treasuring the dream with which his brother had been so careless and so cruel.

But now Chase knew the bitter truth. His destiny, his only destiny always, had been to pursue and conquer evil. He had succeeded in that quest with strangers, journeying into the minds of murderers and putting a stop to their lethal lust. But in the most important pursuit of his life he had failed. The mind to which he should have been the closest—and for which, perhaps, he was the missing conscience—had eluded him. The golden twin had not wanted to be discovered by the dark one, and even in death Chase Kincaid was evil still, brazenly sending his ghost to the deck of *Sea Goddess* to claim his final victim—his brother.

His identical twin had been a monster, and Chase's remarkable gift for evil had failed to find his brother in time to prevent the destruction that Chase Kincaid had caused. As those devastating revelations swirled in Chase's mind, another one surfaced from amid the chaos: Jillian had guessed where Jack's solemn words were leading even before he spoke them. Her hands had turned to ice before Jack revealed what had been found in the car.

As Chase gazed at her now, he saw what he had seen yesterday as the runaway car had sped to eternity—a blend of terror, resignation, and *acceptance*. Jillian was staring straight ahead, as she had been yesterday, her resigned green eyes now focused on Jack. When she spoke, her voice was faraway and lifeless.

"Chase gave me a pair of diamond earrings for our wedding anniversary. Just before Valentine's Day one of the earrings disappeared." She spoke without inflection, and as she continued even her questions were simply statements, a grim recitation of the horrible truth. "The first murder was on February fifteenth, wasn't it, and the victims all had long, dark hair, like mine, didn't they. He must have been very angry with me. I must have done something——"

"Jillian."

Chase's voice startled her, and for a moment she stopped speaking and turned toward him, and when she did he saw apology——and love——and her delicate fingers entwined with his still, loving him, not abandoning him. Her eyes abandoned his though, returning to Jack and resuming the toneless recitation in which she seemed to be assuming responsibility for the crimes committed by her husband.

"He was very tormented during the months before the accident," she said softly. "I tried to get him to tell me what was troubling him, but he wouldn't . . . perhaps he couldn't."

"Jillian," Jack said quietly. "You're talking about Chase as if he isn't even here."

"He isn't here, Jack," she replied simply, her emerald eyes suddenly brilliantly clear and brilliantly innocent. "The man who committed those brutal murders no longer exists."

Last night Chase Carlton had died, a necessary——and so easy——death. He had died so that Jillian would be forever spared a sense of guilt about Chase Kincaid's accidental death. As Chase gazed now at the woman who had forgiven his twin all his betrayals, he realized that Jillian would forgive his brother yet again——and would love him still.

The Guitar String Strangler would go to prison, of course. The best lawyer money could buy and a prestigious panel of neurologists and psychiatrists could probably prevent the death penalty——on the grounds that he now had no memory of his crimes——but the rest of his life would be spent behind bars.

If it would help Jillian, Chase Carlton would willingly spend that life of imprisonment as Chase Kincaid. He had, after all, until her, lived his life in solitude. Jillian had set him free from his lonely and loveless prison . . . and now Chase had to set her free from the imprisonment of having loved the golden twin with the heart of darkness. If he didn't, Chase knew that she would spend her life loving him, visiting him whenever she was allowed, enduring the public scrutiny and censure, and making desperate, anguished pleas to the governor for stays of execution if the jury decided that amnesia or no, Chase Kincaid deserved to die.

"Jillian," he began softly. "Listen to me, please." Chase waited until her eyes met his before continuing. "Listen, please, very carefully. You are not *in any way* responsible for the murders. Serial killers don't kill because they are angry with someone. Yes, they may, before they die, try to blame someone else, but that's just their final selfishness. And they *are* selfish, Jillian. They kill for no other reason than that they want to, because the pleasure of killing is more important to them than anything—or anyone. They make a choice to commit murder. They care about no one but themselves. They don't love. They are unworthy of being mourned. Their death is a blessing. If Chase Kincaid died because he was so distracted that he forgot about the danger of the boom, then so be it. It was good that he died, Jillian, he *needed* to die." Chase drew a steadying breath. Jillian had followed his gentle command, listening intently to his words, but she didn't understand their true meaning, not yet. "He's dead, Jillian. Chase Kincaid is dead."

"I know," she whispered. "All the bad parts died and only the good and loving—"

"No, Jillian. Chase Kincaid is dead. I'm his twin. My name is Chase, but it's Chase Carlton, not Chase Kincaid."

She understood then, with sudden shattering clarity; and with that comprehension Chase Carlton was condemned again to a lifetime of solitude. His prison would be far worse now than it had ever been before, though, because now his heart had known the exhilarating freedom of love.

Jillian had been willing to hold the hand of the twin who in a previous life had been a murderer.

But she was unwilling to hold the hand of the twin who in the past few weeks had so cruelly deceived her. Her deathly cold fingers withdrew from his. Then, with regal dignity, she rose and crossed to the window that gave a panoramic view of the vast sapphire water where her husband had died.

"I grew up in an orphanage in the South of France," Chase began, speaking softly to the taut, slender body that had so purposefully turned away from him. "I knew nothing at all about my family. I had no idea that I had a twin brother until I saw a news report of his disappearance. I've spent the last ten years living in San Francisco, helping the police catch murderers, so——"

Chase stopped mid sentence because it was then that Jillian turned. But her ice-green eyes didn't look at him. Instead they focused, clear and angry, on Jack.

"So Chase called you, didn't he? You told him your suspicions about me and the two of you devised this clever plan to trap a murderess."

It was Chase, not Jack, who answered Jillian's angry accusation, hoping as he did to lure the emerald eyes to return to him.

"I did speak to Jack. He told me that he suspected foul play and was convinced that you were hiding the truth about what really happened that night. But I didn't tell him that I was Chase Kincaid's twin, and he knew absolutely nothing about my plan to return as my brother."

Look at me, Jillian, his heart commanded.

Chase knew that she heard his silent command, and he watched as she defied it, her angry glare leaving Jack and returning to the sea.

The room fell silent then, and for a long time there was only the rhythmic ticking of the Tiffany clock and the sad sighs of a bewildered golden retriever.

Finally it was Jack who spoke. "I'm going to need proof that you're Chase Carlton."

"Of course. Our fingerprints are identical and I assume the same would be true for any genetic studies on our blood. But there are any number of police officers who know me and with whom I share classified information about the cases on which I worked."

Jack believed that he was looking at Chase Carlton, not Chase Kincaid, but he couldn't leave Clairmont until that belief was confirmed. And he wanted to leave, to give Jillian and Chase the privacy they so obviously needed.

"I'm going to give Frank Russell a call right now," he said decisively. "I'll use the phone in the kitchen."

As soon as Jack left the room, Chase said very softly, "Jillian?"

"I have to get something." She spoke to the sea. Then she turned and without looking at him left, too, toward the sweeping staircase that led to the second floor.

Jack returned to the living room first, or perhaps Jillian had simply waited on the stairs until she was sure that Jack was already there, because she reappeared only moments later. She walked past Chase to Jack, her posture straight and proud, her limp almost hidden despite the immense weight of sadness that crushed her battered muscles, and despite the screams of remembered pain from her once-shattered bones.

"Here is the diamond earring that he gave me on our anniversary," she said as she handed the flawless gem to Jack. "I thought it might match one of the ones you found on the victims."

Jack nodded in solemn agreement. He had little doubt that it would be the identical twin to the perfect jewel that had been found in the left ear of the young woman who lost her life on the day after Valentine's Day.

"And," Jillian continued with quiet resolve as she handed him a second earring, "you said that you found four of the five missing earrings in the car. Is this the fifth?"

"Yes," Jack said as his ocean-blue eyes fell on the swirls of gold. "Where did you get this?"

"In his study. In the drawer where he kept extra guitar strings."

"When did you find it?"

When Chase was singing to me. When there was such magic. When we were beginning to truly fall in love.

Banishing the taunting thoughts, Jillian answered, "About two weeks ago." The softness that had come with the unsummoned memory of love vanished as she continued. "I assumed it belonged to one of his mistresses. You can keep both earrings, Jack. I don't want the diamond back."

With that, Jillian returned to the picture window, and after a moment Jack spoke to the dark gray eyes that were staring with such unconcealed anguish at her.

"Let's get this over with, Chase."

"Yes."

From the notes he had taken during his conversation with Frank Russell, Jack asked a series of questions ranging from details known only to the police regarding the Nob Hill Slasher to the name of Frank's cat. Chase answered all the questions swiftly and accurately, satisfying Jack that he was indeed Chase Carlton and stopping the interrogation long before Jack reached the name of the beautiful socialite—Vanessa—who had been the latest in his series of lovers.

"I'm going to go now," Jack said when he had asked more than enough questions of Chase Carlton. "I want to spend some time thinking about the best way to let the press know about this. I won't do anything without letting you know first."

Jack's solemn promise drew the emerald eyes from the sea to him.

"Please don't treat this any differently than you would treat the announcement of the identity of any other murderer," Jillian said quietly. "The victims' families deserve to know the truth as soon as possible, as does everyone who has been worried that even though the killings have stopped, they might start again."

"The announcement won't be treated any differently," Jack assured her. "But unless you tell me otherwise, Jillian, I *will* let you know before making it."

"You don't need to let me know in advance, Jack. It really doesn't matter."

Chase had been wondering if she was ever going to look at him again, but as soon as Jack left, she did—and what Chase saw was pure hatred.

"You're worse than he was," she whispered, a soft, anguished whisper of ice. "He was tormented by what he was doing, but you . . ."

Your eyes became bright blue with pleasure . . . a wondrous blue that was merely happiness at your cruel deceit but which I—so foolishly!—misread as love.

"You loved it, didn't you, Chase? You loved trying to seduce a confession from me." Jillian stopped abruptly as she suddenly realized the extremes to which he had gone to get her to confess. "When simple seduction didn't work, or at least wasn't working *fast* enough, you tried terror, didn't you? There wasn't anything wrong with the brakes, was there? That was just a clever plan you devised to get me to trust you with my life, and my heart—and to get me into bed."

She glared at the winter-gray eyes. They were glacial now, opaque and unreadable. She concentrated on their icy bleakness, trying not to remember how blue they had been last night, how tender, how loving. The memories of their loving came anyway . . . but they brought with them a reminder that fanned even further the flames of her hatred.

"How many *seconds* was it after we finished making love that you asked me to tell you what really happened that night?"

"Just a few seconds, Jillian," he answered, his voice cold and mocking. Chase Carlton wasn't dead after all. He was alive and well, and as infinitely cruel as ever. He forced himself to be—for her. "Just long enough for me to catch my breath."

"I hate you."

"I know," Chase replied, mocking still, indifferent still, making her hate him all the more. She needs to hate me, Chase told the defiant pieces of his shattered heart. She needs to hate me—and then to forget me. Don't let her see that I love her with every ounce of my soul, he silently commanded the whispers of hope that would not die. *Don't you dare.*

As Chase had listened to her, his heart had pleaded desperately that he do everything in his power to convince her again to believe in their love. But Chase had fought the pleas, his ammunition in that ferocious battle of his love for her, the devastating yet confident knowledge that for her sake he needed to get as far away from her as possible as soon as possible. He could not and would not ask her to spend one extra minute, much less a lifetime, looking at the mirror image of a man who had been so evil.

Chase had journeyed to Los Angeles to avenge a murder and to learn the truth about who he was. The yawn of the slumbering sea had already avenged the murders that needed avenging—those of five young women; but he had succeeded in his quest to learn the truths about his heritage. He was a purebred, not a mongrel, abandoned because his parents had needed only one heir, only one crown prince for all their jewels. His twin had been both gifted and tormented, as Chase himself. Together they might have been whole, his conscience controlling his brother's deadly desires; but separately each man was far less than whole, fatally flawed—and so very unworthy of Jillian.

"I'm leaving now."

"Why don't I leave?" Jillian countered swiftly. "Clairmont belonged to your parents. It's rightfully yours."

"There's nothing here that belongs to me." *Especially the only treasure I would ever want—you.*

"Tell me something, Chase. Are you married? Are you returning to San Francisco to a wife and children?"

"No." *I am only—and always—married to you. I am returning to solitude.* Chase fought to keep the love from his eyes as he met the emerald ones that were blazing still, but so terribly hurt and so terribly uncertain. *Hate me, Jillian. Please hate me—and then go on to find a new and worthy love.* His voice was as empty as his heart would be for the rest of his life as he said quietly, "Good-bye, Jillian."

Chase was wearing the blue shirt that Jillian had given him, and the faded jeans which he had worn when he swam ashore near Puerto Vallarta, and a pair of his brother's shoes, and the shiny golden wedding ring that Jillian had gotten for him. Before leaving Clairmont and his dreams forever, Chase removed the wedding band that was never really his and placed it gently, quietly, on the marble table in the foyer.

Jillian didn't follow Chase to the front door. She remained in the living room, with Annie's warm body pressed against her legs, gazing once again at the sea. She neither saw nor heard Chase remove the wedding ring, but at precisely the same moment her trembling fingers removed the pearl earrings he had given her. When they were in her palms, she took her eyes from the sea and stared down at them.

Through the tears that now misted her eyes the magnificent pearls had lost their luster. They were gray and clouded, and the tiny rainbows, and all their wondrous promises, seemed lost forever.

Jack's car was parked on the road just beyond the entrance to Clairmont. After calling Stephanie from his car phone, he had simply lingered there, focusing his thoughts and silently grieving for the victims—all the victims—of Victor Chase Kincaid.

At the sound of footsteps on gravel, Jack turned to the approaching silhouette of one of those many victims. He got out of the car and when Chase reached him, he said, "I know that what you said to Jillian about the selfishness of serial killers needed to be said, and you must know that I have no sympathy whatsoever for what your brother did."

"But?"

"But he did have extraordinary gifts, and there was a sensitivity about him, a compassion that seemed truly authentic."

"Like the authentically sensitive letter he wrote to you when your parents were murdered?" Chase countered harshly. "That sensitive letter was written just a few weeks after he murdered his own parents, his own aunt and uncle, and his own grandfather." *My* parents, *my* aunt and uncle, *my* grandfather. "You know I'm right, Jack. You know the serial killer's fascination with fire, with murder by fire."

Jack's dark blue eyes solemnly acknowledged the truth of Chase's bitter words. It was possible, in fact likely, that Victor Chase Kincaid had set the fatal fire at Lake Tahoe—for no other reason than that he felt like it. He was, perhaps, bored with college and wanted to begin making movies on his own.

"I'm very sorry, Chase."

"So am I, Jack. So the hell am I."

"What now?" Jack asked, even though he had already seen the answer in the tormented gray.

"Now I leave." Chase raised his hand to stop Jack's protest. "She doesn't need any reminders of him—especially not identical ones."

"Where will you go?"

"To San Francisco—and then Puerto Vallarta. My sailboat's underwater off the coast there. As soon as I can get her up and seaworthy, I'll set sail. I'm not sure where I'll be sailing to, but I'll give Frank a general idea of my itinerary in case you need to reach me."

"You mean in case Jillian needs to reach you."

"She doesn't need me, Jack." *I need her. I'm not even sure that my heart can survive without her.*

An image suddenly came to him. He was standing on the deck of *Sea Witch,* distracted by memories of Jillian. The sea yawned, and the boom crashed . . . and then there was peace.

"Can I drive you somewhere?" Jack asked.

Chase considered the question for a moment before answering, "Yes, if you don't mind. I guess I'd like to say good-bye—and apologize—to Jillian's parents."

Chapter Twenty-Nine

Somehow she had willed it. Edward had gone to his study to begin what promised to be a long morning of conference calls on his own line, and she had been sitting in the cheerful kitchen of their Brentwood home, staring at the phone, inexplicably worried. She had wanted to know that both Chase and Jillian were fine, but it was too early and it would be too intrusive for her to call. So she stared at the phone, hoping they would call her.

The call had come, and it had taken Claudia a few moments to even recognize Jillian's lifeless voice, and now the call was over, and she knew the devastating truths, and even though the lifeless voice had claimed to be fine, Claudia knew that soon, very soon, she would find Edward and they would go to Clairmont to be with their daughter.

Soon. But for now Claudia needed a little time to adjust. In a trembling daze she left the cheerful kitchen, wandered to the living room, and stood gazing out the window at the glorious azure and gold day that was unfolding before her.

A glorious day . . . like that distant day in November when her son, her *sons* had been born. Her sons: the gifted golden son who had been a murderer—and the other one, who had been raised in an orphanage in the South of France.

Even as Claudia's trembling heart prayed that his childhood in the orphanage had been a happy one, she knew it was a futile prayer. She had seen the despair that haunted his gray eyes, despair she knew so well: the anguished legacy of loneliness and lovelessness, and the bewilderment of having been abandoned.

Claudia of all people would have wished a childhood like hers on no one, ever, but that was the childhood Chase Carlton had lived, and now he was leaving, perhaps forever, and there were still truths he did not know . . . ones that might even help him.

She would find him, she promised her heart. She would find him and tell him everything.

But Claudia didn't need to look for the son who had been abandoned . . . because as she gazed out at the perfect summer morning, he was suddenly there, walking toward her.

It was too soon. Her heart wasn't yet strong enough to make the confessions he needed to hear.

But you must, a deep voice commanded. He is your son. You owe him the truth.

The front door opened before Chase rang the bell. The light blue eyes which greeted his held no surprise, only fear—as if they knew that they were seeing a ghost.

Chase had once imagined seeing such a look on Jillian's face—the murderess confronted with the ghost of her victim—but now it was Claudia who stared at him with obvious apprehension, and her words, spoken with hushed horror, only confirmed the impression.

"He told me you were dead."

Chase believed he had just heard the confession of a murderess. He believed that Jillian's loving stepmother had just told him that she had been so angered by her son-in-law's cruelty to Jillian that she had hired an assassin to murder him on that foggy night.

Chase Carlton did not want to hear that confession. Not now. Not ever. Victor Chase Kincaid had needed to die.

"Please don't say any more, Claudia. If you hired someone to kill Chase Kincaid, I don't want to know about it. He's dead. He *needs* to be dead. He was a murderer. I'm his twin—"

"I know who you are," Claudia interjected quietly. "Jillian told me. I didn't hire anyone to kill your brother, Chase."

"Then I don't understand. You said you thought I was dead." Chase saw such pain in the fearful blue eyes that he stopped, hoping to find the solution to his misunderstanding himself, to spare her what was obviously going to be a difficult explanation. Finding a plausible solution, he guessed gently, "You knew that Chase Kincaid was a twin? He told you that?"

"No. I'm very sure he knew nothing about you." Claudia took a breath before confessing. "The man who told me that you were dead was Victor Kincaid."

"My father told you that? When? *Why?*"

Claudia bravely met the gray eyes now filled with their own ghosts, anguished memories of the truths that had been, and a gathering storm of dread about the truths that were yet to be revealed. "He told me thirty-four years ago, on November eleventh, just before dawn in a villa at Cap Ferrat."

"You were there? You were in Cap Ferrat the day I was born?"

"I was there." Claudia took a deep breath, hoping for air, for courage, but inhaling only more pain.

She knew with absolute certainty that Chase's lonely childhood had been filled with fantasies about his parents, that they loved him, that they would rescue him. Claudia knew all about such fantasies. For a very long time she herself had survived on them. Her son had undoubtedly survived the horrors of his childhood with such brave hopes, remaining at the orphanage despite everything, afraid to flee because *tomorrow* would be the day when his parents would arrive to save him. At some point the fantasies had been unable to offset the horrors, and he had been forced to abandon the dream, just as he himself had been abandoned.

And now Chase was going to learn the truth about his parents, and amid the pain and fear in the searching gray eyes, Claudia saw flickers of hopefulness, the astonishing resiliency that all orphans shared, the defiant belief that *somehow* they would discover that they had been loved.

Claudia had already told Chase that it had been his father who had told her the lie that he was dead. But still she saw in his eyes the ancient innocence, the bravery of the small boy who hoped that there would be a compelling and loving reason for his father's lie. Claudia knew why Victor Kincaid had lied. She understood it now with painful clarity. His reason had been compelling, yes, but as far away as possible from love.

You owe your son the truth, the voice reminded her, even though it will shatter the hopeful fantasy forever.

"I was there, Chase," she continued finally. "I'm the one who gave birth to twin sons on that morning. I'm your . . ."

She couldn't say it. She could not blaspheme the word "mother." She knew what that word was to an orphan, how filled with hope and love and safety and happiness.

And Chase couldn't say it either. His heart could only ask, a soft whisper of despair, "Why?"

Why. Claudia understood the anguished layers of her son's question. Why was it she—not Rachel Kincaid—who had borne him? Why had Victor Kincaid told her he was dead? And why, why, why, *why* had he been abandoned?

Claudia answered his question with the truth. She began with who she had been then, an orphan too, a young girl who truly believed there would never be love in her life but who had wanted to give everything she had to give, including the greatest gift of all: a baby to parents whom she believed would love and cherish it.

"I was young, Chase, and so very naive. I believed that giving a child to Rachel and Victor Kincaid was good, right, perhaps the best thing I would ever do in my entire life. They insisted on paying me . . . but I didn't do it for the money. I would have done it for nothing."

Her brilliant blue eyes were now as gray as his, and she spoke to him not as mother to son—a relationship which didn't exist—but as orphan to orphan. Chase Carlton heard the words spoken by Claudia Green . . . and he understood. *Because they were so very much alike.* They had come from the same place of lovelessness and hopelessness, and each had sought to redeem that emptiness by giving.

As a teenage girl Claudia had given the precious gift of life, and as a woman she gave that still—to wounded soldiers in Vietnam, and to Edward and Jillian, and to all the children who had been saved by her talented hands. Chase had given, too, journeying into the minds of murderers, enduring that torment despite the cost to himself because it was who he was, all he had, the only gift he could give. And he gave it—despite the cost—just as she did.

As Chase met her eyes he saw the immense cost to her, to her heart, of the first and greatest gift she had given. Very gently he began, "If you had known about me . . ."

"I never would have let you go," she answered softly, swiftly. "Victor must have known that—so he told me you were dead."

"But why? Brad told me that Bradford Chase demanded that each of his daughters present him with a grandchild, but there was no stipulation that it had to be only one."

"I didn't know anything about Bradford Chase then. I just knew how desperately Rachel and Victor wanted a baby. It was only when I heard Brad's bitter recounting of his grandfather's decree several years ago that I understood the need for secrecy, why we spent all those months in the South of France. But it still didn't occur to me that you had survived." She gave a bewildered shake of her head and confessed quietly, "Maybe I wouldn't let it occur to me, Chase. Maybe I was afraid to."

"You had no reason to believe that I had survived," Chase

offered gently, succumbing without resistance to the powerful impulse to reassure her.

"No, I didn't," Claudia admitted. "Certainly not at the time."

"But now? Do you know now why they didn't keep both of us?"

"I think so. Rachel was very delicate, very frail. She'd had a series of miscarriages and when I met her the doctors had just told her that another pregnancy might kill her. I suppose Victor decided that no one would believe that Rachel could have given birth to twins."

"And so," Chase clarified solemnly, bitterly, "he simply left me behind."

The bitterness in Chase's voice created even more despair and more apology on Claudia's beautiful face. And once again he felt the powerful impulse to reassure. He had no wish to punish her. It wasn't her fault. She hadn't known. She wouldn't have abandoned him if she had. Even though she had been young and had believed herself unworthy of being loved, she would have tried to be a mother to him.

And she would have been a wonderful mother, Chase thought. She *was* a wonderful mother . . . to the woman he loved.

Chase saw now in Claudia's apologetic eyes that she wanted to help him, and for a moment he allowed himself a fantasy. Willingly, *so willingly,* he would have his own face destroyed, the bones crushed, the skin tattered; and then he would ask his gifted plastic surgeon mother to create a new face for him, to change him so completely that when Jillian looked at him she would no longer see the mirror image of evil.

Chase would have so willingly permitted his face to be shattered; but, too swiftly, the memory of what Jillian herself had said about plastic surgery came back to him. The eyes don't change, she had said. Nor do the hands, nor does the heart.

Chase Carlton shared, and always would share, his eyes, his hands, and his heart with a murderer.

Claudia wanted to help. But there was nothing she could do. Not even her most generous gifts could change the truth.

Chase should have assured Claudia that the genes of evil that had compelled his twin to such unspeakable horrors had surely been inherited from Victor, not from her. Victor Kincaid had amply proven his own ruthlessness, just as she had proven her generosity. She was not to blame for the monster she had borne.

Chase should have further told her that the things he himself had inherited from her were the very best parts of who he was: the bright blue in his eyes, identical to hers, when he was happy . . . and the gentle place in his heart that knew how to love.

But Chase couldn't speak such assurances. The words were far too emotional and he was already drowning in pain, gasping desperately for privacy in which to think about the twin who had been a murderer . . . and the father who had mercilessly wounded the heart of his own infant son . . . and the woman who would have been such a wonderful mother to him . . . and, most of all, the woman he loved—and had lost.

He needed to leave now, for himself and for Claudia. She, like Jillian, deserved never to see him again, to never again be forced to gaze at the mirror image of cruelty, betrayal, and evil.

It was impossible for Chase to speak all the emotional words that could have been spoken to Claudia; but just before leaving, he managed to whisper the most important truth of all, "Thank you for loving Jillian."

Chase walked outside into the day that such a short time before Jillian had joyfully agreed would be a day to spend resting sore muscles beneath the warm summer sun and listening to songs of love in the rose-fragrant garden.

There was no music in Chase's heart now, and his injured muscles screamed with pain, and he knew that the strident screams would only get louder as he walked farther and farther away from her.

Chase began his journey toward San Francisco without a

cent in his pockets. It didn't matter. He would walk, hitchhike maybe. There was no rush. Chase Carlton was in no hurry whatsoever to reach his destination . . . because the only destination left in his life now was a destination away from love, away from happiness, away from paradise.

"Claudia."

The voice was Edward's, but it was a bare skeleton without warmth or flesh, and even before she turned to face him she knew that he had overheard her conversation with Chase. He knew everything now, all the truths . . . and all the lies.

"Edward," she whispered softly as she met angry eyes that were telling her so clearly that all the years of their love were forgotten, had never really existed at all, built as they had been on shadowy illusions, not the solid foundation of honesty and trust. "Edward, please . . ."

"Why, Claudia? Why didn't you tell me?"

"Because I was so afraid of losing you."

"Because you knew that I might question your motives for marrying me?"

"My motives?"

"To be in Los Angeles, near your son. To one day maybe even find a way to unite your son and my daughter."

She's my daughter too! Claudia's heart cried. "No! Edward, how can you think that?"

"How can I think anything else?"

"You know I had nothing to do with Jillian and Chase meeting each other. You *know* that."

"I don't know anything, Claudia," Edward said grimly. Then, even more grimly, he amended, "No, that's not true. I do know that our entire marriage has been a lie."

"I *couldn't* tell you, don't you see?"

"All I see is a woman who told me that she loved me but obviously didn't."

"Edward, *no*. It was *because* I loved you so much that I didn't tell you. Please understand that. Please believe it."

As Edward had listened to Claudia's emotional confession to her son, his shattering heart had cried, You could have told me, Claudia. You could have trusted me. Why didn't you know that?

But she hadn't told him, hadn't known she could trust him, and now she was telling him that the reason she hadn't told him was that she had loved him so much. Her anguished eyes were so unflickering, as if, somehow, her love for him *had* been the reason she had kept the secret.

"Explain what you mean." It was a gentle command, his voice laced now with a little warmth, a little hope.

"I was afraid that if you knew what I had done you wouldn't want me." Claudia shrugged softly. "I knew that what you felt for me was mostly gratitude for what I had done for Jillian."

"Gratitude?"

"Yes," Claudia answered. Then, urgently, she assured him, "That was enough for me, Edward, *more* than enough."

"You honestly believed that I asked you to marry me because I was grateful for what you had done for my daughter?" Edward repeated with disbelief. When he saw the loving yes in her beautiful blue eyes, he felt a mixture of hope and anger. Had he failed once again to say clearly enough the words of love that should have been said? "I married you because I loved you, Claudia, because I loved you and needed you and couldn't imagine my life without you."

"Edward . . ."

"I love you, Claudia, and I need you, and I can't imagine my life without you."

Claudia's heart raced with hope. But, as always, it quickly stumbled, tripped up by her secrets. Edward knows the secrets now, she reminded her faltering hope. But what if he doesn't, not really? What if there were parts of the conversation with Chase that he hadn't overheard?

"One of my sons was a murderer, Edward," she said. "And because of a decision I made a long time ago, my other son lived a childhood that no child should ever have been forced to live."

"I know," Edward said. He touched her then, his hands tenderly cradling her face, and when he spoke again, his heart reached out with exquisite tenderness to hers. "Let me help you, Claudia. Need me, need *me* as I have always needed you. Will you? Please?"

"Yes," she whispered, curling against him, marveling as she did that the invisible wall of secrets that had always separated them was now suddenly gone. She was in the sanctuary of his arms, drawing strength and courage from his love; but after only a few heartbeats, she pulled away. And then, to the surprised and loving eyes that met hers, she said, "Jillian needs us, Edward. Our daughter needs us."

The newspaper article about the Guitar String Strangler began on the first page of Monday's *Los Angeles Times* and spilled over to the next two pages. The *San Francisco Chronicle* carried an abbreviated version of the same story. Chase read both versions in the privacy of his motel room at Fisherman's Wharf. He had arrived in San Francisco the evening before, explained to the security guard at the Marina Yacht Club that he had found new moorage for *Sea Witch,* and retrieved his car.

Many of the questions that had swirled in his mind as he had walked and hitchhiked up the coast were answered by the articles. That Claudia had revealed the truth about the parentage of the twin boys was immediately apparent. Chase guessed that she had told her family the full truth; but the version that had been provided to the press had been slightly altered, presumably by Brad, to protect the innocent. Victor Chase Kincaid was the *adopted* son of Rachel and Victor Kincaid, the papers reported. The birth parents of the movie-mogul-turned-monster were unknown. The revelation spared Claudia and at the same time relieved Brad of the stigma of having been related by blood to a serial killer.

"I loved Chase as a brother," Brad was quoted as saying. "Of course I don't excuse what he did—it's unforgivable—but I loved him, as did my grandfather." Which meant, the article explained, that even though a claim might have been made that Victor Chase Kincaid had no legal right to the studio, the half of Triple Crown inherited by Jillian Kincaid on her husband's death would remain hers. Brad expressed the hope that someday Jillian would become actively involved with the studio, but for now the devoted schoolteacher would continue her teaching and concentrate on healing the deep wounds of what Brad termed "this unspeakable tragedy."

Part of the healing for both Brad and Jillian would be meeting with the families of the Strangler's victims. The meetings would not be for public consumption, of course, but the public was permitted to know that all profits from *Journeys of the Heart,* the movie that would be Triple Crown's biggest blockbuster yet, would be donated to a fund for victims of violent crime.

There was very little mention of Chase Carlton in either paper. There was the strong implication, however, that the expert in serial killers had sensed that his twin knew something about the Guitar String Strangler, and as a result had appeared, under cover but with the full knowledge and consent of both Jillian Kincaid and Brad Lancaster.

The story given to the press was a masterpiece in public relations. In it Chase saw absolute proof of Brad's gift in that area and was very grateful. The spin Brad had so artfully put on the tragedy made it possible for Jillian to go on with her life as quickly as possible. Brad had protected Jillian, as always, and he had even tried to salvage a shred of dignity for the murderer who had not been his cousin after all: by suggesting that the accident on *Sea Goddess* had perhaps, in fact, been a suicide.

Brad had always been protective of Jillian, and now Chase was forced to face the truth that Brad's concern about Jillian's relationship with his twin, his obvious belief that they would be better off apart, had been entirely correct. And now, too, Chase had to accept the inevitable image of Brad and Jillian . . . together.

Brad, who was untainted by genes laced with evil.

Brad, who was the true hero of the piece.

Brad, who was most worthy of Jillian.

PART FOUR

Chapter Thirty

Los Angeles
October 7, 1994

Chase had believed that all the truths had been revealed and that all the journeys of his own heart were over. In late July, after resurrecting *Sea Witch* from her burial at sea, he had set sail, believing as he did that the only journey left in his life was a solitary one around the world.

Chase was quite certain that this time he would in fact circumnavigate the planet. The dark gift for evil that had always before commanded that he return was surely gone. The restless searching of the tormented conscience for its twin's murderous heart had surely ended forever with the death of that twin.

For many weeks Chase simply ignored the invisible force. It was only his heart, he thought, only that shattered and lonely thing sending a desperate plea for him to return to Jillian, to happiness, to love. Chase ignored the invisible force, believing that eventually it would die, but as he neared the aquamarine waters of the South Pacific, it became even more powerful, its call ever more familiar—and ever more clear—commanding him to return because there was still a death to avenge, a murder to be solved, a killer to be stopped.

Impossibly but so powerfully that it could no longer be denied, the invisible force was telling him that his twin had not been a murderer after all. Impossibly but with powerful clarity it felt to Chase as if the invisible voice that was calling him back belonged to the anguished ghost of that horribly misjudged twin.

Impossibly? No, not really, because compelling evidence notwithstanding, there were things about Victor Chase Kincaid that made him a most unlikely serial killer. True, he had with selfish—or perhaps simply careless—cruelty strangled the gentle hopes of Jillian's loving heart. That in itself was an unforgivable crime.

But it did not make him the Guitar String Strangler.

Chase Carlton knew serial killers. They *were not* kind to animals. A serial killer would not have rescued an abused and orphaned puppy, nor would he have then been so obviously loved and missed by that innocent creature.

And the death by fire of Victor and Rachel Kincaid? Perhaps a tragic accident, after all, not a blazing clue to a future of unspeakable evil.

And the death of the golden twin himself? An accident too, or maybe, as Brad suggested, a suicide. Maybe his twin, stunned by the vicious blow from the boom, had fallen to *Sea Goddess*'s deck to rest, to recover; and maybe in those moments he had made the decision to succumb forever to the intoxicating lure of the sea. But if Victor Chase Kincaid had chosen death, it had been because of what he had done to Jillian, what had driven her to want to end their love, not because he had felt remorse for the murders of five women. Serial killers did not feel remorse, nor did they kill themselves.

The Guitar String Strangler case was unsolved. The murderer stalked still, smug in his victory, and Victor Chase Kincaid's ghost paced with restless anguish, beckoning to his twin to return to avenge the wrong that had been done to him.

The invisible voice beckoned, and it also sent a promise. If you make this right, if you prove that I am not the monster the world believes me to be, then you can ask the lovely emerald eyes to forgive you . . .

* * *

Sea Witch sailed into Marina del Rey shortly after two P.M. on Friday, October 7. Chase guided her expertly into the marina, nestling her midnight-black hull beside *Sea Goddess,* her pure white twin. After securing the two sailboats together, Chase left the safety of *Sea Witch*'s varnished deck and crossed to *Sea Goddess,* to the spot where his twin had died.

He waited, breath held, even though this time he expected warmth, not ice, the welcoming heartcall of the twin who had at last accepted his own death, and who no longer begrudged his brother a chance at happiness, and who now *needed* his brother to clear his tarnished memory.

But what came was pure ice, invading him as powerfully and mercilessly as it had before, threatening to kill him still. Chase fought valiantly to move his frozen lungs, to compel his stilled heart to beat, but he needed more than all his strength and all his will to combat the immense power of evil that enveloped him.

And what Chase found, what came to him as if by magic, was the most powerful weapon of all. Into his frozen heart drifted memories of love, memories of his love for her . . . and memories of the radiant emerald eyes that had once glowed with such love for him. Once before Jillian had saved him from death on the deck of *Sea Goddess*—and she saved him now.

The ice melted slowly, begrudgingly, as before; but it did melt. And when at last it was gone, Chase tried to make sense of what had happened.

It's obvious, isn't it? the taunting voice of his past demanded. Your twin is the murderer. Pretending that he isn't has simply been wishful thinking, a foolish dream of your foolish heart, because you want so very much to find a way back to Jillian. Admit it.

No. The voice came from deep within, defiant, and astonishingly confident despite what had just happened. Victor Chase

Kincaid is not the Guitar String Strangler. Follow your instincts
. . . your gift . . . your plan.

During the long sail back to Los Angeles, Chase had rehearsed his plan a thousand times.

Sail into the marina.

Stand on the deck of *Sea Goddess.*

Rent a car and drive to Bel Air—no, not to Clairmont, to the
Hotel Bel-Air.

Call Jack to arrange a meeting with him to look at all the
evidence on the Guitar String Strangler.

Call Jillian.

That was Chase's plan, and even though what had just happened on the deck of *Sea Goddess* was a dramatic departure
from what he had expected, he would methodically follow the
plan, bypassing no steps, crescendoing in order to what he
wanted most, and feared most: hearing her soft voice once
again.

It was almost five by the time he was settled into his suite at
the Hotel Bel-Air. He placed the call to Jack's office, as planned.
No, he was told, the homicide lieutenant was not in. But he was
expected back within the hour. Chase left his name and number
and replaced the receiver to wait.

"Hi. I took a chance that you'd be—" Stephanie stopped
midsentence and simply stared at her friend. "You cut your
hair."

"Today, on the way home from school."

"Gorgeous," Stephanie enthused honestly as she studied
Jillian's new hairstyle. The auburn was cut very short, a smooth,
glittering cap of fire that fully exposed her beautiful face, making
even more remarkable her huge emerald eyes—her huge
haunted emerald eyes. Stephanie's admiring smile held as she
offered quietly, "Very grown-up."

"It was time for me to grow up, Steph."

"Girlhood myths and legends notwithstanding, being

grown-up does not in fact signal the end of romance or dreams, you know," Stephanie offered gently.

Jillian answered with a soft smile. Romance was over for her forever. She knew that. And dreams? No, she thought, her smile softening even more. She still had a dream, a tiny wondrous dream that was growing bravely deep inside her.

It wasn't by accident that she'd arranged to have her hair cut today. It was a symbol of being a grown-up—a mother—and much more: a symbol of new beginning. If she made today a beginning, not an end, then she and her baby would survive this all-important day . . . she wouldn't lose this precious little life as she had lost her other baby exactly four years ago today . . . this evening . . . at seven P.M.

"I'm leaving the romance to you, Stephanie. So why don't you come in and let's talk about your plans for your wedding and honeymoon."

"Again?" Stephanie teased.

"Again," Jillian confirmed with a twinkle.

"Okay," Stephanie agreed as she followed Jillian and Annie to the living room. But when they were settled, instead of launching into a breathless recounting of every wonderful detail of the small and very romantic wedding that would take place in just eight days, she said solemnly, "There's something I need to tell you first, Jill."

"You sound so serious."

"I am. This is something very important that I should have told you a long time ago. I've just never had the courage."

"What is it, Stephanie?"

"I want to apologize for abandoning you."

"Abandoning me?" Jillian echoed with surprise. "When did you ever abandon me?"

"When? In the hospital, after your accident. I tried to talk to you, but the more I tried, the more I stuttered. It got worse and worse and I became so afraid that I would regress entirely that I stopped visiting you three days before you were transferred to San Francisco." *There,* she had confessed the shameful truth.

But all she saw, still, was surprise. "Don't you remember that? Maybe you couldn't hear me."

"I heard you, Stephanie," Jillian answered softly. "But I chose not to answer you. I blamed myself for what happened, for asking my mother to drive me on that stormy night, and when the guilt became too much for me to bear, I let it spill over to you, blaming you for not coming to my house instead and for having a mother who was so selfish that she would never drive you anywhere. It was irrational, I know that now, but I was irrational then." Jillian drew a breath and then made even more confessions. "I heard you stuttering, Stephanie. I heard you trying to help me, to love me, but I was so hurt that I wanted you to hurt too. You didn't abandon me. I *drove* you away. I'm the one who has needed to apologize all these years, and I'm the one who has never had the courage. That's why I wrote *Journeys of the Heart*. That was my apology to you."

"The reason I turned down the role at first was that I thought it would be hard for you to know that such a wonderful opportunity had been given to such an unworthy human being."

"Oh, Stephanie, I'm so sorry."

"I'm the one who's sorry."

"No. What I did to you was terribly cruel."

"You don't have a cruel bone in your body, Jill. What I did was very cowardly."

"You're not a coward."

"Yes—" Stephanie stopped then, and after a moment she gave a soft, lovely smile. "Shall we stop this?"

"Yes." Jillian smiled too, and then became serious once again. "Thank you."

"Thank *you*. Now . . . change of topic." Stephanie might have breezily moved to something light, or raved again about Jillian's hair, but she saw hesitation in Jillian's eyes that made her ask gently, "What?"

"Brad has asked me to marry him."

"Brad? I hadn't realized . . ."

"Nor had I. We've always been wonderful friends, of course,

and he's always been very protective of me. I know that's what this marriage proposal is really, a way to protect me, although Brad claims it's more."

"So you've already discussed your reaction to his proposal with him?"

"Last week, when he first asked me. I was surprised, stunned actually, and I instantly said no. Brad spent the next two hours convincing me that it was a serious offer and that I needed to give it serious consideration."

"And you have."

Jillian nodded solemnly. "He'll be here within the hour. We're supposed to go to a premiere in Westwood this evening, but he wants my answer first."

"And your answer is?"

"Still no."

"Because of Chase Carlton," Stephanie said quietly, speaking aloud the name that Jillian had resolutely refused to utter at all for the past three months.

Because of Chase, because of Chase's baby, because even though I care for Brad, I don't love him, because I still and always love . . . Jillian drove away the thought.

"Have you heard from him, Jill?"

"From Chase? No, and I don't expect to." Jillian frowned and admitted quietly, "One of the last things I said to him, my parting shot just before he left, was that he was even worse than his twin."

"Well, I know you don't believe that and I'm sure he knows that too. However, since you and I have just proven that apologies can sometimes uncover all sorts of misunderstandings, I think you should talk to him. Jack would be very happy to help you find him." Stephanie gave a thoughtful tilt of moonbeams and sable before offering, "You were really very much in love with him."

"Yes, I was." *More in love with him than I ever was with his brother.* Deep pain filled her haunted emerald eyes. "But for him it was all a pretense. He believed I was a murderess."

"In the beginning, yes, before he ever met you. But not after. Don't forget, Jill, I saw the way he looked at you at dinner that night—and after the accident. He loved you as much as you loved him."

"I'm not going to try to find him." Not *yet,* her heart amended defiantly. But someday . . .

"But at least you're not going to marry Brad."

"No." At the mention of Brad's name, Jillian glanced anxiously at her watch. "I suppose it's time for me to start the transformation from jeans to a dress suitable for a premiere." And for the refusal of a proposal of marriage. Jillian fought the surprising but quite powerful quiver of apprehension with a firm reminder: Brad is a true friend. He'll understand. He'll probably be relieved. The quiver passed, and she smiled at the golden animal curled contentedly at her feet and mused, "It's also about time for me to put Annie outside."

"Outside? Why?"

"Because Brad and Annie aren't terribly close. He always thought we were a little silly about her, but Annie seems to sense his disapproval of her now, so it's easier to put her outside whenever he's here."

All the more reason not to marry Brad, Stephanie thought. After a moment she asked, "Annie still won't use her dog door? Whatever it is that frightens her about the door must be very strong if it keeps her outside even when she'd rather be inside with you."

"Yes," Jillian agreed quietly. Then, smiling at the golden face that tilted with obvious curiosity at the sound of her name, she said affectionately, "She'll stay outside, but she'll whine. Won't you, Annie? Yes, admittedly, it's a very tricky whine, cleverly disguised as a heavy sigh that squeaks."

"I have an idea," Stephanie said. "Why don't I take my favorite dog in the world for a sunset walk on the beach?"

"Really? You want to do that?"

"Absolutely. I'll bring her back sometime after you and Brad have left for the premiere and if you give me a key, I'll let her in."

"You won't need a key. I'll just leave the kitchen door unlocked for you. In fact, maybe I'll tell Brad that I'd rather not go to the premiere after all. In which case, assuming that's okay with him, I'll be here when you and Annie return."

"And if you're not too tired, we could have dinner together."

Jillian suddenly very much hoped that Brad wouldn't mind if she canceled the evening. It was more than a hope, she realized. It was a belief: if she were here, with her best friend—her baby's future godmother—during those all-important moments when the hands of the clock rose toward seven, then those hands would safely approach *and pass* the hour without incident, without tragedy, without loss.

"That would be wonderful, Steph."

"Not completely wonderful," Stephanie countered with a twinkle. "I really think we need to explore further the topic of Chase Carlton." Stephanie paused, and even though she saw far more hope than resistance, she added quietly, "And no matter how annoyed you get with me, you won't drive me away. I will never abandon you again, Jillian, *never,* no matter what."

"My God, what have you done to your hair?"

Jillian frowned at the edge of harshness in his voice. "You don't like it."

Brad smiled an easy, reassuring smile. "I'm just surprised, that's all. It's very stylish, of course, and you look very beautiful." His dark eyes grew gentle but serious as they fell on her earlobes. Always before they had been hidden—at least hidable—by her long, luxuriant auburn hair. But they were fully exposed now, and naked. "You're going to have to start wearing earrings again."

"Yes," she agreed solemnly. She hadn't worn earrings since the day Chase Carlton left, not since she had taken off the pearls he had given her. "I know."

"You have to let it go, Jillian. You have to throw away all the earrings that he—that both of them—ever gave you, and then you have to let me spend the rest of our lives buying new ones for you, beginning with a pair to match the engagement ring I have in mind."

"Brad . . ."

"I take it the answer is still no," he guessed softly of her apologetic eyes. "It's okay, Jillian. I understand. It's still too soon. I should have waited a little longer before asking you."

"It's not the timing, Brad. It's simply not fair for me to let you believe that. I care for you too much."

"You love me."

"Yes, of course I love you. You're my wonderful friend. You've always been there for me, protecting me, picking up the pieces, making me laugh, holding me when I cried."

"I want to always be there for you, Jillian, but not only as your friend. I want to be there as your husband, as your lover." Brad's seductive dark eyes caressed her. "Do you find me so terribly unattractive?"

"Of course not! You know you're gorgeous, Brad. You *know* you could have any woman you want."

"Is that a promise? Because the woman I want is you."

Jillian stepped back a step then, suddenly inexplicably wary. Despite the fact that she had tried to keep the mood light, it now felt dark, ominous.

This is *silly,* she told herself. Brad is my dear friend, the big brother I never had.

Still, as the phone started to ring, she moved to it quickly, relieved at the intrusion, relieved to have an opportunity to put even more space between herself and Brad. "Hello?"

"It's Chase, Jillian."

"Chase."

He had waited for twenty endless minutes for Jack to return his call, eager for that call and even more eager for the one that would follow. Jack still hadn't called, but Chase's heart had finally compelled his fingers to dial Clairmont.

I guess I must have a death wish, Chase had admitted to himself as he dialed. Because what little life is left in my heart will be extinguished the moment I hear her voice, its hatred, its revulsion.

Chase had prepared his heart for hatred, for death, but in the single syllable of his name, he heard welcome.

"Hi," he whispered, a single syllable too, but it held the same joy and wonder now that it had held just moments before they had first made love.

"Hi," she echoed exactly as she had on that night of love. The small but monumental syllables frolicked in the silence for a while, celebrating what had been said, anticipating with pure happiness even more syllables of love. But when Jillian spoke again, her voice was flat. "How are you?"

What had happened? Chase wondered. Had she suddenly remembered all the unforgivable truths? Or was it something else? Please, please. . . . Finally, with quiet hope he guessed, "You're not alone?"

"No," Jillian confirmed as she looked at Brad. His eyes were pure black now—and very angry. "Where are you?"

"At the Hotel Bel-Air. Jillian, I don't think my twin was a murderer. I know that sounds impossible—at least improbable—but it's honestly what I believe. I have a call in to Jack and I'm going to ask him to let me see all the police files on the Strangler." Chase paused for a breath, then said softly, "I was also hoping that I could wander through the house sometime. It might help."

"Of course." Brad had moved closer, his black scowl matching his black eyes. "May I call you back later, Chase?"

"I'll be right here." Waiting for your call, loving you, hoping, hoping . . .

"Okay." Jillian scowled back at Brad. "It won't be long. Good-bye."

Jillian's green eyes flashed angrily at Brad's black ones as she replaced the receiver.

"That was very rude of you."

"He's the reason you won't marry me, isn't he?"

Yes! He's the reason I will never marry anyone. As angry as

she was at Brad, something stopped Jillian from saying the words aloud and provoking him any further. Instead, finding a conciliatory smile, she answered truthfully, "I haven't even talked to him since the day he left here in July."

"Where is he? What the hell does he want now?"

"He's at the Hotel Bel-Air." Her smile became hopeful as she said to the man who had been like a brother to Chase Kincaid, "And Brad, he thinks that someone else is the Guitar String Strangler."

"Really," Brad answered quietly. "Did he happen to say who?"

Chapter Thirty-One

Jack's call to Chase's suite at the Hotel Bel-Air came within a few seconds of the end of Chase's conversation with Jillian.

Chase got right to the point.

"He was my brother, so naturally I want to clear his name. But Jack, my instincts are telling me that it's a lot more than that—they're telling me that the Strangler is still alive."

"Have you connected with him?"

"No," Chase admitted. "But there haven't been any murders since May, have there? In the past, my connections have been with mindprints—or whatever they are—left at the scene of the crime, or with the killer himself when he's actually in pursuit of a victim. I'd like to go to the crime scenes, Jack, and I'd like to take a look at everything you have in your files."

"You're saying that what we found in the Ferrari—and in the study at Clairmont—was planted?"

Chase frowned. He hadn't constructed a theory. He was simply acting on instinct. "I guess I am saying that, yes."

"You know he was a friend of mine. You *know* I would be delighted to clear his name. I'll show you all our files, and we'll go to all the crime scenes, but . . . people don't hold your brother's crimes against you, Chase. The people who care about you can rise above the genetics. Jillian can."

"I don't know, Jack, I think that's really too much to—" Chase stopped cold, *ice* cold. "Oh, my God."

"Chase?"

The ice had invaded him again, but this time it didn't want to kill, only to taunt, to beckon, its ominous message of evil now, at long last, crystal-clear.

"He's at Clairmont."

"Who is?"

"The killer . . . the Strangler. I have to go."

"Wait," Jack commanded urgently as he fought to contain his own rising panic. This was the day that Stephanie had planned to go to Clairmont to apologize to Jillian. "I can get patrol cars there immediately, and a SWAT team."

"No. If he hears sirens, if he feels surrounded . . ." *He will kill her.* The words were unspeakable. Chase couldn't say those words, nor did he need to say them to Los Angeles's most savvy homicide lieutenant. He wanted to leave now, to be with Jillian, but he needed to be very sure that Jack understood. "Listen to me, Jack. No sirens, no storming of the house. *I mean it.*"

"Okay. What else?"

"I'm going to Clairmont now. He wants me there." He wants me too. The eerie realization was strangely comforting. The killer was waiting for him to join them, which meant that Jillian was safe for now, for the moment—until the murderer lost patience with the wait. "I'll just let him talk until I can find a way to subdue him."

A memory suddenly appeared from behind a dark shadow. Chase had said those same confident words in Denver, convincing the police to let him meet the killer face-to-face, knowing the murderer wanted such a confrontation with the man who had journeyed into his mind and accompanied him on his voyages of death. The rest of the memory was still shadowed, what he had said on the ledge of the building, what the killer had said to him, if he had ever even come close to getting the killer enough off guard to subdue him. What Chase knew of those moments he had been told by witnesses: Eventually the two of them had struggled, his bare hands against the murderer's hunting knife. They had fallen off the ledge together, a lethal fall for the murderer but one which Chase had miraculously survived.

And it was all destiny. Chase Carlton had survived that fall in Denver to be here, now, to engage in mind to mind—and then hand to hand—combat with the man whose lust for murder was now focused on the woman Chase loved.

It didn't matter if Chase survived the confrontation that was about to come. All that mattered was that Jillian was safe and that the Strangler was dead.

"You'll have a silent army of backup right outside," Jack promised solemnly. "And Chase, when he lets you in, if you can, unlock the door for me."

"Do you mind if I beg off the premiere this evening, Brad?" Jillian asked casually, finally breaking the lingering silence that had fallen following her revelation that Chase Carlton had returned to clear his twin's name. "It was a long week at work, this year's class of third-graders is the liveliest ever, and I really need an early evening. Stephanie was by earlier—she and Annie are taking a walk on the beach—and we thought we might have a quiet dinner here when she returns. Would that be all right with you?"

"Sure."

Brad turned away from her then, and she followed him as he walked toward the front door. She would hug him good-bye, she decided, a hug for her friend, an apology for the surprising tension of the past few minutes and a promise that the next time they saw each other, everything would be back to normal.

But Brad's destination wasn't the front door. He walked past the marble foyer, down the hall toward what had once been Chase Kincaid's study.

"Brad?"

"I just need to get something from the study," he answered

over his shoulder, his voice pleasant, casual, normal. "Is that okay?"

"Of course it is."

Reassured by the pleasantness of his voice, Jillian followed him in case he needed help finding whatever it was he wanted.

"I'm looking for that heavy knit sweater," Brad explained when they reached the study. "You know, the one you had made for Chase after he won the America's Cup?"

"It should be in here, in the closet, assuming it's not on *Sea Goddess.*"

The hand-knit sweater with sailboats and waves was more jacket than sweater, lined, zippered in the front, with pockets. It was hanging in the closet toward the back. Brad found it immediately, as if he had known it was there, withdrawing not the sweater itself but something from one of its pockets.

Something black, and shiny, and deadly.

"Brad."

"You didn't realize he'd bought a gun, did you?"

"No . . . when?"

"Sometime during the week between the Kentucky Derby and the night he died." Brad held the gun in the palm of his hand, speaking to it, not to her, as he continued. "I imagine he got it because he realized that someday there might be a confrontation with the police, that someday despite his cleverness they might find out about him."

"Are you forgetting that Chase Carlton believes he *wasn't* the Guitar String Strangler?"

"What?" Brad asked, looking up. Then, smiling, he said, "Yes, I guess I am forgetting that."

He was smiling, but when the smile reached his dark eyes there was an expression Jillian had never seen before.

Almost menacing, she thought before dismissing it with the stern reminder that she was being silly.

Still, she wanted him to leave soon—*now.*

"Feel free to take the gun, Brad. I certainly don't want it."

"Thanks." Brad moved away from the closet, but instead of

walking to the doorway and then to the front door, he crossed
to the antique table.

"What time do you expect Stephanie to return?"

The premiere in Westwood was scheduled to begin at seven-
fifteen, which meant that Brad would need to leave Clairmont
by six forty-five at the very latest. That was the time she had told
Stephanie, to be safe, to avoid any overlap, but now because she
wanted him to leave, Jillian answered, "At any moment."

Brad nodded solemnly, then opened the table drawer.

"Brad, what are you doing?" she asked, hearing the silly
quiver of worry in her voice. She should have been angry, not
worried; angry at whatever game he was playing; angry that
now he was looking in the drawer where Chase had kept extra
guitar strings—and where the gold earring had been found.
"Brad?"

"Don't you know?" His voice was soft, seductive, filled with
menace. He wasn't looking at her, but in the drawer, his dark
eyes focused, intent, making a decision. Then, including her in
the decision, he mused aloud, "Let's see, if Stephanie is really
going to be joining us, we'll need twice as many—six, not just
three." Withdrawing an unopened packet of strings, enough
either way, he slipped them into the pocket of his impeccably
tailored suit before turning to her. "Won't we?"

Jillian saw the madness then, the sinister smile, the eyes that
filled with a dark desire for unspeakable terror. She started to
run. But Brad had known that she would run, had wanted her
to, and he moved at the same instant, reaching her swiftly and
imprisoning her in his powerful arms.

"Now you get it, don't you?" he whispered softly.

"No, Brad, I don't get it," she lied. She did understand, of
course, with exquisite and excruciating clarity. "Tell me."

"Gladly. We have time. Even after Stephanie arrives, we may
still have to wait for your lover." At his words, Jillian's eyes filled
with worry for her friend, and then for Chase; in that worry,
Brad saw her remarkable generosity. She had asked him to talk
to her, to buy time, but when she realized that buying time

would only put in jeopardy the people she loved, she was ready to give herself to him to protect them. "Don't worry, Jillian. There's nothing you can do. Stephanie's fate is in her own hands. If she arrives before I need to leave, she dies. If not, she lives. Chase will die. No matter what, he *will* die."

Brad smiled at her terror. Then, wanting to see it more clearly, he released his viselike grip.

"You can't escape, Jillian. You know that. So why don't we go back into the living room? It's more comfortable there. A nice place to chat."

When they reached the living room, Brad indicated that she should sit on the couch nearest the fireplace. Jillian obeyed his silent command, and when she was precisely where he wanted her to be, Brad stood in front of her.

"Look at me, Jillian. Thank you. Now, shall I tell you what I'd like, the perfect scene? All right. It's this: two beautiful women, strangled, lying right here." He gestured with the gun to a place on the plush teal carpet. "I'm annoyed with you for having cut your hair, by the way. I *really* liked the image of nude female bodies dressed only in long hair. The nudity is a departure. That's what you're thinking, isn't it? I *know* it's a departure. I *know* that when I cast Chase Kincaid in the role of the Strangler he always left his victims fully clothed. But now the man playing the Strangler will be his twin, so a little variation is allowed, expected, even. I think I will reprise the earring theme though. You and Stephanie can each be wearing one of the pearls that Carlton gave you. You don't mind sharing with your best friend, do you, Jillian? I assume the pearls are in the same jewelry box where I found the diamonds?"

He was mad, completely insane. But he was also completely in control.

"Brad, please," Jillian whispered with soft horror. "You're ill, you need help."

"But I *don't* need help, Jillian, that's the point. I didn't need

Chase Kincaid's help at the studio, not ever, but everyone decided that he would have the creative genius—like *his* father—and I would have the flair for marketing—like *my* father—and that's the way it was. I lived in his golden shadow for all those years. But I honestly think that with this Guitar String Strangler production—a continuing series, not just a one-time feature—I've more than proven my talents, my mastery of the medium, don't you?" Brad paused for her answer, and when it came, as more layers of terror in her beautiful eyes, his smile was one of pure satisfaction. "So, let me tell you the rest of the perfect scene. The two nude women will be lying here, and over there, with his brains blown out, will be your boyfriend. He will have killed himself, of course, because like his twin his obsession for you had become fatal." Brad frowned briefly before continuing. "I'm not really sure which way causes the most bleeding, a gunshot to the temple or one directly into the mouth. I want blood though, Jillian, because here's the *pièce de résistance.* I've been trying to decide what to do with that stupid dog, whether to strangle her, too, or shoot that ridiculous grin off her face. But I think what will work best, provide the most poignancy for those who love the sentimental, will be to let her live. That way, when Jack Shannon discovers the scene, she'll be in the living room, whining that insipid whine and licking the blood off what's left of Carlton's face. Don't you think that's good?"

"How can you do this, Brad?" Jillian pleaded. "Don't you remember our friendship, how much we've always cared for each other?"

The gentle words had been spoken in hope of finding the Brad Lancaster she once had known; but instead wild fury glittered in his dark eyes.

"What I remember, Jillian, is that you and I were on a date when you met Chase Kincaid."

"It wasn't a date! I was filling in at the last minute because the woman you were dating couldn't make it back from Palm Springs in time."

"You and I were on a date when you met Chase Kincaid,"

Brad repeated resolutely, as if he hadn't heard her. "You left with him, and then you married him. He wasn't worthy of you, Jillian. He knew that you were a princess, of course, and deep down he must have known he was an impostor prince, not the legitimate heir to the crown jewels, because he was *so suscepti- ble* to suggestions of his unworthiness. It was unbelievably easy for me to convince him that he couldn't make you happy no matter how hard he tried, and I even helped him down a path that should have caused the destruction of your marriage. I just hadn't counted on how tenacious you would be, how you would love him and defend him despite his mistresses—and despite what he did when you lost the baby. Would you like to hear how I scripted that marriage-damaging scene?"

"No," Jillian answered softly, a soft protest to the monster, and a soft protest as well to the invisible yet monstrous fingers she now felt deep inside. They were curled around her baby, flexing, clutching, threatening to strangle. You're going to live, my precious little one, you're going to live and your godmother is going to live and your daddy is going to live . . .

"You don't want to hear? That surprises me. You're a gifted scriptwriter, Jillian, and so am I. I thought you'd be interested. You *should* be. So, for your own good, your own enlighten- ment, I'll tell you. Your beloved husband was devastated by the news that the baby had died. He knew that you would be devastated, too, and the moment I told him, he started talking about plans to charter a plane right away to fly home to be with you. I had to stop those romantic plans, of course. I knew that if he came home to you, you'd forgive him all past and future sins and all would be lost. I think what I came up with—on the spot—was quite brilliant, a wonderful plot twist based on an old story line. The reason for your miscarriage, I told him, was your accident. It was highly unlikely that your pelvis would ever be able to carry a baby to term, and even trying again might put your life in jeopardy. I said that you had heard the doctors' prognosis, and were adjusting to it, and that you believed the adjustment would happen more quickly if he didn't come

home. That, I explained to him, would only prolong the grieving."

Jillian's eyelashes fluttered downward, concealing her eyes
and providing necessary privacy for her thoughts. Now she
understood why her husband had never talked about the
daughter they had lost, nor written about her in the long—and,
yes, loving—letters he sent from Africa. And now she knew why
when he suggested that he have a vasectomy, he had withdrawn
the suggestion quickly when he saw how much it saddened her;
and why, after that, he had been so careful with their birth
control.

When she looked up again, her tear-misted eyes defiantly
met the dark smirk of the monster who stood before her.

"You bastard."

"Come, come, Jillian. I was only doing what I thought was
best for you."

"To be with you, not with him."

"You belonged with me, Jillian. It's too late now, you've
revealed your true colors, but you would have been so loved."

"*Loved?*" The word escaped as a startled gasp.

"Don't ever doubt my love for you, Jillian. I loved you. I
killed for you."

"*No,* Brad. I will not allow you to blame me for the unspeakable crimes you have committed."

"Well, well. I'm impressed—and a little disappointed.
You've always been so willing to accept responsibility for everything. But not this?"

"Not this." The words that Chase had spoken to her on that
glorious and then horrible morning in July came back to her
now, giving her strength, and courage, and *hope* as she repeated
them to Brad. "Serial killers are selfish. They kill for no other
reason than that they want to, because the pleasure of killing is
more important to them than anything, or anyone. No one
forces them to kill—they choose to. They care only about themselves, and they do not love."

"That sounds like psychobabble from the twin," Brad ob-

served wryly, his dark eyes filled with contempt. The conde-
scending disdain vanished after a moment, replaced by pure
rage as he hissed, "The *twin*. I was cursed all my life by the
magic of Chase Kincaid, and just when it seemed that I was
finally free of him forever, a carbon copy arrived. The twin was
a poor imitation though, wasn't he? Not quite so magical, not
really the star psychic he claimed to be. Oh, yes, *now* he has
rematerialized, and *now* he may even be on the right track
. . . but in July Chase Carlton bought the brother-as-murderer
scenario hook, line, and sinker. He wasn't supposed to have
lived even to have heard that scenario, of course. He was supposed to have gone up in flames with the car. The police were
supposed to have sifted the earrings from amid the ashes of his
bones." Brad gazed for a moment at the green eyes that had just
learned another facet of his treachery. "I *did* love you, Jillian, no
matter what you say. I would never have put air in the brakes
of the Ferrari if I had known you would be riding in it."

They were interrupted then, not by the melodic door
chimes, but by pounding.

Brad arched an interested eyebrow and smiled his most
chilling smile yet.

"I think lover boy has arrived."

Chapter Thirty-Two

Had the gun that greeted him been pointed directly at him, the fear Chase felt would have been far less than it was. Brad knew that. That was why the barrel was pressed firmly against Jillian's lovely temple, the cold metal crushing mercilessly against her fair skin, the trigger cocked. In one hand Brad Lancaster held the gun and with the other he imprisoned both of Jillian's delicate wrists behind her back.

"Come in, Carlton." Brad's voice held the gracious promise of a host greeting a most welcome guest. "We've been expecting you. I guess this proves you do get vibes, after all, doesn't it?"

"I guess so," Chase answered gravely.

Chase wanted to say a soft "hi" to Jillian, embellishing its single syllable with a thousand layers of love; but he didn't dare provoke Brad any further into the irretrievable madness to which he had already journeyed. Chase looked at her though, and even though his gray eyes were glacier-calm and unreadable to Brad, Jillian saw their deeper messages—and her emerald ones, hidden from Brad, sent greetings of love and courage for both of them.

"Let's go into the living room, shall we?" Brad suggested pleasantly, gesturing with a tilt of his dark head for Chase to

move farther into the foyer, farther away from the door that
Chase had been unable to touch, much less to unlock.

"Why don't you let her go, Brad?" Chase asked when they
reached the center of the living room. "It's me you really want,
isn't it?"

"I *have* you, Carlton. In fact, I think it's fair to say I have you
exactly where I want you. I was just telling Jillian about the
scenario the police will find. We're still giving Stephanie a
chance to arrive." Brad glanced away from Chase to look at the
Tiffany clock on the mantel. The glance was leisurely, not fur-
tive, a silent yet eloquent display of the fact that Brad was in
absolute control. He had no qualms about taking his eyes from
Chase, no fear that Chase might suddenly pounce. That wasn't
going to happen. The panther was completely subdued, tamed
by the gun which was held, cocked, against Jillian's head. "Six-
forty. We'll give Stephanie a few more minutes. After that, even
though I hate to be a party pooper, I really will have to get ready
to go. I have an alibi to make by seven-fifteen. So, what shall we
talk about? I know. I haven't yet told Jillian about what happened that night on *Sea Goddess.*"

"Oh, no," she whispered.

"Oh, *yes,*" Brad countered triumphantly. "This will interest
you, Carlton. You know those tormenting nightmares your
brother started having in mid-February? He was sensing *me,*
what I was up to, just as, I guess, you did this evening. He didn't
know what it was at first, of course, just images of murder and
violence—with feelings to match. For whatever reason, he finally tumbled to it in the winner's circle at Churchill Downs. He
knew he had until the following Tuesday night to stop me. I was
sensing him by then, too, guessing that he had guessed, or at
least was very worried, so I kept myself out of town until that
afternoon. I called him when I returned and listened very patiently to his clever but so transparent plan to arrange a meeting
with me that would keep me busy between nine and ten. I

suppose the idiot thought I'd gratefully confess my sins to him and then beg for his forgiveness and his help. I agreed to meet with him at exactly nine o'clock in the parking lot at Marina del Rey."

"But you didn't show up until later," Chase said quietly, seeing the sudden anguish in Jillian's beautiful eyes as she understood why even on that night, just moments after she had told his twin she wanted a divorce and he had so desperately pleaded with her to give him another chance, he had rushed away from her still, as always. On that night Chase Kincaid hadn't been rushing away from her, but to an appointment with a murderer from which he had promised to return—but hadn't. *I will hold you, and love you, and we will grieve together for my brother,* Chase silently promised. It was only after he believed that Jillian had read his silent message that Chase returned his gaze to Brad. "You didn't show up until after you had murdered Janine Raleigh."

"Bingo. Your brother was in the parking lot, still waiting for me, and he even had this gun. I knew he wouldn't use it, of course. I knew he'd use an entire arsenal of compassionate and sensitive words before ever resorting to deadly force. I told him that I wanted to talk privately and in open water on *Sea Goddess.*" Brad shook his head with disbelief as he mocked disdainfully, "What an *idiot.* It simply didn't occur to him that if he didn't kill me, I would kill him."

Because, Chase thought, when it came to evil, Chase Kincaid had been a novice. His golden twin had had just enough of his own dark gift to be lured to a killer but not enough of his cool indifference to murder him.

Not that he himself had always been that coolly indifferent to killing, Chase realized then as another memory of Denver drifted from the shadows. The police who had witnessed the scene on the ledge of the building told Chase afterward that at one point he had made a gesture that looked almost like an offer to help, as if he naively believed that given the opportunity, the killer would give himself up, relieved perhaps that the ordeal of death and destruction was over. It was during that gesture of help that the murderer had withdrawn the hunting knife from its hiding place in his boot and lunged at Chase.

Even though Chase Carlton had known the Denver killer's evil, and had had no sympathy for it, something deep within him had offered compassion. Something deep within . . . a piece of innocent generosity shared with his golden twin—the same piece of goodness that had permitted that twin to turn his back on Brad just long enough for Brad to make a lethal weapon of the boom.

That's what he had done, Brad was saying now. He had struck Chase Kincaid's foolishly naive head with the boom and then had mocked him as he'd lain bleeding on the deck, pleading for mercy—for himself *and still* for Brad! Chase Kincaid wasn't dead when he was shoved into the sea. But he was dying, and his body was weighted, and there had never been a shadow of doubt in Brad's mind that the man who had appeared in Puerto Vallarta was an impostor.

"I almost left the gun on the boat," Brad explained, his voice conspiratorial, as if Jillian and Chase cared about his crimes and marveled at his genius. "But I thought that might raise questions, so I wrapped it in a plastic bag and tucked it inside the wet suit. Now I'm glad that I did. This gun is going to come in very handy."

What was he planning? Chase wondered as he heard the ominous ticking of the clock. It was moving relentlessly toward a time known only to Brad, when the talking would be over and he would need to act in order to make his seven-fifteen alibi. There was a precise time known only to Brad, and a precise scene he planned to stage.

A murder/suicide, Chase supposed. He guessed that Brad's greatest pleasure would be to kill Jillian first, to watch Chase's helplessness as he witnessed her death. But Brad surely knew that would never happen. Chase wouldn't permit it. Brad would be forced to kill him first; which meant there would be a time when he took the barrel from Jillian's temple and swung it toward Chase.

And that was when Chase would kill him.

For now he could only wait, sending what messages he could to Jillian, and listening to Brad recount with horrifying pride the destruction he had caused—now he was describing with sinister delight the fire he had started at Lake Tahoe—and knowing that even though there was an army of police outside, they were paralyzed, as he was, by the gun pressed into Jillian's fair and delicate skin.

Stephanie was blocked at the entrance of Clairmont by one of what turned out to be many police cars.

"What's going on?" she asked anxiously of the police officer who greeted her.

"You're Stephanie Windsor, aren't you? Boy, is Lieutenant Shannon going to be relieved."

"Is he here? What's happening?" Stephanie got out of her car then, accompanied by Annie.

"Stephanie."

She turned to the familiar voice.

"Jack?" she asked softly of the relieved but still so worried dark blue eyes.

"I think Brad Lancaster is the Guitar String Strangler."

"What? Oh, Jack, he's in there with Jillian!"

"Chase is in there too. He said he thought it would be best—safest—for Jillian if he went in alone." Jack gave a frustrated sigh. "He had hoped to be able to unlock the front door, but—"

"The kitchen door is unlocked, Jack. Jillian said she'd leave it unlocked for me."

Even as she spoke, Stephanie began to move in the direction of the house, the unlocked kitchen door, and her friend. Within two steps Jack had caught her by the arm.

"I want you to wait right here." Jack expected a flicker of

resistance, and then understanding. But what he saw was a defiant shake of shimmering moonbeams and the resolute determination of brilliant sapphire eyes.

"No, Jack. There's a way to get to the kitchen door—through the garden—without being seen. It's too hard to describe, but I can show you."

Jack hesitated only a moment. Stephanie would be safe, of course. He would keep her safe. But Jack prayed that he wasn't allowing her to lead him to a scene of horror that she should never see.

"Okay. Show me."

As they started toward the garden, Stephanie, Jack, and four of LAPD's most expert marksmen suddenly heard a noise— deep, primal, terrifying. At the menacing sound, their silent thoughts all pondered the same question: Was this the inhuman yowl made by a killer when he murdered, a savage cry of bloodlust that predated all history?

No, they realized. The sound wasn't coming from within the house at all. It was much closer than that, beside them, and it came, astonishingly, from the golden retriever.

She wasn't an animal who could logically be named Annie anymore. The smile that seemed a part of her golden face was gone, replaced by a ferocious snarl, and her teeth were fangs now, and her glaring eyes were focused on an enemy which she had sensed but had yet to see. She was low to the ground, her jaunty prance replaced by a purposeful prowl, and as they drew closer to the house, the gait that had been so graceful, almost in slow motion, suddenly accelerated, losing none of its grace but acquiring immense power.

They couldn't have stopped her if they had tried.

And no one tried.

And the dog door that had always been such an obstacle to her, a terrifying symbol of some ancient trauma, was an obstacle no longer. She didn't hesitate, not for an instant.

Jillian and Chase and the Guitar String Strangler all heard the noise that came from the kitchen; but none of them recognized it as the swish of a dog moving through her door. And then came the next sound, the primal growl of rage, and it was only Chase, the abandoned and mistreated orphan, who recognized it for what it truly was—a scream from deep in the soul of an innocent creature who had once been badly abused and now, at long last, would have its revenge.

The growl was swiftly embellished by the appearance of Annie herself, and as Brad Lancaster suddenly felt the helpless terror of a victim who was powerless against a certain and brutal death, he released his grasp of Jillian and frantically pointed the gun at the lethal golden weapon that in another moment would leap for his throat.

Annie leapt, as did Chase, colliding together into Brad, the force of their powerful lunges thrusting him backward, toward the marble fireplace—and instant death as his head struck stone.

Brad was dead, but Annie's powerful jaws were in pursuit of him still, and much of Chase Carlton wanted to let her tear the monster apart; but not in front of the lovely emerald eyes that were safe now, looking up to him with radiant hope from the plush carpet to which she had fallen when Brad released his imprisoning grip.

"No, Annie, *no.*" Chase wasn't sure that just his verbal command would be enough to stop her, and even as he gave it, he moved toward her, to physically pull her powerful body away from Brad if need be.

But the words were enough. Annie stopped instantly, and when she lifted her face to Chase, it once again wore the inquisitive and hopeful look of a much-loved family pet, and when his hands touched her fur and he whispered "Good girl, good girl," her golden tail began to wag.

Then they weren't alone. Jack and the others came through the unlocked kitchen door, and as Jack moved instinctively toward Brad's dead body, Chase and Annie rushed to where they both wanted to be: to Jillian.

Her emerald eyes were all that Chase would get for the moment, because Jillian had a wriggling, lapping, enthusiastic dog to contend with.

"What a heroine you are," she whispered affectionately. "And what a brave girl, dashing through your door as if you'd done it forever. What a brave girl, what—" Jillian stopped abruptly as she felt surprising warmth on the hands that were caressing Annie's luxuriant coat. The warmth was blood, lots of it. "Oh, no. Chase, Annie's been hit!"

Chase's instant response was that she couldn't have been, the gun hadn't even fired.

But the gun *had* fired. The sound had simply been lost in the thunder of Annie's growl. The gun had fired, and there was bright red blood now in the golden coat of the canine heroine, but it wasn't Annie's blood, it was Jillian's . . . and it was gushing from the place in her chest where the bullet had entered.

"Jillian." Chase knelt beside her, pulling her chest to his, shielding her, cradling her, watching as the rapid blood loss pulled the soft pink flush from her cheeks and the radiance from her beautiful emerald eyes. *"Get an ambulance, Jack."*

"Chase?"

"Hi, my darling," he whispered softly. "I love you so much."

"I love you too." Her eyes became radiant again, their glow fueled by pure love, because even as the green filled with its golden light, the rest of her body became ever weaker, more pale, fading, fading. The Tiffany clock chimed then, and for its seven all-important chimes her eyes simply met his. Then, when the chiming stopped, she said with quiet joy, "We're going to have a baby, Chase."

"We are?" he asked, echoing her joy.

"Yes, and she—or he—is going to be fine."

"Yes," he whispered, keeping the fear from his face as he watched her eyes grow cloudy. The ambulance, Jack, his heart pleaded as he placed tender caresses on her ashen face. Hurry, *please*. "Everything's going to be fine, my love."

It seemed that an eternity passed before the paramedics arrived, but in fact they had been waiting outside, one of the emergency teams Jack had already summoned to the scene.

"We're going to the hospital now, Jillian." Chase relinquished his cradling hold of her so that the paramedics could take over. But his hand still touched her pale and lovely face. "I'll be with you all the time."

"My earrings, Chase!" Jillian said suddenly, focusing with solemn urgency on that trivial detail because the blood loss had stolen from her bright mind the ability to distinguish the truly important from the not so critical. "I need my pearl earrings."

"I'll get them." The voice was Stephanie's. She was nearby, on the floor too, her arms gently encircling Annie, her hands tinted red with blood from the golden fur. She repeated quietly, grateful for the chance to help, even this little bit. "I'll get them. Annie and I will get them now."

"Stephanie's getting the earrings for you, darling," Chase said, because Jillian seemed not to have heard Stephanie's words. She seemed aware of nothing now but him. "In a moment they'll be moving you to the ambulance, and I'll be with you the whole time, and everything's going to be wonderful."

"All the promises of rainbows."

"Yes, my love, all the promises of all the rainbows in the world."

Jillian smiled, and there were promises of rainbows in her eyes, and then they became very earnest and very young, and her voice was young, too, as she said solemnly, "It's not my fault, Chase. I'm not to blame for what Brad did. He tried to tell me that I was, but I wouldn't let him."

"Good for you," Chase said gently, proudly, lovingly.

Jillian Montgomery Kincaid wasn't to blame for any of the senseless tragedies that had befallen her, least of all this one. She was the most innocent of victims, struck by a bullet which had somehow fired as two badly abused orphans had lunged with a vengeance at a brutal murderer of dreams.

Chapter Thirty-Three

"Hi," he said softly to the pale and motionless face he loved.

Jillian wasn't sleeping, it was something else, something the doctors couldn't explain. She was in some unknown place between sleep and coma. The bullet had shattered her ribs just as the rocks near Puerto Vallarta had shattered his. There was fire in her chest, Chase knew, a fiery background to whatever dreams or nightmares floated in the never-never land where she had inexplicably dwelled now for over twenty-four hours.

When Chase had been in that place, it had been her voice, her soft promises of love that had finally lured him back to consciousness. He had awakened to her, to the wonderful waking dream of auburn and emerald, and he had been so cruel to that vision of loveliness, mercilessly crushing her hopefulness by pretending to have no memory of her—or of her love.

In Puerto Vallarta Chase Carlton's memory loss had been feigned, a pretense to trap a murderess. But now, Chase knew, it was possible that Jillian might awaken with authentic amnesia. She might recognize his face, but she might remember only his twin, only her deep and steady love for his brother.

"Hi, my love. It's me, Chase Carlton. Remember me?" Chase heard his own uncertainty. It had increased with each passing hour as she hadn't awakened to his loving voice. "You knew me once, Jillian, the most important part of me—my heart. It's a heart that loves you so much, Jillian, *so much.*" Chase paused, fighting his emotion with a smile, and then smiling still as he continued. "There were other things about me that you didn't know. You didn't know, for example, that I'm a pretty good cook. I spent my lifetime—a lifetime of great loneliness until you—cooking just for myself. Last summer you cooked for me, Jillian, and I kept wanting to cook for you, and now, if you give me the chance, I will. Now, if you give me the chance, my love, I'll cook for you and for our baby."

Chase had to stop then as his voice threatened to flood with emotion. Their baby had survived, as Jillian had promised, her dying body generously shunting all of its blood to her womb so that the precious new life wouldn't feel even an instant of deprivation. It wasn't supposed to work that way, Chase overheard the doctors say. It was, they agreed, an extreme example of maternal instinct, and it might cost Jillian her life. Six months from now, after her healthy baby was delivered from her still-sleeping body, her family might be confronted with the most difficult of all decisions.

No. She is going to awaken. Chase forced the fear from his voice and continued. "If you give me the chance, I'll prepare nutritious meals for you and our baby, and I also thought I'd offer my services as a chauffeur, rain or shine, and I will sing to both of you whenever you want. What I'm saying, my precious love, my lovely Jillian, is that I want to spend every second of my life with you, loving you, taking care of you, making you happy—if I can."

You can, Chase, her heart answered.

She heard him, just as he had heard her in Puerto Vallarta, but her eyelids were so heavy, and it felt as if she had to swim through miles and miles and miles of darkness before she could reach the surface, and she was so very weak.

"I love you, Jillian. I know you may not even remember me or our love . . ."

In Puerto Vallarta it had been the uncertain call of Jillian's heart that had compelled Chase's eyes to open, and now, as Jillian heard his uncertainty, her body seemed to soar through those miles . . . and when she reached the bright golden surface her eyelids fluttered open . . . and what she saw when they did were loving gray eyes tinged with the faintest flickers of hopeful blue.

"I remember you," she whispered.

"You do?"

"Yes. You're Chase Carlton, the man who is going to cook delicious gourmet meals for me and our baby." Jillian stopped then, suddenly worried that it had all just been a dream, not really his words, not really the wondrous truth. "Chase?"

"Our baby is fine, darling," Chase assured her gently. "And you're right, I am Chase Carlton, the man who is going to cook delicious gourmet meals for both of you."

"And you're also the man who's going to chauffeur me wherever I want to be driven?"

"If you trust my driving."

"I trust your driving," she said softly, and what she meant, and what the now almost completely blue eyes knew she meant, was that she trusted him *with her life.* "And you're the Chase Carlton who's going to sing to me always?"

"Always," he echoed. "I'm all of those Chase Carltons, Jillian, but mostly—"

His words were stopped by delicate fingers that gently touched his lips. She knew what he was going to say, he had been saying it for the past twenty-four hours, and now it was her turn to say and his turn to hear.

"But mostly you're Chase Carlton, the man I love with all my heart."

As Chase neared the waiting room, he thought about the four people waiting inside—Stephanie and Jack and Edward and Claudia. They were his family now, and forever.

It was every orphan's bravest dream to have a family, and now Chase Carlton had one of his own, and he knew that he was safe with them, that they loved him and cared for him, and always would.

As he entered the small room, he was greeted by faces that were loving, but so anxious, because they had yet to hear his news. Without conscious thought, but compelled by an invisible hand to make the final journey of his searching heart, Chase's eyes traveled to the one among the four who was related to him by blood as well as by love, and who shared with him the spirit of brave dreams that bound all orphans to each other.

Her eyes were bright blue, and when they saw that his were exactly the same color, they shimmered with happiness even before they heard his words.

"Jillian wants you to know," he began, and then stopped. Beginning again, saying it the way it should be said, the way a son would tell the joyous news to his mother, he said softly, "Jillian and I both want you to know that in six months you're going to be a grandmother."